TIMING CANADA

TIMING CANADA

The Shifting Politics of Time in Canadian Literary Culture

Paul Huebener

McGill-Queen's University Press

Montreal & Kingston • London • Chicago

© McGill-Queen's University Press 2015

ISBN 978-0-7735-4598-4 (cloth)
ISBN 978-0-7735-4599-1 (paper)
ISBN 978-0-7735-9772-3 (ePDF)
ISBN 978-0-7735-9773-0 (ePUB)

Legal deposit fourth quarter 2015
Bibliothèque nationale du Québec

Printed in Canada on acid-free paper that is 100% ancient forest free
(100% post-consumer recycled), processed chlorine free

This book has been published with the help of a grant from the Canadian
Federation for the Humanities and Social Sciences, through the Awards to
Scholarly Publications Program, using funds provided by the Social Sciences
and Humanities Research Council of Canada. Funding has also been provided
by Athabasca University.

McGill-Queen's University Press acknowledges the support of the Canada
Council for the Arts for our publishing program. We also acknowledge the
financial support of the Government of Canada through the Canada Book
Fund for our publishing activities.

Library and Archives Canada Cataloguing in Publication

Huebener, Paul, 1980–, author
    Timing Canada: the shifting politics of time in Canadian literary culture /
Paul Huebener.

    Includes bibliographical references and index.
    Issued in print and electronic formats.
    ISBN 978-0-7735-4598-4 (cloth). – ISBN 978-0-7735-4599-1 (paperback). –
ISBN 978-0-7735-9772-3 (ePDF). – ISBN 978-0-7735-9773-0 (ePUB)

    1. Canadian literature (English) – 20th century – History and criticism.
    2. Time in literature. 3. Time – Social aspects – Canada. 4. Time – Political
aspects – Canada. 5. National characteristics, Canadian, in literature. I. Title.

PS8101.T54H83 2015   C810'.933   C2015-905405-2
                                               C2015-905406-0

This book was typeset by Interscript in 11/14 Adobe Garamond.

Contents

Figures

1.1. Standard six-hour trading perspective (Yahoo, 2015). "S&P/TSX Composite Index." Yahoo! Canada Finance. 9 Feb. 2015. Accessed 9 Feb. 2015. https://ca.finance.yahoo.com/echarts?s=%5EGSPTSE#symbol=%5 EGSPTSE;range=1d. Reprinted with permission from Yahoo. © 2015 Yahoo 56

2.1. *Kitchen Door with Ursula* (Christiane Pflug, 1966). Collection of the Winnipeg Art Gallery. Acquired with the assistance of the Women's Committee and The Winnipeg Foundation, G-66-89. Photo: Ernest Mayer, Winnipeg Art Gallery 76

3.1. *The Slave to Machinery* (Alfred Laliberté, 1929–35). Anne Newlands, *Canadian Art from Its Beginnings to 2000* (Toronto: Firefly, 2000), 181. The Montreal Museum of Fine Arts, Purchase, William Gilman Cheney Bequest. Photo: The Montreal Museum of Fine Arts, Christine Guest 119

3.2a and 3.2b. Two pages from Yann Martel's *Self* (1996). Excerpted from *Self* by Yann Martel. Copyright © 1996 Yann Martel. Reprinted by permission of Alfred A. Knopf Canada, a division of Penguin Random House Canada Limited, a Penguin Random House Company. With permission of the author 158–9

3.3. *One Year of AZT/One Day of AZT* (General Idea, 1991). Installation view. Photo: Cheryl O'Brien, courtesy Esther Schipper Berlin 162

Acknowledgments

The research and writing of this book has been a great privilege. I am indebted to many people for their kind and thoughtful encouragement, for directing me toward useful stories, poems, and articles, and for sharing their thoughts on the importance of time to many aspects of life. The seed for this project was planted by a student of mine who, upon reading Emily Carr's description in *Klee Wyck* of Indigenous grave markers that round the time of death to the nearest century, suggested that perhaps "time isn't important to them." Like so many of my own extemporaneous comments, this one contained both an error and an opportunity for further thinking. The particular focusing question that would guide this thinking came to me while reading W.H. New's book *Land Sliding*, in which he seeks to understand "how various *configurations of land* function in literature (and so in Canadian culture at large) to question or confirm configurations of power."[1] What would happen, I thought, if one were to ask a similar question about configurations of time?

For their enduring kindness and expert advice in helping me to complete this project, I am particularly indebted to Lorraine York, Pamela Banting, and Daniel Coleman. I could not have hoped to work alongside such supportive and knowledgeable ambassadors for critical generosity. I am deeply indebted to the members of the editorial team and other departments at McGill-Queen's University Press for orchestrating the transformation of this project into its final form; in particular I thank Kyla Madden for her sustained attention to the book and for allowing me to benefit from her expertise, as well as Kate Baltais for her skilled copy-editing, and Ruth Pincoe for creating the index. I am grateful as well to many current and former members of the Department of English and Cultural Studies at McMaster University, including Roger Hyman, Erin Aspenlieder, Jessica Barr, Peter Walmsley, Jeffery Donaldson, Matthew Zantingh, Matthew Dorrell, Michael Mikulak, Malissa Phung, Antoinette Somo, Ilona Forgo-Smith, Bianca James, and Aurelia Gatto; members of the Department of English at the University of Calgary, including Bart Beaty, Rofina Groebmair, Brigitte Clarke, and Anne Jaggard; my new colleagues in the Centre for Humanities at Athabasca University; and colleagues from other departments and institutions, including Bryan Jung, Diana Brydon, and Nicholas Bradley. I also thank my colleagues at the Time and Globalization Working Group: Liam Stockdale, Susie O'Brien, Tony Porter, and Y. Rachel Zhou; the members of the "Cultures of Time in Canada" seminar at the University of Calgary in 2012: Jennifer Dubon, Jessica Hawkins, Kyla Ricard, Maxine Bennett, and Nicholas McCormick; and the two anonymous reviewers whose close and insightful attention to earlier drafts of this book enabled me to make a much more worthy contribution to knowledge. I have been tremendously fortunate to work within such supportive scholarly communities, and I gratefully acknowledge that this book on the topic of time, as well as the other projects I have worked on alongside it, owe their existence to the sustained and generous gift of time from many colleagues.

I would also like to thank Lisa Szabo-Jones, Pamela Banting, Richard Pickard, Cate Sandilands, and Rob Boschman for fostering the invaluable scholarly community of ALECC (Association for Literature, Environment, and Culture in Canada); the many additional ALECC members who responded to my listserv query about ideas of time; Laurie Ricou and the staff at *Canadian Literature* for inviting me to speak on this topic at their 50th Anniversary Gala in Vancouver in 2009; and Athabasca University, the Social Sciences and Humanities Research Council of Canada, the Ontario Ministry of Training, Colleges and Universities, and the Awards to Scholarly Publications Program at the Federation for the Humanities and Social Sciences for generously funding my work, allowing me the luxury of time that is always necessary for research and writing. I am grateful to my endlessly supportive family: my mother Carol, whose skill and generosity as a parent, a teacher, and a librarian inspired me to pay close attention to works of literature from a young age; my sister Carrie; my father Bruce; my extended family; the Boyd family; and my son Jamie (who was born several years into this project and already knows the difference between a mainspring and a balance wheel).

This book is dedicated to Niki Boyd. If the book has given meaning to my hours at the keyboard, your generous companionship and infinite patience give meaning to all of those moments that make up the wider arc of my time in this world. Thank you for reminding me of the present.

An early version of my vision for this project, drawing mainly from chapter 1, but with variations, appears as "Thoughts on Time-Based Readings of Canadian Literature and Culture" in *English Studies in Canada* 36.2–3 (2010). My readings of works by Gabrielle Roy and Catherine Bush at the end of chapter 2 appear with minor variations as "Subjective Time and the Challenge of Social Synchronization: Gabrielle Roy's *The Road Past Altamont* and Catherine Bush's *Minus Time*" in *Canadian Literature* 223 (Winter 2014).

TIMING CANADA

When Is Now?

In Morris Panych's play *7 Stories*, an unnamed man climbs to the seventh story of an apartment building and contemplates jumping. From his ledge he speaks with several of the building's tenants, though most of them are too preoccupied with their own lives to ask about his dilemma. Only near the end of the play does an elderly woman, Lillian, lean out of a window to ask what is on his mind. He explains:

> You see – my faith in the days of the week has been seriously under-mined. When I woke up this morning, I wasn't exactly sure what day it was. And for that brief moment – it was only a matter of seconds – I think it was seconds – I stood – or I should say I "lay" on very shaky ground. After all – how could I act with assuredness. How could I rise up and plunge headlong into Friday's world, if it was actually Saturday? And so I lay completely still for a moment, pondering this question. That's when I noticed my hands. I'd never noticed them before. How they moved with amazing dexterity. But this flexibility, this movement of hands, can never extend beyond the boundaries of its own flesh – can only reach as far as the fingertips and no further, much as the movement of time is restricted by the days of the week … I saw in the mirror a condemned man, serving a life sentence inside his body.[1]

There is nothing inherent in the flow of time – in the expansion of the universe, the cycle of seasons, or the earth's rotation – to suggest that there is such a thing as a week, or days of the week. The concept of the week is a human invention, one of the cultural constructions by which we order our experience of time. Hellenistic scholars likely adopted Babylonian astrology to develop the seven-day week by dedicating a single day to each of the classical planets – the naked-eye celestial objects that move relative to the seemingly fixed background of stars[2] – an origin that has blended over the centuries with the seven-day creation cycle of the Book of Genesis. And while this seven-day week has been firmly rooted in Canada since it sprung like an introduced species from European ships, all but extinguishing Indigenous time scales in the dominant national consciousness, it is one of any number of possible weeks. Had Indonesians colonized North America, Panych's unnamed man may have been subjected to a five-day week; if ancient Egyptians or the leaders of the French Revolution, a ten-day week.[3] All of these systems have practical difficulties, being unable, for instance, to fit evenly within the period of the earth's revolution around the sun.

But despite the tenuous nature of the concept, the week holds incredible sway over people's daily lives, and it forms one of our most basic cultural assumptions. When Leonard Cohen sings in "Closing Time" that "the place is dead as Heaven on a Saturday night," the relationship between society's weekly holiday and debauched behaviour is immediately understood. Commenting on psychological studies of temporal orientation, William Friedman notes that the weekend holds a special cognitive weight, so that "as the week goes on there is something of a shift from backward-looking thoughts to forward-looking thoughts."[4] The week is necessary not only for scheduling work and play, but also for conducting affairs of all kinds, and the consequences of this dependency range from the trivial to the profound. For George Copway, an Ojibwe man whose nineteenth-century autobiography records his struggle to incorporate the contradictions of European settler culture into his own life, the days of the week become a matter of life and death. Faced with starvation during a prolonged voyage in the wilderness of Ontario, Copway and his party find themselves within reach of the settlement that can save them, but cannot bring themselves to approach. "Nothing to eat," he writes, "and only tea to drink for breakfast, dinner and supper! and yet, only about fifteen miles from La Pointe ; indeed, we could *see* the place; and had it not been that it was the Sabbath, feeble as we were, we would have proceeded. Here, then, we spent the Sabbath."[5] In the twenty-first century, environmental researchers at the University of Calgary have discovered that the five-day work week even holds a special significance for wild bears, cougars, and coyotes in Alberta's Kananaskis Country. The animals are frequent users of hiking trails and backcountry roads, but they tend to avoid the trails on weekends, when humans are more likely to be in the area. Environmental Science and Planning professor Mike Quinn says of the animals, "It seems that they know that when Friday night rolls around, it's time to disappear, and on Monday morning they're back."[6] Eviatar Zerubavel eloquently highlights the importance of the week as a foundational cultural concept:

> Recalling what day today is is one of the first things we usually do upon waking, since it is indispensable for transcending our subjectivity and participating – at least mentally – in a social, rather than a merely personal, world. The uneasy feeling that accompanies our realization that we have lost count of the days of the week is essentially the well-justified anxiety about being barred from full participation in our social environment. In other words, adhering to the week protects us from the dreadful prospect of practical exile from the social world.[7]

The predicament of Panych's unnamed man, then, while sensational, speaks to a concern of genuine importance. How indeed could we act with assuredness if we were to lose track of our culturally mandated patterns of time? Or perhaps more importantly, of what is it exactly that we are being assured when we take these culturally specific categorizations for granted? The unnamed man's fear that it may "actually" be Saturday indicates his absolute investment in – and, as he comes to see it, his enslavement to – the reality of a cultural construct. While his faith in the benign nature of the days of the week may have been shaken, his faith in their reality remains intact; he continues to experience time in terms of a categorization that is seemingly all-encompassing, yet is highly limited and limiting. And this dual function of opening and constricting our experience of time is one that the days of the week share with other temporal categorizations and allocations, from paleontological eras, periods of history, and the hours of the clock, to immigrant residency periods, the number of years a person must live before she can vote in elections, or the systemic allocation of more free time to men than to women.

Certain aspects of time remain generally outside of human control, such as the daily rotation and yearly revolution of the earth, seasonal transitions, mortality, aging, and causality; yet even those categories that have some basis in natural processes (the month, for instance, with its nominal if no longer strict basis in the orbit of the moon) are selected as categories of language and thought and as sites of cultural significance by and for human beings, and carry within them the weight of ideology. As Johannes Fabian explains in his seminal work *Time and the Other: How Anthropology Makes Its Object*, the conceptualizations of time that are built, explicitly and implicitly, into language and other cultural practices are always political. And because language is inevitably temporalizing – because "we must necessarily express whatever knowledge we have of an object in terms of temporal categorization"[8] – the politics of time saturate all human affairs. "Time," Fabian writes, "much like language or money, is a carrier of significance, a form through which we define the content of relations between the Self and the Other."[9]

The difficulty of defining time is well known, for no single definition seems adequate to capture the multiplicity of experiences associated with temporality. Friedman's response to this dilemma is both obvious and brilliant. "Much of the history of the philosophy of time," he writes,

> is a series of attempts to find time's essence, whether in nature or in consciousness. Among those conceptions tying time to the physical world, time has been defined as motions, as the succession of events, and as an absolute, universal framework. Mentalist definitions refer to the perception of succession and simultaneity or the succession of ideas in consciousness. In the midst of all this diversity is a common tendency to treat time as a single thing. Psychologists too seem inclined to seek a single entity, as they write of "the concept," "the notion," or "the sense" of time. Perhaps the fact that we have a single word for time has seduced us into searching for its essence.[10]

He concludes that "it seems far more productive to consider the many things that time is in the world and the many ways in which humans experience it."[11] As Thomas M. Allen puts it, "time is defined in relation to the purposes it serves. Hence, we can never say what time is. Instead, we can only ask what kinds of worlds different forms of time make possible, and what interests are served by the creation of such worlds."[12] While dist-illing a singular definition for time may not be possible, questions of human experience and interests appear inevitable in any human consideration of time, highlighting the degree to which time is always at least partially a cognitive construct shaped by culture. The *Canadian Oxford Dictionary*, which offers more than a hundred meanings and idioms for "time," appropriately begins its entry on the word by acknowledging the inevitable constructedness of the concept: time is "the indefinite and continuous duration of existence seen as a series of events progressing from the past through the present into the future." What begins as a natural entity, albeit an "indefinite" one, is immediately cast through the lens of cultural association and figurative representation, into something "seen as." The word "time" itself is the most frequently used noun in the English language, relegating the word "person" to second place, and the words "year," "day," and "week" all make the top twenty.[13] And yet, the workings of time as a contested site of cultural power in Canada, the specifics by which we *see time as*, have often been overlooked.

Since there is no single construct or metaphor through which we understand time, but rather a cluster of overlapping, sometimes conflicting constructs, several questions arise. How do different structures of time come into existence, and why? Who decides upon the categories through which we plot our locations within social frames of time? How do these patterns reinforce, or disrupt, power relations between individuals and groups? How do personal experiences of time relate to larger cultural patterns? In particular, how have these processes been shaped within Canada, and how do they shape Canada in turn? Or, to revise Northrop Frye's famous question – "Where is here?"[14] – as a focal point for examining Canadian identity, let us ask instead, "When is now?" This book contends that the politics and power relations that saturate Canada's existence are profoundly tied to the broad understandings of time that have been advanced, assumed, and rejected throughout the country's history, and that Canadian literature and other arts are inevitably tangled up in these complex relationships and serve a vital function in both witnessing and questioning them. This study also makes the secondary argument that systemic forms of individual empowerment or disempowerment tied to categories of social existence such as race, class, age, gender, sexuality, and settler-Indigene relations cause significant differences in personal experiences of time, and that these processes, too, can be illuminated through readings of literary and cultural texts. Like the multifarious concept of time itself, the title *Timing Canada* refers to several key operations, some of which borrow from Norbert Elias's elucidation of what exactly is at stake when we perform the act of timing. Elias emphasizes the importance of focusing not on time as an object per se, but on timing as an activity, and one that is bound up in the perspective of those doing the timing.[15] If the act of timing is performed in relation to assumed social and ideological structures, then one of the central ambitions of the critical study of time must be to take the measure of the timing itself, to try to uncover the assumptions that shape our very approach to gauging time. Accordingly, this book discusses the "timing" of Canada as the process by which people bring contested visions of time into existence within the nation, visions of time that in some cases characterize the nation in profound ways; it "times" Canada by taking the measure of how different modes of time function within Canadian society, from broad cultural levels to the more granular levels of individual and group experiences, and by assessing how these contested temporalities operate in concert with different forms of empowerment and disempowerment; and finally it understands time as a verb where Canada is the actor – for the nation itself, and its diverse inhabitants, are continuously engaged in an ongoing process of enacting, constructing, shaping, and imagining the flow of time, with all the complexities and inequities that such a process entails.

INQUIRIES IN TIME

Writers and theorists across many disciplines have enriched our understanding of time, and have investigated the ways in which time is connected to culture, social relations, literature, psychology, phenomenology, concepts of place, collective national projects, and globalization. From Aristotle and Saint Augustine to Henri Bergson and Martin Heidegger, philosophers have described the links between time and mortality, ethics, free will, religion, eternity, and existence itself. For Aristotle, time is linked to motion and change; while motion is not the same as time, one is necessary for the other to exist. "Not only do we measure the movement by the time," he writes, "but also the time by the movement, because they define each another."[16] In his theological treatise, Augustine distinguishes between the human temporality of everyday experience on the one hand and the "ever-present eternity" in which God exists on the other, where "nothing passeth, but the whole is present."[17] He also describes the deep interconnectedness of the past, the present, and the future in the human experience of time, a project that in some ways anticipates Heidegger's attempt to construct new forms of language to better represent the indivisibility of time in phenomenological experience. Bergson's effort to emphasize the subjective experience of duration over an objective sense of measurable linear time has also been highly influential; duration is the experience that occurs when we comprehend a note in a song in relation to the notes that surround it, and this, for Bergson, reflects the true nature of time. Arguing that "real duration is made up of moments inside one another," he finds that the conventional view of time as a linear sequence – a discrete movement from A to B – results from our problematic tendency to conceive of time in terms that apply properly to space.[18] While Bergson's work risks assuming "that time is only an effect of consciousness,"[19] it has been valuable in countering, or supplementing, the purely objectivist understandings of time which fail to account for the intricacies of human perception. Of course, the shift in philosophical thinking from physical to perceptual understandings of time mirrors the shift in the sciences away from Newton's "absolute, true, and mathematical time," which "of itself, and from its own nature, flows equally without relation to anything external,"[20] and toward Einstein's relative time in which "every reference body has its own particular time."[21] As I will discuss in chapter 2, some of the above lines of inquiry have led theorists such as Paul Ricoeur to question the very concepts of "past," "present," and "future," a task that has been guided not only by philosophical and scientific treatises, but also by the thoughtful applications of time within works of fiction.

Notions of history and progress, too, have often taken centre stage in discussions of time. Walter Benjamin's critique of the production of historical knowledge has been influential in its assertion that the idea of historical progress has been tied to "the concept of its progression through a homogeneous, empty time."[22] As Antony Easthope explains, the temporality of a linear calendar system is homogeneous in the sense that it "measures a continuous succession of nows identical in kind."[23] Any critique of the idea of progress, Benjamin argues, must begin with the realization that historical events themselves form "a structure whose site is not homogeneous, empty time, but time filled by the presence of the now."[24] In other words, present events do not merely occupy the empty sequential time of the calendar, but constitute through their particularities the actual flow of temporality, with all sorts of complexities that do not necessarily fit within a broad notion of "progress." Benedict Anderson takes up the idea of homogeneous time in describing how the nation is often perceived as "moving steadily down (or up) history"; he argues that the shared social feeling of simultaneity made possible in Europe in the eighteenth century by the spread of print culture created the sense of an "imagined community," a nation in which individuals move forward together through time.[25] And while Anderson's insights may be more concerned with printing presses, the importance of *clock* technologies for shaping social interactions has, of course, been a frequently discussed topic by many writers. Drawing attention to what he calls "a new time-discipline" that had been imposed through the regularization and monetization of time following the Industrial Revolution, E.P. Thompson diagnoses "mature capitalist society" as one in which "all time must be consumed, marketed, put to *use*; it is offensive for the labour force merely to 'pass the time.'"[26] John Urry similarly suggests that the social importance of clocks is tied to an "orientation to time as a resource to be managed rather than as activity or meaning."[27]

In his influential mid-twentieth-century studies of communications media, Harold Innis argues that large political units, especially empires, tend to succeed or fail in sustaining themselves based on the degree to which they embrace communications media that can address "problems of time" as well as "problems of space."[28] For Innis, the media that "emphasize time" are those that "are durable in character, such as parchment, clay, and stone," while media that emphasize space "are apt to be less durable and light in character, such as papyrus and paper. The latter are suited to wide areas in administration and trade."[29] In other words, the problem of time, for Innis, is the problem of longevity. The need for centralized administrations to transmit information *quickly* – a problem of speed and acceleration – does not arise, for Innis, as a problem of time, but rather is understood as the spatial problem of coordination over large physical areas. His assessment leads him to conclude that empires whose preferred communications media focus on problems of time to the exclusion of problems of space, or vice versa, are likely to fail, while those empires that diversify their media and thus overcome "the bias of media which overemphasizes either dimension" are more likely to persist.[30] The dominance of the light and ephemeral medium of the newspaper in the United States in the eighteenth and nineteenth centuries "led to large-scale development of monopolies of communication in terms of space and implied a neglect of problems of time"[31] – a difficulty that was only exacerbated by the spread of radio broadcasting and cinema, resulting in the dominance of superficiality and the ephemeral. "With these powerful developments," Innis writes, "time was destroyed and it became increasingly difficult to achieve continuity or to ask for a consideration of the future."[32,33] In the end, Innis concludes that the need to balance the concerns of space and time "remains a problem of empire and of the Western world."[34] Innis's arguments have proved influential in the study of communications media and their impact on societies, yet his explanation of the "problems of time" is limited by the assumption that time is essentially synonymous with durability, a significant limitation given the major concerns of speed, acceleration, synchronization, and instantaneity that cannot be reduced to problems of space. His claim that "time was destroyed" through the dominance of mechanized printing, radio, and cinema, sees one particular view of time as the *only* time, and while this comment speaks powerfully to the lack of long-term future orientation in contemporary Western societies, it forecloses the possibility of other important insights into the mobilization of temporal power. In addition, of course, Innis was not able to comment on the new types of media that came about after his death in 1952. The complex forms of media enabled by the era of global Internet and satellite connectivity certainly emphasize instantaneity across vast distances, but their relation to long-term durability is less clear.

Recent cultural studies focusing on time have tended to emphasize the difficulty of overcoming cultural assumptions about time, the use of time as a tool of leverage in maximizing profits or in enforcing social hierarchizations such as those associated with colonization, the complexities of heterogeneous global temporalities, the apparent acceleration of social and technological change and the pace of life, forms of resistance such as the Slow Food movement, and the seemingly instantaneous or simultaneous times brought about by the prevalence of computers and electronic communication networks. In his impressively systematic study, Hartmut Rosa argues not only that social acceleration is quantifiably real, but also that it constitutes the primary mode of experience in contemporary society – that *"the experience of modernization is an experience of acceleration."*[35] Barbara Adam, who has worked to debunk many overly simplistic cultural assumptions about time, shows that the stereotypical opposition between the linear time of developed Western societies and the cyclical time of traditional societies fails to hold up under scrutiny. "It is essential to appreciate," she writes, "that all social processes display aspects of both linearity and cyclicity, and that we recognize a cyclical structure when we focus on events that repeat themselves and unidirectional linearity when our attention is on the process of the repeating action."[36] The utility and the limitations of linear and cyclical visions of time are important concerns throughout this book, as are the differences in cultural views of time, the concerns associated with acceleration, and especially the use of time as a tool of power.

Adam also argues that despite the pervasive and apparently distinctive influence of clock time in Western cultures, clocks can never become the sole bearers of temporal meaning: "the abstract, quantified, spatialized time of clocks and calendars forms *only one aspect* of the complex of meanings associated with Western time."[37] Some theorists, meanwhile, believe that while clock time was of central importance early in the twentieth century, it no longer holds the significance that modernity once afforded it. Urry, for instance, claims that electronic information networks produce a "timeless time" in which global capital's "freedom from time and culture's escape from the clock are both decisively shaped by the new informational systems."[38] He emphasizes "the simultaneous character of social and technical relationships, which replaces the linear logic of clock time, characterized by the temporal separation of cause and effect occurring over separate measurable instants."[39] However, despite the importance of simultaneity and instantaneousness, there is still a persuasive argument to be made that just as clock time modified but did not replace other forms of temporality, so too has the network society modified but not replaced clock time. In the same way that postmodernism, in Simon During's words, "is not just a break with modernism but also represents its intensification,"[40] the contemporary network society is both a departure from and an intensification of modernist clock time. As I will discuss in chapter 1, Sandford Fleming's nineteenth-century push toward standardized time zones was founded on the increasingly urgent need for what he called "a comprehensive view of the globe in considering the question of time-reckoning,"[41] an extension of the sense of simultaneity that Benedict Anderson identifies in the eighteenth century. Visions of globalized simultaneity, then, are not an invention of the computer age, and the clocks that embodied these visions in the past are still pervasive today even if they are now more digital than they are mechanical. New temporal complexities and consequences are always becoming apparent, but the clock itself remains a central and dominating force in the management of everyday life.

Investigations of the role of time in literature have also ranged across wide swaths of territory. Mikhail Bakhtin gives "the name *chronotope* (literally, 'time space') to the intrinsic connectedness of temporal and spatial relationships that are artistically expressed in literature."[42] Through analyzing how such temporal-spatial connectedness functions in various classic forms of literature, he argues that "it is precisely the chronotope that defines genre and generic distinctions."[43] For instance, the plot of a Greek romance follows a particular familiar schema: a boy and a girl of marriageable age meet one another, experience irresistible passion, and then face various obstacles that cause them to be separated before they finally unite in marriage. In Bakhtin's view, this plot schema is chronotopic in that its temporal structure defines the shape of the narrative itself. More importantly, Bakhtin's study leads him to conclude that because of the close relationship between chronotopes and narrative, chronotopes "are the organizing centres for the fundamental narrative events of the novel," and that "any and every literary image is chronotopic."[44] While my approach usually emphasizes the politics of contested temporalities over the temporal characteristics of narrative forms themselves, the concept of the chronotope will be useful here in identifying different types of images or narrative "maps" through which people in Canada understand time to function both collectively and personally. Also of relevance is Paul Ricoeur's seminal trilogy *Time and Narrative*, which focuses on the philosophy and phenomenology of time, and reaches the conclusion that narrative itself is the primary tool that human beings have for understanding time and therefore identity. Ricoeur's work is especially important to my study of subjective experiences of time in chapter 2. Other texts, such as Mark Currie's *About Time: Narrative, Fiction and the Philosophy of Time*, focus on the formal aspects of narratological structures of time, and for the most part lie outside the scope of this book. Scholarly works that have incorporated social, political, and literary understandings of time lie closer to the approach that I am taking here; these include Thomas M. Allen's *A Republic in Time: Temporality and Social Imagination in Nineteenth-Century America*, which "explores the diverse temporal modes of national emergence" by examining "narrative accounts of national identity within time," and connecting these to the context of American nineteenth-century historical developments such as the mass production of mechanical clocks starting in 1807.[45]

My intention is not to provide a comprehensive survey of scholarly approaches to time. While borrowing certain insights from the above works, my book diverges from these studies by approaching the social politics of time from a Canadian perspective, opening Canada's temporal structure to questioning in order to develop a newly complex understanding of how time has been wielded as a tool of power within this nation, and how imaginative responses are key to understanding and questioning this power. At the same time, this book explicitly develops a set of theoretical tools and practices that allow for an approach that I call "critical time studies" – a process of inquiry that advances thoughtful re-evaluations of the social politics of time through the examination of temporal assumptions and the fostering of critical temporal literacy. Below, I explain how I go about these tasks by drawing from existing scholarly work, selecting Canadian case studies, and specifying the critical practices that will be most useful not only in carrying out my own study, but also in equipping others to carry out further work in the critical study of time.

CRITICAL TIME STUDIES IN CANADA: THE APPROACH OF THIS BOOK

How can we go about identifying the particular temporal identity of a nation? In his landmark study, *The Culture of Time and Space 1880–1918*, Stephen Kern discusses cultural and technological innovations in the late nineteenth and early twentieth centuries (the wireless telegraph, cinema, stream-of-consciousness novels, and so on) that "created distinctive new modes of thinking about and experiencing time and space."[46] These new understandings of time included the importance of heterogeneous "private" time, which increasingly came into conflict with "public" time. Alongside this argument, Kern makes a claim about national temporalities. "Nations," he writes, "also demonstrate distinctive attitudes toward time. For example, the contrast between Austria-Hungary, convinced its time was running out, and Russia, which felt it had time to spare, is striking and is revealed repeatedly in diplomatic documents."[47] By carrying out research on diplomatic documents, Kern uncovers temporal attitudes and anxieties that might otherwise have remained hidden. However, by reading these documents as banners of distinctive national attitudes toward time, he is using the name of the nation in question as a metonym for the governing body of the nation at that particular moment, and ultimately for the individual diplomats who wrote the documents. While certain attitudes toward political-temporal opportunities or limitations may have become prevalent in the documents, these statements cannot adequately represent the complexity of temporal modes at work within the nation as a whole. For this reason it is problematic even to speak of a distinctive national attitude toward time.

The matter of national time, then, cannot be addressed solely by examining a narrow range of official documents, or by making generalizations about grand visions of time such as those associated with the idea of progress. Lloyd Pratt identifies a useful methodology on this front. Questioning Benedict Anderson's notion that an overarching sense of simultaneity binds individuals together into a national collective, Pratt argues that the modes of time expressed within nineteenth-century American writing are heterogeneous and contradictory.[48] "This literature," he writes, "articulates a modernity of unequal but coeval orders of time that encourage simultaneous identifications across and within the naturalized boundaries separating colony from postcolonial nation, south from north, future from past."[49] The notion that different concepts of time are unequal and articulated through many voices, yet also coeval – existing contemporaneously with one another – is vital for moving beyond reductive explanations of social, cultural, or national time (a lesson that also applies to individual people, for whom temporal experience is never just one kind of experience).

In a similar vein, the significant point that Daniel Coleman makes in his study of Canadian chronotopes (which I discuss in chapter 1) is that no single image of time is adequate for characterizing something as complex as a nation – an insight that is central to the discussions in this book. The specific chronotopes that Coleman identifies offer only a beginning, since they refer to the broadly understood experiences of a few large social collectivities. The diverse politics of time in Canada have been shaped not only in concert with the broad processes of colonization and nation building, but also through specific policies, events, and productions, ranging from immigration waiting periods to prison sentencing approaches, changes in standard working hours, time-sensitive environmental reviews, controversial time zone boundaries, competing views of temporal justice and accountability, as well as countless personal temporal experiences which in turn are shaped by social categories of gender, age, race, and class.

Through examining many different aspects of temporal existence within Canada I seek to craft an understanding of what "Canadian time" is and how it functions, yet I also argue that identifying the culture of time in Canada is not a question of locating a single factor that sets Canada apart. Rather, such a project involves taking into account diverse modes and frames of time, many of which reinforce, or cast light on, the empowerment or disempowerment of specific groups of people. While it is impossible to account for all of the heterogeneous temporalities within the nation, my approach emerges from the desire to highlight the diversity of temporal ideas that collectively enter into dialogue, the problems of social justice connected to inequitably conceived, enforced, and experienced temporalities, and the processes by which these temporalities are formed, imagined, and reimagined over time. This form of inquiry requires examinations of dominant cultural ideas about time, as well as more granular experiences of time. It requires illuminating the influence that social factors that may appear unconnected to time (such as systemic social biases associated with race and gender, or traumatic events such as rape or war) have on the way that time is felt and understood. It requires particular attention to diverse Indigenous articulations of time, and the complex temporal relationship between Indigenous and settler societies. Finally, it requires an examination of the way that authors and artists in Canada have worked imaginatively to dismantle or reconstruct normative time – processes that have intrinsic value in opening our minds to temporal power and possibility and that can also lead to practical insights in building understandings of the everyday politics of time in complex societies.

The work of several theorists from different disciplines will be central in directing the approach of this study. Johannes Fabian's seminal insight that the functioning of time within human relations always carries a political dimension is a foundational concept in the critical study of time, as are Barbara Adam's revelations about the dangers of oversimplifying social modes of time. In the chapters that follow I will also take up the importance of the acceleration of technological change, social change, and the pace of life articulated by Hartmut Rosa and Robert Levine; Paul Ricoeur's expression of the linkage between time and narrative; and the idea expressed by David Landes, Gerhard Dohrn-van Rossum, and others that the mechanization of time leads to the social development of time discipline. Additional scholars including Rita Felski, Elizabeth Freeman, Georges Sioui, and Taiaiake Alfred offer insights into the role of time in particular aspects of sociality such as gender relations or settler-Indigene relations. The forms of social and personal temporalities that exist in something as complex as a nation are multiple, shifting, and complex, and even while I seek to cast new light on Canada's temporal situation, I am deeply indebted to the scholars whose work has given this investigation much of its analytical direction.

In order to draw meaning from the enormous complexity of temporal relations in Canada, I have selected particular examples for discussion. I examine events and social relations that speak to large concerns, such as the decision of the federal government in the late nineteenth century to set an arbitrary temporal deadline for Métis communities to "develop" their land, or the differences in average working time between men and women and between Canadian regions early in the twenty-first century, as identified by Statistics Canada. I have selected cultural texts that question dominant temporalities and cast the social politics of time under a fresh critical light, as well as those that actively manipulate time for strategic advantage; examples include Newfoundland and Labrador tourism advertisements, statements from politicians and government bodies, and, especially, representations of temporal experience in fiction, poetry, drama, and visual art. While certain forms such as advertisements or government statements may be more obviously constrained by the limitations of branding strategies or political positioning, there is no genre or form that has a monopoly on thoughtful analysis, and the distinction between works that reinforce inequitable temporalities and works that question dominant modes of time is not always clear-cut. Emily Carr's writing, for instance, sometimes repeats racist temporalities even while she carries out a valuable critical analysis of time-based cultural biases. In this sense her work mirrors the statements of all cultural critics, myself included, who are engaged in the always incomplete process of weeding out the injustices enshrined in our own world views. Even those authors who seek to radically subvert the conventions of time held within literary forms, such as Daphne Marlatt or Marlene NourbeSe Philip, are held partially within the grip of hegemonic temporalities. As Lloyd Pratt argues, "The anachronistic formal precedents that inhere in any genre guarantee that this literature also functions as an archive of temporalities drawn from moments other than its own – temporalities that it returns to the present."[50] Individual texts, like the nation as a whole, should be understood as negotiating multiple visions of time and conflicted senses of temporal upheaval in ways that are both explicit and implicit. I have tried to reflect the complexity of the texts and social relations under discussion, but even a lengthy study can only go so far in responding to such wide-ranging material. For instance, while I have attempted to illuminate the temporal concerns associated with francophone culture through discussions of the controversial implementation of Daylight Saving Time in Quebec, the anxious visions of the future held by English-speaking Montrealers in the late 1990s, and a close reading of Gabrielle Roy's short story cycle *The Road Past Altamont* (*La route d'Altamont*), these perspectives do not amount to a fully comprehensive reading of temporal concerns in francophone Canada. Rather than trying to make every possible point about the representation and social functioning of time, my goal is to provide key examples and critical language that will emphasize the important lessons of this research and will enable others to carry out further work in the critical study of time and the fostering of temporal literacy.

In the service of this latter goal, I introduce or reshape several key theoretical concepts that will be of use to others who wish to exercise and promote critical temporal literacy. These include the following:

Temporal Justice. Alongside social justice and environmental justice, temporal justice should be recognized as one of the fundamental responsibilities of a just society. In the context of social policy analysis, Robert Goodin uses the term temporal justice in his attempt to develop a method of "distinguishing how much time one has discretionary control over."[51] If certain people have much greater amounts of flexible, discretionary time, then a measure of temporal injustice is visible. In my usage, though, the meaning of this term is expanded. Temporal justice, I want to suggest, is a measure not only of discretionary time, but of the forms of equity at stake in all of the diverse ways in which time functions socially as a form of currency and a tool of power. My usage, then, is closer to Barbara Adam's plea for "a politics of temporalised democracy." In her discussion of the temporal complexity of environmental problems in the United Kingdom, she concludes that "intergenerational temporal equity, temporal rights, negotiations over temporal conflicts and their arbitration would be integral to the temporalised democracy."[52] Temporal justice, and its inverse, temporal injustice, are foundational concepts in critical temporal literacy.

Temporal Framing. I apply the term temporal framing to the technique of establishing arbitrary conceptual borders around a temporal concept or duration for the purpose of advancing a political agenda.[53] Concepts such as "new," "now," "long-term," and even "first" are sufficiently subjective in their meaning that their use can easily be manipulated. For instance, when a provincial premier remarks, "As I've said from day one, we have been watching this situation closely," she is taking advantage of the fact that, because there is no official or universal designation of "day one" (or similar concepts such as "the beginning" or "always"), this temporal identifier can be moved to a position of strategic benefit, whether this position is explicitly stated or remains vague.[54] The frame of time is composed of conceptual borders that define the moments when the counting of time is initiated or terminated. As I discuss in chapter 1, imagining that the counting of time begins at a certain moment, and not earlier, is often key to the evasion of temporal responsibility and the perpetuation of temporal injustice.

Temporal Resistance. Forms of temporal injustice, like other forms of injustice, can be resisted in various ways, with varying degrees of success. Scholars such as Emily Keightley, Aaron W. Hughes, and Adam Barrows have used the term temporal resistance, albeit briefly, to identify acts that operate against dominant or restrictive modes of social time. As Keightley points out, the Slow Food movement fits into this category, since it seeks to resist the forms of acceleration, speed, and fast profit epitomized by the fast food industry.[55] The term, however, has not been widely taken up. I use it here partly to promote it as a useful name with which to identify active forms of resistance against hegemonic temporalities, and also to deepen our understanding of which kinds of acts can productively be understood as forms of temporal resistance. Given the strong linkage between time and narrative, I am especially interested in how literary texts can carry out temporal resistance by subverting the formal conventions of linear narrative tied to European history, or by telling stories about characters who resist constrictive social categories of time. I also identify the ways in which temporal resistance, like other forms of resistance, is limited by external factors and risks reinforcing the very sites of power it seeks to dismantle, even while it remains a vital method of intervention.

Time Socialization Stories. Though they do not use this exact term, Philip Zimbardo and John Boyd point out that many children's stories "seek to inculcate the audience with socially sanctioned attitudes toward time."[56] Time socialization stories indoctrinate young people into the shared forms of social time that shape the functioning of society and that serve as measurements of individual productivity, success, and belonging. For Zimbardo and Boyd, the primary temporal mode into which children are socialized is future orientation. "The Three Little Pigs," for example, is "a story about the need to prepare for the future," since only the third pig has the foresight to build a durable house.[57] A strong sense of future orientation is important in turn for developing productive habits of adulthood such as goal planning and time management. In addition to borrowing Zimbardo and Boyd's insight to inform my discussion of youth-oriented stories such as *Anne of Green Gables*, I also understand time socialization stories more broadly as narratives that reinforce normative temporal codes for young people and adults alike. The series of bells that rings at any elementary school – one to draw you to class, and one that declares you late if you are not in your seat – is a time socialization story that presents weekdays, working hours, and clock-based punctuality as inevitable. A linear vision of civilizational development is a time socialization story that can reinforce the Eurocentric model of time that casts Indigenous nations as primitive. A federal finance minister who comments that economic growth is "going to come from an accelerated regulatory system" is telling a time socialization story by reinforcing the hegemony of the narrative of rapid development and fast profit. Individuals who have repeatedly been socialized into this latter ideology of time are presumably more likely to agree that *there is no time* for lengthy environmental assessments when corporate executives wish to initiate major new resource projects such as oil pipelines.[58] The ability of works of literature to teach readers how to recognize time socialization stories is an example of how literature can foster the skills of temporal literacy, helping readers to develop the tools of a larger, more socially aware form of critical time studies.

Temporal Discrimination. I argue that temporal discrimination is the entrenched belief that one particular model of time is natural, desirable, and superior to other models of time, that one person's time is inherently more legitimate than another person's time, or that certain times (the present or the short-term future) are more deserving of agency, empowerment, and resource exploitation than other times. Temporal discrimination operates in two key directions. First, dominant cultural models of time can create inequitable social relations and experiences of disempowerment (such as when the Western ethic of rapid land "development" causes Métis homesteaders to be evicted from their land). Second, ingrained forms of social power that may appear unrelated to time, such as those that operate through the categories of race, gender, and class, frequently impact the experience of time for individuals in inequitable ways (this type of temporal discrimination is visible in the fact that women in Canada have less free time, on average, compared with men). Theorists and activists have developed critical vocabularies for identifying racism and sexism, and the forms of discrimination that are tied to these power relationships, so that while the work of countering racist and sexist discrimination remains difficult and complex, to a significant extent people have been equipped with the language and concepts necessary to identify and resist instances of disempowerment based on race, gender, and other categories of identity. However, despite the work of time theorists such as Johannes Fabian, who identifies time as a political site and "a carrier of significance," cultural discourse remains largely unprepared to identify the ways that structures of time inform or reflect relationships of power and disempowerment. I offer the term temporal discrimination to provide a framework and a terminology for identifying, articulating, and responding to unequal valuations of time and the inequitable use of temporal power and privilege.

Multitemporality. In his comparative study of the pace of life across different countries, Robert Levine argues that "one of the most significant differences in the pace of life is whether people use the hour on the clock to schedule the beginning and ending of activities, or whether the activities are allowed to transpire according to their own spontaneous schedule. These two approaches are known, respectively, as living by clock time and living by event time."[59] After considering the biases and misunderstandings that can come about when clock time clashes with event time, Levine proposes the use of "multitemporality" as a coping mechanism, since "the person, or the culture, who combines both modes in a temporal repertoire – or even better, who can draw upon a multiplicity of modes – is more likely to be up to all occasions."[60] For my purposes, multitemporality is a concept that accounts more broadly for the coexistence of many temporal modes and experiences within a social collective. If temporal discrimination theorizes the problems of temporal injustice, multitemporality theorizes the matter of temporal diversity. As I explain in the Conclusion, multitemporality is somewhat analogous to multiculturalism in that it provides an imperfect but important framework for recognizing the existence of multiple modes of time, and for working through the ongoing and provisional process of negotiating temporal differences within a shared social and temporal world. Fostering a sense of multitemporality in the service of social-temporal justice does not require us to make the naïve assumption that all temporal beliefs and experiences are equal. Rather, it can enable us to recognize exactly how temporal inequities are entrenched within social norms, and to envision ongoing negotiations of our shared temporal existence, founded on the premise of mutual temporal recognition.

The above concepts function as part of the larger project of articulating how time functions broadly as a tool of power, privilege, and imagination within large social units such as the nation. As the process of articulating and questioning temporal power, critical time studies involves naming the particular temporal concepts and injustices at stake, and drawing conclusions about the relations of power, diversity, privilege, and typically unquestioned manipulation involved in the application of unequal temporalities.

In the chapters that follow I outline the specific structures of time that serve broadly as sites of power in Canada, and examine literary and cultural texts ranging from the nineteenth through to the twenty-first century in order to explore the difficult negotiations between individual and social experiences of time. From Catharine Parr Traill to Thomas King; from the Mi'kmaq storyteller Susan Barss to Lucy Maud Montgomery, Timothy Findley, and Dionne Brand – these authors' texts reveal that while broad cultural temporalities indeed contribute toward shaping the scheduling and measuring out of individual lives, this shaping process functions differently for different people, and it does not tell the whole story of the relationship between time and social power. Understanding this relationship also requires examining how forms of temporal agency and disempowerment are closely linked to the categories of age, class, race, gender, sexuality, and indigeneity. Exemplary literary texts prove invaluable in teaching us how to read the idea of time critically through the shifting politics of social relations, and in turn to read social relations critically by examining how they influence experiences of time. Alongside other cultural texts including popular news coverage, statements from politicians, and Statistics Canada's Time Use Surveys, works of Canadian literature show us how we can understand, admire, question, resist, and reimagine the dominant structures of time and personal experiences of time that inflect our lives.

The predicament of Panych's unnamed man with which I started this discussion is an illustrative example because it introduces several of the central principles of this book: that while everyday cultural categories of time play a vital role in structuring our social existence, these categories are not permanent and inevitable but are tied to specific ideological frameworks that remain open to critical questioning; that experiences of time have very real material impacts on individual lives, and that these consequences necessitate investigation; and finally, that Canadian artists have frequently played a key role in making the social impacts of time visible, in articulating the shifting politics of time, imagining alternative temporalities, and opening the very fabric of Canada's temporal structure to questioning.

I

Canadian Time: Reading the Politics of Time in Canadian Culture

Myth is an arrangement of the past, whether real or imagined, in patterns that resonate with a culture's deepest values and aspirations ... They are the maps by which cultures navigate through time.[1]

Ronald Wright

Time is a measure of motion and of being moved.[2]

Aristotle

This chapter examines a range of significant developments and representative events in Canadian culture and history in order to develop an understanding of how time has been constructed socially as a form of power within the nation. In the course of building such an understanding, several conclusions come to light. Normative structures of time such as clock time, the Gregorian calendar system, and the linear notion of progress intertwine with powerful social emphases on punctuality, productivity, acceleration, temporal universality, and particular forms of temporal framing through which shorter durations are often seen as more real than longer durations, and through which the prized concept of first-ness and the more ambivalent concept of newness are claimed by certain people and denied to others. This matrix of normative temporal principles creates an important degree of social coherence, but it also tends to construct and reinforce patterns of social power while excluding subaltern groups of people from dominant social and temporal status. As a result, it is vital to realize that there is no singular form of "Canadian time," but rather that Canadian society is just as much multitemporal as it is multicultural, and that the inequitable social playing field that has both plagued and made necessary the concept of multiculturalism also plagues and necessitates a recognition of the twin concepts of multitemporality and temporal discrimination. The tools of critical temporal literacy through which various forms of social temporal injustice can be articulated and critiqued emerge in this way through the study of Canada's complex temporal makeup.

CHRONOPOLITICS: STARTING THE CONVERSATION ON MULTITEMPORALITY

In his influential book *Land Sliding*, W.H. New argues that land "has to be seen as a verbal trope in Canadian writing, not simply as a neutral referent."[3] By interrogating how land is represented across a wide range of texts, New seeks "to explain how various *configurations of land* function in literature (and so in Canadian culture at large) to question or confirm configurations of power."[4] This kind of study would be important anywhere, but it is especially significant in Canada, a place that is so closely associated in the cultural and historical consciousness with its majestic, resource-rich, and contested landscapes. As Thomas King argues in his study of Indigenous-settler relations, "the issue that was the *raison d'être* for each of the colonies, the issue that has made its way from coast to coast to coast and is with us today, the issue that has never changed, never varied, never faltered in its resolve is the issue of land. The issue has always been land."[5] But what about that other, less tangible coordinate of location? Time is just as significant as land to the character of the nation and to the many forms of social relations and injustices that occur within it, yet time tends to remain somewhat slippery and invisible. As Johannes Fabian points out, representations of place are more widely acknowledged as sites of ideological contestation than representations of time. He writes,

> It has long been recognized that imperialist claims to the right of occupying "empty," under-used, undeveloped space for the common good of mankind should be taken for what they really are: a monstrous lie perpetuated for the benefit of one part of humanity, for a few societies of that part, and, in the end, for one part of these societies, its dominant classes. But by and large, we remain under the spell

of an equally mendacious fiction: that interpersonal, intergroup, indeed, international Time is "public Time" – there to be occupied, measured, and allotted by the powers that be.[6]

Fabian goes so far as to argue that because of the temporal framework of "progress, development, and modernity" upon which colonial society was predicated, "*geopolitics* has its ideological foundations in *chronopolitics*."[7] The time socialization stories that underpin much of the discourse of civil society – those deep cultural narratives that teach us that time naturally functions in certain ways – are all the more powerful for the fact that they can be difficult to see.

The chronopolitical position of the Canadian nation has, of course, proven to be a divisive concept in the existing body of scholarly work, partly because of the temptation to identify a singular, distinctive form of national time. While many scholars and cultural figures have commented on the way that time appears to unfold in Canada, no single approach or statement seems capable of articulating the complexities of temporal experience in any place, let alone within a complex and fragile national collective. Northrop Frye, for instance, writing in the mid-twentieth century, resists "the parrotted cliché that this is a 'new' country and that we must spend centuries cutting forests and building roads before we can enjoy the by-products of settled leisure." Canada, he insists, "is not 'new' or 'young': it is exactly the same age as any other country under a system of industrial capitalism."[8] Like so many claims about temporality, this one is true only from a certain perspective. In contrast to Frye, Imre Szeman finds that the Canadian imagination, especially in the context of globalization, does tend to retain "a sense of *belatedness*, of having arrived too late on the historical scene, at the end of a Western modernity that had completely mapped out the global landscape in advance."[9] While the discourse of globalization tends to promote "an image of a world that is *isochronic*, a world in which everything happens at the same time and thus in which the problems and contradictions produced by an earlier, imperialist capitalism are done away with just as surely as are the limitations of time and space," Szeman argues that this discourse in fact reinforces the same political hierarchy established by imperialist capitalism in the first place, since the rules of the global playing field are created by the elite nations and corporations.[10] Stephen Crocker advances a similar argument in his claim that there exists "a form of time-consciousness peculiar to colonialism" that is characterized by a sense of uneven development.[11] While modernity in general creates "the sense of living through a completely novel, unprecedented course of events," colonies (and, for Crocker, post-war Newfoundland in particular) tend to experience a sense of delay in which "the horizon of expectations is defined by a repetition of what is already real and being lived elsewhere."[12] As a result of this pressure to catch up, acceleration can become an obsession, as "the speed at which we can erase the colonial present and replicate the other future space of experience becomes the central motivating force in historical movement."[13] The sense of temporal underdevelopment that colonies around the world can hold in common is apparent in M.G. Vassanji's novel *No New Land* when Nurdin Lalani recalls his childhood in east Africa:

Big Ben says eighteen hours Greenwich mean time, and Father looks up, raises an eyebrow, if you please, and shush, everyone listens to perfect inflections from the BBC, you dare not scrape or cough at this holiest of hours at home and you hold your water and your bowels and your wind, and if a giggle escapes, then the wrath of God, Haji Lalani's cane on your buttocks.[14]

For colonies of global empires, there can be a sense that development, like great art, is something that has already occurred somewhere else, and a feeling that the colony merely listens in on the voice of temporal authority, which comes always from a distant centre.

The notion of Canada's "newness" – when it is not rejected altogether – can thus emphasize several different, sometimes conflicting, temporal experiences: Canada has much growth to do; it is full of promise and free from the tired feuds of previous eras; it is a belated vehicle travelling along a track that others have already laid out; and, like other colonized places, it is a relatively powerless arrival on a pre-existing world stage. Canada, though, is not a simple colony. As the question posed in the title of Laura Moss's book *Is Canada Postcolonial?* suggests, the peculiar configuration of social and historical relations in Canada makes the nation at once a colony whose ownership has never been returned to the place's original inhabitants, and a post-colonial nation defined in accordance with its own social make-up and decision making. In keeping with this ambiguous position, Canada has been seen not only as too young or just old enough, but also as *more* mature than other nations; Sylvia Söderlind points out that amid the late twentieth-century enthusiasm over the promise of a global multicultural future, there emerges a sense that "Canada has gone from running to catch up with the world to having already reached whatever place the whole world is aiming at"[15] – a notion that she denounces as sanctimonious and dismissive of "Quebec's status as the ghost that haunts Canadian self-definition."[16] As Söderlind's and Crocker's comments reveal, not only is the temporal position of Canada as a whole difficult to pin down, but regional differences can easily disrupt claims of supposedly national temporalities – and, as we will see, temporal experiences within a given region are also multiple and contested.

The matter of Canada's relative position in the world's timeline is further complicated when we question the very linear notion of chronological time that permits any claim to newness or oldness, as Frye does when he compares Canadian literature with the traditional canon of English literature. Frye writes,

> To an English poet, the tradition of his own country and language
> proceeds in a direct chronological line down to himself, and that in
> its turn is part of a gigantic funnel of tradition extending back to
> Homer and the Old Testament. But to a Canadian, broken off from
> this linear sequence and having none of his own, the traditions of
> Europe appear as a kaleidoscopic whirl with no definite shape or
> meaning, but with a profound irony lurking in its varied and
> conflicting patterns.[17]

This, too, is an overstatement. Such an assertion not only obscures the multiple forms of non-European lineage from which many Canadians are descended, but also forgets the fact that the sense of irony and amorphousness that sometimes characterizes the Canadian perspective is tempered with a more conservative attitude in which linear history is preserved and reinforced. There is no kaleidoscopic irony in the resolute sense of linear civilizational development that led the Canadian government to confine members of "primitive" Indigenous nations to residential schools.

Recognizing the need for complexity in theorizations of Canadian temporality, Daniel Coleman borrows Bakhtin's literary model of the "chronotope" – a cognitive image that arranges our conceptualization of time's passage – and applies this concept more broadly to the sphere of social relations, identifying within Canadian culture four coexisting chronotopes. The most dominant of these is Isochronic or Imperial Time, which underpins the Canadian invader-settler narrative and "understands everyone in the world to be on a single timeline, with some cultures being more advanced and leading the way into the future while others are more primitive and 'backward.'"[18] The other chronotopes include Nation-Based Post-Colonial Time, which "marks its beginning as the moment when the colony cut its ties to its colonial parent";[19] Diasporic Displacement Time, in which "cultural groups retain their image of themselves in time by reference to the trauma of displacement";[20] and what Coleman tentatively calls Indigenous Concentric Time, in which time is shaped like the concentric circles of a tree trunk, and the past "is not placed in a line of progression where it is seen as superseded by the present," but rather forms "the centre of ongoing life."[21] Wendat scholar Georges Sioui would appear to agree with the latter characterization when he writes that "the Circle is at the centre of our Aboriginal thinking … We believe that the day, the lunar month, the year, even human life itself, are circular phenomena, and that there are cycles of many years, representing the circular reality."[22] Referring to European "linear thought" as a "spiritual and mental affliction,"[23] Sioui suggests that "the thing that is named 'the past' is a European construct and is not part of the Amerindian psyche,"[24] a tension that I will examine in more detail in chapter 4.

The dominance of Imperial Time is closely tied to homogenizing meta-narratives associated with progress, growth, and development, and it is an inescapable presence across many domains of Canadian culture. Because it frames progressive technological and social betterment as both an aspirational dream and an inevitable reality, linear Imperial Time facilitates massive development projects and the envisioning of perpetual improvement to society as a whole. On the other hand, Imperial Time can hold the social imagination hostage, shutting down conversations about the need to radically re-envision the concepts of industrial development and economic growth in order to avoid destroying the ecosystems that keep us alive. Imperial Time also fails to do justice to many members of society because it represents subaltern groups as "backward," or simply fails to acknowledge their experiences. A seemingly innocuous statement, such as E.J. Pratt's comment in *Towards the Last Spike* that the Canadian Pacific Railway *had* to be built because "a nation, like the world, could not stand still,"[25] reveals the dual face of Imperial Time; the linear vision of progressive development fosters the completion of astonishing nation-building projects, yet it also dismisses alternative visions of nationhood and collective temporality as impossible, abhorrently stagnant, or non-existent. Imperial Time has the power to colonize people's perceptions of value, justice, and relevance, embodying one of the key ways in which, in the words of Ngũgĩ wa Thiong'o, a colonized person is "made to see the world and where he stands in it as seen and defined by or reflected in the culture of the language of imposition."[26] In his memoir, for instance, George Copway is internally conflicted about the effect of progress on the Ojibwe people, writing at one point, "O ! tell me, ye 'pale faces,' tell, / Where have my proud ancestors gone ? ... Whose wigwam stood where cities rise,"[27] but later deciding that "multitudes have left their wigwams, their woods, and the chase, and are now endeavoring to tread in the footsteps of worthy white men."[28] In abandoning the literal chase of subsistence hunting, these individuals join the figurative chase of progress toward an Imperial civility that will probably always see them as delayed travellers.

The degree to which linear progressive time presents itself as the *only* time is apparent in the remarkable conclusion – asserted through the time socialization stories of many public figures – that a period of time lacking in economic growth is in fact an absence of time. During the global financial crisis of 2008, US President Barack Obama warned that without government intervention the United States could experience a "lost decade" reminiscent of Japan's economic stagnation of the 1990s.[29] Canada's *Maclean's* magazine picked up on this language with the head-line, "A Lost Decade of Growth: Many Real Indicators Put Us Back to Where We Were 10 Years Ago."[30] Related to this is the frequent character-ization of impoverished people as slow contestants in a race, who struggle to "keep up with inflation" until becoming one of those who "have fallen behind."[31] I will examine the connections between socio-economic class and experiences of time in chapter 3.

The constellation of cultural productions and practices known as post-modernism has waged the most obvious battle against the supposed truth and desirability of the grand notion of progress tied to the linear mea-surement of time, but just as patriarchy and gender bias remain deep social problems long after the first and second waves of feminism, so too do the exclusionary narratives of linear advancement, productivity, and speed retain their hold on cultural discourse. Campaigns of temporal resistance against corporate capitalism's culture of speed, short-term profit growth, and inequitable valuations of different people's time have focused on the desirability of slowness as well as the principles of seasonality and temporal equity; these movements include Slow Food as well as the lesser-known TimeBanking system, whose members barter their own labour in equally valued one-hour segments.[32] These models have offered compelling but irregularly adopted alternatives.

For his part, Coleman identifies linear Imperial Time and the other chronotopes not as absolute categories but as indications that "a diverse civil society cannot establish any one of these chronotopes as its sole narrative."[33] This conclusion makes sense in light of the fact that different timekeeping models frequently blend into one another; for instance, while the linear model of time and its associated notion of progress are pervasive, Zerubavel points out that the ubiquitous concept of the week involves "a *circular conception of time*" in that it "revolves around the experience of *recurrence*."[34] This leads him to conclude that linear and circular conceptions of time "are not necessarily mutually exclusive, and one can very well view time in both a linear and a circular fashion."[35] In chapter 4 I will further highlight how linear and circular models of time are deeply intertwined. Moreover, the conclusion that there can be no "sole narrative" of time is also significant in that large social chronotopes cannot possibly tell the whole story of the conflicting and overlapping temporal maps, both collective and personal, that shape the temporal imagination in Canada. The realization that no single model of time is adequate to represent complex forms of experience is a vital first step.

Coleman suggests that one way to counteract the problematic dominance of Imperial Time, whose single timeline shape is in fact intrinsic to all of the chronotopes that he identifies except for the Indigenous Concentric model, is "to develop an awareness of contending, rather than single, civilities, and this awareness will involve cognizance of multiple, contemporaneous chronotopes."[36] This conclusion echoes Robert Levine's comment on the contrasting approaches of clock-based time and event-based time, that "the person, or the culture, who combines both modes in a temporal repertoire – or even better, who can draw upon a multiplicity of modes – is more likely to be up to all occasions."[37] Levine uses the term "multitemporality" to describe this desired condition,[38] and while his open-ended comment about a "multiplicity of modes" does not specify what additional temporalities might be at stake, it does recognize that alternative, often unacknowledged forms of temporality deserve to be taken into account, and suggests that the idea of multitemporality can usefully be expanded to respond to the need to recognize multiple, contemporaneous modes of time at various levels of social organization. As Homi Bhabha writes, there is "always the distracting presence of another temporality that disturbs the contemporaneity of the national present."[39] The imposition of one dominant form of time onto a diverse population fails to recognize the existence of other models of time, and bestows the vision of linearity with tremendous power in shaping value judgments both large and small. The concept of multitemporality, then, is descriptive in that it articulates the reality of complex and alternative forms of time, and is also aspirational in that it asks us to adjust our everyday conceptions of time in order to challenge dominant structures of temporal privilege and power. And yet, building awareness of multiple legitimate understandings of time is a difficult task, requiring deep questioning of dominant temporal assumptions. Levine's assertion that "no beliefs are more ingrained and subsequently hidden than those about time"[40] signals the difficulty inherent in embracing multitemporality, a problem I will discuss further in the concluding sections of this book. In much of the discussions that follow, I will examine some of the "distracting" alternative temporalities beyond those implied by Coleman's chronotopes, in order to show how focusing on other temporalities in their own right can lead to an understanding of time in Canada that more accurately reflects diverse experiences and inequitable relations of power. First, I will trace some of the primary ways in which normative time has operated in Canada, especially through increasingly standardized clock time, and examine how these dominant modes relate to or impinge on, and thus reveal the existence of alternative experiences of time.

"MORE CLOCKS THAN BIBLES": THE POWER AND LIMITS OF NORMATIVE TIME

When Cartier and other explorers mapped the New World terrain, they domesticated what they saw as an uncharted wilderness not only in terms of a European spatial framework of latitude and longitude, but also within a European framework of time. The temporality of this landscape had already been understood by its inhabitants in terms of creation myths about Raven or Sky Woman, but as the term "New World" suggests these histories were largely forgotten, and were replaced by the Julian and Gregorian calendars. In his journal from 1534, Cartier quickly inscribes European temporality onto the Canadian landscape at Gaspé: "On [Friday] the twenty-fourth of the said month [July], we had a cross made thirty feet high, which was put together in the presence of a number of savages on the point at the entrance to this harbour."[41] Like Cartier's calendar dates and the cross that he erects, the small notation at the edge of Samuel de Champlain's seventeenth-century map[42] of what is now Atlantic Canada, "1612," carries within it the assumption of what Paul Ricoeur calls an "axial moment" in history,[43] the birth of Christ.

Here, David Landes's comment on the practice of Chinese emperors who began their reign by revising the official calendar of their predecessor holds true: "The calendar was a perquisite of sovereignty, like the right to mint coins. Knowledge of the right time and season was power, for it was this knowledge that governed both the acts of everyday life and decisions of state."[44] The centrality of the Christian era was, and is, reinscribed into the collective consciousness not only each New Year's Eve but every time we refer to a year by its sequential number. Even the secular notation – which uses "Before Common Era" in place of "Before Christ" and "Common Era" in place of "Anno Domini" – retains the same culturally specific frame of reference and imposes a particular set of meanings for the word "common," casting other non-Western frameworks of time beyond the pale of normative experience. What is more, a date such as 1612 marks Canada's birth as a delayed one; given the relative starting point, the country is imagined into existence more than sixteen centuries "behind" Europe.[45]

Thomas King takes issue with a closely related problem in his critique of the term "post-colonial," a term that, he says, "reeks of unabashed ethnocentrism and well-meaning dismissal" in its assumption of the arrival of Europeans as the watershed moment against which contemporary culture – even Indigenous literature – must be measured.[46] "At the same time," he writes, "the term organizes the literature progressively suggesting that there is both progress and improvement [and] supposes that contemporary Native writing is largely a construct of oppression."[47] One could easily expand King's criticism to point to the Gregorian calendar itself and its assumption of a Western, Christian framework situated within a path of progress. The Gregorian calendar presents time as a single narrative, and serves as one of the most powerful examples of both the necessity and the inadequacy of dominant temporal registers: a common method of naming and counting the days is necessary for the coordination of shared existence in a social world, yet no calendar system has a neutral relation to cultural history and social power relations. While many alternative date-reckoning systems exist, the narratives of time that they tell have been rendered relatively powerless in Canada since the adoption of Gregorian time.[48] So ubiquitous is the Gregorian calendar that the name itself sounds unfamiliar; in standard parlance it is always simply "the calendar." King's protest that the term post-colonial "is an act of imagination and an act of imperialism that demands that I imagine myself as something I did not choose to be, as something I would not choose to become,"[49] appears in a volume whose copyright is listed as "©1997 the authors": a small example of the ironies that spring from the assumption of a culturally specific time scale. In chapters 4 and 5 I will examine the challenges that literary authors have posed to Gregorian time.

The period of time in which Canada was colonized also overlaps with the period of time in which mechanical clocks became accurate enough to measure minutes and seconds, and grew affordable for individuals. These developments fostered massive social changes, and had especially pronounced consequences in three areas: colonization and empire building; time discipline and its companion concepts of efficiency, punctuality, and productivity; and social acceleration. While these consequences were felt in different ways throughout the industrial world, they achieved a particular constellation of meanings in early Canada, whose settlers were at once ambassadors for the practices of industrial temporal colonization, and outsiders observing the British and American empires with mixed senses of identification and apprehension.

Ancient civilizations had divided the sun's path across the sky into segments thousands of years ago by observing the motions of the sun's shadow; Herodotus's writings suggest that the use of sundials and the twelve divisions of the day come from the Babylonians,[50] while Michael Lombardi claims that the twelve-hour clock has its origin in the ancient

Egyptians' use of a base 12 counting system.[51] Despite this long history of timekeeping, though, David Landes argues in his seminal work *Revolution in Time* that the contemporary social importance of precise time measurement can be traced more specifically "to the invention of the mechanical clock in medieval Europe."[52] This development, Landes notes, "was one of a number of major advances that turned Europe from a weak, peripheral, highly vulnerable outpost of Mediterranean civilization into a hegemonic aggressor. Time measurement was at once a sign of newfound creativity and an agent and catalyst in the use of knowledge for wealth and power."[53] Building on Galileo's knowledge of the temporal reliability of swinging pendulums, the Dutch scientist Christiaan Huygens surpassed earlier mechanical clocks by developing the first pendulum clock in 1656, ushering in the era of timepieces that could measure seconds with reasonable precision.[54] As Levine writes, humanity "had made remarkable progress measuring the seasons, the weeks, and even the hours of night and day as early as thousands of years ago. But it was only at this point, in the last three centuries, that the pendulum clock offered the potential to live by the precise hour, let alone the minute and second."[55] Mariners working on the front lines of intercontinental trade, science, and colonization followed later horological developments closely, since accurate timekeeping at sea would prove invaluable in pinpointing a ship's position; latitude could be measured by observing celestial markers such as the North Star, but accurate longitudinal measurements required knowing the vessel's east-west spatial distance, and thus daylight time differential, from a known observatory such as Greenwich. The lack of stable seafaring clocks during Cartier's and Champlain's voyages resulted in maps of Canada that today look skewed and misshapen, but in 1759, the same year as the Battle of the Plains of Abraham, the self-taught English horologist John Harrison completed his masterpiece chronometer watch, a highly reliable clock that could maintain its accuracy during rough intercontinental voyages.[56] Nautical mapping grew more precise, and the importing of clocks – the objects themselves as well as their increasingly profound cultural significance – went hand in hand with the development of European colonies in Canada and elsewhere. The material significance of timepieces to the colonizing projects of exploration and cartography is visible in the journal of John Franklin, who relied heavily on chronometers for finding his way during his

exploration of Canada's northern coast in 1819, calibrating and recalibrating the clocks' slight rates of error whenever possible. He records an incident where he slips on moss and tumbles into the White Fall river
"betwixt two of the falls," saving himself by catching hold of a willow
branch and waiting for rescue. "The only bad consequence of this accident," he writes, "was an injury sustained by a very valuable chronometer,
(No. 1733,) belonging to Daniel Moore, Esq., of Lincoln's Inn."[57]

The implications of clock development did not stop at the facilitation
of empire building and colonization; the widespread dissemination of
accurate clock time throughout the public sphere, in Landes's words,
"laid the basis for *time discipline*."[58] While "time obedience" reflects the
willingness of people to respond to an external time announcement such
as the summoning of a public bell, time discipline is the *internalized* drive
to be punctual which comes about only when mechanical timepieces are
accurate and ubiquitous. In a complementary thesis, Gerhard Dohrn-van
Rossum finds that a "fundamental change in time consciousness," in this
case characterized by a widespread sense of "time pressure" and time
scarcity, "occurred with the transition from an agrarian to an industrial
society that began in the Middle Ages."[59] Dohrn-van Rossum resists the
conventional notion that the invention of the mechanical clock in the
thirteenth century served to replace "organic" experienced time with
"abstract mathematical time," showing instead that the actual historical
transition took place over a much lengthier period of time and still
allowed for the existence of experiential time alongside objective time.[60]
However, his work still demonstrates, like Landes's, that the pervasive
influence of time measurement, time pressure, time discipline, and the
related concepts of productivity, efficiency, and punctuality – especially
within the industrial era – reflects the new role of clock time in ordering
modern social experience.

The third way in which ubiquitous clock time shaped modern social
development in the Western world was through the processes of social
acceleration. In his comprehensive study, *Social Acceleration*, Hartmut
Rosa finds that the drive toward time discipline and punctuality that
accompanied prevalent clock time is best understood in the larger context of acceleration itself as the defining feature of modernization, "for
the history of modernity can not only be plausibly reconstructed as a history of acceleration; this is in fact the only way in which the unity of

its driving forces, its contradictions, and its historical phases can be revealed."[61] Rosa's insights become especially important in the discussion of late modernity, but for the purposes of examining early Canada, his study effectively confirms Robert Levine's view that the new prevalence of accurate clocks in the industrial era led to a greatly accelerated pace of life, and was in fact the dawn of an entirely new way of inhabiting time. "Clock time," Levine writes, "has revolutionized the cadence of daily life,"[62] largely replacing the slower paced "event time," and driving people to accomplish an ever greater number of tasks per unit of time. Like many scholars of time, Levine repeats Lewis Mumford's memorable assertion that, for the above reasons, "the clock, not the steam-engine, is the key-machine of the modern industrial age."[63]

By the early nineteenth century affordable clocks for everyday use were being mass-produced in the United States, a process that, as Thomas Allen notes, served to replace "expensive, handcrafted items" with "affordable commodities available to all levels of American society."[64] These affordable clocks were soon sold throughout the Canadas. Allen, though, is more cautious in his estimation of the effects of commonplace clocks; while he notes that "temporal modernization" has resulted in "a world made over not only economically but also socially and culturally to suit first the exchange networks of mercantile capitalism and later the clockwork rationality of the free market,"[65] he develops a more nuanced picture through analyses of various actual clocks as well as artistic representations of clocks, arguing that American clock culture did not supplant but instead entered into dialogue with cultural models of time based on nature, religion, and localities: "Clock time was, to be sure, understood as significantly different from natural and religious time, but it was also deeply intertwined with those other temporal modes."[66] Barbara Adam, too, argues that clock time never assumes total significance, but exists in negotiation with other models of time: "While the existence of clock time facilitates context independence and global standardization, decisions about the timing of even the most habitual of actions are made on a one-off basis and with reference to a particular context"; thus, "clock time has not *replaced* the multiple social, biological, and physical sources of time; it has rather *changed* the meanings of the variable times, temporalities, timings, and tempos of bio-cultural origin."[67] The conceptual weight of clock time is so great that the complex interactions Allen and Adam refer to have often been overlooked, as they are in George Woodcock's 1944 essay "The Tyranny of the Clock," where Woodcock draws an absolute distinction between "Modern, Western man" who lives "according to the mechanical and mathematical symbols of clock time" and "the earlier societies" in which "time is represented in the cyclic processes of nature."[68] Still, despite the complex negotiations between clock time and other temporalities, Levine convincingly demonstrates that people within societies that adhere more closely to clock time work more hours per week and tend to be more pressed for time, suggesting that even if the social conversion to clock time is never absolute, clock-based cultures do disclose quantitative and qualitative differences in temporal experience.

These three implications of prevalent clock time in the industrial age – the facilitation of empire building and colonization, the imposition of time discipline and productivity as central values, and the acceleration of the everyday pace of life – all inform the social critique developed in Thomas Haliburton's 1836 collection of humorous Nova Scotian political stories, *The Clockmaker*. While accurate, portable clocks were now becoming ubiquitous throughout the Western world, *The Clockmaker* identifies the particular ways in which the spread of clock time was tied conceptually to the character and anxieties of colonial life in what would become Atlantic Canada. Haliburton's serialized stories follow the titular clock salesman, an American named Sam Slick who peddles clocks throughout Nova Scotia, as seen through the eyes of a Nova Scotian narrator who continually inquires into Sam's methods. From the beginning, Haliburton comments tellingly on the growing primacy of clock time in Canadian life, when the narrator declares that "the house of every substantial farmer had three substantial ornaments: a wooden clock, a tin reflector [oven], and a Polyglot Bible."[69] While this statement places clock time alongside food preparation and Christianity in terms of fundamental importance to daily settler life, Sam goes one step further. When someone tells him that Nova Scotia "ain't a bread country," he replies, "You might as well say it ain't a clock country, when to my sartin knowledge, there are more clocks than Bibles in it."[70] The implication, that clock time has in fact supplanted Christianity as society's foundational source of knowledge, is driven home when a Catholic priest asks Sam, "What are you, Mr Slick?" and Sam replies that he is a Clockmaker.

The priest admits that "every man's religion is his own," though he, tellingly, has already bought a clock for himself.[71] As Haliburton's satirical tone suggests, the view that clock time functions as a form of religion is both absurd and accurate. Adherence to the discipline of the clock carries the weight of faith, devotion, and morality, and Sam's clocks are rapidly converting followers away from the Christian religion that appears in danger, at least satirically, of becoming obsolete; the importance of clock time to everyday matters of social organization has become axiomatic. Kevin Kelly has suggested that "from the very beginning clocks were simulacra"[72] – that is, they manufacture the very temporality they presume to measure – and while a hint of this is visible in the fact that early mechanical clocks in the fourteenth century were designed to help monks keep track of prayer schedules,[73] Haliburton's writing reflects the way that clock time eventually takes on a life of its own, becoming a simulacrum not only of time, but of the religious practice it was intended to facilitate. Instead of winding the clock so we will know what time to pray, we now wind the clock so that we can follow the clock, a reflection of the profound place of time discipline in everyday life – and a notion that carries over, with some degree of irony, into the late twentieth century when Leonard Cohen sings in "Closing Time" of going up "to the tower where the blessed hours chime," not the tower that points to heaven.

When Haliburton's narrator asks Sam how it is "that you manage to sell such an immense number of clocks, which certainly cannot be called necessary articles, among a people with whom there seems to be so great a scarcity of money," Sam explains that he relies on flattery and human nature.[74] Leaving a clock behind at the house of a deacon, another religious figure, Sam confides his covert sales strategy to the narrator: the deacon will not learn "until I call for the clock, that having once indulged in the use of a superfluity, how difficult it is to give it up. We can do without any article of luxury we have never had, but when once obtained, it is not in 'human natur" to surrender it voluntarily."[75] A powerful device that exerts a curious influence over its possessor, the clock becomes a symbol along the lines of Frodo Baggins's magical Ring. And, like Tolkien, Haliburton suggests that the desirable object carries with it a heavy ideological weight. Throughout *The Clockmaker* Sam admonishes Nova Scotians for being "behind the intelligence of the age,"[76] unlike Americans, who "reckon hours and minutes to be dollars and cents."[77]

"We 'go ahead'; the Nova Scotians 'go astarn.'"[78] Beyond selling clocks, Sam wants to convince Nova Scotians to race along the same path of linear technological progress, and to adhere to the same principles of temporal accounting, that he sees the Americans as having perfected. In selling clocks throughout Nova Scotia, Sam is in fact smuggling the ideologies of progress, efficiency, and the acceleration of productivity into Canadian settler culture. Drawing a parallel between clock time and the railroad – that iconic symbol of industrial progress and American expansionism – Sam declares that in the United States, the railroad "*is river, bridge, road, and canal, all in one. It saves what we hain't got to spare, men, horses, carts, vessels, barges, and what's all in all – time.*"[79]

In her historically nuanced discussion of *The Clockmaker*, Oana Godeanu-Kenworthy points out that Haliburton, a lawyer, judge, historian, and politician as well as a successful writer, was highly cognizant of the position of the Canadian colonies, and Nova Scotia in particular, at the delicate "intersection of the British Empire with the new American democratic and republican empire";[80] Haliburton was "a vocal member in the ongoing debate over the fate of the Maritime colonies within the larger family of the British Empire, the available choices being either annexation by the United States or a reinvention of the role of the colonies in the imperial network."[81] Haliburton's satire, Godeanu-Kenworthy argues, emphasizes the perceived shortcomings of American political philosophy, in particular casting doubt on the viability of the American democratic system, and it "can be understood therefore as part of the larger discussion on contested nationalisms and state formation in North America in the nineteenth century, because it dramatizes the competing versions of national identity intersecting in the Canadian colonies at the time."[82] Haliburton's choice of the clock – or to be more specific, the clock-selling business – as the central conceit in the book imbues the clock trade with a political and nationalistic significance as well as a religious one. In Haliburton's Nova Scotia, the somewhat naïve members of workaday settler culture become easy prey for the sophisticated American clock salesman who, in representing the modern ideologies of progress, time discipline, and acceleration, also serves as a figurehead for an anxious belief among the largely Loyalist Nova Scotian population, for whom the War of 1812 was still a relatively fresh memory, that the United States wished to increase its dominance beyond the established American borders. The tools of colonization could include not only ships and guns, but addictive, abundant clocks. Of course, like so many narratives that focus on shared anxieties, *The Clockmaker* presents the normative social group in question, in this case the settler population of Nova Scotia, with a degree of false innocence, obscuring the fact that the British colonies themselves had already carried out a sustained program of temporal colonization, enforcing the Western model of progress in the development of the land, the exploitation of resources, and the suppression of the Mi'kmaq and other Indigenous nations. If the clockmaker is a figure who disseminates the Western temporal ideologies tied to modernity, progress, and colonization, then Sam Slick's customers are just as much clockmakers and clock sellers as he is.

The late nineteenth and early twentieth centuries saw massive changes in the large-scale coordination of clock time as well as the orientation toward time on different social levels. The ethical imperative of time discipline that had established itself with the spread of clock technology had become further pronounced through the availability of pocket watches, and it comes as little surprise that by 1891, twenty-four years after Canada's Confederation, the American Electric Signal Clock Company was marketing temporal precision and punctuality as moral necessities: "If there is one virtue that should be cultivated more than any other by him who would succeed in life, it is punctuality; if there is one error to be avoided, it is being behind time."[83] Peter Galison notes that the massive project of laying intercontinental telegraph lines across the Atlantic Ocean in the mid-nineteenth century created more accurate clock synchronizations between Europe and North America,[84] so that, in Christopher Dewdney's words, "the concept of a global 'now' inserted itself into the average citizen's consciousness, at least in Western nations."[85] For Galison, the extension of the electronically synchronized clock "into train stations, neighborhoods, and churches meant that synchronized time intervened in peoples' lives the way electric power, sewage, or gas did: as a circulating fluid of modern urban life."[86] In his wide-ranging study, Stephen Kern finds that a cluster of changes in technology and culture around the turn of the century – the wireless telegraph, the telephone, cinema, automobiles, and airplanes – "created distinctive new modes of thinking about and experiencing time and space."[87] The telephone, for instance, effectively allowed people "to be in two places at the same time,"[88] and had a levelling influence on historically hierarchical spaces, making "all places equidistant from the seat of power and hence of equal value," and bypassing the hierarchical "protective function of doors, waiting rooms, servants, and guards."[89] In particular, Kern sees a critical tension emerge between a new homogeneous public time and the many heterogeneous private times that public time appeared to suppress. In Canada, several events associated with this new era of electronic time prove especially illuminating in understanding the configurations of power tied to the broad social imposition of clock-based synchronization. The levelling influence of time- and space-collapsing technologies, after all, is far from total. I will discuss the problem of industrial working hours in chapter 3, and the temporal implications of the First World War (through the eyes of Timothy Findley) in chapter 5. But the events that I will consider here have to do with the social politics of the large-scale orchestration of clock time itself through the division of the globe into standard time zones and the implementation of Daylight Saving Time.

The division of the world into "standard" time zones was not a single event, but a process that occurred gradually, first through a national standardized time system in England in 1848, then through a partial system of "time belts" created by railroad companies in North America in 1883,[90] and finally through the slow adoption around the world of the familiar twenty-four global time zones in the years and decades following the 1884 Prime Meridian Conference in Washington, DC, which established Greenwich as the prime meridian of the world.[91] Standardized time has been understood in historical analysis as a landmark in the shaping of modern time consciousness, as well as a source of significant controversy. For Kern, universal time was a key element in the larger conflict at the turn of the century between homogeneous public time and multiplicitous private times. While he notes that "the modern age" as a whole "embraced universal time and punctuality because these served its larger needs," he draws attention mainly toward the passionate debates that emerged through the work of "those novelists, psychologists, physicists, and sociologists who examined the way individuals create as many different times as there are life styles, reference systems, and social forms."[92] Ultimately, for Kern, the central temporal conflict of the age was embodied in the fact that "the imposition of universal public time intrude[d] upon the uniqueness of private experience in private time."[93] Adam Barrows, on the other hand, disputes the idea that the opposition to standardized time occurred primarily at the level of individual private temporalities, arguing instead that modernist writers as well as political delegates from various countries outside of the British Empire objected to the universalization of time in political rather than psychological terms, expressing concerns that globally standardized time would impinge upon their own national and cultural temporalities. For Barrows, the central conflict was "not the tension between public and private time, but rather the tension between national and global time."[94] Other historians examine the arguments about competing time standards that arose between rival observatories, railroad operators, and different levels of government.[95]

And yet, for all of these controversies, it seems that the general public in Canada dutifully set their clocks a few minutes forwards or backwards to match standard time on the prescribed day with little complaint or fanfare. Noting the tendency of studies such as Kern's to evaluate primarily "elite" responses to changing experiences of time in the nineteenth century, Jeremy L. Stein evaluates newspaper and town council archives to arrive at an understanding of how "ordinary Canadians" experienced the transition to standard time. He finds that, aside from practical notices in Ontario and Quebec newspapers reminding people to adjust their clocks on the designated day, the transition "received limited comment in the press, and there was no identifiable public opposition to the change."[96] He speculates that the reception was impassive primarily because "the new system of time-reckoning was steadily introduced on the North American continent over several decades, and because it easily co-existed with other local work routines."[97]

Two important (and to some extent contradictory) principles seem to be at stake, then, in the adoption of standardized clock time. First, it is important to recognize that the imposition of widespread, even global, standardized time structures involves highly ideological dimensions, and it tends to be shaped more by powerful interests than by democratic consultations. The work of Sandford Fleming provides a good illustration of this. The Scottish-born Canadian best known for managing the surveying of the Canadian Pacific Railway became integral to the global adoption of standard time when he advocated tirelessly for what he called universal or "cosmic" time. "We are now obliged," Fleming wrote, "to take a comprehensive view of the globe in considering the question of time-reckoning. We should not confine our view to one limited horizon, to one country, or to one continent."[98] The concept of "local time," he argued, "is entirely incorrect. There is no such thing ... Time remains uninfluenced by matter, by space, or by distance. It is universal and essentially non-local."[99] For Clark Blaise, Fleming's proposal to universalize time under government authority "has Canada written all over it ... He saw time as a free, common resource, not as a privately held property on the order of the American railroads or the sold time signals from the Western Union Company. Fleming was always a government man."[100] The Canada that is "written all over" Fleming's vision of cosmic time, though, is not entirely a genial one, for the idea discloses a highly political ideological underpinning beneath its rhetoric of universality and neutrality. Fleming's system attempted to foist a particular brand of neutrality upon a disparate and unequal world. By dismissing local time as "entirely incorrect," Fleming dismissed any system of time reckoning that falls outside the particular system that was simultaneously cosmic and of his own invention; while brilliantly conceived as a method for coordinating an increasingly interconnected world, his comprehensive view of the globe was not necessarily interested in the perspectives of the people who populate it. What is more, the idea that global standard time is a free resource under government authority conceals much of the true motivation for the global time system in the first place. In his archival study of the 1884 Prime Meridian Conference, Barrows finds that the key motivation, for Fleming and others, for the implementation of global standard time was the facilitation of transnational investment and business arrangements. Arguing that "clock coordination was never purely the outcome of disinterested rationality," Barrows finds that "what is particularly modern about standard time is that it facilitates the unification of global markets to the penetration of capital."[101] To this day, then, the work of Fleming and others to implement global standard time is interpreted variously as a grand vision of neutral public harmonizing or as a transnational corporate effort to pave over the multiple temporalities by which local communities had structured their lives with the new easily traversed singular time of standardized clocks which would facilitate the transactions of wealthy investors.

The problematic homogenizing tendency of the global standard time system is visible in the fact that "local" time in any given place is determined not by the position of the sun or a local observatory, but according to that place's categorization within the standard twenty-four time zones, imaginary constructs in which we have invested heavily, and which, like the days of the week for Panych's unnamed man, both open and constrict our experience of time. For Canadians, standard time facilitates participation in global commerce as well as coordination between geographically diverse Canadian regions, yet clock time is set to a standard that is housed beyond our borders and that does not impact everyone equally, resulting in uneasy tensions when the global system fails to accommodate local concerns.[102] A quick glance at a map of the world's time zones, with their jagged lines and isolated pockets, is enough to identify the clash between local and global time. Saskatchewan, for instance, officially observes Central Standard Time without daylight saving, sharing the same time as Alberta during the summer and Manitoba during the winter, with certain exceptions such as the town of Lloydminster which adheres to Alberta time year-round. The very global connectedness that Fleming saw as the destruction of local time in fact requires local idiosyncrasies to be agonized over. The unifying impulse of global synchronized time highlights the fact that Canada is a conglomerate of many places, and multiple times, rather than a single actor that experiences consistent consequences as a result of temporal standardization.[103]

The second implication – and one that can fade into the background in overly critical analyses of standard time – is visible in the fact that the imposition of a new time standard does not *necessarily* pose any significant problem for the general population, and can indeed represent a welcome adjustment. Stein's realization that the adoption of standard time in central Canada met little public resistance hints at a broad social recognition of the fact that a widely shared system of time reckoning is deeply important for everyday functioning. The process of adjusting local clocks by a few minutes, even if this means abandoning the solar time measurements of a local observatory in favour of imported time signals from a distant centre, can be seen as a fairly trivial measure to take in the service of simplifying communications, travel, commerce, and train schedules. Thus, while calls to recognize the threat that standard time poses to individual "private" times or to national and cultural temporalities implicitly advocate for a greater tolerance for multitemporality, the tremendous value of a shared time standard for facilitating everyday sociality should not be overlooked. Temporal alignment, at least to the extent that human temporal experience can be registered through the hands of a clock, is vital for the coordination of shared social existence, and is not necessarily very difficult to achieve in the age of electronic time signals. The wide distribution of mechanical clock technology in the first place, which instituted clock time itself as well as the imperatives of time discipline, was a much more drastic change to everyday life.

One further example is worth considering here as a kind of limit case. The controversial implementation of Daylight Saving Time (DST) in Quebec early in the twentieth century, as represented through the painstaking archival research of Jarrett Rudy, demonstrates how the amenability of the public to the adoption of new time standards can quickly reach a limit when the time shift is perceived as too great or too inequitable, and it also points to the way that everyday life can descend into a form of temporal chaos when large social mandates for measuring time are simply absent. Daylight Saving Time, which had been adopted in 1916 throughout most of Europe in an effort to align people's productive hours with the early sunrises of summer, was pitched both overseas and in North America as a policy that would increase leisure time and save lighting costs. However, while standard time may have been adopted in central Canada without much in the way of protest, Rudy identifies a series of widespread and extended conflicts around the idea of DST in Quebec. The proposal for DST pitted rural communities, who worried about advancing their already early morning routines and losing out on some of the productive agricultural hours later in the day, against urban communities that placed a higher priority on the concerns of industry. In some cases it pitted anglophone businessmen against leaders of the Montreal Catholic Church, a few of whom "publicly opposed DST on the grounds that it was an attack on the authority of God" and others of whom "argued that DST would cause practical difficulties for the majority of the population."[104] Furthermore, because DST was seen as a war measure, it became "stigmatized among anti-war francophones in Quebec."[105] And finally, once the war had ended the question of DST became even more consequential in the sense that its supporters now emphasized its *permanent* necessity to ensure Canada's place in global economic progress, while detractors continued to point to the lack of sleep, especially among rural labourers, women, and children, that was caused by moving activities earlier in the morning and desynchronizing clocks from the actual position of the sun by as much as ninety minutes.[106] The situation in Montreal, Canada's most populous city at the time, was especially complex because "churches, schools, factories, and courts decided to keep different standards of time,"[107] while the realization that the inclusion or exclusion of women and children from polls on D S T would be significant to the outcome gave rise to contradictory claims of public support or opposition to the measure as well as heated debates over whose will should count in the democratic process.[108] The debate continued into the 1920s, and when members of industrialist lobbies unilaterally switched to D S T, followed by certain schools and churches, "federal government offices began to fall in line, suggesting that they accepted the argument that D S T was the practice of the community."[109]

One of the significant insights that emerges from Rudy's study is that, just as the creation of global standard time was closely tied to the powerful interests of commerce and capital, so too was the question of D S T in Quebec largely an issue of socio-economic class, with powerful business lobbies (mainly anglophone) supporting the measure and a significant portion of the working-class populations opposed.[110] "The institutional power of the largely anglophone economic elite as major employers of industrial labour," Rudy writes, "allowed it to adopt a time regime for a broad swath of Montrealers from all communities,"[111] arguably creating a situation where "democracy was not as strong as economic power."[112] While the adoption of standard time had also arguably produced the greatest benefit for the elites of investment capitalism, it had provided a significant degree of convenience to the general public at little cost. D S T was different because the inequities of the time shift were more apparent, and because moving the clock forward by an entire hour has a much more pronounced physical impact on the human body than the relatively minor adjustment needed to align most local clocks with standard time zones; the rule of D S T strikes people more as an oppressive grand scheme. On the other hand, it was the decision of the federal government *not* to impose a legal D S T time framework for all of Canada which "allowed the church and industrialists to submit Montrealers to dual time regimes."[113]

creating massive amounts of confusion when different transportation networks, businesses, and even different post offices within the same building set their clocks to different times.[114] Thus, while it may be tempting to argue that the imposition of broad socio-temporal mandates such as the synchronization of clocks through standard time zones serves to erase and silence the multitemporal lived realities of diverse communities, there is also a sense in which the absence of large social agreements about temporal measurement result in a very material degree of temporal chaos that can make it exceptionally difficult to facilitate the everyday functioning of social arrangements.

The gradual and sometimes piecemeal synchronization of clocks in the late nineteenth and early twentieth centuries, first through standard time zones and later through Daylight Saving Time, shows that synchronization is never a purely neutral exercise and is rarely even a democratic one, but rather it is always synchronization *with* a particular temporal frame of reference embedded within specific ideological priorities. In the context of electronic clock synchronization, the seemingly inevitable movement toward temporal standardization in the modern age makes the erasure of local multitemporalities seem just as inescapable as the forward march of progress itself. These events also show, however, that temporal homogenization can be very valuable to large segments of the population, and that there is unlikely to be any ideal embodiment of a truly multitemporal society in which many different clocks are set to their own standard, partly because some form of shared time is all but essential to everyday social existence, but also because dominant players within a multitemporal social sphere will tend to exert their own temporal (and therefore financial, political, and even moral) will more forcefully than others. I will comment further on these implications in the concluding section of the book.

Today, the most prominent feature beneath the Canadian flag on Ottawa's Parliament Hill is the Peace Tower clock, an iconic symbol of the importance of clock time and global standard time to Canadian life. When the clock's mechanism failed on 24 May 2006, freezing the hands at 7:28 a.m., the event did not escape the attention of the CBC: "Dozens of tourists crowded around the Centennial Flame snapping photos of Parliament Hill were quick to notice the incorrect time on the clock and the sound of silence."[115] An American company was called in to make the repair, so that Canada's most prominent clock could resume its keeping of British time. But while the problems of supposedly universal clock time that became pronounced with the advent of electronic synchronization still resonate in the twenty-first century, the iconic image of the clock face with its perfectly regular motion is less sufficient to represent one of the more pressing temporal concerns of late modernity that clock time itself has helped to bring about: acceleration. Like standard time, social acceleration is largely a global phenomenon, but one that reveals important elements of temporal politics in Canada, showing that experiences of time do not unfold equally for everyone, and thus that a study of the social politics of time within the nation must account not only for large cultural models of time, but also for the more granular politics of demographic biases, social gender roles, regional variations, and even the selective portrayal of Canada's pace of life in mass media.

Hartmut Rosa, the leading theorist of social acceleration, identifies three distinct types of acceleration within modern societies, each of which feeds into and exacerbates the others. The first type is technical or technological acceleration (the intentional acceleration of particular processes such as transportation or computer processing); the second is the acceleration of social change (i.e., "the acceleration of social changes that are not inherently goal directed," such as "the acceleration of changeover in jobs, political party preferences, intimate partners … or of change per unit of time in occupational and family structures, artistic styles, etc."); and the third type is the acceleration of the pace of life (i.e., "an increase of episodes of action and / or experience per unit of time that is linked with a scarcity of temporal resources").[116] Through a systematic analysis of these structures of acceleration, Rosa finds not only that each type of acceleration demonstrably occurs within modern societies, but also that the three processes fuel one another in a perpetually strengthening cycle of speed: technical acceleration causes an acceleration of social change, which in turn contributes toward the acceleration of the pace of life, which completes the cycle by necessitating further technical acceleration.[117] For Rosa, the consequences of social acceleration include not only the rise of a prevalent sense of time pressure and a loss of overall social stability and predictability, but also the erosion of the viability of democratic "self-steering" as relatively slow-moving political entities struggle to maintain relevance in a fast-moving and unpredictable world;[118] the isolation of young people from old people as "the experiences, practices, and stock of knowledge of the parental generation increasingly become for the youth anachronistic and meaningless";[119] and even the breaking up of "stable, long-term individual identities."[120]

Rosa's landmark study allows for a rigorous understanding of social acceleration, even if some of his conclusions may swing the pendulum a little too far toward a sense of chaos and hopelessness in the face of this seemingly unstoppable speeding up. While he argues that acceleration is tied so deeply into the structure of modernity that it is essentially impossible to resist, there may yet be significant opportunities for societies to envision alternative approaches to time and its accelerative dimensions. As I will argue later on, especially in chapter 5, imaginative literary texts can play an important role in presenting opportunities for rethinking normative temporal structures, and while these works may not necessarily translate into a direct reshaping of modernity, they can indeed contribute to the social awareness of contending temporalities, and their conceptual power should not be overlooked.

Another limitation of Rosa's study is that, in evaluating the accelerative symptoms of late modernity as a whole, it treats modern society as a single entity without investigating how acceleration might unfold differently within different nations, let alone within different regions or populations. One study that begins to address this problem is Robert Levine's comparative study of the pace of life in thirty-one countries, undertaken in 1997 (in Rosa's terminology, by focusing on the everyday pace of life Levine's study investigates only the third type of social acceleration). Levine designed his study to measure three variables in each of the thirty-one countries: "the average walking speed of randomly selected pedestrians over a distance of 60 feet," "the time it took postal clerks to fulfill a standard request for stamps," and "the accuracy of 15 randomly selected bank clocks in main downtown areas."[121] His results point to "five principal factors that determine the tempo of cultures around the world. People are prone to move faster in places with vital economies, a high degree of industrialization, larger populations, cooler climates, and a cultural orientation toward individualism."[122] His overall rankings indicate that clock time is especially significant to the pace of life: the fastest-paced countries are those that run on clock time – Switzerland, Ireland, Germany, and Japan top the list – while the slowest-paced are "event-time" countries such as Brazil, Indonesia, and Mexico.[123] The United States is listed at number 16, followed by Canada at 17. Levine argues that a country's pace of life has "vital consequences for the quality of life," but that these consequences are so mixed as to suggest that "a rapid pace of life is neither inherently better nor worse than a slow one."[124] People in faster places, for instance, are much more likely to die from heart disease, but are also "more likely to be satisfied with their lives."[125] His ranking would appear to indicate that Canada and the United States embody a temporal compromise, avoiding the more extreme tempos on both sides of the scale.

As Levine admits, the methodology of his study suffers from various limitations, such as the fact that postal offices in different countries offer levels of service that vary in ways that are difficult to quantify.[126] But one of the most problematic aspects of his survey is its tendency to group entire nations together into single temporal entities, uniform in time and space. While Levine's study breaks the world down into more granular national units than does Rosa's work, it still presents each nation as uniform within its own borders, and captures results at just one particular moment near the end of the twentieth century, giving little indication of how a society's pace of life may change over time, a significant absence given the widely identified feeling – and as Rosa shows, the demonstrable fact – that the pace of life is continuously increasing within industrialized nations. Certainly there are many subjective indications that the pace of life in Canada is increasing; experimental filmmaker Michael Snow, for instance, commented on his audience's increasing pace of life with the 2003 rerelease of his 1967 film *Wavelength*. The original release, considered a seminal work of avant-garde film, is a 45-minute shot of the interior of a room, slowly zooming in to a photograph on the wall while human figures occasionally perform brief actions. Snow describes the film as "a time monument," the attempt "to make a definitive statement of pure Film space and time."[127] The 2003 rerelease, *WVLNT* (or, *Wavelength For Those Who Don't Have the Time*), consists of "simultaneities rather than the sequential progressions of the original work."[128] Ironic packaging material promotes the film as "Originally 45 minutes. Now 15!" The humour in Snow's commentary reflects the widespread sense of increasing time pressure, but of course, he is not attempting to provide quantifiable diachronic data specific to Canada.

One significant tool that can be used to address some of these limitations is Statistics Canada's *Overview of the Time Use of Canadians*, large-scale surveys that were carried out in 1998, 2005, and 2010. These surveys

provide several insights not available through other means: they specifically address contemporary allocations of personal time in Canada; they
allow for trends to be identified and quantified over a time range of more
than a decade; and in some cases they allow for a more granular understanding of time use across different Canadian regions. Overall, the Time
Use Surveys support the sense that the pace of life is increasing, but the
detailed results show that this trend does not unfold equally for everyone.
While Statistics Canada does not break down results by socio-economic
class, race, or various other possible demographic variables, the results do
indicate significant differences in time use along the lines of age and
sex.[129] Over the course of the years of the surveys, the average free time
for Canadians aged 15 years and over dropped by 21 minutes from 5:48 to
5:27 per day (averaged over the seven-day week). Canadians within the
peak working ages of 35 to 44 worked 9:48 per day in 2010 compared with
9:21 in 1998, an increase of 27 minutes. While certain data may appear to
indicate that the total amount of time Canadians spent working remained
relatively stable over the years of the surveys, and even that the perceived
amount of time stress is decreasing, these apparent trends are largely due
to an increase in the proportion of seniors, whose disproportionately low
amount of working time can skew the overall results, concealing the fact
that working-age Canadians are indeed working more and more over
the years.[130]

When it comes to sex, certain results point toward an increase in temporal equity between men and women. In their own commentary on the
2010 results, Statistics Canada highlights the fact that men "remained
more likely than women to spend time on paid work," but that "the gap
between the sexes continued to narrow," because slightly more women
and slightly fewer men were engaging in paid work as compared with the
1998 study.[131] This would appear to indicate a stronger female presence in
the workforce, and thus greater access to earning power and other forms
of cultural capital for women. However, a different perspective on the
data troubles the optimistic view that gender equity is increasing early
in the twenty-first century. In 1998 men in Canada had an average of
6:00 hours of free time per day (averaged over the seven-day week) compared with 5:36 hours for women.[132] By 2010 this number had decreased
for both genders, but significantly more so for women: men reported 5:46
of free time while women reported only 5:10.[133] If women are gaining

access to more paid work, much of this access seems to come at the expense of women's free time to a more severe degree than is the case with men. There also remains a great disparity in the number of hours spent on paid work (4:15 for men and 3:00 for women in 2010) and unpaid work (2:50 for men and 4:17 for women), revealing that even if women have access to slightly more paid work than they used to, men still dominate the national payroll and still leave most of the unpaid work to women. Thus, while total working hours (combining paid and unpaid work) differ by only 15 minutes across the two sexes, *men earn significantly more money for their work*, even assuming that paid hours are paid equally, which they are not. Also of interest is the fact that the fewer hours of free time available to women appear to reflect not only the extra time spent on total work, but also significantly more time spent on what Statistics Canada calls "personal care," a category that includes sleep, meals, washing, and dressing. Is this an indication that the pressures of cultural beauty standards compel women to spend more time on personal body care? If so, the distinction between "personal care" and "unpaid work" may not be as clear-cut as it appears.

The Time Use Surveys also provide some insight into variations across regions of Canada. While Statistics Canada provides only national averages for its 1998 and 2010 studies, the 2005 study goes on to divide its results into provinces, revealing, for instance, that Prince Edward Islanders spend on average a little more time working, and a little less time sleeping, than British Columbians (information on the territories is curiously absent). These data also provide an opportunity to test one of the widespread mass media representations of a regional difference in the pace of life across Canada.[134] The well-known television advertising campaign from Newfoundland and Labrador Tourism, which has been credited with great success in drawing tourists to the region, uses the province's unique time zone within the standard time system as a hook to strategically characterize the region as a sanctuary from the time pressures of modern life. The television ads feature slow-motion footage of people engaged in leisure activities – hiking, throwing stones into the water, playing music, buying a cake – while a soothing voice says, "When you're always a half hour ahead, you never feel the need to catch up."[135] The province's website elaborates: "We've never been afraid to be ourselves or go at our own pace. And, although we have our very own time zone, we don't really measure time in seconds or half hours, but in moments and experiences. Here, you can set your watch a half hour ahead, or you can just leave it at home."[136] The campaign strategically aligns Newfoundland and Labrador with event time rather than clock time, commodifying the more relaxed feeling associated with events that are allowed to transpire at their own pace. And the data from Statistics Canada in fact bear this out to some degree: the 2005 survey indicates that people in the province work about 18 minutes less per day and have about 24 minutes more free time than the average Canadian.[137] Of course, the province has a higher unemployment rate than the national average, so much of the extra "leisure" time is not necessarily voluntary or stress-free.

While these statistics are illuminating, they offer only broad regional strokes. Levine, too, does not specify where his measurements for Canada were taken, but given his strategy of selecting a large metropolis in each country, it seems likely that his Canadian measurements were taken in Toronto, with Montreal, Ottawa, and Vancouver as alternative candidates. To what extent can such measurements accurately represent the temporal character of the nation, a province, or a city? What deeper variations exist between regions of Canada, or between urban and rural areas of the same region, or even from one household to the next? What relations of power or subjective experiences are at stake in these different uses of time? Broad sociological surveys, like cultural chronotopes, are limited in their ability to capture or explain the temporal character of diverse regions and individual lives. This is an issue to which I will return in later chapters. For the moment, I will examine some of the ways in which Canada's dominant narratives of temporal power serve as strategic temporal frames, and will show how critical temporal literacy can help to intervene in these forms of temporal discourse.

"GUILTLESS BEYOND ALL CIRCUMSTANCE": THE POLITICS OF TEMPORAL FRAMING

The history of clock time in Canada – from the use of clocks to facilitate colonization and establish Western temporal values, to the controversial implementation of Daylight Saving Time – shows not only that ostensibly neutral systems of time measurement are inherently ideological, but also that the ability *to set the clock* on a broad social scale, both literally and figuratively, goes hand in hand with other forms of dominance and control. The more figurative forms of setting the clock will now be the focus. In particular, this section investigates the use of "temporal framing" in Canadian culture, showing how the strategic manipulation of concepts such as "first," "new," "original," "now," and "long-term" serves a critical function in maintaining positions of power, and how temporal literacy must be prepared to recognize the subjective and ideological nature of seemingly neutral frames of time. In a partial echo of Hayden White's assertion that historical narratives ought to be read "as symbolic structures, extended metaphors, that 'liken' the events reported in them to some form with which we have already become familiar in our literary culture,"[138] Craig Ireland writes that narrativity itself

> relates past, present, and future, not in order to recapture an actual or past state of affairs and still less in order to sequentialize empirical brute sense data into the conceptually intelligible, but instead in order to delimit the horizon from which selections will be made and complexity reduced, as well as to establish the threshold where expectations can be violated or disappointed.[139]

The question of whose narrativity – whose temporal horizons and expectations, whose time socialization stories – take precedence is an important one in Canadian society, as the imposition of particular time scales and frames in various social contexts indicates that the use and ownership of time within Canada has been integral to many forms of power struggles and decision-making processes.

The concept of temporal framing is perhaps best evoked by way of an image. Stock market tracking websites, such as TMX Group and Yahoo! Canada, tend to chart on their homepages the progress of major trading indices over the past six hours. The frame of time that this perspective creates, as shown in figure 1.1, defined by the literal frame of the graph's axes, is one that assigns total significance to an arbitrarily limited brief duration, removing any understanding of broader temporal context, and thus limiting the ability of the viewer to make thoughtful or informed judgments about how past events relate to present events, and how the present moment might be understood differently in relation to broader historical processes. A six-hour stock market perspective implicitly

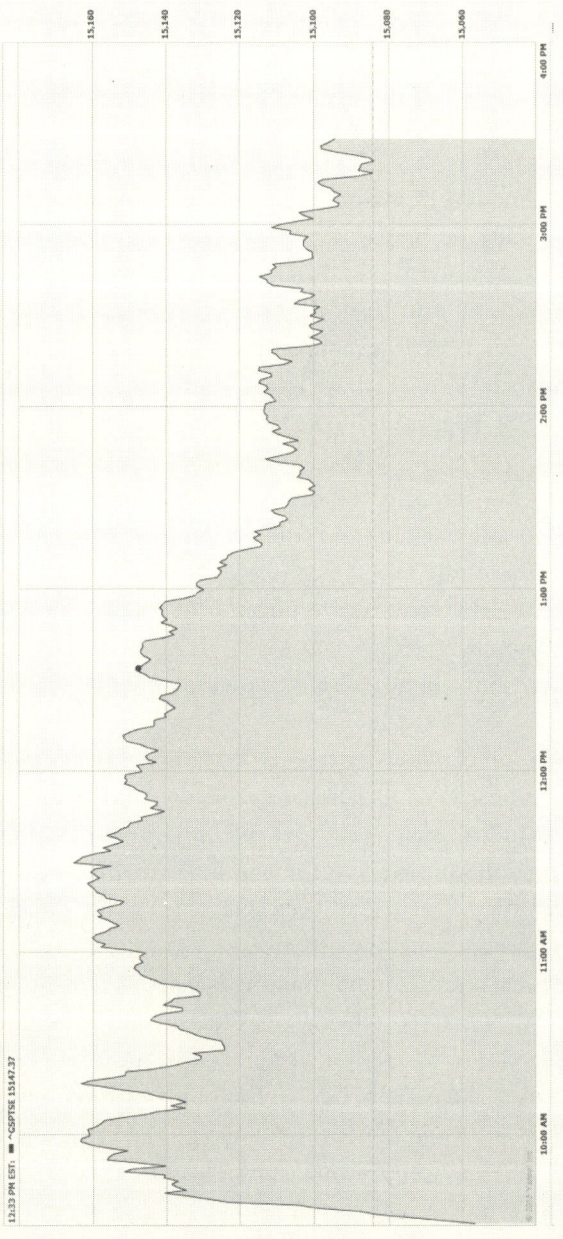

Figure 1.1. Standard six-hour trading perspective (Yahoo, 2015).

assumes that a narrow frame of time is the only frame necessary for making decisions, even though these decisions have connections to distant events in both the past and the future. This type of temporal framing need not occur in visual form; it is equally implicit in the disinclination of the news media (and, we must assume, of their audiences) to trace the origins of current events back more than a few days or months.[140]

A powerful example of the material consequences of dominant temporal framing is found in the life of Maria Campbell, whose autobiography, *Halfbreed*, is intended "to tell you what it is like to be a Halfbreed woman in our country," to "tell you about the joys and sorrows, the oppressing poverty, the frustrations and the dreams."[141] Describing the newly confederated Canada's treatment of her part-Indigenous, part-white ancestors in Saskatchewan, Campbell writes:

> They were squatters with no title to the land they lived on. They wanted assurance from Ottawa of their right to keep the land before the incoming white settlers encroached on them by using homestead laws. Our people believed the lands acts discriminated against them, stating that they had to live on the land and wait three years before filing a claim. They had lived on the lands for years before the lands acts had ever been thought of, and didn't believe they should be treated like newcomers.[142]

Because legal ownership of the land is measured against a very recent moment in time – the creation of the lands acts – the long history of Indigenous inhabitation, and even the shorter history of Métis inhabitation, is immaterial. The broader temporal context of land ownership is erased from the land claims record in accordance with the strategic temporal framing of the dominant authority.

As a result of these events, grievances escalated until the government engaged in a military battle against the Métis and Louis Riel, finally forcing the holdouts to relocate "to the empty pockets of North Saskatchewan,"[143] where they claimed their own homesteads. However, in addition to paying the purchase price of these homesteads, families were required to work the land to the government's satisfaction: "Ten acres had to be broken in three years, along with improvements, before title would be granted. Otherwise the land was confiscated by Land Improvement

District authorities."[144] Unable to afford the necessary equipment, the Métis failed to meet these requirements and "gradually the homesteads were reclaimed by the authorities and offered to the immigrants," thus forcing the Métis, now quite literally marginalized, to take up residence on the strips of land alongside roads.[145] "So began a miserable life of poverty," Campbell writes, "which held no hope for the future."[146] The mandate of progress, of "improvements" to the land, not only imposes a Western ethic of land development that takes no account of long-standing Indigenous forms of land use, but also initiates an arbitrary duration of responsibility, drawing a subjectively defined temporal finish line and creating an unwinnable race against time. The rest of Campbell's autobiography, which recounts her years of poverty and instability, can be understood as a narrative of the broader consequences of the imposition of this temporal frame.

The ability to define the temporal starting point or ending point of any social process – as well as the related ability to declare that certain moments will not *count* toward a total duration – reflects structural forms of power. Consider the asymmetrical waiting periods for citizenship that have been implemented in legal codes such as the 1952 Immigration Act. During this act's tenure, immigrants to Canada acquired "Canadian domicile" after a five-year wait, though any time spent in a prison or a "hospital for mental diseases" did not count toward the five years.[147] Meanwhile, admittance to Canada was denied altogether for those who had "been insane at any time," were "afflicted with epilepsy," had committed "any crime involving moral turpitude," were identified as prostitutes or homosexuals, or advocated subversion of the democratic process,[148] effectively introducing an indefinite waiting period, which lasted until these conditions were loosened in 1976. Such temporal inequities have shifted in recent decades to emphasize different factors, but remain dramatic; in 2010 the *Toronto Star* reported that Canadians applying to sponsor the immigration of a parent or grandparent from Poland could expect to wait for fifteen months, while Canadians with parents in Sri Lanka wait nearly four years.[149]

Confused understandings of when immigrants are considered to have become Canadian are also visible today in the ambiguous meaning of the terms "first generation," which can refer either to foreign-born Canadians or to their Canadian-born children, and "second generation," which can refer either to a foreign-born family's Canadian-born children, or to *those* children's children.[150] Who is first, and when does Canadianness occur? In *What We All Long For*, Dionne Brand takes a satirical jab at the capricious manner in which the dominant culture is able to offer and withdraw membership to minorities. Her character Oku, at a bar with some friends, tells a joke: "What's Canadian in 9.79 seconds and Jamaican in twenty-four hours? Ben Johnson."[151] Oku's reference to the infamous Olympic sprinter whose gold medal in 1988 was rescinded after an incriminating drug test suggests that popular opinion is pivotal in granting social inclusion to those whose status is questionable because of race, foreign birth, or other factors. Underneath the humour one senses an Orwellian tone in the ease with which society is effectively able to claim, at advantageous moments, "Ben Johnson has always been Canadian," or "Ben Johnson has always been Jamaican." The gates of social membership are set to open and close on a timer that keeps desirable people inside the national collective, and keeps undesirable people – however defined at any given moment – out.

Labelling someone "first" is not a neutral act but a political one that indicates an investment in one particular starting point, one particular resetting of the clock. Perhaps this is nowhere more apparent than in Alan Lawson's remark that there are "two First Worlds, two origins of authority and authenticity: the originating world of Europe, the imperium, as source of the Second World's principal cultural authority; and that other First World, that of the First Nations, whose authority the settlers not only effaced and replaced but also desired."[152] Commenting on the Hudson's Bay Company's need for perceived legitimacy in the mid-nineteenth century, Desmond Morton writes that "the Company's prestige depended on an air of permanency, summed up by the rude version of the letters on its flag – 'Here Before Christ.'"[153] Marie Clements resists this association in her play *Burning Vision*, where a Dene widow says, "the Hudson's Bay Store ... seemed like they been here before Christ but not before me. Not before me."[154] Firstness means primacy, and is a prized concept within many political arenas, from the nationalistic "Canada First" movement in the late nineteenth century; to Daniel Johnson's Union Nationale slogan in the 1966 Quebec provincial election, "*Québec d'abord*," which means "Quebec first" but was "discreetly translated for English-speakers as 'A better Quebec for all Quebeckers'";[155] to Stephen Harper's 2008 military

initiative called the "Canada First Defence Strategy." For forest conserva-
tionists, the term "second growth" is a disparaging one.

Daniel MacIvor's play *Never Swim Alone* comments hauntingly on the
politics of firstness, as two nearly identical men engage in inane but
increasingly violent competitions for the privilege of being "the first
man." While the play ends in a Cold War style stalemate between the
two, a penultimate climax speaks to the dominance inherent in the claim
of being "first":

FRANK
The first man is the man
> FRANK *knees* BILL *in the chest.* BILL *goes down.*

FRANK
who is guiltless beyond all circumstance
> FRANK *kicks* BILL.

FRANK
and sure of his right
> FRANK *kicks* BILL.

FRANK
to be first.
> FRANK *kicks* BILL.

FRANK
The first man is the man
> FRANK *kicks* BILL.

FRANK
who can recognize
the second man.
> BILL *lies motionless.*[156]

The related idea of newness, as in the "New World," is famously attrac-
tive and problematic, not only for English colonialists such as Catharine
Parr Traill, who wrote in the 1830s that "Canada is the land of hope; here
everything is new,"[157] or for the early nineteenth-century Métis who saw
themselves as a "New Nation,"[158] but for more recent immigrants as well,
as the self-conscious title of M.G. Vassanji's novel *No New Land* suggests.
More than firstness, the concept of newness has an ambivalent history in
Western societies, with deep ties to value judgments that shift over time.

In Milton's *Paradise Lost*, when the angel Abdiel insists that God created all heavenly beings, Satan refutes the argument with the words "strange point and new!" – the very claim that Abdiel's idea is new casts it under suspicion and deflates the angel's authority.[159] And despite the great attraction of the New World, John Demos notes in his study of American colonial culture that "innovation" was "a favorite term of insult, which Puritans in Old England and their religious opponents regularly flung back and forth at one another."[160] Gradually, the English colonial authority came to be seen as outdated, and America's newness became increasingly desirable, a shift associated especially with the American Revolution.[161] In contemporary global consumer culture newness is perhaps the ultimate virtue, yet it is also increasingly difficult to possess as the new quickly becomes the obsolete. Conversely, while oldness can at times be aligned strategically with primacy, oldness is more typically seen as something distasteful and shameful. In chapter 4 I will discuss how Indigenous writers have responded to Canadian society's practice of projecting an image of oldness onto Indigenous cultures – a process that Fabian calls the "*denial of coevalness,*" a distancing strategy in which the dominant group represents another group as existing in a past era out of which the dominant group has long since progressed.[162]

The ability to frame time, to decide when firstness or newness occurs, when units of time will begin to accumulate, or how much of the past or future a temporal perspective will encompass, is key to the shaping of temporal justice because it allows for the granting or denial of rights to particular people, and relieves those in power of the responsibility to address injustices that occurred before the arbitrary starting point, or will occur after an arbitrary duration runs its course. Maria Campbell's story of disempowerment through temporal framing finds echoes in many contemporary situations in Canada. One common response to Indigenous land claims maintains that the people who now own the land, while descended from settlers whose appropriation of the land may have been questionable, did not themselves engage in this appropriation: any injustice that occurred in the past is not the fault of those now living. Dionne Brand objects to this view by saying that "people use these arguments as reasons for not doing what is right or just. It never occurs to them that they live on the cumulative hurt of others. They want to start the clock of social justice only when they arrived. But one is born into history, one isn't born into a void."[163] Mohawk scholar Taiaiake Alfred, who advocates social and spiritual revolution with the aim of securing autonomy for "Onkwehonwe" – Indigenous people – argues, like Brand, that the clock of social justice started ticking earlier than is usually acknowledged, and that looking further into the past is vital for understanding ongoing cultural disputes. He writes,

> Limited to a discussion of history that includes only the last five or ten years, the corporate media and general public focus on the billions of dollars handed out to the Onkwehonwe per year from federal treasuries and spent inefficiently ... Considering 100 or 300 years of interactions, it would become clear even to the Settlers that the real problem facing their country is that two nations are fighting over questions of conquest and survival.[164]

Relatively narrow temporal frames tend to portray existing configurations of power as natural and even as beyond the forces of politics or causation. In her novel *Salt Fish Girl*, Larissa Lai comments ironically on the need for large corporations to dissociate themselves from the ongoing injustices that are often intrinsic to the production of consumer goods. Her character Miranda, who has been learning about a "disease" that causes people to remember the past in great detail, proposes that the Pallas running shoe company "advertise shoes as protection against the dreaming disease. Memory-proof soles."[165] A successful consumer product, this scene bitterly suggests, is one that "cures" consumers of the pain of calling injustice to mind, of connecting past actions with future consequences. The pun on "memory-proof souls" is no accident.

Official apologies by the federal government for past injustices provide insight into the possibilities of broader temporal framing, but also reveal how even expanded frames can remain shaped by carefully imposed limits.[166] Apologizing in 2008 for the Indian residential schools system, Prime Minister Stephen Harper began his speech with reference to federal government actions in the 1870s, looking back nearly 140 years. In a rather remarkable acknowledgment of broad temporal responsibility, he went on to connect long-standing past policies with the present, saying that "the legacy of Indian residential schools has contributed to social problems that continue to exist in many communities today."[167] As

Matthew Dorrell points out, however, the apology also contained distancing language, relegating the abuses to a past "chapter" in Canadian history.[168] Similarly, when Governor General Michaëlle Jean commented on the relaunched Indian Residential Schools Truth and Reconciliation Commission in October of 2009, she announced that "when the present does not recognize the wrongs of the past, the future takes its revenge."[169] While the past that she has in mind presumably refers to the period in which the residential schools system was active, a still broader temporal frame of several hundred years would provide the perspective that is necessary in order to understand the present state of colonization in its fuller context; if the "wrongs of the past" are understood to have begun around the turn of the twentieth century, the larger patterns of injustice through the longer duration of colonization are dissociated from the present. Taiaiake Alfred's statement that "the crime of colonialism is present today, as are its perpetrators"[170] will likely appear radical and unbelievable to a population whose sense of the relationship between past and present has been shaped by relatively narrow temporal frames. Georges Sioui provides a simple and eloquent example of an expanded temporal frame when he describes European colonists as "our newly arrived Relatives"[171] and comments that "we have suffered a very severe shock these past 503 years."[172] He portrays colonization as a comprehensible, measurable moment in time, a specific duration that increases by one digit each year rather than a vague notion of many centuries. North America's "post-European history" becomes "no more than an accident."[173]

Of course, the temporal frame through which we understand the past can be expanded in even more radical terms into the realms of deep time. For Dionne Brand in *Land to Light On*, the "history of the body" is situated not in Canada or Africa at all, but in the depths of primordial evolution. After tracing the development of life from its watery origins to the appearance of bones, blood, and eyes, she suddenly curtails this inventory, writing, "all that has happened since is too painful,/ too unimaginable."[174] This history not only starts with the pre-national and the pre-human, but actually stops there; all that comes later, all of what we normally consider to comprise "history," is better left unthought. Wai Chee Dimock notes that when seen through a frame of deep time, "American literature emerges with a much longer history than one might think"[175] – a comment that surely applies to bodies of literary and

cultural output from any nation, but whose implications become especially startling within nations that are usually considered young. The
perspective that such a frame might afford on the matters of historical
justice, on "Indigenous" and "immigrant" inhabitants, or on our rapid
obliteration of the ecosystems that sustain us, is profoundly disruptive.
Don McKay speculates, albeit perhaps too optimistically, that seeing ourselves as "members of deep time, along with trilobites" might lead us to
"give up mastery and gain mutuality, at least for that brief – but let us
hope, expandable – period of astonishment."[176]

Taiaiake Alfred also points out that looking to the past at all, no matter
how far back, can be counterproductive: "However noble and necessary
justice is to our struggles, its gaze will always be backward. By itself, the
concept of justice is not capable of encompassing the broader transformations needed to ensure coexistence."[177] The concept of peace, on the other
hand, "is hopeful, visionary, and forward-looking."[178] Alfred would be
aware, though, that looking to the future without accounting for the past
risks treating as equals those who have been placed historically on uneven
ground. Looking forward is susceptible to many of the same issues of
temporal framing as looking to the past. While the long-term maintenance of a society requires a temporal frame that understands the present
alongside the deep future, influential decision making tends to be framed,
at least implicitly, in terms of three-month business quarters and four-
year political terms. Apparent exceptions to this frame occur mainly
for the sake of rhetorical impact and immediate political gain, as when
Sir Guy Carleton said in 1772 that "this country must, to the end of time,
be peopled by the Canadian race,"[179] or when Wilfrid Laurier said in 1904
that "the twentieth century shall be the century of Canada and of Canadian development. For the next seventy-five years, nay for the next hundred years, Canada shall be the star towards which all men who love
progress and freedom shall come."[180] Even Laurier's ostensible appeal to a
hundred-year mindset is short-sighted when compared with certain
Indigenous conceptualizations of time. In an article about the Haida
Nation, the Union of BC Indian Chiefs notes that because the construction of a canoe "requires an 800-year-old tree," second-growth forests "do
not yield the quality of tree needed and for the most part, they will be
logged before they are even half of a century old."[181] The 800-year view
taken here sees centuries, not years, as the basic unit of time for future
planning. Only an Ontarian Methodist preacher, speaking on the eve of

the 1896 election, revealed a broader sense of temporal accountability when he warned that a Liberal vote "would stare the voter in the face at Judgement Day and condemn him to eternal perdition."[182]

Temporal framing discourses are equally present in our relationships with the natural world, and reveal further arbitrary hierarchies. Europeans brought purple loosestrife to North America around the same time, in evolutionary terms, as wheat, but because purple loosestrife is perceived as economically damaging it remains perpetually regarded as a foreign species. In language that is remarkably xenophobic, a single news release from the Office of the Auditor General in 2002 refers to purple loosestrife and other undesirable species introduced in the last few hundred years as "invaders," a "destructive force," "biological pollution," and a "threat" to "Canada's ecosystems."[183] Wheat, meanwhile, which has displaced millions of acres of native grasses, is honoured on the provincial flags of Alberta and Saskatchewan. As Michael Healey, Travis V. Mason, and Laurie Ricou conclude in their study of cultural attitudes toward various invasive species, "the actual roles these species play in nature are secondary to the role, or roles, we assign them. Given that the timeframe of the current proliferation of so many invasive species is relatively short, perhaps the future will tell a different tale, taking some species out of the 'undesirable alien' category and instead setting out for them a welcome mat."[184]

Looking at time and the environment in a broader sense, the anxiety that motivates environmentalism could be described not just as the fear of destroying places but as the fear of destroying time: the time in which human civilization prospers in ways familiar to us. For at the heart of most conservationist impulses is the realization that our degradation of the biosphere inevitably involves dire consequences not only for polar bears and frogs but for us. This anxiety, which looks to the "long term" future of fifty or a hundred years from now, continues under Canada's current socio-political circumstances to take second stage to the widely perceived importance of the more immediate temporal moment. The ideal of sustainability, which requires valuing what we normally think of as the distant future, cannot be realized while the deployment of resources with a view to the short term is seen as common sense. In this regard, little has changed since Catharine Parr Traill, writing in 1834, perceived as inevitable the ideological decision to sell and burn Ontario's trees for short-term gains: "Some years hence the timbers that are now burned up will be regretted. Yet it is impossible to preserve them."[185] While Traill was for the most part optimistic in envisioning the future – "I watch the progress of cultivation among these rugged and inhospitable regions with positive pleasure," she wrote[186] – her confident musings take on a darker tone as we gradually awaken to the consequences of ecological collapse: "Some century hence how different will this spot appear! ... All will be different."[187]

As many of these comments suggest, the fact that the future is a highly contested realm shaped variously by competing hopes, assumptions, and anxieties means that it cannot be envisioned through a single axis, but remains contingent and closely tied up with contending ideologies and senses of individual and social identity. Judith Doyle's study of how English speakers in late twentieth-century Montreal envision the future is illuminating in this regard. Doyle carried out a project of participatory anthropology in Montreal in 1996–97, a time of heightened concern over Quebec nationalism, in order to understand how and why English speakers "imagine the future as uncertain."[188] Aside from the unsurprising realization that her informants held alternate and ambiguous beliefs about the future, including "visions of a successful, independent Quebec, or of a partitioned Montreal, or of an Atlantic Canada absorbed by the United States," Doyle also concludes that the very notion of the future itself is "explicitly tied to identity and politics."[189] Much as Catharine Parr Traill's comments about the seemingly inevitable direction of future development in Ontario suggest that present experiences and ideological assumptions can make one particular version of the future appear to be the *only* future, Doyle's work suggests that conflicted and uncertain visions of the future can be equally revealing in unravelling the ways in which identity and politics inform people's sense of the times to come. In general, then, critical analyses of explicit and implicit visions of the future must interrogate the often unspoken ways in which identity and politics inform the envisioned scenarios, in addition to posing critical questions about the temporal frame within which the future is defined.

Margaret Atwood suggests that Canadians are especially prone to experiencing the future as a source of anxiety:

In my part of the world we have a ritual interchange that goes like this:
    First person: "Lovely weather we're having."
    Second person: "We'll pay for it later."

My part of the world being Canada, where there is a great deal of weather, we always do pay for it later ... What this ritual interchange reveals is a larger habit of thinking about the more enjoyable things in life: they're only on loan or acquired on credit, and sooner or later the date when they must be paid for will roll around.[190]

While the notion that such anxiety is particular to Canada is suspect to say the least, the fact that Atwood associates a fear of the future, or a fear of impermanence, with Canadian life hints at a remaining trace of garrison mentality, at least in her own estimation. Or, as she goes on to argue, the fear of an approaching day of payback may in fact be a guilty acknowledgment of ecological unsustainability. Ultimately, fear of the future is tied to mortality itself; the concept of linear progress is always haunted by the spectre of death. "Are all fears, at bottom," Don McKay asks, "fears of endless uninflected time?"[191] The further we probe such anxieties, the further away we are taken from any indication that Atwood's "ritual interchange" is uniquely Canadian. But the questions of who gets to draw the boundaries of the temporal map, of who gets to set and reset the moral accounting clock, and for what purpose – the real questions at stake when we consider how far back, or forward, we ought to look – are closely tied in Canada to the issues we have been discussing. Canada's particular histories of indigeneity, colonialism, immigration, expansive territory, resource use, and variable ecologies do create a unique matrix of temporal framing patterns, even if some aspects of this matrix are universal.

CANADIAN TIME AND TEMPORAL DISCRIMINATION

In 1904, the Arthur Pequegnat Company based in Berlin (now Kitchener), Ontario, began to manufacture what has always been a fairly rare commodity, Canadian-made clocks. The company ceased production in the Second World War due to a shortage of brass, but its clocks remain among the best-known and most desirable for collectors of Canadian timepieces.[192] One of their popular wall clocks, known as the "Canadian Time" model, is emblazoned with the words "Canadian Time" on the glass pane through which the swinging pendulum is visible.[193] The time that the clock keeps, of course, is the standard twelve-hour time that has evolved for millennia and is recognizable around the world, but there is truth to the slogan in the sense that the particular histories, materials, and social meanings connected to this clock are tied to the unfolding complexity of time reckoning within the Canadian nation. Canadian society itself has inherited various long-standing socio-temporal structures nested within homogenizing globalized patterns; our time is in many ways a reflection of the global reach of the Gregorian calendar, the twenty-four-hour clock, and the normative concepts of progress and development. Yet the nation's particular cultural and temporal situation is the product of a unique history of Indigenous inhabitation, expansive and diverse northern territory, colonization, and multiculturalism.

All of our systems for measuring time – our clocks, calendars, globalized synchronizations, temporal framing devices, and personal and social narratives – are forms of language. They attempt to witness, describe, and model the world, yet can never complete the task; there will always be aspects of time, whether functions of physical relativity, personal subjectivity, or cross-cultural disparity, that these models fail to encompass. Canada has learned to speak particular temporal languages just as it has grown around English, French, and other verbal languages; we live immersed within them, adapt them to meet our particular needs, and sometimes struggle against them. Identifying the cultural construction of time in Canada is not a question of locating a single factor that makes Canada different. Canada's clocks do not contain an extra digit; our calendar does not use a special Canadian month. The degree to which Canadian temporality is unique is an emergent property of the complex combinations of cultural and ecological relationships that exist nowhere else. And while certain models of time are entrenched, Canada's temporal maps, like its spatial maps, inevitably shift over time.

The significant lesson that emerges here is less about the question of identifying a uniquely Canadian time and more about the recognition of disparate social relations. Shared conceptualizations of time in Canada have helped to orchestrate the broader coherence of the nation, whether through a formalized calendrical and clock system that allows for the coordination of everyday events, or through grand visions of progress that have guided major infrastructure projects and shaped sustained aspirations of democratic social betterment. The cases discussed in this chapter, though – the imposition of "standard" measurements of time onto diverse populations, the devaluing of temporalities that fall outside the mandate of development and productivity, the enforcement of inequitable waiting periods for citizenship, the priority given to relatively narrow frames of temporal accountability – all compel us to acknowledge not only the existence of multitemporality (the fact that many different visions and experiences of time circulate within a complex society), but also the existence of *temporal discrimination*, the entrenched belief that one particular model of time is natural, desirable, and superior to other models of time, that one person's time is inherently more legitimate than another person's time, and that certain times (the present or the short-term future) are more deserving of agency, empowerment, and resource exploitation than other times. As the rest of this book will make clear, the concepts of multitemporality and temporal discrimination can provide a terminology and a potential framework for thinking through the politics of contested cultural temporalities.

As some of the discussions in this chapter have further indicated, the issues surrounding the cultural construction of time in Canada, like all issues of social concern, frequently manifest themselves overtly in literature, and some texts consciously critique dominant modes of time reckoning. But even those texts that do not set out to engage such matters, or are not normally read as doing so, find themselves inextricably involved with them. Thus, reading the cultural construction of time as a backdrop to any Canadian text can prove illuminating. Authors who may have no particular interest in the politics of time often write stories in which dominant modes of time reckoning enhance, or perhaps more often restrict, a character's physical or cognitive latitude. As I will show in chapters 3 and 4, stories are also common in which the constraints that characters face in terms of gender, class, race, and so on translate into constraints on the way they inhabit time.

Whatever the particulars, the myriad opportunities for witnessing and manipulating the human experience of time arise because of our common immersion in time, a commonality that contains as much potential for solidarity as it does for exploitation. As Margaret Atwood writes, "time is a condition of the life of our physical bodies: without it we can't live – we'd be frozen, like statues, because we wouldn't be able to change."[194] Or, in the words of time itself, as imagined by Brian Bartlett, "I am the space between heartbeat / and heartbeat ... Yes, I am merciless, / but I'm mercy too."[195] The point is well taken by Panych's unnamed man, still standing on his precarious seventh-story ledge, pondering his captivity in the days of the week. In the final moments of the play, with Lillian's encouragement that he will "be an inspiration to others,"[196] he does indeed leap into space. But he falls *up*, flying impossibly across to another building and, according to the stage directions, "through the stars,"[197] metaphorically embodying the potential to disrupt normative understandings of time and other cultural categorizations. But, while liberating, overstepping the boundaries of normative time is also perilous; when the man returns to his ledge he finds that Lillian has disappeared, perhaps having fallen to the ground. The play ends as the man urges himself to "just wait for the wind again," while a police megaphone orders the crowd (and the theatre audience) to "break it up now and go home ... The show's over."[198] Temporal resistance, like other forms of resistance, is confined by personal limitations and voices of authority. Still, the image of the man flying through the stars remains vital in its suggestion that the constraints of temporal categories are partial and pliable.

2

Negotiating Subjective Time in a Social World

Each character had his own time zone, his own lamp, otherwise they were just men from nowhere.[1]

Michael Ondaatje

The after is complicitous with the before.[2]

Smaro Kamboureli

Margaret Atwood's short story "Hack Wednesday" begins by juxtaposing personal and social concerns. The first paragraph introduces Marcia, who is dreaming about her conflicted desire to have another child, while the second paragraph begins, "Downstairs the news is on. Something extra has happened, she can tell by the announcer's tone of voice, by the heightened energy. A disaster of some kind; that always peps them up. She isn't sure she's ready for it."[3] Marcia's uneasy task of deciding which concerns, the personal or the social, deserve the more prominent place in her mind goes on to form the crux of the story, and is expressed repeatedly in terms of her anxiety about the passage of time. She buys a piece of the Berlin Wall as a souvenir "not of a place … but of a time," and in the next breath focuses on her family life, "squirreling away bits of time – a photo here, a letter there."[4] She works for a Toronto newspaper called *The World*, writing about contemporary social issues such as malnutrition, violence toward women, and overcrowding in prisons, all the while believing "that life is something that happens to individuals, despite the current emphasis on statistics and trends."[5] She eats in her kitchen, while outside "the world shifts and crumbles and rearranges itself, and time goes on."[6]

All of this culminates in Marcia's reflections on passing time as she prepares to host her now grown-up children at Christmas:

> She will cry because the children are no longer children, or because she herself is not a child anymore, or because there are children who have never been children, or because she can't have a child anymore, ever again. Her body has gone past too quickly for her; she has not made herself ready.
>
> It's all this talk of babies, at Christmas. It's all this hope. She gets distracted by it, and has trouble paying attention to the real news.[7]

This final sentence of the story leaves open the question of what constitutes "the real news." Are the stories of unfolding social injustice the real news, or is the real news the day-to-day moments in time that slip by unnoticed, yet comprise Marcia's actual life with her family?

This question is an important one for understanding the temporal structure of life in Canada, or anywhere. What is more "real," the broad cultural chronotopes that shape the workings of social structures and historiography, or the experience of time's passage on the level of the individual? How do we locate ourselves on our overlapping layers of temporal maps, since, as Christopher Dewdney writes, "our collective sense of the present, the one we all agree upon, is not the same as our private sense of 'now'"?[8] It is one thing to examine large cultural modes of time such as standard time zones and normative temporal frames, but the operation of time as a site of meaning, experience, and differential power also functions at much more intimate levels. While the previous chapter offered an overview of Canadian cultural temporalities and discussed certain examples of how large cultural models of time can impact social relations, this chapter turns the focus to personal subjective temporalities, partly because personal temporal experiences are significant in their own right, but also to demonstrate how subjective time is connected to broader forms of social and temporal relations. The project of understanding how time functions within a large social collective will remain inadequate if it does not take into account subjective experiences of time, and I examine here how such experiences are shaped in negotiation with several factors, including not only the human condition of mortality and experiences that are unique to each individual, but also cultural conventions of narrative and language, the desire for various levels of social synchronization, the ongoing significance of past events, and encounters with voices of authority and socio-cultural structures that may appear to have little to do with time. If chapter 1 argued that certain normative temporal structures have taken hold in Canada and that these modes of time frequently shape inequitable social relations, chapter 2 argues that temporal experiences for individuals do not represent merely a filtering down of large cultural temporalities, but are also a product of, and a window into, other forms of social power.

NARRATIVIZING SUBJECTIVE TIME

"What justifies our taking the subject of an action," Paul Ricoeur asks, "so designated by his, her, or its proper name, as the same throughout a life that stretches from birth to death? The answer has to be narrative ... Without the recourse to narration, the problem of personal identity would in fact be condemned to an antinomy with no solution."[9] The perception of any constant identity or relationship is possible only through the perception of continuity, the perception that past events are related to present and future events, and that one moment in time can be understood in terms of another. The word "continuous" etymologically means "hold together," and it is through the impression of a continuous world that particular moments in time, like words in a sentence or individual human beings, hold meaning. Recalling the entry for "time" in the *Canadian Oxford Dictionary* – "the indefinite and continuous duration of existence seen as a series of events progressing from the past through the present into the future" – we may notice a striking similarity to the definition of "narrative" as "a spoken or written account of connected events in order of happening."[10] Both processes involve the defining of relationships between events, the *seeing as* of particular moments; the significant difference appears to be that we do not expect time to have an ending (though, as I will discuss in chapter 5, apocalyptic stories may envision the end of a particular social model of time). The central thesis of Ricoeur's seminal three-volume work, *Time and Narrative*, is that "time becomes human time to the extent that it is organized after the manner of a narrative," an observation that finds its mirror image in the claim that "narrative, in turn, is meaningful to the extent that it portrays the features of temporal experience."[11] The relationship between time and narrative thus involves a type of circular logic in that each appears necessary to formulate the other, though Ricoeur argues that this relationship is best understood not as a vicious circle, but rather as "an endless spiral that would carry the meditation past the same point a number of times, but at different altitudes."[12] The coherence of temporality and narrative build continuously upon one another.

If identity itself requires the use of narrative, which in turn is nearly synonymous with the construction of temporality, then personal identity is shaped not merely through isolated subjective experiences, but also through the social conventions of narrative that exist all around us. In his study of the everyday use of autobiographical storytelling as a fundamental part of personal identity formation, Paul John Eakin uses the term "narrative identity" to argue for the existence of "an extremely close and dynamic relation between narrative and identity, for narrative is not only a literary form but part of the fabric of our lived experience. When it comes to our identities, narrative is not merely *about* self, but is rather in some profound way a constituent part *of* self."[13] Autobiography in particular, Eakin suggests, "is not merely something we read in a book; rather, as a discourse of identity, delivered bit by bit in the stories we tell about ourselves day in and day out, autobiography structures our living."[14] These everyday stories that we tell about ourselves in order to lend coherence to our own existence from one moment to another may take the form of conversations with our companions, official written documents, informal messages, or entirely imaginative narrations within our own minds – and the use of the autobiographical form in structuring many *fictional* narratives (such as *The Road Past Altamont*, discussed later in this chapter) reflects the importance of the narrative construction of identity in life as well as in art within a society that values the notion of individualism. Importantly, though, we do not create these everyday stories in a personal vacuum with absolute freedom and spontaneity. Eakin mentions the case of an American man who was arrested for stealing a car, and then refused to tell the police his name. Not knowing how to process him within their systems of record keeping, the police imprisoned the man indefinitely until his name – and therefore, his story – was revealed.[15] For Eakin, the consequences of this man's refusal to participate in the "narrative identity system" highlight the social existence of invisible rules and forms of discipline that ensure that our narrative identities fit within "normative models of personhood."[16] There is a deep social expectation that individuals will construct their own lived temporalities in the familiar terms of a life story, which is then delivered (depending on the appropriate context) in the form of official documents, relevantly filtered statements, or simply a name. In this sense, just as individuals are expected to internalize the normative understandings of time encapsulated within the large cultural narratives that function as time socialization stories, so too are individuals expected to tell familiar narratives about their own personal time in order to demonstrate their socialization into the narrative identity system. The social constraints that contribute toward the shaping of personal narrative identity include not only the compulsion to communicate with figures of authority, but also the principles and conventions of narrative forms themselves, since our identity stories allow us to fit comfortably within our social world only to the extent that they meet at least the basic expectation that "the subject of an action," in Ricoeur's words, must be understood "as the same throughout a life that stretches from birth to death."

From a phenomenological standpoint, the unfolding sensations that constitute ongoing temporal experience do not necessarily align in any obvious sense with linear narrative forms that envision a human life following the unidirectional trip along time's arrow from birth to death. The absolute sequentiality of clock time, the epitome of a perfectly uniform narrative in which each moment is directly superseded by the subsequent moment, stands partially in contrast to direct subjective temporal experience, which tends much more toward non-linear associative relations. Subjective time draws complex, often counter-logical connections between different moments, so that even while narrative identity is important for shaping temporal experience into coherent stories, tension exists between subjective associative time and the more objective social templates of narrative identity.

While the nearly synonymous relationship between temporal cohesion and narrative means that literary texts are especially well suited to articulating and interrogating the concepts through which we understand ourselves in time, the ability of art to reflect the tensions of subjective time is, of course, not particular to literature. Christiane Pflug's 1966 painting *Kitchen Door with Ursula* exemplifies the capacity of art to highlight the

Figure 2.1. *Kitchen Door with Ursula* (Christiane Pflug, 1966). Oil on canvas. Collection of the Winnipeg Art Gallery. Acquired with the assistance of the Women's Committee and The Winnipeg Foundation, G-66-89. Photo: Ernest Mayer, Winnipeg Art Gallery.

associative aspects of human temporality, to construct a very human narrative even in a single image. The portrayal of a neighbourhood in wintertime seen from the inside of a house is made counter-logical by the reflection of a spring scene in the glass door. The simultaneous presence of objectively discrete temporal moments speaks to the inevitable circumvention in the human mind of the absolute flow of time – whether through memory, longing, or imagination – as well as the ability of art to "mirror" subjectivity. In other words, the painting does not misrepresent reality so much as it truthfully reflects subjective experience. Pflug said of her work, "I would like to reach a certain clarity which does not exist in life."[17]

The uneasy coexistence of objective and subjective time is the central theme of W.H. New's long poem *Along a Snake Fence Riding*, which is largely an attempt to articulate how subjective associative time operates, and how the negotiations between associative and objective time unfold. According to New's note to the reader, the poem contains the voices of "the Newtonian Clock (which is constant throughout), and six others."[18] The six "others," which appear to be human characters (though the wording above suggests that they may also be clocks of a kind), speak in numbered sections "which appear non-sequentially, by association – like the process of memory or recognition – as the book moves forward into story."[19] The result is a pastiche of voices and narrative fragments; while the Newtonian Clock chants short rhythmic phrases in block capital letters on the bottom of each page, the human voices along the top of the page speak in no clear order, often on unrelated topics. There are several ways of reading the book: starting on the first page, one can read the human fragment and the Newtonian fragment, then turn to the second page and so on until the end; or, one can read across the top of each page to hear the human voices without interruption, then return to the beginning and set out again with the Newtonian voice; or, making note of the relative positions of the sixty-six non-sequential numbered sections, one can flip maddeningly forwards and backwards in an attempt to sequentialize the narrative.

However one turns the pages, various revelations about the human experience of time come to light. The non-sequential sections, by mirroring the workings of "memory or recognition," indicate that subjective time operates in a fundamentally different way from the regular forward beat of absolute clock time and the idealized narrative form that it appears to embody. An epigraph taken from Australian writer Tim Winton's short story "Aquifer" signals a possible basis for this theme: "*When a wave breaks, the water is not moving. The swell has travelled great distances but only the energy is moving, not the water. Perhaps time moves through us and not us through it ... the past is in us, and not behind us. Things are never over.*"[20] This reading sees consciousness as the medium within which time takes shape; the associative quality of memory serves to produce ripples of temporality in different directions, so that a person's experience of the present moment is always coloured by the simultaneous presence of certain pasts. Time in this sense is a product of subjectivity more than it is a separate dimension of the world, an echo of Henri Bergson's famous assertion late in the nineteenth century that "real duration is made up of moments inside one another."[21] Similar perspectives have remained influential in recent investigations into temporal experience, as in the sociologist Michael Flaherty's view that "human beings make time by sifting the fragmentary dynamics of experience through the reflexive 'unity of consciousness.'"[22] The associations that subjective experience creates between different moments of time function in a similar way to metaphorical thought processes by which counter-logical relationships are formed between different domains of reality; the jumps between non-sequential moments in the story are a form of metaphor.

Despite the distinction between subjective time and clock time, in New's poem the juxtaposition of the two modes of temporal experience indicates that they are inevitably intertwined and perform complementary functions. Throughout *Along a Snake Fence Riding* neither the human voices nor the Newtonian voice ever speak without the other also speaking on the same page, suggesting that while the two may appear distinct, one cannot exist without the other. After all, phenomenological time requires the imposition of a narrative structure in order to cohere into the experience of identity, while the perfect objectivity of clock time exists only insofar as there are human beings to conceive of it. Psychologist Klaus F. Riegel uses the term "dialectical time" to describe the same principle. He argues that like a polyphonic musical composition, dialectical time "indicates that any experience of time involves the interaction of at least two event-sequences, for example, the phenomena observed and the measurement taken."[23] In New's poem, the dialectical nature of this formal juxtaposition mirrors the content of the dialogue when the Newtonian voice notices that time is not rigid and singular. "TIME / STRETCHES / TIME SHRINKS," it says;[24] and later it seems unable to fix temporality into any one register, asking not just *what time*, but "WHICH TIME / SUMMERTIME / WINTERTIME / WHICH TIME / DINNERTIME / WHICH TIME."[25]

Associative subjective time, then, cannot be reduced to straightforward forms of linear narrative, yet it remains perpetually engaged in negotiation with the formalizing structures of thought that seek to transform fragmentary experiences into comprehensible stories. Whether through the social requirements of narrative identity or through the pressure to measure the experiences of a human life against linear chronologies such as those supplied by clocks and calendars, the subjective process of temporal association-making involves the same narrativizing tendency that is at work in historical narratives. Recalling Hayden White's comment that historical narratives are in fact "symbolic structures, extended metaphors, that 'liken' the events reported in them to some form with which we have already become familiar in our literary culture,"[26] New's description of the past as a "makeshift territory, / the one we learned later / to call time −"[27] frames subjective time, like historical narrative, as a product of fluid symbols shaped and selected retroactively (even if the "retro" in question is no further than the slippery instant when the present becomes the past).

Alongside the formal conventions of narrative, the mechanics of language and grammar also contribute to the ways in which personal experiences of time can be articulated. The power relations at stake in the narrativizing of identity frequently operate through temporal indicators as innocuous as verb tenses, a process of which literary authors tend to be highly cognizant. Ricoeur notes that the structuring of verb tenses "varies from one language to another," forming intricate cultural apparatuses that "cannot be derived from the phenomenological experience of time and from its intuitive distinction between present, past, and future."[28] While the tense system of a given language "allow[s] the structuring of the time appropriate for the activity of narrative configuration,"[29] it also prescribes and delineates this time. But even though authors are bound to the restrictions of linguistic temporal indicators, they can construct narratives that reflexively question these restrictions or foreground the assumed connotations of different verb forms.

In her short story "Powers," Alice Munro describes a conversation between Nancy, whose husband Wilf is suffering from dementia, and her estranged friend Tessa. Tessa mentions a deceased mutual friend, whose death comes as a surprise to Nancy:

> "*Ollie*? You mean Ollie's dead?" …
> "I thought you would've known. Didn't Wilf know?"
> "*Doesn't* Wilf know," said Nancy in an automatic way, defending her husband by placing him amongst the living.[30]

Brad Fraser's character Shannon, in his play *Poor Super Man*, also attaches the weight of life and death to verb tenses. As Shannon nears death, succumbing to AIDS and cancer, she says, "I've already started thinking of myself in the past tense ... Everything's then. Nothing's now."[31] For the narrator in Yann Martel's *Self*, events of great personal significance refuse to be relegated to the past tense, signalling their undying importance: "In my memory the past and present tenses do not measure out temporal sequence, but emotional weight. What I cannot forget repeats itself in the present tense."[32] Margaret Atwood, meanwhile, in her short story "The Age of Lead," recounts her character Jane's confusion over a television documentary about the Franklin Expedition to the supposed Northwest Passage. John Torrington, a victim of the doomed expedition, has been excavated from the ice after 150 years, looking nearly the same as when he was buried. Atwood writes, "The man they've dug up and melted was a young man. Or still is: it's difficult to know what tense should be applied to him, he is so insistently present."[33] By choosing one verb tense over another, a speaker can accommodate a subject within the ongoing present, or slot it, him, or her categorically into the past, to be entrapped in the deathly realm that Atwood refers to as "previous layers of time."[34] While I hold that thematic and formal concerns of contested temporalities in literature are vital for reflecting cultural-temporal issues, Karen Newman, Jay Clayton, and Marianne Hirsch go so far as to argue in *Time and the Literary* that "the systematic grammatical contrasts that express time in language are perhaps the most fundamental way the literary continues to structure thinking about time."[35]

Other components of language shape the human experience of temporality in less obvious ways, and important differences exist in this regard between different languages. Commenting on their own English translations of two Mi'kmaq stories that had been recorded in their original language in the nineteenth century, Elizabeth Paul and Peter Sanger note:

> There is one great absence in the English translations which cannot be remedied by literality or any other solution. Mi'kmaq categorizes nouns not only by gender and number but also in terms of animate and inanimate. Animate nouns include growing trees, stars, household goods and hunting weapons. The consequent play within the Mi'kmaq language of life and death cannot be reproduced by the neutrality of tree, star and arrow in English.[36]

Dewdney agrees that while verbs "mediate the influence of time on our lives," English nouns "are almost entirely timeless, except when they refer to *elements* of time such as sundials, hours, schedules or seasons."[37] Taiaiake Alfred, following Leroy Little Bear, identifies a similar differentiation as a systemic one within larger language groups. European languages, he says, "centre on nouns and are concerned with naming things, ascribing traits, and making judgments. Onkwehonwe [i.e., Indigenous] languages are structured on verbs; they communicate through descriptions of movement and activity."[38] Alfred concludes that "the European way is to see the world organized in a system of names and titles that formalize their being. Onkwehonwe recall relationships and responsibilities through languages that symbolize doing."[39] While such a broad generalization is troubling – is there really a "European way"? – it is intriguing to consider the ways in which the English language can serve to essentialize subjects, to regard people or other things as static in time rather than as ongoing processes being continuously enacted.

Such tendencies have been countered somewhat by theories of relational identity that hold that identity is not essential and stable but rather performed and negotiated – not permanent but momentary. Charles Taylor describes this as the "fundamentally dialogical character" of human life.[40] He writes, "My discovering my own identity doesn't mean that I work it out in isolation, but that I negotiate it through dialogue, partly overt, partly internal, with others ... My own identity crucially depends on my dialogical relations with others."[41] Ecological theorist Neil Evernden even suggests that "we might more closely approximate the facts of existence by regarding ourselves less as objects than as sets of relationships, or as processes in time."[42] These approaches focus more on theoretical or subjective knowledge than on the structure of language, but they resist the idea of the world as a formalized system of names and titles, investing instead in the transformative power of ongoing relationships.

However, theories of dialogical identity notwithstanding, the weight of often traumatic histories across many forms of narrative, literary and otherwise, indicates that while the past may be partially revisable in the sense that ongoing experiences allow for altered perspectives on events, pervasive understandings of identity remain ensnared by essentialization, centring on past events and "permanent" characteristics such as race or gender. Entire novels may follow a character's struggle to "move on" from the continuous present of an unwanted past, and even when such a story ends, as is often the case, with some degree of success, the intensity of the struggle itself signals the oppressive weight of essentialized pasts.

"THIS UNBEARABLE ARCHAEOLOGY":
EVENTS THAT SHAPE SUBJECTIVE TIME

As we have seen, the expectations of socialization, the formalizing structures of narrative, and the grammatical conventions of language are not
alone in shaping articulations of subjective time. Specific events and relationships at various scales from the personal to the social and the cultural
are also deeply important components of the processes by which individuals
understand their own temporal existence, agency, and disempowerment.

The use of a pivotal or watershed moment, usually a negative one, as
the defining feature of a character's life story is common in literature,
reflecting broadly perceived anxieties about the perpetual influence of
past events. Alice Munro's short story "Post and Beam" offers a vivid portrayal of such anxiety when the character Lorna convinces herself that her
older sister has likely committed suicide. This is "the time before," she
tells herself. But once she finds the dead body everything will be "the
time after."[43] In another story, "Trespasses," prickly burrs that stick to
Lauren's ankles while she helps to bury her adopted sister's ashes – an
event mired in secrecy and trauma – become a metaphor for thorny pasts
that cannot be detached. Lauren tries to pull the burrs from her legs, only
to find them stuck to some of her fingers, and then more fingers: "She
was so sick of these burrs that she wanted to beat her hands and yell out
loud, but she knew that the only thing she could do was just sit and
wait."[44] Occasionally, though, Munro grants her characters some leeway
in shaping the past to fit their needs, articulating the useful imaginative
potential of the ability to reconceptualize the flow of time from past to
future and back again. In "What Is Remembered," the protagonist Meriel
remembers only particular aspects of her one-time lover, realizing years
later that if she had been unable to suppress her suspicion of his infidelity,
"Her life might have been different."[45] She begins now to remember him
in this new light, wondering "if he'd stay that way, or if she had some new
role waiting for him, some use still to put him to in her mind, during the
time ahead."[46]

The oppressive weight of the past in the ongoing formation of identity
is also a central motif in Dionne Brand's body of work, and the circumstances that surface in her writing often explicitly reveal the complex
ways in which subjective time, while deeply personal, is inevitably tied to

relations of social power and systemic injustices. Describing the life of slave plantation workers in *In Another Place, Not Here*, she writes, "And the living, they lived in the past or had no past but a present that was filled, peopled with the past. No matter their whims and flights into the future some old face or old look, some old pain would appear."[47] Any woman, she writes, is "full of all the things that had happened to her … One way or the other, a woman was always pregnant."[48] In *What We All Long For*, Brand describes the grief of a couple who lost their young son while fleeing Vietnam several decades earlier. The remaining daughters become reminders "of their parents' past, their other life; the life that was cut in half one night on a boat to Hong Kong."[49] Cam, the mother, rarely sleeps, obsessively imagining "over again and again the scene at the bay when they both lost sight of Quy … trying to alter the sequence of events so that she would arrive at herself in the present with her family and her mind intact … Why couldn't she reclaim the time?"[50] In her poetry collection *Land to Light On*, Brand describes being pulled over, along with two other Black friends, by a police officer whose gaze constrains them, forcing their pasts upon them, fastening their identities as members of a subjugated race: "The snow-blue laser of a cop's eyes fixes us / in this unbearable archaeology."[51] For people of African descent in the Americas, Brand writes in *A Map to the Door of No Return*, "History is already seated in the chair in the empty room when one arrives."[52]

These examples suggest that a past event can be a defining feature of a person's identity because she perceives it to be so, or because it is imposed as such by some form of authority. While either possibility could be construed as a failure of dialogic identity-making, the two can more usefully be articulated in terms of dialogism by saying that the past event or characteristic continues to make its presence felt in perpetuity; the past event remains a present participant in the ongoing dialogue through which identity is constructed.[53]

One of the factors at stake here, particularly in *Land to Light On*, is the potential conflict between personal and broader cultural conceptualizations of time reckoning. The police officer who looks with suspicion into the stopped car constrains the group of travellers in the "unbearable archaeology" of the inequitable social construction of race, an act that carries within it, and reinforces, the actual history of systemic racism in Canada as well as the cultural chronotope of civilizational advancement in which, as Daniel Coleman says, "the idea of progress itself is deeply informed by a central value of whiteness."[54] This cultural chronotope is obviously at odds with the personal temporal motivations of the friends in the vehicle, and this situation is an example of what Coleman describes as the fraught process of the negotiation of chronotopes: "We construct chronotopes in an ongoing dialogue between individual and collective experience, and much of our personal sense of belonging has to do with the fit between our individual time-space maps and those of the communities in which we live."[55] This suggests that the conflicts that emerge between subjective experiences of time and broader cultural frameworks of time indicate that the social concept of temporal discrimination inevitably becomes important to understanding the temporal experiences of individual people. Not only can grand cultural concepts like linear progress fail to hold equitably for all members of society, but even for individuals who in some respects subscribe to them these narratives will almost certainly fail to articulate particular aspects of the actual lived experience of time. Any attempt to reconstruct temporal experience – to overcome past traumas or reimagine goals for the future – must negotiate not only the rehearsed timelines belonging to the individual in question, but also the cultural hierarchies of privilege tied to broader social concepts of time.

Still, the act of the police officer only indirectly involves the cultural model of time that equates whiteness with progressive civility. At a more direct level his act is a component of systemic racialization, and is thus more a matter of ingrained inequitable social power relations than it is a matter of social concepts of time. Personal experiences of time, then, are shaped through negotiations not only with grand cultural chronotopes, but also with *other forms* of social relations, including relations of power such as those associated with race, gender, or class. As long as social categories of identity infused with status, power, and privilege continue to operate, they act as present participants in the ongoing construction of narrative identity. The ability of individuals to conceptualize their own existence in any temporal direction is at least partially shaped by such relations, since social interactions necessarily impact on perception (the present), along with memory and expectation (the past and future), delineating the horizon of expected temporal possibilities as well as more immediate temporal experiences.

SUBJECTIVE TIME AND THE CHALLENGE
OF SOCIAL SYNCHRONIZATION

I will close this chapter with two case studies reading the tensions between subjective time and sociality in Gabrielle Roy's short story cycle *The Road Past Altamont* (*La route d'Altamont*, 1966), and Catherine Bush's novel *Minus Time* (1993). While the two books examine strikingly different temporal circumstances – francophone settler culture in early twentieth-century Manitoba, and the implications of orbital space travel for a Torontonian family near the end of the twentieth century – both works clarify the ways in which broad social temporalities must be understood through individual temporal experiences, as well as the ways in which subjective time, and thus the very notion of identity, must be understood through the context of social factors that include not only cultural chronotopes, but also other forms of social circumstance such as the need for intimacy with others, the flux of familial relations, and the ambivalent effects of new technologies.

Like Gabrielle Roy herself, the protagonist Christine in *The Road Past Altamont* is born in Manitoba early in the twentieth century to francophone parents who had immigrated to the prairies from Quebec. While some critics refer to the book as a novel, it is usually seen as a short story cycle, in that the four sections, which examine four different periods of time in Christine's youth and young adulthood, are comprehensible on their own but are best understood as building on one another to establish a fuller perspective on Christine's growth into adulthood and her decision to become a writer (as such, the book is a *Künstlerroman*, if we allow that a work that leans more toward the short story cycle form can still usefully be described as an "artist's novel"). Critical commentary on the book has often focused on Roy's representation of the prairie landscape, but the subjective experience of time in informing both personal identity and intimate social relations is also a central theme in the work. As Christine gradually comes of age, she learns through interactions with those close to her that the temporal bonds that tie family members and friends together simultaneously preclude the possibility of complete temporal coexistence. While individuals are connected to one another by virtue of the fact that everyone ages, by partially overlapping lifespans, by the inevitability of death, and by social customs that create a sense of community in a particular time and place, each of these things also ruptures interpersonal relations: no two people are exactly the same age, no one's lifespan overlaps completely with anyone else's, the timing of death is unique to everyone, and, especially in modernity, the social customs to which one is accustomed shift over time, separating oneself not only from those who are younger or older, but also from one's own past way of life. This knowledge of temporal connections and ruptures in turn becomes a form of self-knowledge, informing the discoveries that Christine makes about her own identity as a young but aging person navigating complex relationships with the people around her.

David Williams sees *The Road Past Altamont* as an "imagist novel"[56] that transforms problems of time into spatial figures such as the tapestry or the womb, which respectively symbolize Maman's telling of the changing family history and her realization that the aging individual metaphorically gives birth to her ancestors and her children through hard-won comprehension of the needs and anxieties of people of different ages. For Williams, the "linked story form" allows the novel to create "its series of lyric instants";[57] indeed, seeing the book specifically as a short story cycle can draw out several temporal aspects of the form. Gerald Lynch argues that the form of the short story cycle itself is "a distinctly Canadian genre" that "allows for a new kind of unity in disunity, reflecting a fragmented temporal sense."[58] The popularity of the form, he points out,

> coincides with the arrival of the modern world, when the revolutionary impact of Darwin, Marx, Freud, and Einstein was being cumulatively felt and all traditional systems were coming under a destabilizing scrutiny ... including the tradition of the realistic-naturalistic novel. Viewed in this context, the short story cycle can indeed be considered as a kind of anti-novel, fragmenting the continuous narrative's treatment of place, time, character, and plot, and often offering simultaneous multiple perspectives in a manner paralleling that of cubist painting.[59]

J.N. Nodelman briefly mentions that Lynch's argument could be applied directly to *The Road Past Altamont*, but does not comment further on the implications of this fragmented temporal sense, focusing instead on the various modes of spatial transport in the book – including stilts, horse-drawn carts, trains, and cars – that cause people to conceptualize and interact with the landscape in particular ways. Lynch's generalization on the short story cycle does accurately reflect the fragmented temporalities created by the way in which each of the four stories that constitute *The Road Past Altamont* covers an isolated period of time, even while the stories taken together develop a more unified sense of Christine's growing comprehension, a formal trait that is entirely appropriate to the representation of temporal bonds that connect people even while they divide individual experiences. The form of the book mirrors its thematic preoccupation with subjective temporalities that are both fragmented and coeval. Still, this does not make it an anti-novel as such. Modern and postmodern novels, after all, had carried out similar rejections of continuous linear narrative by the 1960s. Rather, the form of *The Road Past Altamont* disrupts the conventions of continuity that were tied more specifically to nineteenth-century novels invested in what Lynch calls "the realistic-naturalistic" tradition, and in this way the form also mirrors the experiences of the characters who find themselves living in a world where the social conventions of the previous century have given way to shifting and complex new realities. Monsieur Saint-Hilaire's complaint that his grandchildren "weren't unkind or heartless but suffered from the malady of the times: a fondness for speed and cars and motorcycles and also for spending money as quickly as they could ... and that he felt too old now to be able to adapt himself to the frenzy of the day"[60] is appropriate not only thematically, but formally insofar as it appears within a short story cycle that eschews a regular narrative progression in favour of the modernist "frenzy" of a more rapid pace of change.[61]

While the spatial metaphors that Williams sees as the key to the book's commentary on time are indeed important, the notion of identifying what he calls "the ultimate spatial form for time"[62] risks moving the conversation somewhat away from temporal concerns per se and toward debates over the significance of different spatial images. Hence, Williams's argument that the image of the womb makes Roy's modernist vision of time quintessentially feminine. Hence, too, the long-standing critical debate over whether time in the book is best understood as cyclical or linear. Nodelman points out that, for M.G. Hesse, "Essentially time is conceived as a cycle, so that the future contains the past while the past anticipates the future," while for Paula Gilbert Lewis the characters' desires for cyclicality "imply a lack of any forward movement" along the linear path of time.[63] Nodelman refers to "Christine's deepening sense that life is a great circle," but suggests that the debate remains open, that the central question in the second story of the book, for instance, is "whether our passages across the landscape are cyclical (in the sense that we can experience several different times of our own lives, and those of others, at once) or linear (meaning that the past is forever lost, and the generations cannot truly connect)."[64] Williams correctly sees this choice as a false one, arguing that "time is neither cyclical nor lineal but both: the round womb of time gives birth again to linear development,"[65] a comment that reflects the conclusion in the critical study of time that, in Barbara Adam's words, "all social processes display aspects of both linearity and cyclicity, and that we recognize a cyclical structure when we focus on events that repeat themselves and unidirectional linearity when our attention is on the process of the repeating action."[66] Roy draws our attention to both of these aspects in turn.

In some ways, then, the more interesting approach does not have to do with identifying the type of spatial image that best represents the book's concern with time, but rather examines the properly temporal concerns of troubled simultaneity and synchronization. Amid the fractured and divided temporalities that Christine encounters in her relationships with her mother, her grandmother, and her elderly neighbour Monsieur Saint-Hilaire, she develops a deep desire for her own life to be *synchronized* with the people she loves, a contradictory desire that is associated with sorrow and solitude as much as it is with intimacy and connection. The temporal gap between individuals takes its clearest form as a gap between generations, and becomes the concluding thought to the first story in the collection, "My Almighty Grandmother." In this story the six-year-old Christine stays for part of the summer with her grandmother, who has become elderly and forgetful. When her grandmother uses spare household materials to make an elaborate doll for her, Christine is delighted at the act of pure creation, and begins to wonder about the relationship between the youthful, active grandmother of the past, and the increasingly frail and incapacitated grandmother of the present. Looking through an old album, Christine finds a photograph of her grandmother as a young mother: "This old photograph fascinated me so much that I forgot everything else. Through it, at last, I think I began to understand vaguely a little about life and all the successive beings it makes of us as we increase in age."[67] Christine's realization that the experience of temporality makes "successive beings" of individuals is, paradoxically, also the realization that the *same* person undergoes remarkable changes over the course of a lifetime. When Christine takes the album to her grandmother's bedside, "to show my grandmother the portrait she no longer resembled," Maman appears at the doorway wearing "a sad and very tender little smile." The story ends with Christine (the adult narrator) thinking back and wondering: "But why did she look so pleased with me? I was only playing, as she herself had taught me to do, as Mémère also had played with me one day … as we all play perhaps, throughout our lives, at trying to catch up with one another."[68]

This final line of the story presents the irresistible but impossible desire to "catch up with one another," to achieve interpersonal synchronization, as an expression of the tension that arises through the human coexistence of temporal intimacy with temporal solitude. In her study of time and feminist theory, Rita Felski suggests that the term "synchronous nonsynchronicity" – a phrase that she borrows from Ernst Bloch – may offer "the most promising way of approaching the cultural politics of time. Quite simply, it acknowledges that we inhabit both the same time and different times: individuals coexist at the same historical moment, yet often make sense of this moment in strikingly disparate ways."[69] A key point here is that temporal identities, like other forms of identity, are always partial. As Christine realizes, though, it is not just that people make sense of their historical moment in different ways, but that individuals actually experience different times within the "same" absolute moment by virtue of their own temporal situatedness. The state of synchronous non-synchronicity, while paradoxical, accurately reflects the internally conflicted sense of subjective time in a social world. Indeed, after the first story ends with Christine's supposition that people endlessly try "to catch up with one another," the remaining stories in the cycle confirm that the attempt to synchronize amid inevitable non-synchronicity is a project that does in fact continue "throughout our lives."

If the first story identifies the need for temporal alignment in the fostering of human intimacy, the second story, "The Old Man and the Child," confirms the impossibility of synchronization. Christine, now eight years old, becomes friends with the elderly Monsieur Saint-Hilaire, though to Christine he is simply "the old man." When he invites her on a day trip by train to Lake Winnipeg, which Christine has never seen, she enters a frenzy of excitement. Upon arriving at the beach, the old man explains that the lake "was older than the soil of Manitoba and that it would still be there when millions of years had passed. For the eternity of time, he told me."[70] To sit in front of the lake, then, is to encounter eternity, yet even in the face of the ultimate human commonality – the knowledge that one will die while the world carries on – Christine is struck by the gulf of time separating her from her companion. After writing a figure eight, her own age, into the sand, she experiences a sensation of distress: "I suppose I could not bear the joy of being at the beginning while he was at the end."[71] The old man then whispers his own age to the girl, which she writes alongside her own "as a sum in arithmetic." The temporal gap between eight and 84 is then displayed for her, in the most transient form of writing, in the sand before the eternal lake:

> I was stricken by what remained to me and seemed to separate us
> from each other by a stretch of time even more mysterious than the
> extent of water and earth ... I was rather disheartened, I think, by a
> sense of the inequality and injustice of life. Why, I wondered, did we
> not all reach the same age at the same time.
>   "It would be dull," he pointed out, "all the old folks together – or
> only the young."[72]

While the desire for temporal alignment is an ache that never goes away, the old man's comments begin to reflect the fact that absolute synchronization, completely shared experiences of time, would also mean completely shared narratives, and therefore shared identities. The unbridgeable temporal gulf between Christine and the old man is part of what it means for each of them to have their own identities, and the ache for synchronization is thus the confirmation of subjectivity. Our experiences of time are our stories, and even while we all share the experience of temporality itself, the infinite variations in personal temporalities establish our identities as individuals.[73]

Importantly, though, this story does offer several forms of synchronization to Christine and the old man, even if these remain partial and temporary. First is the obvious but important sense in which the two companions are able to spend time together, conversing, interacting, and experiencing the world simultaneously. Second, as Williams points out, by telling Christine stories about his travels in Europe, the old man "offers her another way of 'catching up with one another' through time. For his stories of the many countries to which he has travelled inspire in her a desire for imitation."[74] Many years later Christine will be in a position to replicate some of these travels in his memory, just as Maman relives her own mother's experiences of old age as she begins to become elderly herself. While this eventual reliving is among the most nonsynchronous forms of synchronization, it speaks to the exemplary power of temporal alignment through storytelling. Narratives, or personal articulations of time, not only shape phenomenological experiences into coherence, but also transmit subjective temporalities into the consciousness of those around us, allowing for intimate sharing of personal temporal experiences, even if the sharing may occur across a wide gulf of absolute time. The final form of synchronization in "The Old Man and the Child" occurs as Christine and the old man share their final moments together before the lake. Throughout the earlier parts of the story the two of them had become drowsy at different times – Christine nearly falls asleep on the beach only to have the old man wake her to walk into town, then the old man falls asleep at a restaurant while Christine watches nervously from across the table – but as the story draws to a close, the two achieve a momentary alignment when, "Alone now on this long beach before immensity, we slept shoulder to shoulder."[75] In the face of eternity, and through a basic human act of replenishment, the two become synchronized, even if this moment of alignment is a small part of their extended temporal experiences.

By the eponymous final story of the collection, "The Road Past Altamont," Christine is entering adulthood herself, and she is driving her mother along the unmarked prairie roads that seem to intersect at random across the landscape, until the pair stumble upon a series of hills surrounding the tiny village of Altamont. When Maman reminisces about the hills in the region of Quebec where she had grown up, Christine is dismayed that her mother is so deeply attached to a period of her life to which Christine has no access: "I was astonished to see Maman pass over her adult existence in Manitoba to go to the most remote part of her life in search of those images, unknown to me yesterday and now seemingly more pleasing to her than any others. I was perhaps even somewhat vexed."[76] The concern wears at Christine throughout the story: "come to think of it, it was only since the reappearance of hills in our life that I had noticed that attention to voices from the past that I found so bewildering and that took her to some extent away from me."[77] Maman's reminiscing about times that occurred prior to Christine's existence separates the two of them, even while they sit together travelling in the same car.[78]

Once again, though, the story juxtaposes these unsettling forms of temporal disconnection against opportunities for temporal alignment. One such opportunity, a massively social one which is tied to the passage of the seasons, occurs when a large group assembles at Uncle Cléophas's house for harvesting: "These people ... came from every corner of Canada, I should perhaps say of the world, for that was the most astonishing thing of all, that men of such diverse nationalities and characters were gathered together in our remote farms to harvest the wheat."[79] And once again storytelling emerges as a binding force, as the men "were never so tired that they did not attempt, when night came and the whining of the machines was silenced for a few hours, to share something unique to each of them that might draw them for a moment closer to each other."[80] While the old man's story at the beach had itself fostered a form of temporal alignment, the harvest gathering shows how an instance of temporal alignment – in this case one tied to seasonality and communal food production – can foster other forms of social connection. The ache for synchronization sees one of the fruits of its fulfillment here, as the participants are drawn closer to one another through actual shared temporal experience as well as the more abstract shared temporalities of storytelling. Christine reflects: "It is from those evenings, unfolding like competitions of songs and stories, that my desire, which has never since left me, to learn to tell a story well undoubtedly dates, so much was I impressed at that time by the poignant and miraculous power of this gift."[81] The adult Christine, we learn, has become a writer, and the narrative reflections that constitute *The Road Past Altamont* represent her articulations, in form and content, of the gradual temporal shaping of her own subjectivity as well as the larger family history through which her temporal existence takes shape.

The intergenerational experiences of Christine and her mother, alongside the memory of Christine's grandmother, open up the remaining opportunities for non-synchronous synchronization. Maman recalls that, as she grew older, she began to resemble her own mother both in appearance and in personality: "Only with middle age did I catch up with her, or she caught up with me – how can you explain this strange encounter outside time? ... Besides, I'm no longer angry about it, since, having become her, I understand her."[82] Here the old man's hint to Christine that temporal difference constitutes identity reaches its logical conclusion, that "catching up" with another person means that one *becomes* that person. The transformation is not literal, of course, but confirms that to the extent that sharing the temporality of another person is possible, such an experience forms a connection as intimate as the sharing of an identity. Even while Christine and her mother drift apart toward the end of the story when Christine travels to Europe "to learn to know myself and to write,"[83] Maman leaves her with a final insight on temporal identity and intimacy. The period of adulthood, Maman explains, in which "parents truly live over again in their children" even while they also relive "the lives of [their] own parents" is "perhaps the most illuminated part of one's life."[84] Through carefully constructed narrative, the artist illuminates the ways in which subjective experiences of time effectively constitute identity, always partially overlap the temporalities of others, and draw us inevitably toward one another even while they hold us at a distance. Just as the implications of the modernist frenzy of changing social temporalities become most clearly meaningful to the extent that they are actually embodied through individual experiences, so too can subjective experiences of time be understood only through an examination of the broader social circumstances within which they take shape.

Catherine Bush's novel *Minus Time* offers a nuanced investigation of the interactions between several of the issues important to the discussion of time, subjectivity, sociality, and narrative: the ways in which personal identity is shaped by past events; the fragmentation and internal conflict to which an individual's sense of time is often susceptible; the problematic negotiation between personal and collective chronotopes and the impossibility of separating one from the other; the difficult but important feat of aligning one's temporal maps with those of one's family and peer groups; and the consequences of conflicting visions of temporality for people and the rest of the biosphere.

The novel tells the story of Helen Urie, a young adult in Toronto whose mother Barbara is famous not only for being a Canadian female astronaut, but for attempting to set a new record for the amount of time spent living in space. The title *Minus Time* refers to the anxious duration of the countdown before the space shuttle launch (as in the phrase "T minus three minutes"), but also takes on a figurative association with the intense temporal anxiety and sense of loss surrounding Helen's realization that her mother "had left the planet and they had no idea when she was coming back again … The time and space that lay between was not traversable. She was speeding into the future."[85] Looking up at the overwhelming Florida sky into which the spacecraft has disappeared, Helen experiences a mixture of elation and panic: "She had concentrated so hard on the launch and now she'd surged beyond it. In that instant, everything had changed. Her life, too, split into before the launch and after. She wanted to reach for the sky and howl out loud like a wolf – *what now?*"[86] The liftoff itself becomes a watershed moment of the kind articulated in many works of literature, figuratively launching the emotional arc of the story. For critic John E. MacKinnon, the novel's title refers to "an interval in Helen's life" that holds "her future in abeyance, as if suspending her in time."[87]

This sense of trauma causes Helen to look for meaning in the events leading up to and following the launch, and to single out those whom she sees as complicit in forming the temporal chasm. She comes to identify as antagonists everything from her mother, whose life ambition to become an astronaut has interfered with her ability to spend time with her children; to her father, who copes with family stresses by spending years in distant countries helping the victims of natural disasters; to the alienating socio-technological infrastructure that carries her mother indefinitely into space even while gradually poisoning her home through chemical spills, species loss, and interpersonal fragmentation. "You've got these video screens all around you," Helen's brother Paul explains about watching the shuttle launch, "and the launchpad almost looks like it's balanced right on top of the digital clock on the ground in front of you, the clock that shows the countdown. It *is* scary, in a way."[88] As a metaphor for pervasive techno-science, the countdown clock forms the unstable ground upon which the key moments of the family's lives precariously sit. Its starts, stops, pace, and authority are outside the family's control, yet the clock governs the creation of personal temporal chasms and leads seemingly toward widespread ecological apocalypse. Helen decides to collaborate with Elena, an animal rights activist who wants to construct a "huge clock or some kind of timer that would count out each time another species disappeared,"[89] a project that emblematizes the fraught relationship between techno-scientific tools and the actual people whose use of such tools both causes and condemns ecological destruction.

While the consequences of technologically mediated temporality may affect everyone, they do not do so even-handedly, and contested temporalities within familial groups are susceptible to similar imbalances. Despite being subjected to the same brief media spotlight as the rest of her family, Helen's feeling of alienation from her parents continues to grow: "Time itself seemed suddenly compressed and uncontrollable. Faster, faster. Didn't everyone feel it? Was I the only one whose stomach was being turned inside out?"[90] She accuses her mother of having "hurled us with you into the dangerous future,"[91] while Paul describes their relationship with their perpetually absent father as an asymptotic line graph: "It's like these waves on a graph and they keep getting closer and closer as they run toward infinity but they never touch. That's what it feels like."[92] The space agency, meanwhile, warns Helen that because astronauts and their families inevitably change over the duration of their separation, she should expect a traumatic experience when her mother eventually returns to earth: "Only it wasn't exactly a return: The woman who left did not come back. Those she'd left behind were not the people who came to greet her."[93]

The tension culminates in Helen's angry confrontation with her mother – a conversation that is both intensely personal and mediated by the technology of the space station videophone hookup. When Barbara insists that it will remain "possible to be close to you, even from here," Helen replies, "What if I don't see the future the way you do? ... I *do* have some sense of the future – but what if I see it being here, right here? ... We have to change things here, the whole way we think about things here. I don't think it's good to act as if everything might get better by being someplace else."[94] Growing desperate, Barbara says "I would give you a whole new world if I could," but Helen shouts back, "I don't want a whole new world ... Don't you see? I want this one. I want a future here."[95] For Helen, the anxieties of increasing technological alienation, looming ecological collapse, skewed social chronotopes that treat individual people as momentary objects of interest, and discordant familial visions of temporality have culminated in a personal temporal crisis.

Attempting later on to catch a glimpse of the space station as its orbit passes above her, Helen walks "through a wilderness of satellite beams and radio waves, somewhere beyond Sudbury, through a world that seemed to her like a map of voices in the darkness, lost voices … Time itself seemed vaporous, lapping in small waves around her."[96]

Despite this sense of conflict and fragmentation, the concluding scenes of the novel emphasize the potential for stability, reconciliation, and solidarity. This shift occurs partially on a personal level, as Helen finds within the resiliency of narrative identity an ability to locate a stable sense of self emerging from her own past, a past that trails behind her "like comet trails, vaporous and filled with detritus. In the present, receding into the future, she still multiplied and divided, seeing through several eyes, longing for too many things at once, but in the past she was singular; her past made her singular, it was hers and no one else's, and whatever else happened, she still carried it with her, like a portable home."[97] But the most meaningful shifts toward solace occur on a social level within Helen's immediate family, and, like Gabrielle Roy, Bush accomplishes this transition through images of synchronization. Growing accustomed to her father's presence after his unexpected return, Helen feels that "already something like habit was binding itself between them, dissolving the time that separated them into almost nothing."[98] Sharing an intimate moment with her lover, Foster, Helen's "skin grew as springy as moss, as if touch itself could redefine the two of them, hurl them into the present, clear some space and time for them."[99] Barbara makes the metaphor explicit when she asks Helen to look up toward the night sky that evening and locate the space station, promising to return the gesture: "Whatever happens, I'll look down tonight. Your night. We'll synchronize our watches."[100] The intentional unification of the watches marks a deep alignment in temporality and purpose, even while the phrase "Your night" acknowledges that the two people inevitably remain partially absorbed in asynchronous registers of time. The fact that they can experience precisely the same minute even while occupying different portions of the day-night cycle – a cycle so disrupted by space travel that Barbara experiences sixteen sunrises each day[101] – indicates that temporalities, like other aspects of identity, are always partial, and that meaningful alignments can occur even while some aspects of temporal identity remain divergent. Just as the concept of synchronous non-synchronicity is key to *The Road Past Altamont*, where subjective temporalities remain separated even while the ache for alignment is soothed momentarily through shared times and shared stories, so too is it central to understanding Helen's experience and her musing, "It was as if they were all still walking through their own version of minus time, toward the moment of cumulative choice."[102]

The final scene of *Minus Time* depicts Helen arriving at the lake that has been selected as the family meeting point, while Barbara floats overhead: "The dark lake and dark sky shone before her like a doorway, shimmering in time ... *A small step into tomorrow*."[103] Paul and David arrive to join her, and the novel ends with: "She held out her hands to them, and stepped through the doorway."[104] The triumph suggested in the story's conclusion is a result of all four family members finally inhabiting the same subjective moment, sharing a sense of companionship, purpose, and movement into the future. While temporal alignment on the broader social and ecological scales remains worryingly elusive, synchronization is achieved, even if only momentarily, within the familial circle. While *Minus Time* contends with temporal relativity in ways that were unforeseen in past eras, the novel supports Ricoeur's view that "the major contribution of fiction to philosophy does not lie in the range of solutions it proposes for the discordance between the time of the world and lived time but in the exploration of the nonlinear features of phenomenological time that historical time conceals."[105] More than this, the novel articulates how phenomenological time and historical time themselves are internally contested and unstable, bearing witness to the difficulty, and the importance, of enacting fleeting moments of synchronization.

FROM THE SOCIAL TO THE PERSONAL AND BACK AGAIN

Through investigating some of the issues at stake in subjective experiences of time, we see that because a sense of narrative is necessary for conceptualizing both time and identity, literary arts are particularly well suited to serve as exemplary modes for thinking about how time configures, and is configured by, subjectivity. At the same time, the examples that I have discussed here indicate that in trying to understand how individuals experience time we are led inevitably back to considerations of social relations, ranging from the intimate workings of families and peer groups whose temporal experiences fluctuate within synchronous non-synchronicity, to the accelerative impulses of modernity and the ingrained configurations of social power that operate on systemic and cultural levels. The specifics by which these larger configurations of power impact the lived and imaginative realities of time for individuals now become the focus; the following chapter surveys Canadian works of literature to examine how experiences of time are connected to particular socially defined categories of identity formation and systemic forms of power.

3

Reading Time and Social Relations Critically

They weren't the same people who had taken that train to Toronto fifteen years ago. Well, no one ever is, but they weren't those two people much more so than they'd imagined. They weren't the people they were going to be or had set out to be, the people they had envisioned. Look, okay, they hadn't *envisioned*. Who does, except rich people?[1]

Dionne Brand

Unrolling the past through her mind, she knew very well how much of her life had been a matter of waiting upon others, waiting for their decisions, adapting to their plans and days.[2]

Rachel Wyatt

"Over the millennia," writes Christopher Dewdney, "our penchant for technology and abstract thought has helped us to construct an empire of time, a chronological culture within which our lives are scheduled and measured out."[3] While Dewdney's reference to "our" chronological culture appears to reflect a singular social entity, his use of the phrase "empire of time" also hints at the unequal and divisive nature of normative temporality; like all empires, an empire of time inevitably contains deeply entrenched biases and power divisions. I have discussed some of the ways in which human culture colonizes time, and in particular the ways in which the European colonization of Canada involves the construction and perpetuation of ideological frameworks whose foundational principles are just as much temporal as they are spatial. I have also looked at how personal experiences of time both depart from, and remain inevitably tied to, broader chronological cultures. What I would like to do now is examine how particular works of literature take up the complex relationships between time and social power in Canada. Diverse literary texts in Canada make abundantly clear that while broad cultural chronotopes indeed contribute toward shaping the scheduling and measuring out of individual lives, this shaping process functions differently for different people, and does not tell the whole story of the relationship between time and social power; in order to understand this relationship it is necessary also to evaluate the impact that systemic forms of social hierarchization have on lived and imagined experiences of time. I suggest that these relations can productively be understood in terms of several categories of subject positions; in particular, I examine how the relationships between time and power in Canada revolve around the categories of age, class, gender, sexuality, race, and, in the next chapter, indigeneity.

Throughout these discussions, the theoretical concepts associated with critical time studies remain vital for the coherence of particular readings as well as for the development of broader insights. For example, the concept of the time socialization story is crucial for understanding the relationship between time and age in *Anne of Green Gables*; temporal resistance is important for reading the intersection of time and socioeconomic class in Tom Wayman's poetry or the intersection of time and gender in Daphne Marlatt's fiction; and the linked concepts of temporal discrimination and multitemporality remain important throughout these conversations, allowing for the development of a larger vision of time and power in Canadian culture. The tools of critical time studies form the impetus for the lessons drawn from these readings, even while the organization of the chapter by categories such as race and gender emphasizes the links between temporal power and particular axes of social experience.

Categorization always comes at the risk of oversimplification, and my approach involves at least two limitations. First, the categories that I have chosen are by no means the only subject positions by which individuals or groups may identify themselves or be identified by others. People may belong to, negotiate, or resist being associated with many categorizations of identity, including religion, physical appearance, occupation or organizational membership, city or region, consumer habits, various types of kinship ties, different forms of ableness, and so on. Because I cannot hope to account for all the complexities of subjectivity, I have tried to identify those categories that appear most prominently, or are represented as having the greatest importance for social existence, in Canadian texts. A second limitation of my method is that, by discussing each text under a particular heading – race, class, and so on – I risk creating the impression that each work speaks to just one category of social existence. The texts that I am discussing are works of great complexity, and it would be a disservice to reduce them to the confines of a single rubric. While the purpose of dividing my analysis into categories is to identify prominent areas of concern, and to try to understand why particular subject positions appear again and again as sites of preoccupation, I will attempt to do justice to the fact that these works could be discussed within alternative or multiple frameworks; in some cases I will examine how different categories like race and class can overlap, and at times I will discuss a particular text under more than one heading. To emphasize the importance of seeing different categories of identity as correlated, before breaking Canadian literary representations of time into prominent clusters I will offer one case study to indicate how a single work of literature can speak to temporal experiences associated with many different subject positions.

Marie Clements's play *Burning Vision* (2003) is a polyphonic, fragmented story that examines the social disruptions surrounding radium mining and atomic weapons manufacturing. Women who are hired to paint glowing radium faces on military equipment dials encounter unexpected health consequences, as do the Dene and white men who are hired to mine the radium from the ground in the Northwest Territories, having been told that the radium will be used to cure cancer. The atomic bombs called Fat Man and Little Boy are personified, respectively, as an atomic test dummy and a "beautiful Native boy," the latter also representing "the darkest uranium found at the center of the earth."[4] The different characters exist in different time periods – the late nineteenth century, the 1930s, the Second World War, the Cold War era – yet are present during the same scenes, and at certain moments actually interact with one another, blurring past and present, race and class, language and origin, into the common frame of shared consequences. As Allison Hargreaves notes, while many works that investigate past injustices can unintentionally form a temporal barrier in which present-day life is seen to be removed from the past, *Burning Vision* expresses "the truth that this history – as well as its consequences and casualties – is present among us still."[5] Indeed, by articulating the many particularities, from race and class to place and historical moment, that factor into the experiences and causes of injustice, the play simultaneously breaks down all of these divisions by stressing the ultimate intersectionalities of cause, effect, and mortality.[6]

In the first scene, a *"scared and huddled"* Little Boy speaks to competing claims of firstness and priority, while uranium prospectors close in on him:

> Every child is scared of the dark, not because it is dark but because they know sooner, or later, they will be discovered. It is only a matter of time …
>
> *The radio footsteps and laboured breath get closer.*
>
> … before someone discovers you and claims you for themselves. Claims you are you because they found you. Claims you are theirs because they were the first to find you, and lay claims on you …
>
> *The radio footsteps and laboured breath get closer and closer. The two beams of light circle towards him.*
>
> … Not knowing you've known yourself for thousands of years.
> Not knowing *you* are not the monster.[7]

Clements thus questions colonial claims to primacy along with the notion of the "discovery" of ancient natural resources. Yet the influence of colonization on temporal experience remains pronounced; the Dene widow of a uranium ore carrier indicates that her social conceptualization of time has been severely disrupted by the colonial logic of progress and capitalism. She recalls her husband explaining that he must take the uranium job, because "times are changing my girl. Times are changing and we have to change with them or be left behind. It is for our family."[8] The widow laments the loss of her earlier life, in which time was measured by a different framework: "We used to be able to tell where we were by the seasons, the way the sun placed itself or didn't, the migration patterns of the caribou. Time."[9]

Temporal disruption and subalternity are not limited to Dene or Métis characters. Captain Mike, the Icelandic captain of a barge that transports radium toward the atomic bomb research facilities, complains:

> Why'd I have to work in da only goddamn part of da country where da daylight hours in da day is da hol' goddamn day and nit.

Twenty-four goddamn hours a day we gotta keep dis boat goin' and dose poor assholes gotta haul dose sacks. I'm sittin' in da pilot house of dis goddamn *Radium Prince* and if we don't go nowhere in a goddamn hurry we won't be goin' anywhere goddamn soon.[10]

The "captain" turns out to be a working-class labourer just like the miners, a slave to the time clock that takes cruel advantage of the long periods of Arctic daylight, and whose confused but irrefutable logic is reflected in the temporal incoherence of the last sentence.

Fat Man, the American bomb test dummy who speaks with the voice of normative power, advocates a fast pace of atomic weapons deployment even though the process will mean the destruction of his own house in the test site: "We don't want studies. We want tests. We don't want thinking, we want reaction. Highly skilled unthinking reaction."[11] "I mean let's get real," he adds, "it's just about making yourself feel better in the now."[12] This short-term–oriented temporality accompanies an anxiety-ridden survivalist mentality that casts the earlier discussion of firstness under an even more ominous light. "If you can imagine the end of the world," Fat Man says, "you can imagine making the world end for someone else first."[13] As the representative of hegemonic power, Fat Man is the only character in the play who appears to have control over the management of time, and he manipulates temporality to his own ruthless and short-sighted advantage.

For Frances, the radium painter, the sense of time running out is captured by the clock dials that she paints "so that men at war can see the face of their watches when it's dark."[14] She places the radium-painted clocks in a circle so that "*they all begin to tick loudly. / The sound of a heart beating.*"[15] "Tick ... tick ... tick ..." she says. "Time can be ugly but your face is beautiful. I made you beautiful and what will you do for me?"[16] Clements's historical timeline at the beginning of the script makes clear what the clocks will do; from 1925 to 1930, "Radium watch-dial painters, all women, were encouraged by their employers to lick their paint brushes to give them a sharp point for better application of the luminous paint. The ingestion of radium resulted in severe anemia, 'radium' jaw and bone cancer."[17] While the beautiful clock faces obscure the injustices surrounding their creation, a foreboding sense of inevitability emerges as Frances ineffectually asks the clocks to "Slow down ... please slow down."[18] As an employee whose role is to ensure that military personnel can function efficiently within the strict pacing of absolute clock time, she finds that her own time as a living subject is nearing its end with equally ruthless unstoppability.

In this final scene of the play, the stage notes indicate that the course of events "*starts out slowly and begins to escalate in fear as characters and worlds collide.*"[19] The sounds of the radium clocks ticking, the miners' Geiger counters clicking as they approach the radium, an atomic bomb radar target beeping as it draws near, and the beating human heart, all overlap until "*a huge white light whites out their world into blackness.*"[20] The scene indicates that each character is both cause and victim of impending apocalypse; the various subject positions to which we might assign the characters – Dene, Métis, white, male, female, working class, privileged, child, adult, nineteenth-century or Cold War era, in the centre of America or geographically marginalized from power – are represented as intensely important in the determination of agency, yet also blend into a single scene, a single temporal moment of common failure and consequence. As the Dene See-er says, "Can you look through time and see the future? Can you hear through the walls of the world? Maybe we are all talking at the same time because we are answering each other over time and space. Like a wave that washes over everything and doesn't care how long it takes to get there because it always ends up on the same shore."[21] The categories by which we divide people into groups are indeed vital for understanding the flow of power and temporal agency, yet they can never be absolute divisions in the ongoing shared conversation of social existence and mortality.

AGE

Age is an important rubric for understanding people's relationship to time in two senses: it can classify the phases of an individual's life measured in numerical years or social status categories from infancy to old age, or it can refer to the social era in which a person exists, whether a longer-term category like "the industrial age" or a shorter-term one like "the 1950s" or "the Trudeau years."[22] Both types of age affect a person's experiences of time, but caution is necessary in understanding these effects since both types of age are frequently subjected to temporal stereotyping

("Old people live in the past"; "nineteenth-century life was primitive").[23] Identifying the personal aspects of age as "an undertheorized site of difference in cultural studies," Amelia DeFalco points out that "if aging can be regarded as a manifestation of human time, narrative and aging are intrinsically, if not constitutively, bound."[24] She argues that the importance of age for thinking through identity and time becomes especially pronounced in narratives of old age, since the "uncanniness of aging into old age can teach us that the self is always other than it was, other, even, than it is."[25] Margaret Laurence's protagonist Hagar in *The Stone Angel*, for instance, enacts a typical "life review" narrative centred on the attempt to reconcile an entire lifetime of subjective experiences into a coherent whole, but "despite her desire to discover, even enforce, a singular, authentic identity, divergent, even contradictory narratives thwart her efforts, exposing the mutability and multiplicity concomitant with temporal identity."[26] Old age serves to heighten the complex and shifting ties between time, subjectivity, and narrative that I discussed in chapter 2. And while DeFalco focuses mainly on questions of subjective experience, her study also usefully highlights the politics of "popular media representational practices, in which aging functions as a dangerous villain that must be battled at every opportunity, with the various providers of anti-aging products and services promising effective weapons of defense."[27] The desire to stop time, a desire sold through the commercial idealization of youth, simultaneously marginalizes and profits from old age.

On the other end of the spectrum, important insights into the social politics of normative temporality become visible in narratives of youth. Philip Zimbardo and John Boyd point out that many children's stories serve as time socialization stories, since the process of aging from childhood into adulthood is figured socially as the acquisition of time management skills and future orientation. "The Three Little Pigs" is "a story about the need to prepare for the future," since only the third pig has the foresight to build a durable house,[28] while *Peter Pan* "is a story about the magic of the present and a boy who refuses to grow up. By not growing up, Peter avoids the future orientation that is necessary to cope with the demands and responsibilities of adulthood … In the end, Peter's refusal to grow up prevents him from leading a normal life."[29] While the category of children's literature is a contested one, certain youth-centred works of Canadian literature have indeed taken future orientation as a dominant theme. Robert Munsch's classic *Love You Forever* (1986) follows the life of a child from the troublemaking of toddlerhood all the way to the adult responsibilities of caregiving for an elderly parent and raising a baby of the next generation. The book is a profound demonstration of the notions that aging and death occur naturally through time, that human life renews itself through slow generational cycles, and that famil-ial relationships must be nurtured for an entire lifetime. Like many simi-lar works, though, *Love You Forever* also takes genuine delight in the immediate present-oriented joys of childhood, prompting a sort of pre-emptive nostalgia at the thought that adult maturity risks dampening such pleasures.

L.M. Montgomery's *Anne of Green Gables* (1908) provides insight into the role of normative temporality in a particular cultural age – Maritime settler culture at the turn of the twentieth century – but speaks especially to the social roles assigned to, and sometimes resisted by, people of differ-ent chronological ages from youth to adulthood. The book tells the story of the orphan Anne Shirley's adoption into a Prince Edward Island fam-ily, and her subsequent rocky but progressive indoctrination into norma-tive early twentieth-century social existence. Montgomery makes clear from the outset that one of the most vital conceptual frameworks existing in the village of Avonlea is the normative temporal framework that struc-tures and reinforces patterns of work, religion, ethics, and relationships. The first chapter opens with a description of Rachel Lynde, a busybody Avonlea matriarch who immediately discerns that something unusual is happening at Green Gables, the Cuthbert homestead, because "Matthew Cuthbert ought to have been sowing his [turnip seed...]. And yet here was Matthew Cuthbert, at half-past three on the afternoon of a busy day, placidly driving over the hollow and up the hill."[30] The cause of this inter-ruption to Matthew's usual timetable is Anne's arrival at the train station, and Anne soon reveals herself to be at odds with many foundational prin-ciples of social decorum, a conflict repeatedly expressed in temporal terms. While Joy Alexander sees the characters' confusion about the arrival time of Anne's train as proof that "the Avonlea world is apparently not tyrannized by time and pays scant regard to clock-rule,"[31] Rachel Lynde's judgment about what Matthew Cuthbert "ought to have been" doing at "half-past three" is just one of many clues suggesting that not only clock time itself, but also the related social expectations of time discipline are deeply important to the Avonlea community. Drawing from the work of Maria Nikolajeva, Alexander suggests that Anne's gradual shift from a childlike mythical temporality to a more linear sense of time mirrors the movement of the broader community "toward modernity."[32] While this approach provides a valuable reading of the large social transformations that Montgomery hints at through images of train lines and telephone cables, it neglects the extent to which the Avonlea society is *already* structured very closely around rigid scheduling before Anne arrives on the scene. I would suggest, then, that while the novel is partially a story about the modernization of Prince Edward Island, it is more essentially a time socialization story that portrays Anne's gradual and compulsory indoctrination into normative time as a definitive component of the maturation process from youth to adulthood.

Montgomery uses Anne's relationship with Marilla Cuthbert in particular to construct a distinction between the child's emphasis on idle dreaming and imagination, and the adult world of schedules and timetables. The distinction appears clearly upon Anne's waking up after her first night at Green Gables:

> Anne dropped on her knees and gazed out into the June morning, her eyes glistening with delight. Oh, wasn't it beautiful? Wasn't it a lovely place? Suppose she wasn't really going to stay here! She would imagine she was. There was scope for imagination here ...
>
> She knelt there, lost to everything but the loveliness around her, until she was startled by a hand on her shoulder. Marilla had come in unheard by the small dreamer.
>
> "It's time you were dressed," she said curtly.[33]

The voice of authority interrupts the child's idle dreaming through the language of temporal obligation. The centrality of time discipline and its associated values of punctuality, strict scheduling, efficiency, and future planning, is itself a kind of metaphorical clothing, a garment of social belonging with which Anne is expected to dress herself. The Green Gables house contains, among the other usual fixtures, a "clock shelf,"[34] and the centrality of clock time to Avonlea life forms a gravity that repeatedly pulls the young Anne back to earth from her "raptured voyages of exploration ... made in the odd half hours which she was allowed for play."[35]

Marilla continually reminds Anne of her temporal obligations, warning, "You're not going to play all the time nor most of it. You'll have your work to do and it'll have to be done first."[36] When Anne is more than half an hour late to return home after playing with her friend Diana, Marilla is emphatic about enforcing the rule of clock time:

> "Just look at the clock, if you please, Anne. What time did I tell you to come in?"
>
> "Two o'clock – but isn't it splendid about the picnic, Marilla? Please can I go? Oh, I've never been to a picnic – I've dreamed of picnics, but I've never –"
>
> "Yes, I told you to come at two o'clock. And it's a quarter to three. I'd like to know why you didn't obey me, Anne."
>
> "Why, I meant to, Marilla, as much as could be. But you have no idea how fascinating Idlewild is. And then, of course, I had to tell Matthew about the picnic. Matthew is such a sympathetic listener. Please can I go?"
>
> "You'll have to learn to resist the fascination of Idle-whatever-you-call-it. When I tell you to come in at a certain time I mean that time and not half an hour later. And you needn't stop to discourse with sympathetic listeners on your way, either."[37]

Anne, in Marilla's view, "never think[s] once about the time or her duties … She may be bright and sweet enough, but her head is full of nonsense and there's never any knowing what shape it'll break out in next."[38] Anne likewise has difficulty with the concept of school hours, and her teacher reprimands her for tardiness.[39] The clock becomes a particularly potent enemy when, after Anne accidentally inebriates Diana, Diana's mother forbids their friendship. Diana comes to say a final goodbye, her mother having said "I was only to stay ten minutes and she's timing me by the clock." "'Ten minutes isn't very long to say an eternal farewell in,' said Anne tearfully."[40] For Marilla, the sense of time discipline structured by the clock is the *only* form of temporality that has any purchase on everyday social existence, leaving other forms of temporality to be dismissed under the umbrella category of "nonsense," hence her conclusion that Anne's nonconformity with clock time means that she *never thinks about the time*. As we see from Anne's comments, though, the young girl thinks frequently about time, especially when her preferred form of spontaneous present orientation comes into conflict with the time discipline of the clock. Anne's consciousness of time is of great importance to her experiences, but to the extent that it fails to repeat the temporal expectations of the broader community it is constantly under threat of erasure.

While Anne's good-natured nonconformity, temporal and otherwise, is seen within the Avonlea community as a cause for concern – and has been seen for generations of readers as one of Anne's defining characteristics and a source of her famous charisma – a recent critical reading of the novel posits a controversial new understanding of Anne's behaviour. Paying a "clinical" form of attention to Anne's predilection for "impulsiveness," "daydreaming," "inattentive unpredictability," "susceptibility to tangents," "poorly timed interruptions," "problems with time," "symptomatic difficulties with conceptualizing and managing time," and her apparent lack of an "internal time clock," Helen Hoy argues that this set of characteristics, and the frequency of their occurrence in Anne's character, "creates the behavioural matrix or phenotype of a disorder that has been recognized as such only since 1973: Fetal Alcohol Spectrum Disorder (or FASD)."[41] While Marilla and other adults in the novel see Anne's approach to time as an admittedly exasperating eccentricity that needs to be corrected through repetitious lessons in time discipline, Hoy's contentious reading deepens the level of concern over Anne's behaviour through the discourse of pathology. The inclination to understand Anne as a person suffering from a disability may be reminiscent of the alarmingly high rate of diagnoses, at the turn of the twenty-first century, of pathologies such as attention deficit hyperactivity disorder in young people, and represents a stark contrast to the assertion by Zimbardo and Boyd that *every* human baby is simply a "present-oriented hedonist," and that only the long, gradual processes of formal and informal education instill a sense of time discipline, eventually making young people "more future-oriented."[42] While Hoy's thesis may seem shocking initially, her nuanced reading of the novel itself as well as the social meanings and values attached to the labelling of impairments such as FASD lead her to the conclusion that the novel successfully confounds "the all-too-familiar distinction between fully human people and deficient people, between able and disabled," illuminating "the degree to which the meaning of disability is a product of the social imagination."[43] If *Anne of Green Gables* is a time socialization narrative, telling the story of Anne's gradual acceptance into society through her slow adoption of time discipline, Hoy's reading further elevates the stakes, showing how a society in which time discipline is key to enculturation can easily represent the disinclination to internalize time discipline not just as a matter of youthful impetuousness, but as the symptom of a medical disorder.

The final sections of the novel mark the eventual triumph of temporal socialization; as Anne grows from the age of eleven into her teens she begins to undergo a subtle transformation, gradually internalizing the normative principles of temporality. "I had such an interesting talk with Mrs Allan about besetting sins last Sunday afternoon," Anne tells Marilla. "There are just a few things it's proper to talk about on Sundays and that is one of them."[44] After her first trip to a larger town, she decides "that I wasn't born for city life and that I was glad of it. It's nice to be eating ice cream at brilliant restaurants at eleven o'clock at night once in awhile; but as a regular thing I'd rather be in the east gable at eleven, sound asleep."[45] Returning to Green Gables, she declares, "It's so good to be back ... I could kiss everything, even to the clock."[46] She begins to repeat the teachings that have been impressed upon her, commenting that she and Diana

feel that we are so much older than we used to be that it isn't becoming to talk of childish matters. It's such a solemn thing to be almost fourteen, Marilla. Miss Stacy took all us girls who are in our teens down to the brook last Wednesday, and talked to us about it. She said we couldn't be too careful what habits we formed and what ideals we acquired in our teens, because by the time we were twenty our characters would be developed and the foundation laid for our whole future life.[47]

While Anne had initially operated under a form of event time in which present experiences carried total significance, she has gradually learned to adopt the principles of clock time and the related concepts of punctuality, scheduling, and future orientation. While familial and other social interactions are significant drivers of this socialization, the school system also plays a key role, for, as Zimbardo and Boyd point out, "schools teach delay of gratification, goal-setting, cost-benefit analysis, and abstract thought" – principles that are necessary for inculcating the "remarkable tolerance for monotony and boredom" necessary for holding repetitive jobs.[48] School presents standard weekdays, long working hours, and the completion of repetitive tasks as pre-existing and inevitable temporal organizing principles. Clearly, the near-constant exposure to such temporally socializing forces eventually causes a radical shift in Anne's attitude toward time. Significantly, by this point in the novel, Marilla and Mrs Rachel begin to *approve* of Anne's behaviour, declaring her for the first time to be "a real smart girl," "real steady and reliable now."[49] Anne sounds more and more like Marilla herself, remarking, "There's so much to learn and do and think that there isn't time for big words ... The story club isn't in existence any longer. We hadn't time for it."[50] She dedicates herself to studying for her secondary school entrance exams, thinking seriously about her future life and career options.

Anne's gradual temporal socialization reflects the importance of deeply rooted social values necessary for workaday settler existence. When she arrives on the scene she disrupts the usual scheduling of events, and is considered foolish and irresponsible. But once she internalizes and even promotes the importance of scheduling and future planning, she is welcomed as a responsible member of society. Zimbardo and Boyd's point that many children's stories "seek to inculcate the audience with socially sanctioned attitudes toward time"[51] resonates here. Time socialization stories serve to indoctrinate their characters or readers into the shared forms of time that shape the functioning of society – the forms of time that serve as measurements of individual productivity, success, and belonging. *Anne of Green Gables* is a more complex time socialization story than "The Three Little Pigs," partly because it articulates some of the deeper conflicts, both internal and social, associated with the drawn-out reshaping of a young person's encounters with time, but also because it presents the possibility of escape from the confines of entirely practical temporality as somewhat wonderful and charming. Thus, even while the novel emphasizes the importance of normative time, the sense of temporal freedom associated with not-yet-fully-socialized youthfulness offers at least a gentle critique, suggesting that the adult world of clocks and schedules is not totalizing, and that seeing it as such risks denying certain facets of human emotional existence.[52]

A century later, we find that the distinction between youthful imaginative freedom and adult scheduling and timetabling remains firmly entrenched, and that the socialization of young people into normative temporality remains a process of vital importance to society, yet one that is often tinged with regret over, as Anne would say, reduced scope for imagination. Rachel Wyatt's novel *Time's Reach* offers a look at an early twenty-first century version of childhood temporal socialization, when Greg, the protagonist's grandson, overhears his parents arguing, and worries that his life may be split traumatically into two recurring temporal fragments. If his parents separate, he will have to "live like half his friends: Couldn't do my homework, the books are at my dad's place. I'm with my mom Wednesday to Saturday. Those guys survived but their lives were cut in half."[53]

Perhaps the most memorable commentary on the confluence of personal age and cultural age is Douglas Coupland's 1991 novel *Generation X: Tales for an Accelerated Culture*, which popularized the term Generation X as a name for the post–baby-boom generation born in the 1960s and 1970s. The main characters, Andy, Dag, and Claire, are three friends approaching the age of 30, living in the late 1980s or early 1990s. As they share stories about their lives they reveal a deep sense of malaise, "futurelessness,"[54] and resentment toward their parents' generation – attitudes toward time, which, in Hartmut Rosa's view, encapsulate the "simultaneity of frenetic change and historical lack of development."[55] While the subtitle of the novel and the bricolage form of the narrative speak to the forces of acceleration by drawing attention to the relentless social changes of late modernity, the characters simultaneously feel adrift in an aimless temporal moment that leads nowhere, largely because the baby boomers have sucked society dry of most opportunities. Andy opens the novel by recalling a solar eclipse that he witnessed as a child. The sight of the sun being extinguished, an interruption of its predictable daily path that fills him with "a mood of darkness and inevitability and fascination,"[56] becomes a metaphor for the perceived lack of future prospects for young adults of his age. Like Andy, Dag both envies and despises the baby boomers, accusing his "embittered ex-hippie boss, Martin" of having won his million-dollar home "in a genetic lottery ... sheerly by dint of your having been born at the right time in history."[57] When Dag vandalizes a car whose bumper sticker reads "WE'RE SPENDING OUR CHILDREN'S INHERRITANCE" [*sic*], Andy supposes that Dag "was bored and cranky after eight hours of working his McJob ('Low pay, low prestige, low benefits, low future')."[58]

While the three friends appear to feel that things may improve in some vaguely imagined future – they tell themselves "that the only time worth living in is the past and that the only time that may ever be interesting again is the future"[59] – they also suffer from a sense of impending doom, characterized in particular by fears of nuclear war and toxic environments. One result of their malaise is a susceptibility to "terminal wanderlust," described as "a condition common to people of transient middle-class upbringings. Unable to feel rooted in any one environment, they move continually in the hopes of finding an idealized sense of community in the next location."[60] Sure enough, the final chapter sees Andy leaving his temporary apartment in California to follow his friends in their attempt to start a hotel business in Mexico. While an earlier chapter describing an imagined nuclear doomsday scenario had been titled "December 31, 1999,"[61] the final chapter is titled "Jan. 01, 2000,"[62] suggesting the possibility of new beginnings after a traumatic endpoint. Andy stops at the side of the road to see a burned field promising renewed growth, "now that so many new and wonderful tropisms had been activated by fire."[63] Yet this hopeful ending gives way to a darker appendix called "Numbers," in which Coupland offers sobering statistics on the precarious future of Social Security benefits, the increasing percentage of income required for a down payment on a first home in the 1980s compared with the 1960s, and so on.[64]

Generation X has been celebrated for offering a clear picture of a generation that is often considered to be highly distinct from the baby boomers, yet Coupland later resisted the use of the titular phrase, apparently growing uncomfortable with the delineation of generational categories altogether. Upon the publication in 2009 of *Generation A*, a novel that uses the same broad structure as *Generation X* but follows the lives of early twenty-first-century youths, Coupland claimed in an interview that "neither of the books is about a generation per se, as they are more tombstones to the notion of generations."[65] While Coupland's attempt to distance himself from the very articulation of generational distinctiveness that his writing so convincingly performs may not be entirely credible, his comment in the interview does speak to the fact that the concept of a generation can usefully be understood as a cultural construction along the lines of race, in that it names categories that are not objectively distinct but are subject to shifting and contradictory social forces. Does Generation X end with people born after the mid-1970s, or does it include those born up until the early 1980s? Has the twenty-first century created a culture where, as *New York Times* writer Brad Stone suggests, "the ever-accelerating pace of technological change may be minting a series of mini-generation gaps, with each group of children uniquely influenced by the tech tools available in their formative stages of development"?[66] Contested generational definitions abound, with partially overlapping categories vying for popularity including the Net Generation, the iGeneration, Generation Next, the Millennials, Generation Y, Generation Z, Generation Screwed, and so on. One can see how the very concept of generations is limited by a lack of objective delineation, and is limiting in the conceptual boundaries it risks imposing on individuals. Paul Ricoeur notes that theoretical understandings of generational divisions have centred on locating particular influences and events to which all members of a generation are thought to have been exposed, or on identifying, as Karl Mannheim does, "disinclinations as well as propensities to act, feel, and think in a certain way."[67] Ricoeur is quick to point out that such theories remain troubled by the fact that all contemporary persons "are not submitted to the same influences nor do they all exercise the same influence."[68]

Still, the cultural events and changing circumstances or technologies that inspire generational terms are often very real, and social factors such as economic depressions, wars, and changing demographics have often led to changes in cultural habits of all kinds. Even Anne Shirley, whose story Montgomery continued to tell through various sequels, sees her own children encounter very different circumstances from those of her youth. In *Rilla of Ingleside* (1920), Anne's daughter Rilla watches anxiously while her brothers and her love interest leave to fight in the Great War, a far cry from the young Anne's preoccupation with picnics and schoolroom insults. Psychologists Bernard Gorman and Alden Wessman note,

> The problem of separating age-related variance from generation-related variance is especially critical in time research ... Thus, a statement of the form "Elderly people are less oriented toward the future

and more oriented toward the past than younger people" may have to be modified by considerations of when the people were "elderly" or "young."[69]

Perhaps, like racial categories, generational divisions should be understood as constructs that do not represent essential differences, but do correspond with actual sociological consequences, both in the sense that they label patterns of cultural thought, and that for better or worse they create perceptual distinctions that cause people to see themselves and others in a certain way.

As far as the study of temporality in Canada is concerned, the potential exists to organize an entire such project by cultural ages, tracing how social constructions of time shift along the chronological route from pre-colonization to the First World War to the era of official multiculturalism. I have not used a chronological model as my primary system of classification for several reasons. First, a purely chronological study of time in Canada would in some ways mirror the work of countless historical studies, and I wish to show that the critical study of temporality – which investigates relationships between power structures and experiences of time – is distinct from historiography, which investigates the representation of historical events and therefore emphasizes shifting power relations over the actual course of time. History looks at processes *in* time, while critical time studies looks at the function *of* time. Second, a study that uses chronological divisions as its primary model would risk suggesting that populations are best understood as being split categorically into different time periods, and that some sense of progress emerges along this timeline, when in fact many experiences associated with social constructions of temporality resonate across long periods of time. Finally, such a study would risk obscuring the importance of various other subject positions, to which I will now turn.

CLASS

Time functions in connection with socio-economic class in multiple ways. Perhaps most obviously, the working time investments of those belonging to wealthier socio-economic classes are typically compensated at a higher rate than those of wage workers, a gap that in some cases is staggeringly wide, and which has consequences for the sheer amount of time a person must spend working, as well as for the perceived character of working and leisure time. Questions of individual time orientation toward the future or the present are also closely, and controversially, connected with socio-economic class. And finally, in a broad social sense, the pace of life can be said to accelerate roughly in concert with the processes of industrialization and the increasing influence of modern consumer culture. Literary and artistic representations have taken up these issues, and have frequently probed the experiential meaning of the cultural link between time and money, questioning the assumption that society operates on an upward progressive trajectory of increasing wealth in which hard work is rewarded financially through time, questioning the idea that individuals who happen to earn low incomes are deficient in temporal awareness, demonstrating that listening to typically silenced voices and temporalities can create deeper understanding of class-related conflicts, and articulating the ways in which racism and other social injustices shape and reinforce experiences of temporal poverty.

Various scholars have observed that hierarchies of income and social status correlate with differences in the experience of temporality, such that materially impoverished people are perceived to have less influence over their own use of time, and to be more present-oriented than future-oriented. In *The Spectrum of Social Time* (1964), French sociologist Georges Gurvitch writes, "The social classes are exceedingly complex and are of major importance as social frameworks for the study of the multiple manifestations of social time and their hierarchized time scales. More ostensibly than any other partial collective unity, each class possesses its own dynamic and its own time scale."[70] Gurvitch argues that the "bourgeois ideology of progress" creates the illusion of time "leaping forward," but that because "the bourgeois class must, in order to persist, partially subordinate the proletarian and peasant classes," any supposed social advance "is realized only for a narrow, privileged stratum. The other classes have to wait patiently for a long period of time for the questionable benefits of this advance."[71] Jeremy Rifkin makes the related observation – perhaps a self-evident one given the prevalence of the "time is money" metaphor – that "in industrial cultures, the poor are temporally poor as well as materially poor."[72]

Scholars have disagreed, though, over what lines of causality may exist in the relationship between class and temporal orientation. In a particularly contentious claim, Gurvitch writes, "Let us say bluntly, the passive masses are not capable of becoming conscious of time in the proper meaning of the term, nor do they make the least attempt to master their time. They produce a specific time and move in this time, but they do not take account of the time in which they live."[73] And Edward Banfield similarly finds fault with the poor: "Extreme present-orientedness, not lack of income or wealth, is the principal cause of poverty in the sense of 'the culture of poverty.'"[74] William Friedman comments on psychological studies that have found that "income was strongly related to temporal attitudes. People with the lowest incomes showed the highest levels of Present Hedonism and Present Fatalism, whereas the high-income respondents believed most strongly that the future statements were characteristic of them."[75] Friedman is cautious, though, about locating causality in this relationship, writing with a more neutral tone than Banfield that "perseverance and planning are clearly associated with higher levels of achievement in our society, whereas a sense of the futility of trying to influence the future and a greater commitment to short-term rewards are characteristic of poorer people."[76] Friedman is much more willing than Gurvitch and Banfield to admit that broad social distinctions cannot hold in all cases, though certain questions inevitably remain unanswered; for instance, how might impoverished immigrants who foster a powerful vision of futurity for their children fit within this model? Zimbardo and Boyd, too, hedge their bets by suggesting that "social class is both a contributor to and a consequence of time perspective."[77] Still, they argue that future-orientedness "is a prerequisite for membership in the middle class. Ambition and need for achievement drive a future orientation that focuses on work, savings, and planning for a continually better life through one's efforts."[78]

Far from condemning people with low incomes for their present-orientedness, Craig Ireland locates a historical basis for the belief that class privilege actually fosters future-orientedness. "We have earlier seen," he writes, "that modern future-oriented temporality ... is not only a historical phenomenon that surfaces with consistency at the turn of the eighteenth century – it is also a phenomenon that initially manifests itself within a very limited segment of the population, namely, the rising late-eighteenth-century industrial bourgeoisie."[79] Looking at sociological trends at the turn of the twenty-first century, Ireland concludes,

> as predictable long-term wage-based employment shifts, as it has been exponentially doing since the 1970s, to precarious contractual work or disposable part-time labour, the exigencies of immediate economic survival literally absorb the time of increasing sectors of the general population, thereby compromising the ability to allocate resources beyond the short term and the immediate and, in so doing, ultimately wreaking havoc on an extended sense of self – a situation recently diagnosed by Richard Sennett as a "corrosion of character."[80]

For people belonging to the working classes, the necessity of bowing to "the exigencies of immediate economic survival" is, of course, traceable further back than the 1970s. Alfred Laliberté's sculpture *The Slave to Machinery* (c. 1929–35) exemplifies the all-consuming urgency of the worker's relationship to backbreaking labour. Anne Newlands writes, "Laliberté employs the mythological figure of Ixion (whose punishment by Zeus was to be forever bound to a fiery wheel) as a fitting metaphor for his view of society's relationship to industrialization. The weary figure of the nearly naked man slumps against the winged wheel, his independence sacrificed to its mechanical revolutions."[81] The hopeful wings become a bitter symbol for the human toll taken by an ideology of unrelenting progress, while the worker's agonized posture lends credence to the view that future-orientedness is an unattainable luxury for people trapped within merciless socio-economic conditions. Though he spent most of his life in Montreal, Laliberté was born into a Québécois farming family and remained associated with the *terroir* movement and its resistance against the processes of modernization. Newlands comments that "his attachment to the old ways made it difficult for him to accept the pace of modern life."[82] Indeed, *The Slave to Machinery* can be read as a general warning against modernization, urbanization, and industrialization. The winged wheel, with all of its mechanized speed, will destroy those who would subscribe to the ideologies of modern progress. In this reading, the inhuman pace of industrialized existence impoverishes the quality of life for all who participate in it, rendering a crushing form of

Figure 3.1. *The Slave to Machinery* (Alfred Laliberté, 1929–35). Painted plaster.

temporal poverty a blanket condition of modernization rather than just a symptom of more literal impoverishment.[83]

The Slave to Machinery also hints at the fact that the acceleration of technological developments in industrial capitalism is closely connected to the overall acceleration of the pace of life. In his systematic study of social acceleration, Hartmut Rosa finds that the three primary forms of social acceleration operate within a self-propelling loop: technological acceleration (the increasing rate of the developments of new technologies as well as the increasing speed at which machines carry out specific tasks) causes an acceleration of social change – the "change per unit of time in occupational and family structures, artistic styles, etc."[84] – which creates acceleration in the pace of life – "*an increase of episodes of action and/or experience per unit of time* that is linked with a scarcity of temporal resources and the resulting 'lack of time'"[85] – which in turn encourages further technological acceleration. For Rosa, this cycle of social acceleration is not only historically visible primarily within the modern period of capitalist industrialization, but is in fact its defining characteristic: "Progress and acceleration were indissolubly linked together from the very beginning," so that "*the experience of modernization is an experience of acceleration.*"[86] Acceleration, then, is key to understanding the connections between socio-economic conditions and temporal experience.

In his study of the pace of life across different cultures, Robert Levine also finds that modern industrialization indeed goes hand in hand with a faster social tempo. It is somewhat of a paradox that as industrial progress ostensibly increases the total wealth of a society, individuals find themselves increasingly strapped for time, so that while there may be a degree of truth to Zimbardo and Boyd's claim that "the rich or upper class can afford to take any time perspective they want,"[87] people in general tend to become increasingly busy. Levine notes that people in non-industrialized societies regularly work fifteen-hour weeks, while "the shift to plow cultivation, which requires feeding and caring for draft animals, pushes the work week of men to 25 to 30 hours."[88] "The single most crucial watershed event in the acceleration of the tempo of the Western world," he writes, "was the Industrial Revolution."[89] Noting that the factory system brought about increased working hours as well as an increasing intensity of working time, Gerhard Dohrn-van Rossum finds that "work time has been one of the great themes of social conflict since the beginning of industrialization."[90] Through the insights of Marx and Engels in particular, Dohrn-van Rossum argues, "The alienation of the worker from the possibility of an autonomous control of time had thus been discovered as a characteristic feature of modern capitalism."[91] Workplace punch clocks were developed in New York in the 1880s, and "efficiency engineering" led to factory consultants "filming a worker's every movement, with the dual goals of breaking down a company's tasks into their component parts and establishing standard times for each bodily motion."[92]

Levine explains the increasing tempo of industrialized society by observing that "almost every technical advance seems to be accompanied

by a rise in expectations" – for instance, the availability of vacuum clean-
ers raises people's cleanliness standards, causing individuals to "invest the
time needed to propel these products against the suddenly defeatable
household grit."[93] For Rosa, email is a perfect example of the way in
which technological acceleration, by allowing us to complete tasks more
quickly, alters "the implicit temporal standards and rationalities of action:
we send an e-mail message instead of a letter because this saves time
resources (and of course also mental energy) and thereby risk already getting an answer a few hours (instead of several days) later and hence once
again being under pressure to act."[94] By allowing us – and therefore compelling us – to accomplish more tasks per unit of time, supposedly time-
saving technologies actually increase our pace of life. Allen Johnson links
this trend to consumer culture in particular, noting that "as a result of
producing and consuming more, we are experiencing an increasing scarcity of time ... Free time gets converted into consumption time because
time spent neither producing nor consuming comes increasingly to be
viewed as wasted."[95]

The above principles illuminate important aspects of the history of
time and labour in industrialized nations. The standard work week in
Canada at Confederation – a time of rapid industrialization and increasing reliance on clock time – measured in at sixty hours: ten hours a
day for six days a week.[96] Within the next five years, though, citizens
exhausted by long working hours had begun to organize a series of pro-
tests that became known as "The Nine-Hour Movement." A commemo-
rative sign in Victoria Park in Hamilton, Ontario, reads: "Inspired by
British and American examples, Hamilton unionists launched a crusade
for a shorter workday in January of 1872. The workingman, they argued,
needed more time for family, leisure, education and civic life. Soon the
Nine-Hour Movement had branches across central Canada." "The issue
of shorter hours," Levine writes, "was at the heart of the labor movement
from the beginning ... 'Eight hours for work, eight hours for sleep, eight
hours for what we will,' was the cry of turn-of-the-century unionists."[97]
In the United States in 1930, W.K. Kellogg of breakfast cereal fame was
widely celebrated for introducing a six-hour working day in his plant.
But while the trend toward increasing leisure time has remained somewhat steadier in Europe, the North American post-war consumer bonanza
saw a marked reversal: people demanded *more* working hours.[98] This
desire, of course, is a deeply conflicted one; in the late twentieth century

Levine notes that two-thirds of Americans, if given the choice, would opt for salary cuts in exchange for more time off work.[99]

In Canada, as in the United States, the standard work week hovers at least officially at forty hours over five days, and even while both countries celebrate Labo(u)r Day each September to honour the unionist movements that ended the sixty-hour week, the desire for increased leisure time remains in conflict with the desire for new consumer experiences, the increasing relative cost of living, and the pressure in many fields of employment to demonstrate heightened productivity through long hours of overtime. Statistics Canada measures the total average working hours per day for Canadians over the age of 15 – including paid work, unpaid work, and education, averaged over a *seven*-day week – as 7.9 hours in 2005.[100] These responses vary by region, with the fewest hours of work reported in Quebec (7.6 hours), and the most in Alberta (8.5 hours).[101] They also vary by age, with working hours increasing from 7.3 between the ages of 15 and 24, to a maximum of 9.6 between the ages of 35 and 44, down to 4.5 hours for those aged 65 and over.[102] The Canadian Index of Wellbeing notes that in 2005, 16.6 percent of men and 22.7 percent of women experienced high levels of "time crunch," or pressure to meet competing temporal demands; the CBC reported this news under the headline "More Canadians Pressed for Time," citing such causes as "greater consumer demand for services outside weekday hours, urban sprawl and workplace technologies such as email and smartphones that increasingly demand employees be 'perpetually on call.'"[103] With the rise of mobile Internet connectivity, concepts such as time crunch and multi-tasking become increasingly important; for people in certain types of employment the traditional differentiation of time into working hours and leisure hours dissolves, and the limited ability of time use surveys to account for blended and overlapping spheres of work and personal life becomes more apparent.[104] While the devastating problem of wage slavery is well documented, the notion that members of the so-called leisure class have greater agency in determining their own working and holiday hours carries a significant risk of oversimplification; working hours even for society's wealthier members can frequently stretch into long days, evenings, and weekends, especially with the ubiquity of mobile connectivity. The fact that terms like "wealthy" are pliable enough in their meaning to support contradictory conclusions is significant here. While the data in Statistics Canada's Time Use Surveys are not broken down by income or education level, the 2013 American Time Use Survey in the United States shows "that Americans with a bachelor's degree or above work two hours more each day than those without a high-school diploma."[105] One factor in this result is that high unemployment among low-skilled workers can skew the average working time for people with less education, so that anxious periods of unemployment can sometimes be misinterpreted statistically as leisure time. But another key factor here is that "highly educated" is sometimes seen as a synonym for "rich." The *Economist*, for instance, reported on the above education-related data with the subheadline "Why the Rich Now Have Less Leisure than the Poor."[106] This conflation conceals the complexities of different layers of wealth, and ignores the fact that there is not always a direct correlation between university education and income or asset levels.

Of course, such measurements offer only a broad stroke in portraying socio-economic temporal demands. Yann Martel's unnamed narrator in his novel *Self* gives an indication of what the statistical split between paid work, unpaid work, and free time can actually look like for an individual. The narrator, who is writing a novel, spends much of her free time with her lover Tito, and supports herself with a waitressing job that she refers to as Slave Work: "I had a schedule in my life now, time imperatives that I had to contend with. There was Slave-Work Time, Novel-Work Time, Miscellaneous-Things Time and Tito Time."[107] In her mind, the moments that comprise her life are inevitably divided into categories associated with necessity or pleasure. While Rosa argues that the time stamp clock has become obsolete in late capitalist production – that "in the context of late modernity it has rather become quite generally inappropriate as a sequencing instrument"[108] – such a statement may fail to account for the experience of workers in various employment sectors where the clock retains its iron grip on the distinction between working hours and leisure hours. The blended spheres of work life and home life brought about by Internet connectivity are less relevant for many wage workers.

For an exemplary portrayal of the psychological cost of the industrialized obsession with precise, controlled temporal units of work in clock-based employment settings, we must turn to Tom Wayman's sardonic poem "Factory Time" (1977):

The day divides neatly into four parts
marked off by the breaks. The first quarter

is a full two hours, 7:30 to 9:30, but that's okay
in theory, because I'm supposed to be fresh, but in fact
after some evenings it's a long first two hours.
Then, a ten-minute break. Which is good
another way, too: the second quarter
thus has ten minutes knocked off, 9:40 to 11:30
which is only 110 minutes, or
to put it another way, if I look at my watch
and it says 11:10
I can cheer up because if I had still been in the first quarter
and had worked for 90 minutes there would be
30 minutes to go, but now there is only
20. If it had been the first quarter, I could expect
the same feeling at 9 o'clock as here I have
when it is already ten minutes after 11.

Then it's lunch: a stretch, and maybe a little walk around.
And at 12 sharp the endless quarter begins:
a full two afternoon hours. And it's only the start
of the afternoon. Nothing to hope for the whole time.
Come to think of it, today
is probably only Tuesday. Or worse, Monday,
with the week barely begun and the day
only just half over, four hours down
and 36 to go this week
(if the foreman doesn't come padding by about 3
some afternoon and ask us all to work overtime).
...

But even when I quit
the numbers of the minutes and hours from this shift
stick with me: I can look at a clock some morning
months afterwards, and see it is 20 minutes to 9
– that is, if I'm ever out of bed that early –
and the automatic computer in my head
starts to type out: *20 minutes to 9, that means*
30 minutes to work after 9: you are

50 minutes from the break; 50 minutes
of work, and it is only morning, and it is only
Monday, you poor dumb bastard ...

And that's how it goes, round the clock, until a new time
from another job bores its way into my brain.[109]

By portraying the human employee as a type of reluctant cyborg driven
to madness by an obsession with the clock, Wayman satirizes the dominance of a socio-temporal structure designed around inhuman principles
of pure efficiency. We are not told what goods this factory is actually producing, for clearly its central purpose from the employee's point of view is
to manufacture time itself, metering out hours and minutes to exacting
specifications. Eventually the employee too has become a time factory,
"typing out" the temporal allotments whose fragility of meaning is
heightened when they are removed from the context of the workplace.
The dominant sensation in the poem is one of mind-numbing, purpose-
less duration and the endless performance of repetitive, anonymous
work. The factory itself is both a form of hell that traps wretched souls for
all eternity, and a kind of clock that chimes regularly with rigidly defined
break whistles throughout the day. The robotlike sequences echoing
through Wayman's head recall the inflectionless yet accelerating voice of
the "Newtonian Clock" in W.H. New's long poem *Along a Snake Fence
Riding*, which declares: "THESE ARE THE TIMES / WORK TIME / THAT
TRY MEN'S SPIRIT / BROKEN TIME / TIME CARD / WORK TIME /
TIME CARD / DO IT AGAIN."[110] But while Wayman's poetic speaker is
indeed temporally poor, he is by no means incapable of becoming conscious of time; he reveals through his obsessiveness that his consciousness
of time has actually been *heightened* by the strict time pressures that control his every waking moment. His options for resistance appear limited,
but the scathing satire of the poem itself serves as a highly conscious articulation of, and a form of resistance against, industrialized time.

Despite the onset of a post-industrial era, Wayman's agonizing portrayal
of the endless work necessary for eking out a living has only increased in
poignancy over the decades since it was written, as wealth is increasingly
concentrated in the hands of the few. The Canadian Centre for Policy
Alternatives (CCPA) reports that in 2009, a year of deep recession, the

top-paid CEOs in the country each made more than 330 times the annual
income of the average minimum wage worker, a figure that has increased
dramatically since the 1990s.[111] A person making minimum wage would
have to work for 330 years to earn what a top CEO makes in twelve
months, not taking into account stock option tax subsidies that boost the
total amount of take-home pay for the wealthy. As Hugh Mackenzie
of the CCPA points out, this means that "Canada's best paid 100 CEOs
earn a year's worth of minimum wage work by 3:15 p.m. on New Years
Day."[112] For shift workers, the taxing and often inflexible timing of work
"days" not only can interrupt basic social and family schedules, but also
can lead to a chronic lack of sleep. Calling sleep deprivation a "national
epidemic," *Globe and Mail* writer Ian Brown laments "the growing popularity of night shifts, early starts and extended hours," all of which are
intended to save costs.[113] The phenomenon does not escape Wayman,
who, in his poem "Overtime," gets into his car after an overtime shift
and realizes, "There are 12 hours / until I have to be out of bed for
more."[114] Brown notes that sleep loss has been linked to "hyperten-
sion, heart disease, diabetes, obesity, memory loss, bipolar disorder,
reduced immunity, mood swings, impaired carbohydrate metabolism
and increased heart-rate variability," as well as impairment of "the ability
to make moral judgments."[115]

While temporal disempowerment may be especially pronounced for
wage workers, the middle classes are by no means exempt. Gurvitch argues
that the middle classes, as a result of being the least conscious of their class
groupings, "do not produce their own time scales. They are tossed between
diverse social times and are unsuccessful in finding even a tenuous cohesion."[116] In *Generation X*, Coupland's character Andy agrees, in a sense,
that middle-class life involves to some degree an *absence* of distinction.
And yet, contrary to Gurvitch, Andy clearly feels that this negation contributes toward a very particular middle-class character and temporality:

> You see, when you're middle class, you have to live with the fact that
> history will ignore you. You have to live with the fact that history can
> never champion your causes and that history will never feel sorry for
> you. It is the price that is paid for day-to-day comfort and silence.
> And because of this price, all happinesses are sterile; all sadnesses
> go unpitied.

And any small moments of intense, flaring beauty such as this morning's will be utterly forgotten, dissolved by time like a super-8 film left out in the rain, without sound, and quickly replaced by thousands of silently growing trees.[117]

Of course, as this passage ironically attests, literature is one form through which history is made to *remember* the hopes and anxieties that authors perceive within the diverse members of society, middle class or otherwise.

Margaret Sweatman's novel *Fox* (1991) takes socio-economic class divisions as its central concern, and connects the recognition of multiple temporalities with an acknowledgment of unequal access to temporal privilege and futurity. The story traces, in a fragmented and multivocal way, the events surrounding the Winnipeg General Strike of 1919, a well-known and controversial labour disruption that Reinhold Kramer calls the "originary moment of Canadian socialism."[118] While the two central characters, Eleanor and Mary, are daughters of wealthy Winnipeg families, their position of privilege is held up to sustained questioning, both through their direct experiences with working-class lives and politics, and through the form of the narrative itself, which intersperses scenes that focus on the wealthy families with various alternative voices including vignettes of impoverished wage workers and fragments of propaganda from news publications that speak for the establishment and the striking workers in turn, as well as letters, diary entries, and advertisements.

The juxtaposition of Eleanor's and Mary's experiences against many other voices becomes what Herb Wyile calls a "dialogic narrative collage."[119] "If an important dimension of social history," Wyile writes, "is the recognition of history as the product of multiple subjective perspectives rather than of an objective, unitary view, *Fox* takes that multiplicity as the departure point for its investigation of class conflict in a time of crisis (while demonstrating that even a notion such as 'crisis' is class-specific)."[120] The use of multiple perspectives involves an implicit emphasis on multitemporality, since the fragments that make up the narrative collage form windows into different experiences of time, different visions of the future, and different events that occur simultaneously. Following Homi Bhabha's assertion that the complexity of subjective identities "demands a 'time' of narrative that is disavowed in the discourse of historicism," Gabriele Helms argues that *Fox* "creates that temporality of the in-between and shows how the performative can operate through a narrative restaging of the Winnipeg General Strike."[121] Specifically, Helms notes that *Fox* speaks to temporalities beyond the dominant narrative of history because "the chronological progression of events seems to pause by counterpointing activities that occur at the same time or by focusing on one event seen from the perspectives of different characters,"[122] and that "the strategy of counterpoints also conveys a sense of simultaneity; the novel thus not only moves forward but also broadens its scope by embracing multiple viewpoints and thus expanding laterally."[123]

The positioning of radically different perspectives alongside one another means, for instance, that when Mary becomes engaged to the wealthy land developer Drinkwater, delighting in the thought that "forever after life will be a calm ocean crossed in the luxuryliner of joint fortunes,"[124] this scene is inevitably haunted by scenes where impoverished characters experience a distinct lack of futurity as they struggle to survive on a daily basis. Aileen, who works in Ladies Wear at the T. Eaton Company department store, earns such a small wage that she cannot afford to replace her worn-through gloves and boots, let alone live up to her boss's expectation that she appear fashionable in front of the upper-class customers. As her sister puts it, "there's no goddam way Aileen's gonna spend her entire month's pay on one of them dresses she sells at T. Eaton bless his ass."[125] One day as the two sisters are walking home from work, a car stops near Aileen, who speaks to the man inside and then gets in. She arrives half an hour later at the flat that the sisters rent for five dollars a month, where "she puts five bucks on the dresser and she says he screwed her in the back seat."[126] The urgent demands of immediate survival suggest that socio-economic privilege is largely a prerequisite for making long-term productive life decisions, and foreclose the possibility of a visionary future perspective that, to Mary, is simply a component of her expected life narrative.

Even for those upper-class characters who have the luxury of future orientation, though, Sweatman explicitly reveals contrasting visions of the future in a series of scenes that end with glimpses inside the forward-looking thoughts of different characters. Looking at a plot of his undeveloped land, Drinkwater thinks not of the fate of the construction crew that abandoned the project the day before due to the strike vote, but rather "sees a finished house, expensive, brick covered with Virginia creeper, unabashed imitations, Tudor, Dutch colonial, Georgian … DW, sticking to the leather upholstery of his roadster, sipping brandy from a silver flask, looks into the stark early spring night and he sees *the future*."[127] Three pages later, Mary gazes upon Drinkwater and "breathes deeply, her hands lightly stroking her satin robe, stroking her narrow thighs, her eyes on DW's mouth, his masculine chin slightly bearded, she likes his neck in its starched collar, Mary's hands stroking, caressing, wakening, *the future*. And she sees, that it is *good*."[128] And after another three pages, we see Eleanor lamenting the death, one year ago, of her brother, to whom her attraction was profound and even sexual. As she does many times throughout the novel, Sweatman here offsets the text into fragmentary thoughts:

And the Lord have removed men far away,
And there be a great forsaking in the midst of the land
And Eleanor sees the future. *And it is missing.*[129]

There is a clear implication in the Drinkwater and Mary scenes that great wealth affords the luxury of future planning, life narrative formation, and the realistic envisioning of individual progress toward the culmination of projects and the fulfillment of desire. Eleanor, though, complicates this association – not only because she comes to sympathize, at least to an extent, with the wish of the strikers to disrupt the inequitable distributions of wealth and power from which she benefits – but also, in this scene, because the trauma of her brother's death and the disrupted personal sense of time that it creates transcends class divisions and shows how a person's subjectivity is always circumscribed by mortality regardless of how it might be aligned with wealth.

The radical potential of the strike itself to bring about new conditions of social existence is embodied in the way the sudden cessation of labour seems to create a new form of time. The first day of the strike "is like other first days, when your child has arrived, or the new year, it is a day of celebration and wonder … No one gets much done today. The man with the child in his arms doesn't fix the front gate like he would if this were a Saturday, or a holiday. There is no name for a day like this. It's the first day, and nobody can say how many days there will be."[130] By unravelling and unnaming the normative progression of working days, the strike holds a utopian promise of renewal, suggestively recasting what would have been an ordinary day into something not yet defined, giving birth to a novel temporality that will become whatever the people choose to make of it. The ability, though, of established socio-economic relations and consumer culture to resist such change is expressed in an advertisement in the *Winnipeg Tribune*, which uses its own language of utopian temporality to confirm the alignment of upper-class wealth with temporal power:

> Did your Washerwoman Show Up on Washday? Hasn't the Strike brought Home to you the fact of how Dependable a *Time Saver Electric Washer* would be in your Home? *Think*! Your washerwoman is asking 40 cents an hour and you can't be sure she's coming. And the *Time Saver Electric Washer* is Always at your Command, costs 2 cents an hour to operate, and will last a Lifetime.[131]

The ability of the wealthy to allocate financial-temporal resources for the purpose of sustaining luxury and privilege seeks to neutralize any leverage that the strike may have afforded the working classes in repositioning these resources. Even while the ability of the washing machine to save time and money on a permanent basis with absolute dependability is exaggerated in the advertisement for the purpose of increasing profits for the manufacturer, the actual financial-temporal benefit of the machine is available only to those who are wealthy in the first place, presumably leaving the "washerwoman" to identify some other marketable talent within herself. The time that the "Time Saver" washer ultimately saves is the established temporality of progressively increasing wealth for corporate executives and the upper classes, and the continued impoverishment of the lower classes.

As the novel draws to a close, Sweatman demonstrates the urgent and violent means by which the establishment must protect their wealth and status. Eleanor's love interest, MacDougal, is arrested for sedition because he runs a bookshop that stocks writings by authors such as Karl Marx. The "Specials" – a police force brought in to serve the interests of the elite with greater reliability than the public police force – break into and ransack the homes of MacDougal and other strike sympathizers, leaving the arrested men's families to face the destroyed remains: "And so for the children of the *Reds* who are now sitting in Stony Mountain Penitentiary, it is a trauma so unimaginable as to falter on the steps of their memory, and it will repeat itself over and over like the tripped needle on a phonograph."[132] Meanwhile, Mary marries Drinkwater in a lavish ceremony that culminates in her father giving the newlyweds "a grand house" across the street from his own.[133] Thus, while the families of those arrested for sedition experience a watershed moment of terror, separation, loss of property, and the violation of the sanctity of home, the elite families experience the joy, togetherness, and futurity of marriage and the renewal of their enclosed wealthy neighbourhood.

Class divisions often overlap with other social divisions, and the connection between class and race is particularly prominent (much of the social tension in *Fox* has to do with the contested status of immigrants as wage earners in Canadian society). M.G. Vassanji's novel *No New Land* follows the protagonist Nurdin Lalani, a man of Indian descent whose family moves to east Africa; when Nurdin then immigrates to Canada, he marvels at the opportunities that await him. His age of 46 years is "about the average life expectancy where he was born, but here in Canada you got an extended lease on life."[134] And yet, because Nurdin's potential employers in Canada are reluctant to hire him – his race, of course, being the unspoken reason – the "extended lease on life" turns out to mean that Nurdin has more time to spend in menial, unsatisfying jobs. Hours of undesirable work, which provide a basic living, become a kind of currency in and of themselves, as Nurdin learns that by giving his first week's salary to his supervisor at a subway car cleaning job, he will be allowed to spend most of his shift playing cards with the other workers[135] – a lowly but attainable temporal victory.

Shani Mootoo's novel *Cereus Blooms at Night*, which takes place on a fictional island probably based on Trinidad, expresses in temporal terms the class divisions that accompany racialization and spatial distance from the colonial centre. Chandin's father, an indentured labourer from India, obsesses over the relationship between time and personal finance. "The old man kept himself awake," Mootoo writes,

by worrying about the future of his only child. He had been turning mathematical estimations this way and that, inside out and upside down in his head. He had, as usual, whipped himself up a headache with his obsessive predictions of what the state of his finances could be if he and his wife, Janaki, were to work one hour more, or even

two hours more per day, so that enough funds might be accrued to
send Chandin to a college in the capital, or even abroad to study a
profession. [He...] calculated how many years it would be before
Chandin were eligible for enrollment in a college, how many extra
hours there were in that many years – times two if his wife were also
to work the extra time, factoring in a possible raise in their salaries –
and he even went so far as to do a little division and addition to
account for the inevitable rise in the cost of living.[136]

As with Tom Wayman in "Factory Time," Chandin's father obsesses over
both the minutiae and the expansiveness of his work time. Here, though,
religion is also at stake in the financial predicament. When a reverend
from the "Shivering Northern Wetlands" – England – adopts Chandin
into his seminary, news quickly spreads that Chandin's parents have converted to Christianity in order for the adoption to proceed. As one person in the village puts it, "If it is the only way for your child to get
education and not have to work like a horse sweating and breaking back
in the hot sun for hardly nothing, you wouldn't convert?"[137] Conversion
to Christianity becomes a way for people of Indian descent to excise, at
least partially, their racialization and corresponding financial and temporal poverty – a tempting option for Chandin's parents, and one that con-
verts religion itself into a matter of sheer practicality. But while Chandin's
father's obsession with time does open the door to a kind of escape from
temporal poverty, this escape remains partial and problematic. Many
years later Chandin becomes horribly abusive to his own family, raping
his daughter Mala who succumbs to madness and becomes lost in time,
being unable to tell the difference between the past and the present.[138] It
is as though Chandin's father's attempt to escape temporal impoverishment, while valiant, ultimately cannot prevent the destruction of coherent temporal existence for his descendants. Like many other authors,
Mootoo is sensitive toward the temporal power of individual decisions,
yet resists the notion that temporal impoverishment is a simple vice, suggesting instead that complex entrenched social factors of race, religion,
and unequal wealth are weighted toward maintaining existing patterns of
financial and temporal poverty.

One of the dominant assertions across many works of literature is
that, despite apparent opportunities for escape such as the problematic

conversion outlined above, members of the working classes tend to find themselves in a frustrating rut or cycle, a temporal whirlpool of poverty. Mordecai Richler's Duddy Kravitz is a powerful example of a working-class character who believes in idealized linear progress, who wants to experience time as a series of achievements escalating toward wealth and fame, yet even after repeated failures cannot bring himself to critically examine the linear model. Despite his plans to become wealthy through savvy land purchasing and developing deals, Duddy finds himself betrayed by the linear model as he spirals again and again into financial and psychological ruin. "Time," Richler writes, "became an obsession with him and he was soon trying to do two and even three things at once. He kept self-improvement books beside him in the car to glance at when he stopped for a red light. He did exercises while he listened to his records and in bed with Yvette he memorized stuff from *How to Increase Your Word Power*."[139] All of this results in a nervous breakdown, but Duddy musters his strength and takes on even more entrepreneurial projects. "You are looking at the man," he says near the end of the novel, "who is going to build a town where only bugs and bullshit was before ... I have to do everything alone. I can see that now. I can trust nobody."[140] By the final scene Duddy has made a rural land purchase, achieving some degree of material wealth, but the victory is precarious and comes at the expense of his moral centre and personal relationships. Still penniless despite the land title, Duddy is thrilled when a restaurant waiter agrees to take his lunch bill on credit. This final accomplishment is such a minor one that it serves as an effective parody of the classic capitalist success story; even if Duddy fails to learn from his own history, Richler's readers are left with the distinct impression that linear temporal progress toward wealth may largely be an illusory concept. While the novel is partially an indictment of ruthless ambition, Richler is also interested in questioning the linear model of time by showing that no amount of future-oriented time consciousness can circumvent the essential cruelty of a socio-economic system whose existence actually requires that most people will lose out on temporal and economic wealth.

David Fennario affords an entire cast of temporally constricted characters in his bilingual play *Balconville*, which follows the lives of poor working-class neighbours in a run-down area of Montreal. Metaphors of physical immobility, such as Thibault's delivery bicycle with the perpetually flat tire, create an equally powerful sense of temporal immobility, as the neighbours complain endlessly about dead-end jobs, hopelessness, and familial poverty cycles. Johnny, like many of *Balconville*'s characters, claims to have plans for the future – "Yeah," he says. "I'm gonna call up some people, try to get something together, as soon as I get my first cheque"[141] – but instead embodies a class-based temporal paralysis as he spends the entire play waiting for the cheque that never arrives. Gurvitch, despite his accusatory attitude toward the impoverished, is perhaps accurate when he writes that "the consciousness of time in the working class often takes the form of fatigue, expectation, or hope."[142] Visible in portrayals like Fennario's is the perversion, the apparently inevitable failure, of the grand model of progress; Johnny thinks in terms of society's dominant linear model, but actual progress in terms of an improved quality of life never materializes, and he wakes up each day only to repeat the cycle of dashed hopes. While models of time that intentionally emphasize circularity (such as certain Indigenous models I will discuss in chapter 4) offer a positive conceptualization of recurrence and cyclicity, the experience of time for a working-class character like Johnny is *accidentally* cyclical – it is a negative experience, the inward collapse of the desired linear model.

If these texts are any guide, Canadian authors have had a stake in countering temporal discrimination by questioning the notion that economic impoverishment is the result of, or even corresponds with, a lack of time consciousness. They reveal a deep desire to resist and challenge explanations of poverty that rely on the assumption of personal temporal failures, suggesting instead that poverty is an inherent part of the socioeconomic system and is tied to cultural structures of value and power. These works argue that just as poverty can force people to obsess over money it can also heighten people's consciousness of time, even while it tends to mould the experience of temporality into a fatiguing cycle. As with many of the works discussed in this chapter, such texts can teach us to recognize time itself as a category of domination, a socially constructed site where power is enacted and agency negotiated. By questioning the inequitable distribution of temporal wealth, such works socialize their readers into perceptions of time that run counter to the dominant narratives of linear progress and increasing wealth for all, while acknowledging the entrenched power of temporal inequities. These works help us to articulate both the possibilities and the limits of temporal resistance.

GENDER AND SEXUALITY

In her book *Doing Time: Feminist Theory and Postmodern Culture*, Rita Felski asks whether it is reasonable to conceive of women as inhabiting a fundamentally different temporality from men, whether it is possible to "talk meaningfully about men's time and women's time."[143] In this project, Felski is building partially on the work of Julia Kristeva, who notes that "the feminist movement both inherits and modifies" normative understandings of time.[144] To break the question down into specific components, Felski envisions "a tentative distinction between three temporal levels": everyday time (the day-to-day phenomenological experience of time), life time ("the process of understanding one's life as a project that encompasses and connects the random segments of daily experience"), and large-scale time (processes of history and myth that "transcend the limits of our personal existence").[145]

First, Felski notes that Western ideological structures have tended to link women conceptually to cyclical or repetitive modes of time, contrasted with the masculine associations of linear progressive time. This notion, Felski argues, emerges partially from the cultural phenomenon that while "biorhythmic cycles affect various aspects of male and female behavior ... menstruation and pregnancy become the preeminent, indeed the only, examples of human subordination to natural time and a certain feminine resistance to the project of civilization."[146] Perhaps even more significantly, the linking of women with repetitive time emerges from the everyday temporal experiences that have traditionally been associated, through social constructions of gender, with the two sexes: "women are primarily responsible for the repetitive tasks of social reproduction: cleaning, preparing meals, caring for children. While much paid work is equally repetitive, only the domestic sphere is deemed to exist outside the dynamic of history and change."[147] Felski suggests that while the oppressiveness of these repetitive tasks has contributed to the idea that women are removed from the linear pace of progressive history, it may also reveal an *increased* reliance on strict temporal accounting. "Rather than being elemental

creatures attuned to natural rhythms," she writes, "many women nowa-
days are, if anything, even more preoccupied with time measurement than
men. Caught between the conflicting demands of home and work, often
juggling child care and frantic about their lack of time, it is women who
are clock watchers, who obsess about appointments and deadlines, who
view time as a precious commodity to hoard or to spend."[148] Despite the
apparent "dramatic contrast between the grand narratives of male historical time and the repetitive everyday time of women,"[149] the complexities
of everyday time for both women and men complicate the assumption
that this contrast reflects any essential difference.[150]

On the level of "life time," too, Felski notes that "traditionally men (or
rather, white men of the middle class) were encouraged to think of their
lives in linear terms [as] a project," whereas women "did not for the most
part have the luxury of imagining a self-directed future" and instead
experienced life as "a series of fragments, not a carefully choreographed
upward ascent."[151] Still, she says, it would be a mistake "to conclude that
women never think of their lives in developmental terms and to oppose
female formlessness to male linearity."[152] Seeing contemporary self-help
manuals as an example of a genre "aimed primarily at women" that "presents female lives as a movement through a series of stages toward ever
greater self-knowledge," she suggests that women "are knitted ever more
deeply into the rhetoric of self-development and are encouraged to view
their lives as a meaningful and coherent story."[153] Finally, on the level of
large-scale narratives of time, Felski resists the notion "that women are
essentially at odds with such narratives. On the contrary, they have often
been passionate believers in national progress, racial uplift, women's
growing freedom, and many other big historical stories."[154] The feminist
movement itself "is clearly indebted to forms of historical thinking made
possible by modernity"; because it "aspires to a better future," feminism
is "a *project*, requiring a purposeful and hopeful relationship toward
future time."[155]

Felski concludes that "it is hard to argue for a distinctive 'women's
time' without oversimplifying the links between gender and temporality."[156] Given that many apparently feminine temporal associations are
the result of culturally assigned and unstable gender roles, and that
women have both adopted and challenged large historical narratives like
modernism, "women can neither be subsumed within conventional

periods nor segregated within a separate 'women's time.'"[157] Only through taking into account the "dense entanglements and disjunctures within and between specific male and female experiences of history and time" can we do justice to the relationship between gender and temporality.[158] In this way Felski's work concurs with the idea that I have been developing throughout this project, that grand cultural chronotopes are limited by their inability to account for the complications and idiosyncrasies of specific temporal experiences. Still, bearing witness to the effects that cultural constructions of gender and time have had on women's experiences, and vice versa, allows for a larger and more nuanced picture to emerge. Kristeva argues that "it is in the aspiration toward artistic and, in particular, literary creation that woman's desire for affirmation now manifests itself,"[159] and while literature can indeed serve as a site of outright assertion, it can also reflect in more subtle ways the complex relationships between experiences of gender and time.

Catharine Parr Traill's experience upon her ship's arrival in the Saint Lawrence in 1832 is emblematic of the complex relationship that Felski and Kristeva identify between gender and temporality. Commenting on the villages and logging operations visible on either side of the ship, Traill writes, "I watch the progress of cultivation among these rugged and inhospitable regions with positive pleasure."[160] Yet despite her enthusiasm for the grand cultural notion of progress, by the very next page she has been denied equal participation in the project of exploring and cultivating the terrain: "I felt a longing desire to set my foot on Canadian ground, and must own I was a little disappointed when the captain advised me to remain on board, and not attempt to make one of the party that were preparing to go on shore: my husband seconded the captain's wish."[161] Traill continues to watch and *wait* throughout the extended passage toward Montreal, pleading in vain to be let off the ship. Margaret Atwood describes a similar experience in her *Journals of Susanna Moodie*, a collection of historical-fiction poems that explores the life and thoughts of Traill's sister. Atwood's Moodie sits anxiously in her small cabin, surrounded by dangerous wilderness, "waiting / for my shadowy husband."[162]

The experience of waiting, of being left out of the linear progressive project, while significant, is part of a more complex temporal position. As Traill takes up residence in her own pioneering cabin she becomes an expert autodidact, learning to produce maple sugar, vinegar, soap, candles, and pickles: tasks that are repetitive, surely, but not necessarily any more repetitive than the male-gendered tasks of chopping wood or trading for supplies. What is more, Traill's domestic chores are an essential part of the progress-oriented project, gradually drawing her household forward along the path of civility through the accumulation of desirable everyday amenities. Such "comforts," Traill writes, "are the reward and the slow gleaning-up of many years of toil"[163] – toil that is shared in different ways across both genders, even if, as Felski observes, "the domestic sphere is deemed to exist outside the dynamic of history and change."[164]

One component of the exclusion of women from full participation in higher cultural pursuits is the historically male focus of educational systems. Commenting on how education in general tends to foster an increased future orientation, Zimbardo and Boyd write that "societies that offer less opportunity for education are likely to have more citizens whose focus is limited to the present. This is especially the case where even minimal educational resources are unavailable for women; when women's educational level advances, their children and social class also advance."[165] Here we can recall the young Anne Shirley's socialization, in *Anne of Green Gables*, from an insubordinate present hedonism toward a community-sanctioned future orientation; her basic social education under the tutelage of schoolteachers, community members, and especially her adoptive parents stretches her time perspective until her behaviour meets with approval from her elders. However, once Anne has attained this required level of socialization and has gained enough of a future-oriented work ethic to take up her designated place in the perpetual maintenance of the social order, the community *resists* the idea of educating her any further. Near the end of the novel the neighbourhood matriarch Rachel Lynde visits Green Gables and says, "Well, Anne, I hear you've given up your notion of going to college. I was real glad to hear it. You've got as much education now as a woman can be comfortable with. I don't believe in girls going to college with the men and cramming their heads full of Latin and Greek and all that nonsense."[166] While Anne's education and expanded time perspective, up to a certain point, were unequivocal requirements of her acceptance into the community, she faces a backlash against pursuing the higher forms of education associated with male-dominated grand cultural achievements. Anne's defiant resolve to study college material after all – which causes Mrs Lynde to lift her hands "in holy horror"[167] – is tempered with her agreement to take up the more conventional day job of teaching at the Avonlea school; she will study the college texts only from home, on her own time as it were.

Interestingly, when Anne runs down toward Diana's house to share this news, Mrs Lynde muses that "there's a good deal of the child about her yet in some ways,"[168] suggesting that Anne's stubborn and contrary desire to continue her education sends her backwards, not forwards, along the normative linear measurement of maturity (meanwhile, no such judgment is made of Anne's male friend Gilbert who also plans to study at college). Marilla takes issue with this assessment, replying, "There's a good deal more of the woman about her in other [ways]."[169] All of this reveals that the perceived correct amount of education and participation beyond the domestic arena for women remains a contested topic within the Avonlea community; Anne is both progressive and regressive for testing the boundaries. In the closing lines of the novel Montgomery leaves Anne entirely satisfied with the domestic restrictions that have come to define her life options: "if the path set before her feet was to be narrow she knew that flowers of quiet happiness would bloom along it. The joys of sincere work and worthy aspiration and congenial friendship were to be hers."[170] These lines can be read as an acknowledgment of the genuine pleasures that daily life can afford regardless of any grand cultural project, or as the final domestication of Anne's rebellious spirit as she fully internalizes the circumscription of her life project.

The gendered infantilization hinted at in Anne's experiences is central to the cultural link between masculinity and advancement, maturity, and progress. If men are seen as the drivers of cultural development, then women are necessarily underdeveloped and childlike, perpetually located further back along the linear model of time. In her short story "What Is Remembered," Alice Munro describes a young couple, Meriel and Pierre, as they try to adjust to married life in the mid-twentieth century. The narrative reveals how normative gender roles direct women into an adulthood of perpetual perceived underdevelopment, but Munro is also sensitive to the stark repetitiveness and temporal restraints to which men are subject:

Young husbands were stern, in those days. Just a short time before, they had been suitors, almost figures of fun, knock-kneed and

desperate in their sexual agonies. Now, bedded down, they turned
resolute and disapproving. Off to work every morning, clean-shaven,
youthful necks in knotted ties, days spent in unknown labors ...
What a lot they had to learn, so quickly. How to kowtow to bosses
and how to manage wives. How to be authoritative about mortgages,
retaining walls, lawn grass, drains, politics, as well as about the jobs
that had to maintain their families for the next quarter of a century.
It was the women, then, who could slip back – during the daytime
hours, and always allowing for the stunning responsibility that had
been landed on them, in the matter of the children – into a kind of
second adolescence. A lightening of spirits when the husbands
departed. Dreamy rebellion, subversive get-togethers, laughing
fits that were a throwback to high school, mushrooming between
the walls that the husband was paying for, in the hours when he
wasn't there.[171]

Earlier in the twentieth century the German writer Sigmund von Radecki
declared the wristwatch "the handcuff of our time,"[172] and the strict temporal regulation facing Pierre and his contemporaries takes on an equally
ominous tone in the image of the "youthful necks in knotted ties"; the
restrictive garment, reminiscent of a noose, must be tightened onto the
body every morning with precise punctuality. Pierre's behaviour is a perfect example of what David Landes calls "time discipline," the internalized drive to be punctual that is produced and reinforced in a highly
clock-driven society.[173] No one else pulls the tie around Pierre's neck, or
drags him out of bed early in the morning; he has assimilated the necessity of these actions and regulates his own life around them in order to
meet the future-oriented responsibility of securing his family's long-term
finances. As Hartmut Rosa notes, the internalization of normative time is
accomplished primarily not through "direct *coercion*," but rather through
"all the institutions of modern society in which corresponding orientations and practices are inculcated as *habits*, for instance (along with the
factories), hospitals, prisons, asylums, kindergartens, and, above all,
schools. On a closer look time proves to be the main instrument of the
disciplinary society analyzed in particular by Michel Foucault."[174] However, while Pierre is flung forward into this intensively regulated adulthood responsibility, Meriel appears to move in two temporal directions

at once: she travels forward into the responsibility of motherhood and simultaneously "slips back" into childhood, much how Anne Shirley is seen as both progressive and regressive, both adult and child. Normative gender roles cause men and women to age at apparently different and even internally contradictory rates, but neither gender is free from culturally imposed temporal restraints.

Texts that question the linear shape of narrative itself – or, to use Bakhtin's term, texts that resist standard literary chronotopes – can be particularly adept at challenging the dominance of masculinist assumptions of linear progress. The concept of *le nouveau roman* advanced by the French writer Alain Robbe-Grillet in the 1950s and 1960s served as a manifesto for experimenting with alternative forms of narrative centred on objects rather than plot, and while the difficulties of this type of experimentation can serve partially to reinforce the inevitability of narrative concepts like sequence, the impulse to question dominant narrative forms has also opened up vital methods of resistance against entrenched structures of power. In Canada, Daphne Marlatt and Kristjana Gunnars have been especially notable for enacting political resistance through formal manipulations of narrative.

Marlatt's 1988 novel *Ana Historic* self-consciously probes the limits of objectivist history, telling the story of Annie, a woman who questions official records of the past, and figures the flow of events as a shifting, multi-layered composition – "a tangle of hair," as the epigraph's phrasing has it. Echoing this tangled shape, the novel itself weaves Annie's present-day reflections with the recollected and imagined history of "Ana," a resident of pioneer-era Vancouver. The link between normative historiography and patriarchy is repeatedly made clear throughout the story, as Annie notices that women such as Ana are largely absent from the official late nineteenth-century archives. Historical documents focus on civic developments and property sales, while "amidst all this there are brief references to women."[175] Even the name Ana is a speculative invention that Annie produces upon discovering that the "Mrs Richards" briefly mentioned in the archives is left without any name other than her deceased husband's surname. The novel itself, then, becomes an alternative form of archive in the sense that it dedicates time and attention to the lives of women, as well as in the sense that it eschews linear narrative sequence in favour of woven, or tangled, threads of experience, memory, and

speculation. Meanwhile, in response to the fact that city patriarchs articulate history using the typographical convention of initial capital letters
"to convince themselves of its, of their, significance,"[176] individual sentences throughout the novel begin with lower-case letters, suggesting that
far from being a new beginning stamped with a declaration of official
(i.e., masculine) historiography, each moment in time reflects subjective
experience and is always already underway, flowing in a slippery continuity from what came before. Events in the novel similarly recast expected
notions of sequence and linearity, as in the climactic scene where Jeannie's
labour and childbirth are juxtaposed against a newspaper report of a
men's boat race. While the boat race and its historical representations
assume that firstness takes priority – "that worth be established by com-
petition" – the birth scene portrays Jeannie as a woman "in touch with
her body its tides coming in not first nor last nor lost she circles back on
herself repeats her breathing out and in two heartbeats here not winning
or losing labouring into the manifest."[177] Through the story's framing of
linear competitiveness as a masculine enterprise that cannot encompass
women's continual cooperative practices, and through the form of the
book that weaves past and present, history and imagination, poetry and
prose, the novel constructs a temporality modelled after the principles of
complexity, solidarity, renewal, and multiple times, emphasizing coexisting truths rather than a victorious singular truth.

Herb Wyile describes *Ana Historic* as "a narrative that assumes the freedom of imaginative projection to be not only a justifiable option but
indeed a necessary corrective to the marginalization and patriarchal
inscription of women in a linear, phallocentric, male history."[178] As a
result of Marlatt's innovations, Wyile argues that this novel, "perhaps
more than any other 'historic' fiction in Canada," supports the idea that
"scepticism about traditional historiography along epistemological, political, and gender lines necessitates a new approach to the form of history."[179] Lloyd Pratt's cautionary insight on formal manipulation is
significant here, in that the "anachronistic formal precedents that inhere
in any genre"[180] mean that even those works that strategically manipulate
the formal conventions of the novel still in a sense replicate and thus
implicitly confirm the traditional temporalities and related structures of
power that are embedded in the novel form. As is so often the case,
though, the fact that an act of resistance partially confirms the very power

it seeks to subvert does not render the project of resistance meaning-less. If, as Smaro Kamboureli says, "The after is complicitous with the before,"[181] it is inevitable that formal innovations will innovate *from* past conventions, but this type of manipulation remains precisely that process that can compel normative forms to evolve over time in order to question dominant discourses and reflect alternative priorities. A different possible interpretation here – the conclusion that *Ana Historic* is not properly a novel at all – is one that Marlatt anticipates with the statement (appar-ently Annie's) that "a book of interruptions is not a novel."[182] The state-ment is, of course, largely ironic, since *Ana Historic* proves that a book of tangled, non-linear narrative fragments can indeed serve as a novel, and a significant one at that. For Gabriele Helms, the book is paradoxically "both a novel and a work full of interruptions."[183] By straddling the line between being a novel and not being a novel, *Ana Historic* adjusts the notion of what a novel can be, recalibrating the expected forms of tempo-rality and power that go along with it.

Homi Bhabha's commentary on the temporality of nationhood also provides a useful perspective on *Ana Historic*. Bhabha argues that in order for a nation to present an image of itself as a coherent, unified collec-tive moving comprehensibly through time into modernity, "the scraps, patches and rags of daily life must be repeatedly turned into the signs of a coherent national culture."[184] As Bhabha's image of scraps and rags sug-gests, however, there is "always the distracting presence of another tempo-rality that disturbs the contemporaneity of the national present."[185] Indeed, there is not just "another temporality," but many temporalities that make up what Marlatt figures as the "tangle of hair." Wai Chee Dimock's explication of Bhabha's concerns involves the realization that "in escaping homogenization, experiential time works against the puta-tive unity of *any* construct, not least the construct called the nation. For Bhabha, then, the breakdown of a single, enforceable chronology stands as one of the most powerful challenges to the sovereignty of the state."[186] Thus, while Marlatt's novel has typically been read as resisting the tradi-tional linear sense of masculine history and the subaltern status that this normative history affords women, Bhabha's comments may lead us to see this critique as one that can implicitly expand to challenge the sover-eignty, unity, and linear trajectory of the nation itself. The novel shows that the scraps and rags of daily life need not be tied precariously together into a sequential narrative of coherent national culture, but rather can illuminate heterogeneity, inequities, and multiplicitous alternative histories. While the formal innovations of Marlatt's novel, like any variations on traditional forms, function imperfectly to resist normative modes of temporal power, the act of resistance remains potent on many different levels. At the same time, reading *Ana Historic* through Bhabha's commentary on time and the nation revises our understanding not only of the novel, but potentially also of Bhabha's theory, which can usefully be applied not only at the scale of the nation-state, but also within smaller social collectives such as regions, cities, or other less geographically circumscribed imagined communities. The assemblage of scraps and rags that constitutes *Ana Historic* specifically revises the ostensibly unified, linear temporality of Vancouver and the West Coast.

Kristjana Gunnars's 1989 book *The Prowler* enacts a similar interrogation of temporally linear plot, but while many of the same conclusions on *Ana Historic* can usefully apply to *The Prowler*, Gunnars's text also seeks to question the binding of particular temporalities to different genders. *The Prowler* is told from the perspective of a girl growing up in Cold War era Iceland, where trade monopolies and foreign military occupations have left the population impoverished and malnourished. The narrative is broken into 167 short fragments told through a logic of subjective experience and memory rather than through the linear trajectory of chronological order, and the fact that these fragments are numbered while the pages themselves are not seems to suggest that the conceptual experiences of the mind form a more meaningful sequence than the arbitrary and uniform page divisions of a text leading from beginning to end. As the narrator says, "I have sometimes thought: it is possible there is no such thing as chronological time. That the past resembles a deck of cards. Certain scenes are given. They are not scenes the rememberer chooses, but simply a deck that is given. The cards are shuffled whenever a game is played."[187] In this sense, *The Prowler*'s perspective on subjective temporality is similar to W.H. New's perspective in *Along a Snake Fence Riding*, though Gunnars's narrator pays special attention to the connection between linear time and masculinity. As with *Ana Historic*, there is some degree of uncertainty as to whether *The Prowler* should properly be considered a novel – an ambiguity that the book's subtitle, "A Novel," does little to resolve. Méira Cook argues that because Gunnars "conflates the prose / poetry binary," the 167 sections "may equally be defined as stanzas if this text is to be described as a long poem, or as paragraphs if it is to be considered a prose work."[188] For Cook, Gunnars "appears to be extending the borders of genre, the implication being that only through unusual subterfuges may the love story be adequately communicated as a discourse that alternately requires and resists form."[189] While the problems of the love story are of significant concern in the book, the refusal to adhere to traditional literary forms is also a comment on the limitations of linearity for articulating human experience more generally, and is especially important in the context of social constructions of gender.

"I have read treatises on male writing," Gunnars's narrator says. "The male line. The masculine story. That men have to be going somewhere. Men are always shooting something somewhere. And that women do not. That women can grow all things in one place. That the female story is an unfolding of layers."[190] This comment mirrors the assertion in *Ana Historic* that masculinity is associated with competitive linear time that emphasizes winning or arriving first at a destination, while women's time can better be represented as a collaborative, productive process that is more concerned with growth or continuation rather than with reaching a particular end point. This distinction is highly reminiscent of the distinction that James P. Carse draws between finite games and infinite games, where "a finite game is played for the purpose of winning, an infinite game for the purpose of continuing the play."[191] Because finite games have definite beginnings and endings, "we can speak of finite games as having temporal boundaries";[192] infinite games, however, are "not bounded by time. Indeed, the only purpose of the game is to prevent it from coming to an end."[193] While the two game types of this theory can be mapped quite clearly onto the male and female genders, respectively, in *Ana Historic* in order to illuminate the book's critique of masculine historiography, Gunnars takes a more cautionary approach in *The Prowler*. Immediately after Gunnars's narrator draws the above distinction, she adds, "I do not know if this is true. It is incidental."[194] Linear time and its tendency toward domination must be interrogated because of the constraints they impose on perception and subjectivity, but, importantly, these constraints remain significant even if the gender associations through which they are sometimes understood turn out to be tenuous. Gunnars, it seems, would concur with Rita Felski's conclusion that seemingly feminine temporal modes are frequently the result of culturally assigned and unstable gender roles, and that "it is hard to argue for a distinctive 'women's time' without oversimplifying the links between gender and temporality."[195] Instead of envisioning her own story as a linear, chronological line, or as a supposedly feminine alternative to the linear mode, Gunnars's narrator allows her narrative to circle back upon itself within a process of questioning, so that the teller and the listener alike experience an unfolding process of discovery in which gender associations begin to fade into the background. Like Marlatt, Gunnars is highly conscious of the ties between patriarchal power and linear time, but while Marlatt highlights the masculinity of linear time in order to locate resistance within women's multiplicitous narratives, Gunnars shows that experiences of time are always multiple, suggesting that pure linearity fails to articulate temporal experience for men as well as women. Like the reader whose gender is indeterminate, the writer too remains ungendered while operating as "a prowler in a given story that emerges in time."[196]

Among the most eloquent literary articulations of the relationship between gender roles and experiences of time is Margaret Atwood's 1988 novel *Cat's Eye*, which follows the life of Elaine Risley, an artist who reflects back on her childhood in 1940s Toronto as she prepares to attend a retrospective of her own career in the present day. The narrative structure of reminiscences that build gradually up to a fuller understanding of the present is significant to our understanding of Elaine, but it is also a formal technique common to many novels. Instead of focusing primarily on formal manipulation like Marlatt or Gunnars, Atwood develops a complex thematic assessment of gender and time, which can usefully be understood as taking two parts. First, Atwood investigates how normative gender roles within a patriarchal society restrict the ways in which women are expected to spend their everyday time and to envision the temporal possibilities of their lives, and suggests that these gender-based social restrictions cause women's time to be distributed, experienced, and valued inequitably compared with men's time. Second, the novel is intensively preoccupied with childhood bullying among girls, and shows that the trauma of this bullying causes the protagonist's experience of time as an adult to be confused, layered, and fractured. As a result of the convergence of these two thematic concerns, the novel suggests that negative personal temporal experiences, especially for women, should be understood through their connections to systemic social inequities as well as through more intimate social relations such as bullying, even while these latter interpersonal relations in turn have ties to the widespread sense of shame and weakness that patriarchy instills within female children.

An early hint of the significance of normative gender roles occurs when Elaine recalls being perplexed, as a young girl, over the fact that girls and boys are required to enter the school through separate, gendered door-ways, a division that expands into other aspects of life; her brother Stephen relates easily to Elaine when they are alone, but during school hours he takes on a separate existence, disengaging himself from his sister through snowball fights with loud groups of boys. Adults, too, are separated through gender roles in time and space. For adult women, spending one's time at home as a mother is the acceptable plan, while men are expected to disappear from the home during daylight hours, taking on a shadowy and mysterious existence; "daytime is ruled by mothers. But fathers come out at night. Darkness brings home the fathers, with their real, unspeakable power."[197] Even in the otherwise unusual Risley house-hold Elaine's father enjoys a grandiose vision of time, musing over the eventual fate of the human species and the polar ice caps, while Elaine's mother attends to immediate household needs, serving "coffee soufflé for dessert."[198]

As a young adult Elaine finds that the act of painting serves as a form of resistance against the expected uses of her time. With her daytime Art and Archaeology course serving as a cover for her "real life," which "takes place at night,"[199] she enrolls in an evening Life Drawing course where instead of observing other people's art she creates her own. She keeps this night life secret from the Art and Archaeology world, where "my botched attempts at drawing naked women would be seen as a waste of time. Art has been accomplished, elsewhere. All that remains to be done with it is the memory work."[200] Her nighttime painting resists not only the man-dated uses of women's time, but also the view of meaningful art as some-thing belonging to a previous (and male-dominated) era.

When she becomes pregnant, Elaine worries that she is losing her abil-ity to control time – "My body is a separate thing. It ticks like a clock; time is inside it. It has betrayed me, and I am disgusted with it."[201] The more significant temporal tension here, though, again turns out to be social rather than primarily biological; while raising her infant daughter, her efforts to resist normative temporality become a central point of tension in her arguments with her partner, Jon. As she spends her days at a new job to pay the bills, Elaine takes to painting at night or early in the morning when the baby is asleep, causing Jon to complain: "Jon does not like me painting at night. 'When else can I do it?' I say. 'You tell me.' There is only one answer, one that would not involve the loss of his own time: *Don't do it at all.* But he doesn't say this."[202] Elaine soon discovers that Jon has been sleeping with another woman, and she bitterly recalls the advice that would have been offered "in women's magazines, of a decade ago: wait it out."[203] But the passive feminine temporality envisioned in such magazines is inadequate. She accuses Jon of cheating, and when he accuses her right back, she replies, "Me? … I don't have the time. I don't have time to think, I don't have time to paint, I barely have time to shit. I'm too busy paying the goddamn rent."[204] As her relationship implodes she has to give up painting altogether and focus exclusively on day-to-day necessities: "I push myself through time, to work, to the bank to get money, to the supermarket to buy food."[205] Gradually Elaine begins to associate with a group of feminist artists and activists, who argue that "what is wrong with us the way we are is men … They are violent, wage wars, commit murders. They do less work and make more money. They shove the housework off on women."[206] The inequitable valuing and distribution of time between work and leisure across genders, which Elaine has experienced firsthand, is a central driver of these women's politics. Thus, the novel gives voice to the forms of temporal disempowerment tied to the social construction of gender, and points toward multiple forms of resistance – the reclaiming of personal time through artistic practices and the alternative use of nighttime hours, as well as the social organization of feminist activism – but also leaves readers with the understanding that the gains associated with these forms of resistance are hard-won and limited.[207]

This brings us to the second thematic concern. While Atwood is clearly interested in the direct impacts that patriarchal social structures have on women's experiences of time, *Cat's Eye* also examines the temporal consequences of relationships between women, focusing especially on bullying among girls. For Elaine, the gender-based temporal disempowerment discussed above combines with a sense of temporal fracturing brought about by childhood bullying, suggesting that, just as time itself is never only one thing or one experience, disruptions of subjective time do not have a single root cause; these disruptions must be understood in the context of constructed social gender roles as well as intimate personal relations.

Elaine's childhood friends, Grace, Carol, and especially Cordelia, subject her to endless cruelties and psychological tortures, constantly watching over her and telling her that everything she does is wrong. At one point Cordelia digs a hole in her backyard and the three girls lure Elaine inside, trapping her. "When I remember back to this time in the hole," the adult Elaine says, "I have no image of myself in the hole; only a black square filled with nothing, a square like a door. Perhaps the square is empty; perhaps it's only a marker, a time marker that separates the time before it from the time after. The point at which I lost power."[208] The experience becomes a watershed moment, dividing Elaine's life in two, and she perceives the time afterward as "the endless time when Cordelia had such power over me."[209]

As the daily tortures continue, Elaine forms a habit of obsessively peeling the skin from her own feet, and contemplates burning her hand in the toaster: "All of these are ways of delaying time, slowing it down, so I won't have to go out through the kitchen door."[210] On the radio she listens to "the Dominion Observatory Official Time Signal: first a series of outer space beeps, then silence, then a long dash. The long dash means one o'clock. Time is passing; in the silence before the long dash the future is taking shape. I turn my head into the pillow. I don't want to hear it."[211] Time itself has become a slow torture, as the unfolding of each day inevitably brings unbearable new forms of abuse, while at the same time, Elaine's act of listening to the unerring public time signal holds out the promise of an effortless progressive synchronization that cannot be fulfilled (much like the ache for synchronization in Gabrielle Roy's *The Road Past Altamont* and Catherine Bush's *Minus Time*). Eventually Elaine learns a new skill, fainting at will, which allows her to escape some of the worst encounters with the girls: "Fainting is like stepping sideways, out of your own body, out of time or into another time. When you wake up it's later. Time has gone on without you."[212] The relief of dissociation afforded by fainting soon creeps into the waking moments of Elaine's life: "I begin to spend time outside my body without falling over. At these times I feel blurred, as if there are two of me, one superimposed on the other, but imperfectly."[213]

Longer-term consequences of this phenomenon are visible in the adult Elaine's narrative, where she occasionally experiences disconnected temporal skips: "I find myself standing in the middle of the main room, not knowing exactly how I got in here from the kitchenette. A little time jump";[214] "I get on the escalator, but suddenly I'm going up. This is bad, confusing directions like that, or am I jumping time, did I go down already?"[215] The effect is compounded by brief but increasingly prevalent narrative moments whose temporal setting is ambiguous; do Elaine's comments about walking through Toronto or arguing with Jon refer to the "present" of her adult life, or are they recollections from decades ago? Aside from vague anxieties about Alzheimer's and other "diseases of the memory,"[216] the adult Elaine has no awareness of where her tendency to experience temporal fragmentation comes from; her childhood traumas have a profound effect on her life, yet remain unavailable to her conscious mind.

If the experience of being trapped in Cordelia's backyard dungeon is the moment when Elaine loses power, Cordelia's most dangerous act of torture becomes, paradoxically, the moment when Elaine gains control. In the depths of winter Cordelia throws Elaine's hat over the edge of a wooden footbridge into the ravine below and insists that Elaine climb down to retrieve it. Abandoned in the icy water, Elaine nearly freezes to death and has a hallucinatory, detached experience. After recovering over the subsequent days, though, she discovers that she is no longer bound to obey Cordelia's demands. She stops listening to the taunting voices of the girls and gradually goes on to forget her entire tortured childhood. When she reflects on Cordelia, Grace, and Carol, she finds that "there is no emotion attached to these names. They're like the names of distant cousins, people who live far away, people I hardly know. Time is missing."[217] Her childhood traumas run so deep that Elaine has taught herself to disconnect her life into separate temporal existences. It is only decades later, while helping her dying mother clean out the cellar, that Elaine recovers her lost time. She stumbles across a cat's eye marble that she had hidden away as a girl, a marble that, during her torture, she had endowed with a symbolic and hopeful power of protection. "I look into it," she says, "and see my life entire."[218] The inevitable temporal connectedness of human subjectivity, the fact that all of a person's life moments build upon one another and contribute to the full character of ongoing existence, now becomes as clear to Elaine as it has been within the narrative structure all along.

The two issues of concern here – the inequities, temporal and otherwise, associated with the social construction of gender, and the temporal fracturing brought about by childhood bullying – are linked not only in the sense that they both inform Elaine's subjective experiences of time as she grows into adulthood, but also because bullying is a microcosm and replication of larger social power relations. Inquiring into the possible cause of Cordelia's exceptionally ruthless behaviour, Theodore Sheckels writes,

> Perhaps Cordelia is just a vicious young girl, or, perhaps, she is being pushed to victimize Elaine because she herself is a victim. That "perhaps" takes us from the small group structure of these girls to the small group structure of their families where the girls may be learning about power before passing on those lessons to the naïve, power-down ones such as Elaine.[219]

Even if Atwood never explicitly declares the source of Cordelia's behaviour, Sheckels's interpretation makes good sense, since the gender-based power dynamics of families are prominent throughout the novel and strongly suggest that "the viciousness Cordelia shows toward Elaine seems to be based in and a reflection of Cordelia's own victimization at the hands of her father."[220] More than this, though, because the novel is also deeply concerned with the *larger* group structures shaped through socially mandated gender roles, the book implies a link between broad systemic forms of gendered power and discipline, and the smaller-scale echo of these power relations within female-gendered peer groups. If women, to borrow Sheckels's terminology, are "power-down" in society at large, then for the girls who are discovering their own power-down status through the socializing processes of childhood, the most obvious opportunity to become "power-up" is to dominate their peers. In this way the temporal disempowerment tied to the social construction of gender multiplies rather than dissipates within small group structures.

Because *Cat's Eye* strongly suggests a causal relation between systemic sexism and peer-group bullying, the obvious convergence of the effects of these power relations on Elaine's experience of time becomes all the more notable. Elaine's brother Stephen, who becomes a leading expert in physics and cosmology, provides various insights into the physical nature of time – into the way that time can bend, or the way that all of the stars are "fragments of the past"[221] – and these comments serve, through Elaine's reflections, as metaphors for subjective time. As Fiona Tolan writes, "Atwood draws a parallel between the psychologist's exploration of the mind and the physicist's exploration of the universe."[222] While Stephen's research builds toward a grand "Unified Field Theory" of the universe, *Cat's Eye* itself is an attempt at a unified field theory of human subjective time, and asserts that relationships both across and within gender categories can profoundly influence the connectedness or dislocation, the empowerment or disempowerment, of temporal experience.[223]

Like gender categories, sexualities carry deeply rooted cultural associations that tend to reinforce hierarchies of privilege. In Canada, as in other places, discrimination against people of minority sexual identities has often constrained individuals' experiences of time, and artistic representations play a key role in articulating these experiences. At the same time, the politics of queerness can be especially well suited for questioning the "straightness" of the normative modern sense of linear development and productivity. Queerness thus operates both as a temporal liability within a heteronormative society, and potentially as an important site of temporal resistance.

In his 1993 play *The Stillborn Lover*, Timothy Findley frames the Japanese board game "Go" as a metaphor for human agency through time; once the game's stone pieces have been set in place, "they cannot be withdrawn. Their positions are locked, irrevocable. Like the moves and gestures we make with our lives."[224] The past is laid out in an unalterable configuration, and this locks the circumstances of the present into place, confining future possibilities as well. For Harry Raymond, the Canadian ambassador to Moscow who has been framed for a crime because his homosexuality is politically embarrassing, agency is constrained by a figurative playing field whose pieces have been arranged in accordance with systemic homophobia. Michael, the minister of external affairs, explains that Harry has two choices: return to Moscow and face unjust punishment, or stay in Canada and confess to crimes of which he is innocent. In Richard Cavell's words, "What Findley seeks to show is that deceptiveness and intrigue characterize both the communists and the RCMP who have been sent to interrogate Raymond, and that this deceptiveness is founded upon sexual duplicity."[225] As the deadline for a decision draws near, Harry's wife Marian hands him a stone and says, "Here. It's your move,"[226] implying that Harry has the power to choose and create his own future. But the two futures that he has to choose from are unreasonable products of sexual regulation, and the power is illusory. His influence over the direction of his life through time is metaphorically no greater than that of a stillborn baby, his agency having effectively been extinguished before he has a chance to exercise it.

Findley's representation of temporal disempowerment tied to minority sexual identities recalls various aspects of Canada's historical treatment of same-sex relationships. In 1965 Everett George Klippert of the Northwest Territories admitted to police that he had engaged in homosexual sex on various occasions; he was deemed a dangerous sex offender and was sent to prison to serve an *indefinite* sentence – temporal disempowerment indeed. Partially as a result of this case, Pierre Elliott Trudeau soon passed legislation decriminalizing homosexuality, and Klippert was released in 1971.[227] Long legal and parliamentary struggles through the 1980s and beyond have gradually led to the prohibition of discrimination on grounds of sexual orientation, to the ability of same-sex partners to collect spousal pensions under the Old Age Security Act, and to the legalization of same-sex marriage. The questions of when such rights are acquired, and how much time elapses during the various rulings and appeals are of no small concern to those affected. The matter of retroactive rights is also complex; the 2003 granting of spousal pension payments to same-sex partners retroactive to 1985 (the date when equality rights were established in the Charter of Rights and Freedoms, or, as comedian Rick Mercer jokes, the date when "gayness was invented") led to an appeal by the federal government that argued "that it needs to be able to make laws and set its own payment dates."[228]

Discrimination against people of minority sexualities tends to rely on the claim that heterosexuality is a normal, stable, natural identity, relegating other sexualities to the status of deviation. The word "deviate" itself etymologically means "turned out of the way," suggesting a distortion of some expected linear path. In her book *Time Binds*, Elizabeth Freeman describes this expected linear path as "*chrononormativity*, the interlocking temporal schemes necessary for genealogies of descent and for the mundane workings of domestic life."[229] Normative modernity, she argues, is intent on linear productivity and sees time "as seamless, unified, and forward moving."[230] In response, she analyzes a range of texts to identify forms of opposition to monolithic chrononormativity, focusing on

> moments of asynchrony, anachronism, anastrophe, belatedness, compression, delay, ellipsis, flashback, hysteron-proteron, pause, prolepsis, repetition, reversal, surprise, and other ways of breaking apart what Walter Benjamin calls "homogeneous empty time" ... Queer temporalities, visible in the forms of interruption I have described above, are points of resistance to this temporal order that, in turn, propose other possibilities for living in relation to indeterminately past, present, and future others: that is, of living historically.[231]

These types of opposition to "straight" time are, of course, intrinsic to many everyday forms of experience as well as narrative. In a sense, many of the forms of resistance against normative time that I have been discussing throughout this book could be described as queer temporalities, modes of time that present alternatives to the dominant forms of regular forward motion. As Ben Davies and Jana Funke argue in *Sex, Gender and Time in Fiction and Culture*, "Possible forms of deviance and resistance [to linear straight time] have been acknowledged in discussions of diverse temporal practices that are subsumed under the umbrella term *queer temporalities*."[232] Thus, while there is much debate over "just what a queer relation to time entails – and who can participate in it,"[233] to the extent that queer time deviates from straight time it can function as a site of intentional or embodied resistance. Davies and Funke are careful to complicate the supposed distinction, though, between queer and straight time, making the point that heterosexual people can engage in queer experiences of time, that "life – queer or straight – does not unfold in a strictly linear fashion,"[234] and that queer individuals can participate in future-oriented projects (such as the desire for reproduction or for increasing civil rights over time) typically associated with straight linear time. Even the simple desire for personal agency over time that we see in Findley's representation of Harry Raymond articulates an obvious way in which queerness is entirely compatible with the human craving for "straight" temporal coherence. Still, despite the need to question the supposed straight-queer binary, Davies and Funke recognize that "discussions of queer temporality tend to focus on LGBT sexualities."[235] Their conclusion, then, concurs with Freeman's realization that texts that show a particular engagement with the politics of queer sexualities can be especially well suited for questioning the "straightness" of chrononormativity. Considering these points alongside the history of the social treatment of queer individuals in Canada reveals that the discussion of the forms of social power involved in the relationship between queerness and time must be conscious of two different processes: on the one hand the inequitable social regulation of sexualities causes temporal disempowerment for individuals, and on the other hand large social concepts of time tend to exclude (and thus remain vulnerable to) the metaphorically "queer" forms of non-linear temporality that operate within many different domains of everyday experience.

One of the most notable applications of what could be called queer temporality in Canadian literature occurs in Yann Martel's 1996 novel *Self*, which highlights both of the above processes of queer time. The book disrupts the notion that sex identities and sexualities are constant over time, thus questioning the idea that human experience can be understood through the dominant social chronotope of normative linearity. At the same time, the book bears witness to the personal temporal devastation brought about by sexual violence, a form of disempowerment that is associated with the social regulation of sexualities but also requires its own consideration. The shattering of the protagonist's experience of time after a man rapes her speaks to the personal forms of temporal disempowerment caused by sexism and patriarchal power, and also suggests that sexual violence itself can exacerbate the already inevitable separation of the temporal experience of individuals from the grand social chronotope of progressive linear regularity.

Following the model of Virginia Woolf's *Orlando*, the landmark fictional treatment of the constructedness of social gender roles, Martel has his protagonist spontaneously switch sexes at different times in the narrative; at first the sex of the protagonist is unspecified, then he is definitely male, then spontaneously becomes female, and finally after seven years as a woman wakes up a man once more. From the protagonist's childhood point of view human metamorphosis is completely natural: "I had already gathered evidence on the metamorphosis of day and night, of weather, of the seasons, of food and excrement, even of life and death, to name but a few ... I envisioned life as a series of metamorphic changes, one after another, to no end."[236] Upon being told that sex identities, far from being fluid and various, are in fact limited to precisely two – male and female, husband and wife – the protagonist states, "I became an indubitable boy."[237] Years later, though, on his eighteenth birthday, he wakes up a woman.[238] If sex identities must exist in the form of a binary opposition, a notion the protagonist deeply resists, then the possibility of inhabiting multiple or fluid identities simultaneously is precluded, and fluidity must be realized in transformations that occur *over time*. The occasional sex metamorphoses that the protagonist experiences are both unremarkable, barely more surprising than putting on a new set of clothing, and also revolutionary, defying the notion that binary sex identities themselves are natural and permanent, and thus resisting the adequacy of larger notions of "straight" linear experience.

The final act of the novel, however, radically shifts the focus of the story to an examination of rape and its consequences for the victim, including personal temporal disempowerment. While Timothy Findley's character Harry finds his temporal agency thwarted by systemic homophobia, Martel's protagonist, who has developed a keen desire for temporal empowerment and enjoyment, finds this preoccupation devastated by the catastrophe of brutal sexual assault. When the protagonist encounters a neighbour who enters her rented office space and refuses to leave, the narrative splits into two columns: her first-person account of the attack runs down the left, while her fragmented feelings of pain, fear, and shock run down the right. "Things went from normal to terribly wrong in a fraction of a second," she says as the man begins his attack.[239] This fraction of a second becomes a watershed moment that opens into an extended duration, a lifetime, of terror: "It was a long assault. It felt as if it lasted hours. How otherwise can I account for so much fear? ... The problem with rape is that it ruins your life, the whole rest of your life, because the fear spreads. When I think back, he was there maybe twenty minutes."[240] The chaotic temporal expansion that she experiences during the attack is mirrored in the intense sparsity of those few pages that are left almost or entirely blank, as well as the right-hand column where time is measured only by the recurrence of fear and pain.

The split-column narration, a technique that Martel uses briefly at different moments throughout the novel to represent the internal experience of simultaneous thought processes or language translation, continues in this scene for an agonizing thirty pages during which the protagonist falls into a temporal vacuum, causing the reader, too, to lose any clear sense of passing narrative time – at one point during the sequence the protagonist realizes that she has not fed her dog in two days. Early in the novel the protagonist had spent one night as a male child in bed with a girl named Marisa, and upon being kissed, he says, "I wanted time to stop, I wanted the night never to end, I wanted the sun to be gutted."[241] Later, as a woman, she similarly describes slow-motion film as "that cinematic elixir of life that allows a second to live for twenty."[242] The rape scene serves as a bitter perversion of these romantic sentiments, a slow-motion elixir of death in which the stopping of time is a poisoned, shattering experience.

The novel's remaining pages see the narrator painfully becoming male once more, contemplating suicide, and eventually meeting a female lover, this last event suggesting an initial gesture toward healing. The final four lines, a list of banal autobiographical details titled "Chapter Two," form an abrupt end to the story – "I am thirty years old. I weigh 139 pounds ... I am Canadian. I speak English and French"[243] – with no reference to gender. That this sole chapter division occurs on page 331 out of 331 suggests that the protagonist has at long last succeeded in embarking on a new stage of life no longer dominated by the shadow of the attack, but also indicates that the first chapter, which encompasses her entire lifetime up to this point, remains dominant, unsurmounted, and inevitably complicit in what comes after.

Self has generally not fared well with critics, who have been put off by the novel's apparent aimlessness; the strange weighting of trauma near the end of the story indeed frames the majority of the narrative as a protracted rising action in such a way that the novel as a whole appears not to attain a satisfactory degree of coherence.[244] It is as though the narrative has not found its true shape, or has taken on the form of a monstrously distended short story in that the opening stages – here nearly 300 pages – are understood primarily in terms of a late revelation. This may be a

Self 287

react, to take measures. No.
I even had my boots off,
had removed them upon
entering.
  It was a long assault. It
felt as if it lasted hours. How
otherwise can I account for
so much fear? Can fear be ...... fear ..... fear .....
concentrated? Can it enter .... fear .....
your life like a few drops of
food colouring, a few drops
of red that plop in and dilute
and taint your whole life?
The problem with rape is .... fear .....
that it ruins your life, the .... fear ....
whole rest of your life,
because the fear spreads. .... fear ....
When I think back, he was
there maybe twenty minutes.
  He didn't have a knife or
a gun. He didn't need one.
He did nothing more threat-
ening than pull my hair with .... pain ....
all his strength and slap me .... pain ....
and punch me and kick me. .... pain .... pain ....
  His fist flew out and hit .... pain
me square on the cheek. I
lurched to the side and
collapsed.
  "Get up."
I did so, mechanically.

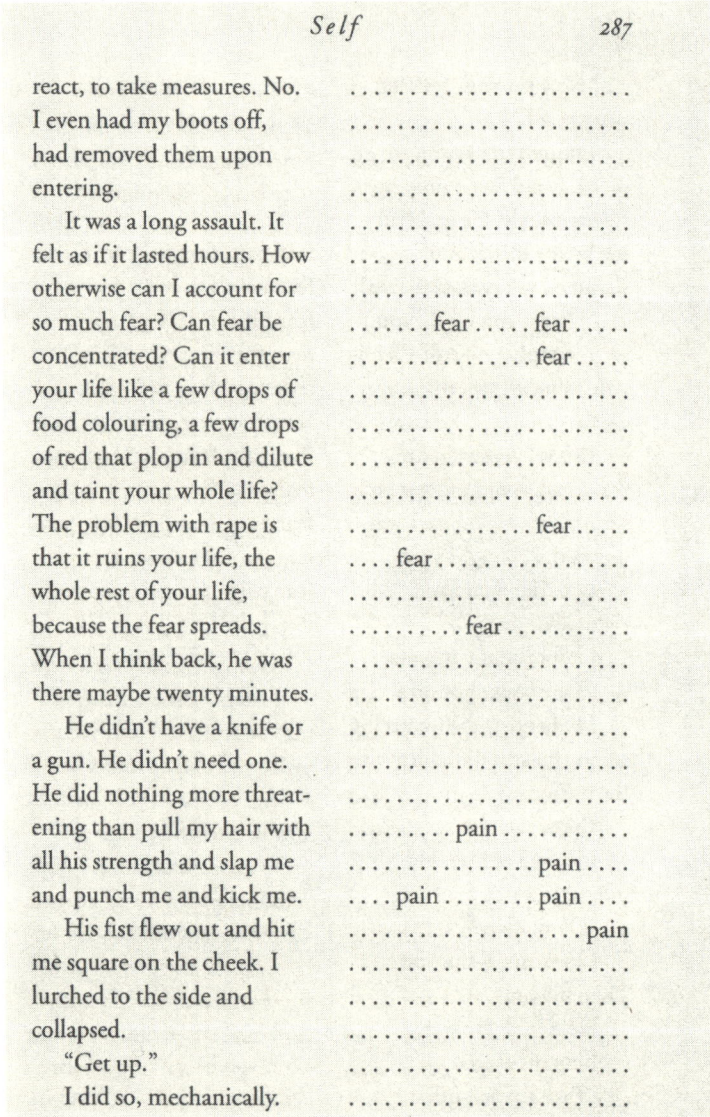

Figures 3.2a and 3.2b. Two pages from Yann Martel's *Self* (1996).

failure on Martel's part, but the peculiar narrative shape can also be read as a carefully crafted formal manipulation of plot and chronotope, a recognition of sexual assault as an explosive and devastating temporal disruption. While the largely empowering non-linear experience of queer

298 *Yann Martel*

. . . .
. . . .
. . . .
. . . .
. . . .
. . . .
. . . .
. . . .
. . . .
. . . .
. . . .
. . . .
. . . .
. . . .
. . . .
. . . .
. . . .
. . . .
. . . .
. . . .
. . . .
. . . .
. . . .
. . . .
. . . .
. . . .
. . . .
. . . .
. . . .

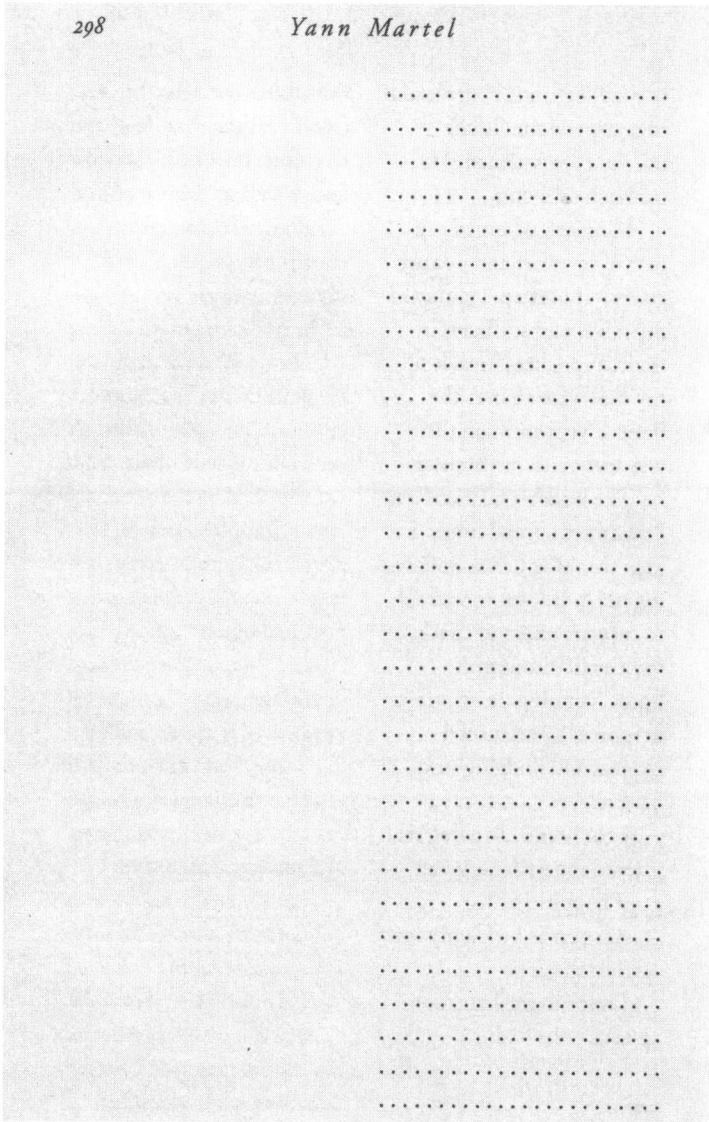

temporality through spontaneous sex-shifting is integral to the life of the protagonist before the assault, the later disruption of progressive time is a direct result of sexual violence imposed by a representative of the same masculine authority that is associated with linear time in the first place.

Chrononormativity, the novel suggests, not only fails to describe the range of human experience, but also contains the seed of its own destruction, even while it retains very strong ties to systemic social power.

The temporal dislocation that Martel's protagonist experiences as a result of the attack echoes that of Robert Ross, Timothy Findley's protagonist in his 1977 novel *The Wars*. When Robert is sexually assaulted and beaten by fellow military soldiers in a pitch-dark room near the First World War battlefields in France, he loses consciousness and along with it his sense of time: "After a while – (it might have been an hour or a minute) – he could feel the others retreating."[245] A chapter division occurs at this point, and the narrative picks up with Robert standing in a room; we do not know how much time has elapsed, and the ongoing passage of time remains obscure as each fragment of thought is broken into lines of sparse, disconnected prose:

> Robert stood in the centre of the room.
> He wanted a clean shirt.
> He wanted a clean pair of underwear.
> He wanted his pistol.
> He looked behind the door.
> He looked underneath the bed.
> He pulled out the drawers of the dresser one by one.
> He dumped them on the floor. ...
> He knelt beside the bed and ripped at the mattress, pulling out great loops of horsehair and dropping them onto the floor.
>
> He tore the ticking off the pillows and the air filled up with feathers.
>
> Gun. Gun. He wanted his gun.
>
> Somebody knocked at the door.[246]

Because the basic maintenance of human subjectivity requires continuously reinforced connections between past and present experience, the division of Robert's thoughts into repetitive disconnected fragments indicates that the very core of his identity – his temporal coherence – has been mangled.

Earlier in the novel a group of fellow soldiers in training had taken Robert with them to a brothel outside of Lethbridge, Alberta. When Robert first sees the prostitutes, Findley writes that "the women – (or girls: they were really both) – at first appeared to be dressed like actresses in a play."[247] Like the young soldiers who must take on the adult burden of military service emblematized by the official garb they wear while on duty, the prostitutes in their own garb are simultaneously young and old, children and adults. Findley is suggesting that the dangerous roles these young people find themselves in actually disrupt the normal flow of aging and time, a notion that is heightened later on in the attack – both military and sexual – that leaves Robert, and Findley's readers, dislocated in time.[248]

In *Cereus Blooms at Night*, Shani Mootoo also associates the trauma of rape with temporal dislocation. After she is raped by her father Chandin, Mala watches as her companion Ambrose runs away in terror; at that moment Mala recalls watching her mother, also terrified of Chandin, run away with no time to save her daughter, an event that happened "long ago. Today."[249] With these words Mootoo indicates that Mala's sense of time, her ability to differentiate the past from the present, has been shattered; Mala disconnects from the ongoing present and perpetually inhabits a remembered past. For the rest of her life Mala remains unable to piece the fragments of her experience into a coherent temporal order. Growing old, "she did not ascribe activities to specific times. When doziness pawed at her, she responded regardless of the time of day or night, curling up in the yard or on the verandah."[250] When the morning light in her backyard mimics the appearance of the day her mother ran away, "time would collapse," throwing her into renewed paroxysms of terror.[251]

The spectre in the late twentieth century of HIV, which appeared at first to target gay men in particular, has at times served as a focal point for artistic representations of sexuality, and the power of AIDS to cause profound suffering and severely reduce the lifespans of those affected ties the disease inevitably to experiences of time. A styrene and fibreglass art installation called *One Year of AZT / One Day of AZT* displayed in the National Gallery of Canada in 1991 portrays the antiretroviral drug AZT as a temporal monument, a statement on the way that HIV-positive status requires patients to remain perpetually hyper-conscious of their limited remaining days and their perpetual ties to the health care system.

Figure 3.3. *One Year of AZT/One Day of AZT* (General Idea, 1991).

General Idea, the artist collective behind the installation, was a collaborative project of three Toronto-based artists working under the pseudonyms
AA Bronson, Felix Partz, and Jorge Zontal.[252] Anne Newlands writes that
the installation "fills a large room, lining its walls with shiny white capsules that symbolize a year's dose of AZT, the drug alleged to impede the
spread of HIV. On the floor, five giant capsules (a day's dose) evoke futur-
istic coffins that vacillate between clinical innocence and the macabre."[253]

Time in this installation is measured solely through the required daily
dosage of drug capsules (whose blue bands along the wall appear to shift
against the line of sight, curving like the phases of the moon), reducing
each day to the repetitive act of consuming the medicine – medicine that
creates its own painful illness in the form of wide-ranging side effects.
The capsules are oppressive in their insistence on absolute temporal regularity, staring the viewer down in larger-than-life form and seeming to
erase all particularities of temporal experience, even while they hold out
the hope of allowing the person who swallows them to survive for some
precious number of additional days. When installed in the Power Plant
gallery in Toronto (see figure 3.3), the work fills a narrow corridor rather

than a more spacious room. In this configuration the installation appears to create a path – both miraculous and ominous – toward a brightly lit exit, while the capsules themselves entirely dominate (and even obstruct) the path of prolonged life that they enable. General Idea persisted as a group until 1994, when "Partz and Zontal died of AIDS-related illnesses."[254] Life expectancies for persons who test positive for HIV and have access to adequate health care have increased significantly over the last two decades to the point that AIDS is now often considered a manageable chronic condition, though HIV-positive status still ties patients to a close lifelong relationship with the health care system.

Brad Fraser's 1995 play *Poor Super Man* comments on the personal consequences of widespread social homophobia as well as the toll of HIV on infected individuals, showing that the temporal disempowerment that affects LGBTQ people through the social pressures of heteronormativity in some ways parallels the temporal trauma of AIDS itself. If AIDS is a disease that primarily affects LGBTQ individuals and reduces temporal agency, then heteronormativity functions as a figurative temporal disease, constraining the experience of time for those who are not heterosexual or cisgender. In Fraser's play, the figure of Superman, a hero who must conceal his identity every day in order to enjoy some semblance of ordinary life, comes to represent the experience of LGBTQ people who feel compelled to put on an everyday performance of heteronormativity. Shannon, a man in the process of becoming a woman, is especially sensitive to the limits of the normative social framework in which gender and sexuality are seen as permanent, essentialized identities. Commenting on a male acquaintance who is married to a woman but attracted to another man, Shannon says, "Maybe fag and lesbian aren't nouns. Maybe they're verbs."[255] This brief statement radically deconstructs the normative essentialization of sexuality, arguing that sexuality is a shifting, flexible form of identity best understood within the temporal pools of specific acts rather than as a permanently fixed binary. The statement also speaks to the dominance of heteronormativity, though, because the very terms "fag" and "lesbian" appear inevitably essentializing; the shift in linguistic usage that Shannon advocates is one that she simply cannot bring about on a large social scale.

Meanwhile, the social pressures of heteronormativity combine with the temporal losses associated with HIV; by the end of the play Shannon has died of complications from AIDS, and her companions have suffered losses of friends and personal relationships. Even Superman himself, in a newly published comic, has been killed by a monster that appears almost to be a symbol for HIV: a "nameless unknown killer with no origin and no apparent purpose except to kill Superman."[256] In the play's final moments the phrase "The Future" is projected onto the stage, prompting Shannon's friend David to say, "Goodbye";[257] the act of saying goodbye to a friend is simultaneously the act of saying goodbye to the very possibility of a desired future. As soon as the sorrow of permanent loss is acknowledged, though, one final projected caption appears before the stage fades to black: "Beginning."[258] Just as Superman's death is inevitably followed by his rebirth and reinvention, Fraser too signals a flickering hope in the idea that even while the dual crises of AIDS and homophobia are irrevocably devastating for those affected, new stories of some kind remain to be told.

The power of story itself as a method of articulating and reshaping temporal experience is central to many of the representations of gender and sexuality discussed here. Thoughtful portrayals of the consequences and complexities of such experiences demonstrate that while temporality is often closely tied to gender and sexuality, such connections inevitably shift along with changing social configurations over time. These portrayals reveal that challenges to gender inequality and homophobia can productively take the form of challenges to normative temporality, because even the acknowledgment of the non-straight character of much human temporal experience challenges the legitimacy of dominant progressive chronotopes. When it comes to experiences of time, we are all "queer" in different ways, and the empathy implied in this recognition of partially shared identity can be a powerful tool in expressing the limitations of assumed chrononormativity. At the same time, even if queer temporality is a term that can usefully describe certain forms of experience for all people, stories that articulate the fact that LGBTQ individuals experience disproportionately severe forms of temporal disempowerment also remind audiences of very real forms of discrimination and the deeply shared humanity that is at stake in structures of hierarchization. Temporal disempowerment is a form of disempowerment with which all mortal people are in some way familiar, and the recognition that certain individuals are subjected to severe temporal disempowerment within patriarchal, heteronormative societies should serve as a strong foundation for the promotion of social equity.

RACE

In *White Civility*, Daniel Coleman traces how the concept of civility functions historically in Canada to combine "*the temporal notion* of civilization as progress" with "*the moral-ethical concept* of a (relatively) peaceful order."[259] He discusses the prominent belief in Canada in the late nineteenth and early twentieth centuries that "some societies were farther ahead on the single timeline of civilization, while others were 'backward' or delayed," and finds that racialization was closely linked to this distinction, as "the idea of progress itself is deeply informed by a central value of whiteness."[260] As Coleman points out with reference to Imre Szeman's research on time and globalization, "this dense interweaving of White enterprise and civility as progress insists upon an isochronous temporality (i.e., a single timeline); it does not consider the possibilities of 'allochrony,' that different civilizations might operate on different temporal scales of progress, ingress, or regress."[261] The alignment of whiteness with progress and non-whiteness with backwardness is a central problem in the ongoing history of settler-Indigene relations in Canada, and one that I will examine in the next chapter; for the moment, though, I will investigate the articulation within literary texts of how dominant Canadian ideologies have reinforced temporal disempowerment for non-Indigenous racialized minorities. As we have seen in other cases, the social politics of time connect with categorizations of race in two significant ways: first, the large social chronotope of civilizational progress tends specifically to cast non-white societies as backward, a conclusion that, in many cases, seemingly justifies inequitable treatment; and second, firsthand experiences of racist discrimination, whether such discrimination is tied to the ideologies of social chronotopes or to some other ostensible justification, often result in experiences of temporal disempowerment.

Lawrence Hill's novel *The Book of Negroes* illustrates how the eighteenth-century slave trade aligns the dominance of Western models of time with hierarchies of racialization. Aminata Diallo is born in the village of Bayo in West Africa, but as a child she is captured, sold to white slave traders, and sent to North America where she gradually internalizes the English model of time, using Gregorian numerical years in place of her earlier temporal concept of "rains." Her description of the physical layout of an American town mirrors the way in which Western linear time imposes a rigidly progressive structure over cyclical seasonal changes:

"In my homeland, the towns I knew were set up in a circle so everybody could be together. In this place, people walked off in all directions, taking dusty roads running either side by side or at sharp angles to one another. I didn't believe I could ever find my way in such a place."[262] She grows to understand Western temporal and spatial concepts, but she also becomes trapped within them, as symbolized by the badge she must wear in public stamped with her Anglicized name, Meena, and the Gregorian year, 1762.[263] Upon running away from her captor during the chaos of erupting violence between American rebels and the British, Aminata declares, "It was late in the afternoon of April 23, 1775, and I had taken back my freedom,"[264] her internalization of the English language and Gregorian time casting an ironic light on this assertion. Her oppressive experiences as a "free" person in Nova Scotia, where the wait for restitution and equality appears endless, reinforce the fact that the obstacles to freedom are not just legal, but deeply social, and are highly resistant to change even over the period of a lifetime. Slave traders themselves, meanwhile, justify their profession by venerating the linear model of cultural progress, arguing that the civilizing influence of the slave trade "saves Africans from barbarity."[265]

During her time in slavery, Aminata's questioning of the nature of enslavement is often expressed in temporal terms; she wonders if her captor "owned me at all times, or only when I was working for him. Did he own me when I slept? When I dreamed?"[266] She comes to describe slavery itself as a condition of temporal impoverishment: "That, I decided, was what it meant to be a slave: your past didn't matter; in the present you were invisible and you had no claim on the future,"[267] a statement that resonates with Northrop Frye's comment that "the deeper forms of human dignity and self-respect are bound up with whatever seems to connect the past with the future."[268] Aminata's vow, in the face of this oppression, to remember her past, becomes a potent form of resistance, perhaps the only one available to her during much of her enslavement. Her eventual autobiographical act, then, in which she has the authority to narrativize and publicize her own personal timeline, is a symbolic reclamation of temporal authority, even while it is written, inevitably, in the English language.[269]

The temporal-racial categorizations that allowed for the justification of slavery have, of course, evolved in various ways over the centuries.

Examining social discourse of the early twentieth century, Daniel Coleman and Donald Goellnicht understand the social Darwinist method of hierarchization as a system of knowledge that "allowed turn-of-the-century Canadian nationalists to advocate racist immigration and Indian policies without considering them racist."[270] E.W. MacBride's 1902 article in the *McGill University Magazine*, for instance, divides humanity into apparently natural racialized categories ranging from primitive to advanced, making unequal treatment appear not only acceptable, but necessary:

> The primitive type of man at present existing is the Negro, who, like the Apes most nearly allied to Man, is essentially a tropical animal, and does not flourish in cold countries … As the Negro race, however, spread, it gradually reached the temperate regions, and here the struggle with Nature became fiercer and the whole civilization underwent development and a higher type of man – the yellow or Mongolian race was evolved … [Eventually] the highest type of man was evolved – the Nordic type or white man.[271]

In his memoir *Paper Shadows*, Wayson Choy recalls his childhood in Vancouver's Chinatown during the Second World War, and highlights the anti-Chinese practices that were implicit in Canadian social structures, as well as those explicitly enforced by the Head Tax (which demanded a large financial penalty from Chinese immigrants to Canada from 1885 to 1923) and the Exclusion Act (which denied such immigration altogether, with few exceptions, from 1923 to 1947). Choy's descriptions of Chinatown life reveal that significant temporal inequalities are intertwined with these legal and social race-based exclusions; the implementation of the Head Tax itself marks the end of a specific period of time in which Chinese immigrant labour was considered desirable for the dangerous work of building the Canadian Pacific Railway. "After the 'Last Spike' of 1885," Choy writes, "the pioneer Chinese labourers' usefulness ended. Instead of finding themselves returned to China, as many had been promised, thousands of railway labourers, and some women who worked as prostitutes, were betrayed and abandoned in near-poverty."[272] While immigrants from Britain were granted Canadian domicile after three years, the time that Chinese immigrants invested in building Canadian infrastructure did not result in equal status. "Until after the

Second World War," Choy writes, "no Chinese, even those born in Canada, like me, were given citizenship: I was a *Resident Alien*, forbidden to vote or to enter any profession, including law, teaching, medicine and engineering."[273] Rocío Davis points out that even the physical segregation implicit in the boundedness of the Chinatown neighbourhood establishes a perpetual sense of disconnection from Canadian society for young residents: "Chinatown constantly reminds these children that they are considered Chinese, even as the context of the site ... beckons to the children as, in a sense, their true place."[274]

Wayson's father, Toy, whose Chineseness severely restricts his employment options, finds work on a steamship carrying goods between Vancouver and other ports along the west coast; throughout Wayson's childhood, Toy's work schedule requires that he be away from home for weeks at a time. "When Father came home," Choy writes, "he seemed more a visitor to me than a parent."[275] The transience of Toy's presence in his own household goes hand in hand with exceptionally long workdays, and Choy recalls that "the combination of twelve- to fourteen-hour shifts, cramped working conditions and the superior attitudes of his white supervisors created in him a bursting rage that he had to struggle hard to contain."[276] Still, Choy points out, "many Chinatown fathers were away for long periods, earning money in lumbering and fishing camps, so I didn't feel too deprived."[277] The separation of family members over long periods of time becomes, for Chinese immigrants, a normal state of affairs.

These labour-based separations are themselves fleeting compared with the longer-term segregation of Chinatown's inhabitants from those family members who remain in China. Recalling his various "uncles" – men who have left their families behind in the hopes of earning enough money in Canada to finance their collective futures – Choy describes the years of loneliness these men faced. People in Chinatown

spoke of the day when they would be reunited with their families. Tragically, the passing of the 1890s Chinese Head Tax, a tax raised from fifty dollars to five hundred dollars by 1904, had proved prohibitive for those who earned seasonal wages of twenty-five cents an hour. After Parliament's passing of the Exclusion Act of 1923, which forbade any Chinese from immigrating to Canada, except for a few merchants or scholars, Vancouver's Chinatown entered what historian David C. Lai has called "the withering stage."[278]

Recalling his "Third Uncle" in particular, Choy notes that this man had not seen his wife and son in Hong Kong for seven years, and that "it would be another ten before they would reunite."[279]

Regardless of the families they may have left behind in China, these Chinatown men are referred to perpetually as "bachelor men"; impoverished wages and ongoing restrictions on immigration prevent the arrival of existing or potential wives, effectively freezing the men within a stage of life normally considered temporary. Choy recalls that "when they weren't labouring, many of the bachelor men gambled, socialized, drank and fought, kept women or kept to themselves – did what men might do to keep their sexual and mental sanity, separated these five, ten, twenty years from their wives and children."[280] One way for the men to cope with "the empty hours they faced in cell-like tenement rooms" is to entertain neighbourhood children like Wayson, hence their status as "uncles."[281] All the while, a sense of what Coleman calls Diasporic Displacement Time – in which "cultural groups retain their image of themselves in time by reference to the trauma of displacement"[282] – pervades the experience of Chinatown's immigrant inhabitants, whose wish to return to China remains potent throughout their lives, and even after death. "Spirits wait for the war to end," Wayson's aunt explains. "Wait to go back to family."[283]

Intertwined with these descriptions of immigrant life is the story of Choy's remembered childhood, which itself is framed against the discovery many years later that his parents are in fact adoptive, not biological. "The past, as I knew it, began to shift," he writes upon being told that his mother is not his "real" mother.[284] Reacting to the person who has broken this news to him, he asks, "Where should I begin?"[285] – a question that could be called the central inquiry of the book, as it highlights the thematic suggestion that despite the constraints of mortality, a human life has no clear beginning or end but extends into ranges of complex relationships with ancestors, descendants, and other ghostly presences. This theme finds its material incarnation in the tassel that the young Wayson recovers from a discarded Chinatown wind chime; the tassel has "a beautiful knotted design in the middle of it," which Fifth Aunty describes as the traditional Chinese icon of "the endless knot."[286] When Wayson asks why it has no end, she replies, "Oh, stupid boy ... Life like that! Love like that! Everything like that!"[287] Later on, at the end of his reminiscences, Choy writes: "All lives are ten *times* ten thousand secrets. Even those who are quite sure of themselves, they, too, are made up of mystery, defined by secrets told and untold. Whose life, I wonder, is not an endless knot?"[288] Choy's life story is wrapped up in the secrets of false family names acquired for immigration purposes, his own adoption kept silent by his entire Chinatown community, and unspoken encounters with various kinds of ghosts – yet his concluding thought indicates that all lives involve concealed relationships and hauntings whose conse- quences reverberate forwards and backwards through time. His memoir, then, is a narrative of how every life is an endless temporal knot, even while it tells the particular story of how racist exclusions have fractured the experience of time for many Chinese Canadians.

Racist categorizations not only fracture temporal experience for indi- viduals, but also are themselves subject to ruptures and mutations over time. Following theorists such as Stuart Hall, Coleman notes that racial and ethnic terminology "floats, changing in salience with the context. One day you're a Canadian citizen, after Pearl Harbour you're an Enemy Alien Japanese; you've long been considered Black Irish, but when you compete for a job with African Americans, suddenly you're White; one day you're a Canadian citizen, after September 11, 2001 you're an Islamic terrorist."[289] The grounding for the selection of racial categories changes over time "from genetic ancestry to national heritage to religious history to political form – all within a generalized, assumed discourse of civility."[290]

The sudden identification, during the Second World War, of Japa- nese Canadians as Enemy Aliens is portrayed most memorably in Joy Kogawa's novel *Obasan*. Like *Paper Shadows*, *Obasan* affords a central position to the temporal disjunctures and disempowerments associated with racist exclusions, but, more intensely than Choy, Kogawa empha- sizes the lasting damage of traumatic events that reverberate through time. Naomi, who narrates from her present in the 1970s, establishes a frame narrative through which she remembers the persecution of her family during the war. Reading through her Aunt Emily's journal entries from 1942, Naomi recalls the rapid imposition of social policies limiting the freedom of Canadians of Japanese descent. While the most notorious policies eventually called for Japanese Canadians to be dispossessed of their homes and relocated to distant camps, one of the first signals of these looming exclusions is the initiation of a decidedly temporal restriction. "A curfew that applies only to us was started a few days ago," Emily writes. "If we're caught out after sundown, we're thrown in jail. People who have been fired – and there's a scramble on to be the first to kick us out of jobs – sit at home without even being able to go out for a consoling cup of coffee ... We look in the papers for the time of next morning's sunrise when we may venture forth."[291] Strict temporal limits on the activity of Japanese Canadians work in concert with the enforcing of strict spatial limits during internment, and the two types of restrictions are mutually amplifying. Naomi recalls a newspaper article from 1948 announcing that the House of Commons has voted to extend the duration of the spatial restriction by one more year, emphasizing the malleable temporal nature of place-based policy.[292] The article quotes one Member of Parliament as saying that "the government was wise in giving the old sores another year to heal."[293] "Another year?" Naomi thinks to herself. "Which year should we choose for our healing? Restrictions against us are removed on April Fool's Day, 1949. But the 'old sores' remain."[294] Highlighting the temporally unstable nature of racist anxiety itself, Naomi comments, "In one breath we are damned for being 'inassimilable' and the next there's fear that we'll assimilate."[295]

As Naomi describes the traumatic events that occurred during her childhood – the forced evacuation of her family from Vancouver, as well as the agonizing death of her mother in the aftermath of the atomic bombing in Nagasaki – the central problem of the novel comes to light: how can Naomi and her family learn to cope with a devastating past that cannot be erased? "Life is so short ... the past so long. Shouldn't we turn the page and move on?" Naomi asks Emily. "The past is the future," Emily replies.[296] Naomi herself is haunted by a dream in which she and her unnamed companions "toil together in the timelessness," in a mysterious place where "the endlessness of labour has entered our limbs."[297] Significantly, Kogawa never offers a clear resolution to Naomi's temporal entrapment; the act of narration itself, though, creates some degree of solace, as the process of recalling the past works gradually toward the idea, if not the complete realization, of acceptance. "You have to remember," Aunt Emily says. "You are your history. If you cut any of it off you're an amputee. Don't deny the past. Remember everything."²⁹⁸ Ben Lefebvre expands a similar perspective to encompass not only *Obasan* (by far Kogawa's most discussed book) but also the larger body of her collected works of fiction. While "reconciliation would necessitate a forgetting, a turning of the page," Lefebvre writes, the tendency of Kogawa's narrator-protagonists to engage in an ongoing "struggle to transform their traumatic memories into trauma narratives" suggests that "Kogawa's seven works of fiction can all be read as part of an ongoing process of mastery and control as one part of the healing process."²⁹⁹

As they continue to trace Canada's vacillating history of racialization, Coleman and Goellnicht note:

> With the defeat of Nazism and the discrediting of eugenics in the postwar period, Canada in the midcentury decades of the 1950s and 1960s turned gradually away from race-based legislation and policy … All discriminatory laws against Asian immigrants were repealed by midcentury, and the 1967 Immigration Act "liberalized" immigration from Third World countries, thus leading to a rapid increase in racialized minority populations, especially in Canada's large urban centres, during the next decade.³⁰⁰

Canada became well known in the late twentieth century for its official endorsement of multiculturalism, a policy that has served as a source of national pride even while it has been criticized, ironically, for homogenizing the differences between the cultural groups under its purview. Racialized divisions, both long-standing and evolving, remain potent sites of contested power relations. In M.G. Vassanji's novel *No New Land*, the Lalanis, a family of Indian descent, reflect on having moved to Canada three years previously. "The children were well on their way," Vassanji writes, "'Canadians' now, or almost."³⁰¹ The structure of this simple statement – the hesitancy of the quotation marks around "Canadians," the back-pedalling of the "almost" – reveals that the process of transcending racial divisions is exactly that: a process, a continuous negotiation of obstructions.

Dionne Brand's work is among the most eloquent recent writing in bearing witness to experiences of racialization, and as a member of the African-Caribbean diaspora she is particularly conscious of the disconnections – spatial, social, and temporal – associated with being cut off from one's origins. Like some of the other figures discussed here, Brand experiences a form of Diasporic Displacement Time in which her present is always informed by the remembered trauma of displacement, yet in Brand's case the memory is inaccessible and therefore unavoidably imaginative. The moment in which her African ancestors boarded slave trading ships, she writes, initiates "a rupture in history, a rupture in the quality of being."[302] She recalls asking her grandfather the name of the people in Africa from whom they are descended, and being deeply disappointed by his inability to extend his memory back to the time before the rupture. "Having no name to call on," she writes, "was having no past; having no past pointed to the fissure between the past and the present. That fissure is represented in the Door of No Return."[303] Of course, *every* moment in time is a door of no return; there is always an irrevocable fissure between past and present. The difference, for Brand, is that as an unwilling diasporan she has been cut off violently even from *looking* back. For Brand, this door "signifies the historical moment which colours all moments in the Diaspora";[304] the watershed moment upon which her experience of time centres itself is a direct product of racist colonialism, and continues to resonate long after the institutionalization, in her adopted home, of official multiculturalism. Vikki Visvis argues that the ongoing experience of oppression for Black people in the Americas means that the past can be unrecoverable not only because of what Brand calls the Door of No Return, but also because the lack of "a safe place to remember and ameliorate trauma" turns the very process of recollection into "a luxury unavailable to the socially marginalized."[305] Brand's comments on this problem are strikingly similar to those of M. NourbeSe Philip, in her essay "Taming Our Tomorrows," where she writes:

For us Africans in the New World tomorrow is a constant problem. We are the only group brought forcibly and unwillingly to the New World, this touted utopia, to help create utopias for others. Cut off from our yesterdays – in fact told that we had no yesterdays, no history – forbidden to live out the promise of the tomorrows of progress of which the New World boasted, we were and still are condemned to a today in which we are intended to be nothing but hewers of wood and drawers of water.

In an odd and disturbing way, time stands still for us Africans. Sometimes it even repeats itself. The promise of tomorrow never comes. Consequently time and its representations present a constant challenge. This is all the more ironic for the fact that African cultures understand in profound ways the fluidity and non-linearity of time.[306]

The problem of time and its representations – of past disconnections that continue to shape the present – remains a relentless one for Brand and Philip.

Brand's first novel, *In Another Place, Not Here*, takes up the relationships between racialization, diasporic displacement, and temporal fragmentation; like her poetry collection *Land to Light On*, the title of the novel portrays connection to place as inevitably fragile and temporary. The first section of the novel follows Elizete, an indentured plantation worker in the Caribbean who has been cut off from her African ancestry. "Nobody here can remember when they wasn't here," Elizete says, her experience of temporal dislocation resembling that of Brand herself.[307] A person in this position, Elizete tells us, "needed history, something before this place, something that this place cut off";[308] she inhabits the paradoxical position of centring her experience on a past that cannot be remembered. Her oppressors, meanwhile, "who measured time in the future only and who discarded memory like useless news,"[309] are invested in ensuring that the past remains cut off, since a progress-oriented legacy of wealth built on racist colonialism can sustain itself only through a wilful denial of past injustice. The lack of belonging that Elizete experiences as a result of this temporal dislocation finds its symbolic counterpart in the chewed paths of wood lice etched into the wall of her temporary dwelling place: "She tried to trace them home, yet perhaps home was these paths, she thought, or their way of not being seen, waiting and listening."[310] The drawn-out experience of a lack of belonging gradually becomes its own form of belonging, yet one centred on watchfulness and anxiety.

The second half of *In Another Place, Not Here* follows Elizete's lover Verlia, who, not held in slavery herself, tries to convince the plantation workers to stage a revolution. Frustrated by her companions' obsession with the irrecoverable past, Verlia wishes to escape the constraints of temporal existence altogether, a contradictory desire that threatens to tear her apart. She "fears that any mortal self is heavy and persistent, full of presentness, which jostles the air and is unpleasant ... She'd like to live, exist or be herself in some other place, less confining, less pinned down, less tortuous, less fleshy to tell the truth."[311] While Elizete's feeling of disconnection causes her endlessly to seek "another place" so that the wandering itself becomes a kind of uneasy home, Verlia's "other place" lies beyond the temporal confines of mortal existence itself. The present for Verlia is "a waiting room," a temporary stopover on the way to somewhere else.[312] When Verlia spends time in Toronto trying to advance the cause of the revolutionary struggle for racial justice, we see that her ambitions are twofold: she aims to turn the slave plantation into a cooperative organization, and to promote self-determination for Black North Americans. Her personal desire to be "less pinned down" mirrors her political philosophy, which holds "that it was possible to leap, it had to be, out of the compulsion of things as they are or things as you might have met them."[313]

This image of leaping becomes a prominent theme in the narrative, and signals Verlia's desire to escape the long history of racist exploitation by which present reality is constrained. When Abena, Verlia's lover and fellow activist, warns that the revolutionary struggle must proceed at a slower pace, that "you can't be ahead of the people," Verlia responds, "It's never going to be the time ... When the hell is the time? You have to leap sometimes don't you? Sometimes you have to be ahead?"[314] Tormented by her inability to pull time forward into a moment when her politics will be fulfilled, Verlia repeatedly expresses her frustration in terms of temporal blockages. Recalling Macbeth's tirade against the futility of human temporal existence, Brand writes, "She didn't want to wake up tomorrow and tomorrow and tomorrow feeling the same, in the same spot."[315] For racial injustice to be extinguished, Verlia admits, "so much would have to have not happened. It's like a life sentence. Call it what we want – colonialism, imperialism – it's a fucking life sentence. Nobody I come from knows these words but they do the time. You can't catch five fucking minutes of sleep without it, you can't drink a beer, some fucking breeze passes over your lips smelling of molasses."[316]

It is perhaps this realization that partially motivates Verlia's final act in the novel, an act that embraces her own capacity to "leap" into a different time and place even while it gruesomely accentuates her failure to halt the broader historical time of racial injustice. Caught up in an American bombing raid on Grenada, being driven back by gunfire, Verlia runs at the edge of a cliff and leaps toward the sea. The novel ends with: "She's leaping … Her body has fallen away, is just a line, an electric current, the sign of lightning left after lightning, a faultless arc to the deep turquoise deep. She doesn't need air. She's in some other place already, less tortuous, less fleshy."[317] The leap takes Verlia beyond the physical and temporal constraints of her own existence, but comes at the cost of her life. This event recalls the ending of Morris Panych's play *7 Stories*, in which the unnamed man, lamenting his imprisonment in the days of the week, jumps from the seventh story of an apartment building. But while Panych's character *decides* to jump and falls *up*, embodying the potential to escape the constraints of social time, Verlia's deadly jump is necessitated by brutal American gunfire. For Vikki Visvis, even though Verlia's leap fulfills her earlier wish "for a place devoid of social oppression," it is ultimately "bereft of agency and suggests an act of subjugation."[318] Verlia remains caught in the literal and figurative gravity of her world and its long-standing histories, even while the tone of triumph with which her death is narrated highlights the elation of her control, however limited, over her own temporal destiny. Verlia's effort to resist oppressive temporal experience is remarkable, even if it cannot overcome the fact that, as she admits to herself in a diary entry, "five-hundred years is a long time to undo."[319]

SOCIAL RELATIONS AND TEMPORAL RESISTANCE

The works considered in this chapter show that the ties between social power structures and temporal experiences run profoundly deep; that forms of social hierarchization focused on age, class, race, gender, sexuality, and other categories are complicit in the reduction of temporal agency for individuals; that social chronotopes are frequently implicated in systemic forms of inequity in Canada, even while forms of social injustice that cause temporal disempowerment have many additional complex causes and justifications; and that time itself is a socially constructed site where power is enacted and agency is negotiated. These works give insight into the possibilities of temporal resistance, whether through the delight that Anne Shirley takes in transgressing the confines of the adult world of clocks and schedules, through the mockery that Tom Wayman makes of purely efficient industrialized time, or through the bitter but triumphant leap that Verlia takes to escape a present shaped by long histories of exploitation. As Verlia's leap makes clear, though, even those authors who find promise in 'temporal resistance have often been highly conscious of the constraints such resistance faces in the form of past events, social discord, categories of identity, voices of authority, and the inevitable passage of time itself. Temporal resistance both responds to and highlights the existence of temporal discrimination.

Many Canadian authors – in fact, all authors – have borne witness to, if not attempted to recalibrate, the dominant cultural clocks that tick around and within them. But whether texts are speaking from within unexamined temporal structures or explicitly questioning the role of time in subjectivity and social relations, critical time studies equips us to ask questions such as "What does this text assume (and what do we assume) about how time functions in society?" or "How does this text question (and how can we question) the way that dominant structures of time and individual temporal experiences reflect relations of power?" Exemplary texts such as those discussed here are particularly useful in teaching us how to read time critically through social relations, and to read social relations critically through time. In chapter 5 I will examine M. NourbeSe Philip's attempt to imagine a reconstruction of the history that prompts Verlia's leap. First, though, I will turn to the temporal issues surrounding Indigenous identities in Canada.

4

Imagining Indigenous Temporalities

The Elvis clock says the time is seven-thirty, but it's always either an hour ahead or an hour behind. We always joke that it's on Indian time.[1]

Eden Robinson

Talk to her of post-modern deconstructivism
She'll say, "What took you so long?"[2]

Beth Cuthand

In chapter 1 I briefly traced the idea that Indigenous representations of time tend to emphasize the circular or concentric shape of temporal existence. In the words of Wendat scholar Georges Sioui,

> The Circle is at the centre of our Aboriginal thinking ... We believe that the day, the lunar month, the year, even human life itself, are circular phenomena, and that there are cycles of many years, representing the circular reality. We also believe that all circular phenomena have four parts, or movements: spring, summer, fall and winter; morning, noon hour, evening and nighttime; infancy, youth, maturity and old age. Also, most things in nature are round, or rounded: the sun, the earth, the moon; the rocks, after prolonged action of the elements; plants, trees, fruits, seeds, vegetables, the bodies of humans and animals, the nests of birds, their eggs – in brief, almost everything is round.[3]

There is something compelling about Sioui's sense of conviction, but part of the danger in speaking about "the" or "our" Aboriginal way of thinking is that such language homogenizes diverse individuals associated with many different First Nations, Inuit, or Métis identities. As Daniel Heath Justice says, Indigenous literary traditions speak through many voices, and "insistence on artificial purity erases the real and valid life experiences of many Indigenous people throughout the Americas, and it assumes a static, monolithic Native identity that belies the diversity of history and experience of the thousands of Indigenous Nations in this hemisphere."[4] Still, Sioui's claim that "all along, our societies have faced an ideological impasse because of our different understanding of time, of history, therefore, of life,"[5] has much to offer in a consideration of how contested temporalities have functioned in settler-Indigenous relations. Indeed, if Sioui is correct, divergent representations of time are in fact central to the long history of settler-Indigenous conflict and misunderstanding. But it is important to remember that no single "understanding" of time is adequate to represent the views of all people of Indigenous (or European) descent. Bearing this limitation in mind I will trace some of the differing representations of time, and contested visions of the place of Indigenous peoples within time, that have been advanced in what is now called Canada. My aims here are to show how these models have both informed and resisted the embattled history of settler-Indigenous relations, to identify how temporal discrimination is closely tied to the ongoing colonialist project, to recognize Indigenous representations of time as meaningful in their own right and not merely as "others" to the Western norms, to emphasize the limitations of the supposed distinction between circular and linear models of time, and to identify literary works that have questioned and reshaped representations of Indigenous temporality.

This latter concern is especially crucial. While Canadian society has a long history of framing Indigenous nations as relics of an outdated past, Beth Cuthand's comment in "Post-Oka Kinda Woman" that serves as an epigraph for this chapter implies that it is in fact the mainstream Euro-descended majority, and not the Indigenous world, that is delayed in its conceptual progress and development toward insight. Cuthand's post-Oka woman is emboldened with a new sense of confidence and political strength after witnessing the intense physical resistance of the Mohawk community in Oka, Quebec during the famous land dispute in 1990, and, as a result, she now refuses to be silenced in asserting her own temporal and political perspective. The marginalization to which Indigenous people in Canada have been subjected, this poem suggests, long ago endowed them with the strong sense of irony and critical questioning that mainstream Canadian society has adopted only slowly and belatedly through the Western concepts associated with postmodernism. Cuthand's statement thus radically reorients the dominant sense of Indigenous out-datedness as well as the assumed notion that the settler society is the more advanced one. As a result, the temporal character of settler-Indigene relations themselves is also cast in a significant new light. Of course, like the "post" in the term "post-colonial," the "post" in "Post-Oka Kinda Woman" turns two ways: it declares that the woman has moved beyond the forms of conflict with dominant authority emblematized by the Oka Crisis, but also suggests that she remains haunted and partially defined by this confrontation. The ability of Cuthand's post-Oka woman to reframe received temporal relations cannot be absolute, yet her statement illustrates how literature itself can function as a critical tool in the ongoing projects of temporal resistance and decolonization.

The promise, and the limitations, of temporal resistance in "Post-Oka Kinda Woman" can be seen as a reflection of the important work that contemporary Indigenous literature is carrying out more broadly, not only to counter the notion that Indigenous societies are stuck in the doomed backwaters of civilization, but also to dismantle and rearticulate the most basic, and damaging, temporal assumptions that have coloured settler-Indigene relations in Canada and North America for such a long time. The later sections of this chapter are especially concerned with this project, arguing that contemporary Indigenous literature plays a vital role in countering the forms of temporal discrimination that have targeted Indigenous societies, and advocating for the self-conscious adjustment of everyday language, especially that of the Canadian Euro-descended majority, for the purpose of resisting temporal discrimination and recontextualizing the temporal relations between Canadian society and the original inhabitants of the land.

BEYOND CIRCULAR AND LINEAR MODES

Just as the idea of time cannot be reduced to a singular form or expression within any diverse society, the much-discussed distinction between linear and circular time is also tied to significant oversimplifications. The linear model of time – whether we know it through the language of civility, progress, economic growth, Imperial Time, or so on – is inevitably inflected with circular experiences, and vice versa. As Barbara Adam writes, "It is essential to appreciate that all social processes display aspects of both linearity and cyclicity, and that we recognize a cyclical structure when we focus on events that repeat themselves and unidirectional linearity when our attention is on the process of the repeating action. Whether we 'see' linearity or cyclicity depends upon the framework of observation and interpretation."[6] Nevertheless, linear and circular chronotopes remain powerful images that hold great influence over how people "see" the nature of temporal experience. The conceptual grip of circular thought is evident in Georges Sioui's statement that "the Circle is at the centre of our Aboriginal thinking," while the conceptual grip of linear thought tied especially to contemporary economics is equally evident in Fredric Jameson's famous observation that "it is easier to imagine the end of the world than the end of capitalism";[7] in this vision the straight progression of linear advancement would come to a complete end before it would dare take on an alternative shape. As a result of the power of these chronotopes, an examination of Indigenous temporalities and settler-Indigene temporal relations must take the history of circular and linear modes into account, while also developing methods of moving beyond the limitations of this distinction. In this section I trace the significance of circular models of time and the social dialogue between circular and linear modes, and propose conceptual tools for complicating this troubled binary in the service of resisting temporal discrimination.

Inuit artist Kenojuak Ashevak's lithograph titled *Nunavut (Our Land)* offers a striking visual representation of cyclical time. Anne Newlands writes that Ashevak

was commissioned in 1992 by the Department of Indian Affairs and Northern Development to produce a work to commemorate the signing ceremony for the Tungavik Federation of Nunavut Settlement Agreement in Iqaluit in 1993. Unusual for its narrative structure, *Nunavut (Our Land)* is a round lithograph. In the centre of the Inuit universe, the sun and the moon reign eternal throughout the changing seasons, overseeing the cycle of life on the land, where igloos give

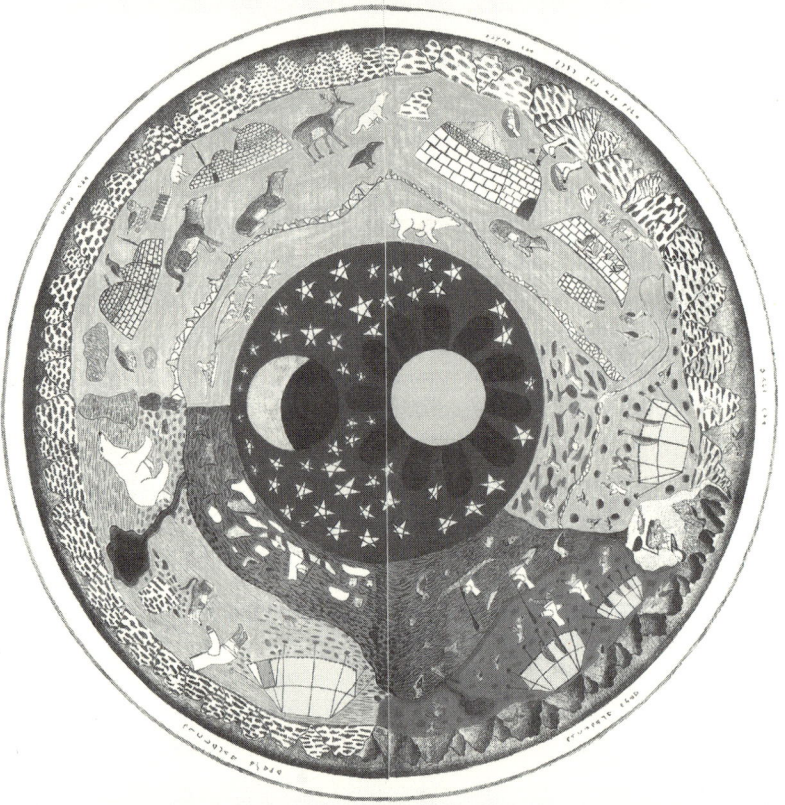

Figure 4.1. *Nunavut (Our Land)* (Kenojuak Ashevak, 1992). Lithograph-hand-coloured watercolour.

way to snow tents and ice melts to water for kayaking and fishing. The distant mountains circle the land, declaring the homeland for Inuit of the eastern Arctic.[8]

While the image is indeed structured as a form of narrative, the circularity of the sequence confounds those who may expect the traditional Western narrative shape of beginning, middle, and end. Instead of offering a single starting point, the image reveals that the entire story is always already being enacted. Every point along the outside lies at an equal distance from the point of orientation at the centre, and no "moment" in the narrative fades into the past, even if viewers may focus on one particular area at a time. The time represented here can be understood both as an eternal "now" and as a cyclical vision emphasizing endless recurrence. Consciously or not, viewers may find themselves rotating their heads in a circular motion to try to orient themselves to the elements that appear upside down, or wishing that they could rotate the lithograph itself. Sioui's belief that European linear thought is foreign to Indigenous representations of circular time and reality finds an eloquent expression here in the absence of straight lines and corners.

Poet and editor Peter Sanger has also described the circular form of narrative that is central to traditionally oral cultures, a feature that is especially significant when we recall Paul Ricoeur's belief that the construction of narrative is inextricably connected to the human experience of temporality. In 2007, Sanger, along with Elizabeth Paul, released a volume called *The Stone Canoe*, which contains Mi'kmaq and English transcriptions of two "lost" Mi'kmaq stories from the nineteenth century. The first of these stories, told in 1847 by Mi'kmaq storyteller Susan Barss, and recorded on paper by the missionary Silas Tertius Rand, tells about Little Thunder's quest to find a wife with exuberant help from the figure whom Elizabeth Paul translates as "Wolverine." This story, Sanger notes, "is probably the earliest piece of indigenous Canadian literature recorded in its original language."[9] Sanger explains that various aspects of the story may appear odd to anglophone readers, not only because of the quirks of translation that inevitably run through the English version of the text, but because of the very shape of the narrative. Storytellers within an oral culture would not conceptualize a story as a linear narrative running from left to right, leading the reader down the page toward a conclusion; instead, Sanger suggests, such storytellers would shape their narratives by drawing on other forms of human interaction with the world – forms based on the idea of *process*. Such a narrative should not be approached with the assumption that a series of rising actions will progress toward a climax, but rather should be thought of as taking the form of a continuous or circular process such as the weaving of a basket.[10] In the case of the 1847 story, while anglophone readers may expect the story to conclude after Little Thunder acquires his new bride, Barss's narration continues beyond this event, relating how Little Thunder retraces the steps of his journey, staying overnight at all of the places where he had stayed during the first half of his quest before finally arriving back home. The story ends where it begins.

Sanger also suggests that the mythical time in which Barss's story takes place is connected, through the traditional Mi'kmaq storytelling mode, to the literal present time in which the story is spoken. The words with which Barss begins her story – *Wikijik kisiku'k* – become, through Elizabeth Paul's English translation, "The old people are encamped."[11] By figuring the live audience of the storytelling performance – the listeners assembled around the storyteller – into the narrative itself, this "formulaic beginning for a Mi'kmaq legend"[12] highlights what Sanger calls the "immediate presence" of the mythic time of the story.[13] The temporal structure of the myth, then, does not relegate it to a linear "past" that is over and done with; rather, the events of the story and the "literal" present moment are mutually enacted within one another. Sanger compares this perpetual making-present of mythological events to the framework of Christian belief within which the figure of Christ is "eternally present"[14] – a fascinating comment that highlights one way in which structural similarities may exist between the mythic forms of different cultures. These mythic temporalities, though, still allow and require sequences of events that occur one after another: at first Little Thunder does not have a wife, but later he does. All of this suggests that while Indigenous and Western models of time may emphasize different aspects of circularity or linearity, structural similarities run deep within these modes so that each culture inhabits a time that is *simultaneously* circular and linear.

These different emphases come to light in various ways, but one of the most interesting accounts comes from the early twentieth-century American anthropologist A. Irving Hallowell, who attempted at various times to immerse himself in Indigenous culture. In the summer of 1932 he spent several months living with residents of the Pikangikum or Saulteaux nation, a branch of the Ojibwe people, on the Berens River east of Lake Winnipeg. While anthropologists, in Anne Fausto-Sterling's words, "must invent categories into which they can sort collected information" – a process that inevitably draws from "the anthropologists' own unquestioned axioms of life"[15] – Hallowell is remarkably sensitive to the legitimacy of cultural structures different from his own. While we would not want to consider his outsider's account to be a definitive description of what he calls "Saulteaux" culture – the word itself is a European ethnographic marker – we can see within his remarks an attempt to transcend the ethnocentric racism that has plagued many other such accounts. "These contrasting differences in the temporal orientation of Saulteaux culture and of western civilization," he writes, "undoubtedly imply profound differences in the psychological outlook which is constituted by them. Such differences are not functions of primitive mentality or racial make-up. They are a function of culturally constituted experience."[16]

While many Pikangikum people had converted to Christianity and adopted other Western cultural practices in Hallowell's time, he notes that communities situated further away from colonial settlements relied more heavily on traditional cultural frameworks and temporalities. Attempting to understand the Pikangikum temporal vocabulary, Hallowell learns that while the period of daylight is not divided into hours or minutes, a precise terminology serves to differentiate between different stages of the day:

> When streaks of light, distinguishable in the east, announce the first signs of coming day, although darkness still reigns on the earth, this is pi·tában, dawn. When darkness is dispelled so that one can discern terrestrial objects at some distance, but the sun has not yet risen above the tree tops [sic], it is tci·bwaságàtik, "before coming out from the trees (the sun)." Soon the light from the rising sun reddens the treetops. This point of time in the new day is called miskẃɑnagáte, "red shining (reflected) light." In addition, there are two other expressions that refer to the position of the sun before it emerges into full view. One of these connotes the point in time when the sun is still behind the tree-tops [sic], literally, "beneath trees when hangs (the) sun," änämatikèpi·ʼágotcinggí·zis; the other, when it reaches the tops of the trees, "tops of trees when hangs (the) sun," ékwɑnákɑk épi·ʼágotcinggí·zis.[17]

These divisions become broader as the sun approaches its zenith; but even with the use of these concepts Hallowell finds it difficult to arrange appointments with residents of the area. He would ask one acquaintance to come to his tent in the "morning," and another to come in the "afternoon," but the two would sometimes arrive within a few minutes of one another. "The lack of common reference points," Hallowell writes, "made it difficult to coordinate our activities efficiently."[18] Eventually he learns to work within the structure of what Robert Levine calls "event time," asking the first visitor to arrive "as soon as you have lifted your nets," this being a consistent early morning activity.[19]

Hallowell also learns the Pikangikum divisions of the annual sequence of the moon's phases; each lunar cycle is named according to "such non-celestial phenomena as the appearance in the country of certain birds, the condition of plant life, the rutting of animals, human economic activities," and so on.[20] Meanwhile, the divisions of the year that correspond roughly with the Western concept of seasons are six in number, not four.[21] So while the Western models of time divide the daylight period into uniform numbered hours, and name the months, or "moons," after Roman gods, emperors, or numerical sequence (March is for Mars, July is for Julius Caesar, and September, which used to be the seventh month of the year, comes from the Latin for seven), the essential concepts of days, moons, and seasons, all of which derive initially from obvious *recurring* changes in sunlight, lunar brightness, or climate, are at least recognizable across both cultures.

One of the most obvious differences, for Hallowell, between Pikangikum and Western models of time is the absence of weeks and fixed dates in his hosts' system. "I lost track of the days of the month," he writes, "since I did not have a calendar with me; the days of the week became meaningless."[22] Likewise, when his watch stops running he can no longer count the hours of the day. Still, he does not find these changes entirely disconcerting:

> My "disorientation," of course was only such relative to the reference points of western civilization to which I was habituated. Once the usual mechanical and institutional aids to these were removed, the relativity and provinciality of western time concepts became obvious. But the significant fact is that since I remained associated with human beings it was a very simple matter to make their temporal reference points my own.[23]

Where Hallowell identifies more significant differences is in the apparent disinclination of the Pikangikum to count years in a formal linear chronology, or at least a numerical one. Events that would have occurred many years in the past are described not through a numbered sequence, but in relation to the relative ages of the people in question, significant events such as local marriages or the First World War (several Pikangikum enlisted in the military), or the lifespans of deceased relatives. Hallowell finds this genealogical history to be accurate, and while he claims that this method is incapable of recuperating more than the past 150 years,[24] the stories that he describes as mythology may articulate a deeper sense of the past; the precise extent of Pikangikum historical consciousness is difficult to assess through his limited records. The ages of people themselves, meanwhile, are counted not numerically, but in terms of transitions between different stages of life roughly aligned with childhood, puberty, young adulthood, marriage, and old age.[25] While the Pikangikum chronologies, then, appear to function without an abstract numerical counting system, the essential concepts of sequence – *before*, *after*, and *no longer* – are easily identifiable in the relationships between past events and present circumstances. We might say that numerical and relational chronologies are both successful in articulating the concept of sequence, but that a numerical chronology, while potentially affording greater precision in recording the timing of past events, is more likely to conceal the cyclical patterns at work within sequences of events. Naming a past moment by assigning it a numerical marker far removed from the present moment's numerical marker can serve to *disassociate* past from present events even while connecting events along a linear representation, compared with chronologies that emphasize recurring patterns of birth, aging, and death.

The structures of Pikangikum mythology, as Hallowell understands them, also emphasize a temporality similar to that which Peter Sanger understands as the "eternally present" aspects of Mi'kmaq mythology. Hallowell writes:

the most prominent anthropomorphic characters of mythology like wísakedjak and tcakábɛc are not only living beings, they are conceived as immortal. They were alive when the earth was young and they assisted the Indians then. They are still alive today and continue to aid mankind, this latter fact receiving empirical demonstration in dreams and by the manifestation of the presence of such beings in the conjuring lodge. The conventional pattern of dream revelation and the conjuring lodge are, then, institutional means of keeping mythological beings and spiritual entities of other classes constantly contemporary with each new generation of individuals, despite the passage of "time."[26]

Significantly, though, at the same time that the beings from mythological time are "constantly contemporary," Hallowell also argues that "a temporal distinction is recognized between those days and the present."[27] Certain "monster species" such as "Great Snake" and "Great Mosquito" that existed in mythological times are "now only represented by smaller varieties of their kind," and particular myths suggest that at one time "all human beings were covered with hair" and "winter lasted all the year round."[28] A conception of time, then, that emphasizes recurrence and identifies deep structural connections between past and present does not preclude the notion that certain past circumstances no longer hold in the present moment.

In his 1990 study on the psychology of time, William Friedman comments on Hallowell's experiences, and sees the apparent coexistence of cyclical and linear temporality in Pikangikum culture as a lesson in resisting simplistic characterizations of Indigenous or Western models of time. There is a temptation, Friedman writes, to claim "that people in traditional cultures have no way of conceptualizing series of unique, nonrecurrent events, and that people in modern cultures cannot appreciate repetitive temporal patterns. This is clearly not the case."[29] He concludes that "attributing either a linear or cyclic view of time to a culture ignores the fact that time is understood by many representations."[30] To the extent that they exist, then, structural similarities between Indigenous and Western models of time reckoning reveal that Indigenous cultures and Western cultures may employ both circular *and* linear models of time, so that instead of identifying Indigenous time as purely circular and Western time as purely linear, it makes more sense to say that Indigenous temporality may emphasize circularity while Western temporality emphasizes linearity. Or to push the notion a little further, the very difficulty of categorizing temporal models as either linear or circular suggests that, like other binary structures, the linear-circular dualism obscures important complexities.

While there are occasions when a focus on one particular linear or circular representation can be necessary, there may still be a way to conceive of diverse models of time within a framework that allows for a greater degree of complexity. Because cultural models of temporality, as well as personal experiences, can rarely be understood either as a straight line with no recurrences or as a circle in which the notion of sequence is obscured, a more viable image for time's motion may be found in the helix. The shape that a wire takes when wound around a cylinder carries both the sequential and circular aspects of temporality, and it remains possible to focus one's attention on either of these characteristics at any given moment. More precisely, we might say that time is a *fractal* helix: a helix that loops back upon itself in such a way that larger and larger cycles emerge out of the linear structure (imagine that the cylinder itself takes the shape of a helix rather than a straight line, and that the wire in turn is wrapped around this already curved form). This image is useful in demonstrating how different emphases can exist within a model that incorporates both linear and circular shapes; it helps us recognize that elements of recurrence exist within apparently linear processes, and that, as Barbara Adam explains, "cyclical processes *by definition* involve the combination of repetition with variation, linearity and progression."[31] Of course, the attempt to envision a common framework of temporality carries its own precarious assumptions of universality, so while I propose the fractal helix as a tool for introducing a greater degree of complexity into the dualistic linear-circular models, I caution against the characterization of any single representation of time as complete or universal.

Keeping this model in mind, when Georges Sioui, for instance, writes that European settlers "had forgotten about the Circle and had come to believe that life is a linear, evolutionary process, in which they, the European and Christian, are to lead the rest of humanity and nature itself in a certain enlightened direction,"[32] we are led to understand European linear thought as a deeply biased perspective that endows the linear progression of the fractal helix with total significance while neglecting its cyclical patterns. At the same time, though, we can recognize that Sioui's language serves to conceal the fact that cyclical patterns of days, weeks, months, years, and generations remain potent sources of knowledge within Western traditions. Christian rituals themselves are deeply invested in the recurring patterns of the Sabbath, Easter, and Christmas; even the development of mechanical clocks, whose minutes and hours endlessly recur while simultaneously progressing in sequence, was tied to the regulation of European prayer schedules. In his book *Circles and Lines*, John Demos notes that early Euro-descended colonists in the United States were no exception to the fact that the cycles of day, night, and lunar brightness are deeply important for any society without electric lighting, and that seasonal cycles, too, were critical in determining warmth, coldness, diet, the type of work available, and the timing of conception, birth, illness, and death.[33] For Demos, it was the American Revolution that installed linearity as the desirable and seemingly inevitable basis for temporal experience in the United States, while the increasing significance of life choices and career options in the eras following the revolution (at least for white men of a certain economic position) cemented the importance of future-oriented linear life narratives.[34] This is not to say that the cyclical patterns of days, seasons, and human generations become inconsequential in modern Western societies; rather, the progressive aspects of the helix shape come to be perceived as more socially significant.

Of course, the ability of Western scholars to identify apparently linear sequences of events within Indigenous models of time does not entail the existence of progress in the Western sense of advancement toward a more theoretically ideal condition. In this regard, Sioui's identification of a peculiar Western belief in linear movement *toward* an enlightened state carries more weight; whatever circular patterns may exist in Western models of time become effectively flattened out, carrying meaning only insofar as they contribute toward the linear motion. As a result, Western cultural temporality is able to discount the importance of those events or societies that do not appear to participate as leading actors in the linear progression of advancement. Tracing the "view of Indigenous people as delayed in the race of civilizations" that was central to the institutionalization of European settler culture in Canada, Daniel Coleman discusses what he calls "the racialized concept of time, which equated whiteness with modernity and the administration of industrial development and non-whiteness with pre-modern backwardness and manual labour. The simple sequence of racialized time meant that it was impossible to weave First Nations culture into the progressive narrative of Canadian development."[35] A comparative perspective on the combined linear and circular modes across various Western and Indigenous societies may have made such racist justifications much more difficult, but the discounting of the cyclical aspects of the helix precluded such an outlook, and the helical journey of civilizations became, for mainstream Canadian society, a linear "race." The word "primitive," which comes from the Latin *primus*, essentially means "first" or "original," yet the connotation of backwardness, of a lack of civility and progress, has turned the word into a pejorative that reinforces racial-temporal divisions. The consequences of such segregations are vast; the dual notions of backwardness and development have coloured the orientation of settler culture toward First Nations since the groups' first contacts, justifying reductions in land and resource rights as well as the creation of the residential schools system, and Indigenous cultures themselves have often struggled to determine their place within, or without, the notion of linear temporal progress.

The concept of temporal discrimination is especially useful here in identifying the closely related beliefs that one particular model of time is natural, desirable, and superior to other models of time, and that certain times (the present or the short-term future) are more deserving of agency, empowerment, and resource exploitation than other times. Following the model of critical race studies that works to resist racist discrimination, the concept of temporal discrimination can provide a terminology and a potential framework for thinking through the politics of contested cultural temporalities. For instance, just as racism requires, and even creates, supposedly objective categories of races – categories that inevitably break down under scrutiny – so too does temporal discrimination rely on, and create, different times. Sioui's notion that "the thing that is named 'the past' is a European construct and is not part of the Amerindian psyche,"[36] as well as Ricoeur's belief that the indivisibility of the past, present, and future may "require that the very terms 'future,' 'past,' and 'present' be abandoned,"[37] highlight the cultural construction of temporal categories that are (often unwittingly) necessary to temporal discrimination.[38] Of course, just as we must be wary of framing the fragility of racial categories as the ultimate justification for equality because of the risk that the discovery or invention of clear genetic racial markers would then appear to destroy the case for equality, we should also be cautious in describing the fragility of temporal categories as the justification for temporal equality. Whether we highlight time's linear, cyclical, or indivisible aspects, respect for different temporalities itself must be seen as having intrinsic value if it is to maintain purchase. Articulating the very existence of alternative models of time is an important step in countering the hegemony of a singular temporal ideology, and in this regard the comments of writers like Sioui – who claims that "yesterday is today and tomorrow is yester-day: time is one, life is one"[39] – play a vital role in critical time studies.

SEEING AND FAILING TO SEE ALTERNATIVE TEMPORALITIES

The ability to examine temporal assumptions critically, to envision modes of time outside those that emphasize linear progress, has an important but troubled history in Canadian and Indigenous writing. I have already mentioned the struggle that George Copway records, in his nineteenth-century autobiography, as he attempts to reconcile Western ideals of progress with his Ojibwe background. He vacillates between anger at the imposition of cultural and technological progress onto his way of life, and gratitude for the opportunity "to tread in the footsteps of worthy white men"[40] – a conflict with no easy resolution. Pauline Johnson, who was born in 1861 to a Mohawk father and an English mother, also reveals a degree of internal conflict in her writing from the turn of the twentieth century. In one of Johnson's stories in *The Moccasin Maker*, the European settler Charlie marries a young half-Indigenous woman named Christie, who explains that when her own parents were married the community prepared a feast, but did not perform a ceremony. "There is no ritual to bind them," she explains; "they need none; an Indian's word was his law in those days."[41] But while Christie takes pride in this tradition, Charlie is furious at what he sees as a scandal, claiming that in the absence of a Christian ceremony Christie's parents were never actually married. While previous generations of the family could not have known better, he says, "Your father and mother live in more civilized times. Father O'Leary has been at the post for nearly twenty years. Why was not your father straight enough to have the ceremony performed when he *did* get the chance?"[42] In response to Charlie's rhetoric of "civilized times" and "straight" behav-iour, Christie emphatically resists the notion that the Western perspec-tive is more advanced, and she does so through images of simultaneity and recurrence:

Why should I recognize the rites of your nation when you do not acknowledge the rites of mine? According to your own words, my parents should have gone through your church ceremony as well as

through an Indian contract; according to *my* words, *we* should go
through an Indian contract as well as through a church marriage.
If their union is illegal, so is ours. If you think my father is living in
dishonor with my mother, my people will think I am living in dishonor with you. How do I know when another nation will come and
conquer you as you white men conquered us? And they will have
another marriage rite to perform, and they will tell us another truth,
that you are not my husband, that you are but disgracing and
dishonoring me, that you are keeping me here, not as your wife,
but as your – your – *squaw*.[43]

But while Johnson is eloquent here in interrupting the racialized model
of time that privileges Western culture as advanced, she also reinforces
the idea that aspects of Indigenous culture are backwards and not yet
developed. Earlier in the story, Johnson describes the initial meeting of
Christie's parents in terms of their relative positions along the arrow of
civilization:

The country was all backwoods, and the Post miles and miles from
even the semblance of civilization, and the lonely young Englishman's
heart had gone out to the girl who, apart from speaking a very few
words of English, was utterly uncivilized and uncultured, but had
withal that marvellously innate refinement so universally possessed
by the higher tribes of North American Indians.
 Like all her race, observant, intuitive, having a horror of ridicule,
consequently quick at acquirement and teachable in mental and
social habits, she had developed from absolute pagan indifference
into a sweet, elderly Christian woman ...
 He had given their daughter Christine all the advantages of his
own learning – which, if truthfully told, was not universal; but
the girl had a fair common education, and the native adaptability
to progress.[44]

The uncritical language of development, progress, and the acquisition
of civility troubles the plausibility of the story's apparent repudiation of
these concepts. Whom are we meant to believe: Johnson's narrator, or
Christie? Like George Copway, Johnson appears to have internalized two

contradictory models of temporality, and her own articulations of progress – as both an unquestioned truth and a culturally biased assumption – are fractured and inconsistent. In their detailed examination of Johnson's work and life, Veronica Strong-Boag and Carole Gerson write, "By claiming and expressing the sensibilities of both Aboriginal margin and European centre, Johnson ultimately confounds the simple dichotomies that underpin Western consciousness."[45] This complexity, though, may reveal an unresolved inner tension as much as it enacts a questioning of normative power.

Writing by Canadians of European descent sometimes reveals similar vacillations, though the bias toward a racialized, progress-oriented model of time has often been a dominant force. Duncan Campbell Scott, the poet and deputy superintendent of the Department of Indian Affairs from 1913 to 1932, is infamous for his support of the mandatory residential school system that separated Indigenous children from their families and cultures. Like many of his contemporaries, Scott saw Indigenous peoples as an inherently backwards race, and, as Lisa Salem observes, the policies that he orchestrated were "based on the idea that the Native peoples possessed an essentially 'savage' nature and therefore needed to be guided into civilization by the representatives of the British Empire."[46] In Scott's own somewhat contradictory words, the inevitable disappearance of Indigenous peoples would be accomplished "not by race extinction but by gradual assimilation with their fellow citizens."[47] His 1898 poem "The Onondaga Madonna" portrays a woman of the Onondaga First Nation as living proof of the inescapable demise of her people; she belongs to "a weird and waning race,"[48] and the fact that she is never named fits the notion that she is a representative of a type rather than an individual. While the woman holds a newborn child, normally a sign of regeneration and futurity, the baby is merely "the latest promise of her nation's doom";[49] he sulks moodily with "the primal warrior gleaming from his eyes."[50] For Scott, the collective "promise" of Native peoples, their very future, reveals only violence and ruin. Reading the baby's "paler" skin as a sign of interracial lineage, Salem writes that "Scott uses the mother and child tableau in 'The Onondaga Madonna' to represent, not the hope and promise of the Madonna and Christ-child of Christian iconography, but the impending death of the Indian race through miscegenation."[51]

This racialized view of cultural temporality carries through into many twentieth-century works, but it also becomes a target for critical resistance. Emily Carr, who is best known for her paintings of Indigenous art and west coast landscapes early in the twentieth century, also wrote creative non-fiction accounts of her travels, and while the assumption of racialized temporality is sometimes visible in *Klee Wyck* – Carr's collection of short autobiographical stories that won the Governor Gereral's Award – she moves much more toward a critical understanding of cultural bias. Her stories bear witness to the imposition of Western temporality onto west coast Indigenous cultures, and reveal how a transition toward an acceptance of alternate, simultaneous presents can unfold.[52]

In the first story in *Klee Wyck*, Carr watches while a missionary in Ucluelet blows on a cow's horn, signalling the beginning of the school day; "the blasts were stunning, but they failed to call the children to school, because no voice had ever suggested time or obligation to these Indian children. Then the Greater Missionary went to the village and hand-picked her scholars from the huts."[53] This scene establishes two of Carr's beliefs that will gradually be questioned and dismantled during the course of her experiences. First, she believes that the Western model of time is the *only* model; if the children have not been trained about school days and working hours, they must have no understanding of time. Second, the connection of time with "obligation" reveals that adherence to Western temporality through the internalization of time discipline involves a moral dimension. Like citizens of the twenty-first century who feel compelled to respond quickly to electronic messages lest they be seen as unreliable and out of touch, Westerners at the turn of the twentieth century are held captive by the moral, almost sacred importance of clock technology. In Ucluelet, the reluctant Indigenous students begin "squirming out of their desks" while the missionary writes the English alphabet on a chalk board.[54] This schoolhouse is clearly a place where the dominance of Western cultural forms is inscribed, but while the English language lesson is an overt example of cultural politics and the alterity of Indigenous knowledge, the very fact of the children's attendance at particular times of day serves to indoctrinate them into the Western models of clock time, working hours, and weekdays. The authority of Western time reckoning is always the schoolhouse's message, regardless of the particular topic of each day's lesson.[55]

While Carr begins tentatively to question her own assumptions in "Ucluelet," realizing that she is "to them a child, ignorant about the wild things which they knew so well,"[56] her later story "Greenville" is especially significant in the way it traces her gradual understanding of alternative temporalities. When she hires a ride to the town of Greenville from an Indigenous man named Sam, she asks what time the boat will depart. "Eight o'clock," he replies, but on the appointed day Carr sits waiting "on the wharf from eight o'clock till noon" while "Sam and his son sauntered up and down getting things as if time did not exist."[57] As in the Ucluelet scene, the Indigenous man's failure to adhere to Western standards of punctuality means, in Carr's eyes, that he operates as though he is outside of temporal existence altogether, Western temporality being the only form with which she is familiar. The perceived necessity of Western temporality for life itself becomes apparent when she finally arrives in Greenville and enters the abandoned schoolhouse that is to serve as her lodging. She notes that "the hum of the mosquitoes had stopped, as every other thing had stopped in the murky grey of this dreadful place, clock, calendar, even the air – the match the Indian struck refused to live."[58] Recoiling at the room's "strangling deadness," she decides to improve the situation as best she can: "I turned forward the almanac sheets and set the clock ticking. When the kettle sang things had begun to live."[59] The regular ticking of the clock is associated here with comfortable living space and the forward motion of normal existence, and yet, the fact that the clock and calendar function only when Carr is present to activate them suggests that Western temporality, far from being omnipresent, is a specific socio-technological practice that she herself brings with her into a place where it would not otherwise exist.

As Carr spends time in Greenville she begins to find evidence that the choice between Western temporality and stifling atemporality is a false one, for along with their languages, arts, and forms of spirituality, her Indigenous hosts adhere to alternative forms of time reckoning. On the verge of this discovery, Carr notes that the typical method of house construction in the village follows (or fails to follow) what she considers to be a slack schedule: "As soon as a few boards were put together the family moved in, and the house went on building around them until some new interest came along. Then the Indian dropped his tools ... and after a long pull on his pipe he would probably lie round in the sun for days doing nothing."[60] While "the Indian" is troublingly cast here as a type rather than an actual person, Carr's observations call to mind Robert Levine's distinction between clock time and event time, where he concludes that "one of the most significant differences in the pace of life is whether people use the hour on the clock to schedule the beginning and ending of activities, or whether the activities are allowed to transpire according to their own spontaneous schedule."[61] While Carr expects construction to follow a rigid timetable organized around predictable assembly milestones, the people building this house may have decided that the construction has proceeded as far as necessary for the moment. Cultures that operate on event time, Levine argues, may resist the Western linkage of time with money, and may have no use for the concept of "wasted" time; he quotes Jean Traore, a student from Burkina Faso in Western Africa, as saying, "There's no such thing as wasting time where I live ... How can you waste time? If you're not doing one thing, you're doing something else."[62]

The concept of event time, then, goes part of the way toward articulating the experience of time that Carr is seeing. And yet, something more is at work. Peering into empty houses that have clearly been rapidly vacated, she realizes that "because the tide had been right to go, bedding had been stripped from the springs, food left about, water left unemptied to rust the kettles. Indians slip in and out of their places like animals. Tides and seasons are the things that rule their lives: domestic arrangements are mere incidentals."[63] The notion that the villagers spring into rapid action when the tide is "right to go" suggests that they are perfectly quick to act when need be. Scheduling one's activities in strict accordance with tides and seasons is neither clock time nor event time – it is a form of ecological time in which actions are coordinated around naturally recurring changes. While Sam's departure had been four hours late by the clock, another form of punctuality now becomes visible, one based on a keen awareness of changing marine conditions. Of course, the tide-based temporality that Carr identifies is not a definitively Indigenous mode; indeed, her experience is as much an encounter between the temporality of an urbanite and the temporality of mariners as it is an encounter between Western and Indigenous time. Still, the temporal emphases that strike her as unexpected reveal the contrasting elements foregrounded by alternative forms of social time reckoning. It is important to remember here that just as the Indigenous mode involves event-based, ecological, and other temporal factors, so too does Western temporality consist of various complex layers. As Adam writes, "the abstract, quantified, spatialized time of clocks and calendars forms *only one aspect* of the complex of meanings associated with Western time"; social interactions and environmental concerns remain potent sources of time reckoning.[64] Carr's gradual realization that multiple forms of time are significant for the functioning of everyday life in Indigenous communities is thus also a comment on her own culture's understanding of time. While clock time may appear totalizing for those who adhere to it, multiple forms of social and environmental time retain a significant degree of influence. Carr is slowly awakening to the existence of multitemporality – a concept whose implications I will clarify more fully in the next chapter.

Carr's earlier accusations that Sam and the schoolchildren had no understanding of time now take on an ironic tone, as we realize that Carr herself has been failing to understand *their* sense of time. At this point in the story Carr writes in detail about the totem poles she encounters nearby, and her growing willingness to accept cultural modes different from her own becomes apparent. The carver of the poles, she muses, "cut forms to fit the thoughts that the birds and animals and fish suggested to him, and to these he added something of himself. When they were all linked together they made very strong talk for the people. He grafted this new language onto the great cedar trunks and called them Totem poles and stuck them up in the villages with great ceremony."[65] Importantly, Carr chooses this moment to reveal the Indigenous name for Greenville: "Lakalzap."[66] The languages, arts, and cultural forms that have been made invisible under Western colonialism begin to become apparent now in Carr's eyes, and she grows increasingly critical of the missionaries who "came and told the Indians this was all foolish and heathenish."[67] As she prepares to leave Greenville at the end of the story she has grown to see Western temporality – along with Western art and language – not as inevitable and singular, but as a limited framework, a construction that she carries with her in her travels, and that, like the colonialist agenda itself, is sometimes better left behind. "I let the clock run down," she writes. "Flapped the leaves of the calendar back, and shut the Greenville schoolhouse tight."[68]

In one of the late episodes of *Klee Wyck*, Carr highlights the importance of alternative forms of timekeeping directly in the title of the story: "Century Time." Describing an Indigenous graveyard, she writes:

In the late afternoon a great shadow-mountain stepped across the lake and brooded over the cemetery. It had done this at the end of every sunny day for centuries, long, long before that piece of land was a cemetery ... Indians do not hinder the progress of their dead by embalming or tight coffining. When the spirit has gone they give the body back to the earth.[69]

This passage frames human lifespans as insignificant in comparison with the geological time of the earth; the language reveals a willingness to entertain an elongated perspective on time, and the statement about giving human bodies "back" to the earth sees long-standing earthly processes as primary sites of ownership and importance.

Noting that the cemetery itself contains a blending of traditional Indigenous burial conventions with more recently learned Christian practices – wooden crosses and written words – Carr reads the lettering on the grave markers:

SACRED OF KATIE – IPOO

SAM BOYAN HE DIDE – IPOO

RIP JULIE YECTON – IPOO

JOSEPH'S ROSIE DI – IPOO[70]

Carr does not understand the word "IPOO," so she asks a woman in the village what it means. This results in a convoluted linguistic struggle as the two women try to understand one another across their cultural and language differences:

"Mean die time."

"Die time?"

"Uh huh. Tell when he die."

"But all the graves 'tell' the same."

"Uh huh. Four this kind" (she pointed separately to each of the four letters, IPOO) "tell now time."

"But everybody did not die at the same time. Some died long ago and some die now?"

"Uh huh. Maybe some year just one man die – one baby. Maybe influenza come – he come two time – one time long far, one time close. He make lots, lots Injun die."

"But, if it means the time people died, why do they put 'IPOO' on the old graves as well as on the new?"

> Difficult English thoughts furrowed her still forehead. Hard English words came from her slow tongue in abrupt jerks. Her brown finger touched the I and the P. "He know," she said, "he tell it. This one and this one" (pointing to the two O's) "– small – he no matter. He change every year. Just this one and this matter" (pointing again to I and P). "He tell it."
>
> Time was marked by centuries in this cemetery. Years – little years – what are they? As insignificant as the fact that reversing the figure nine turns it into the letter P.[71]

Visible in this conversation is the gradual convergence of two radically different conceptualizations of time. While Carr cannot understand why "old" and "new" graves would be marked with the same time of death, the Indigenous woman cannot understand the distinction that Carr is trying to make; for her, Carr's notions of old and new both fall within the duration that she calls "now." The landscape itself, we now realize, with its many centuries of daily cycles, had been hinting all along at the importance of this longer-term view.

Explaining his desire for Western societies to develop a longer-term perspective, Stewart Brand asks, "How long *is* now, usually?" For most of us, "'now' consists of this week, slightly haunted by the ghost of last week. This is the realm of immediate responsibility, one in which we feel we have volition, where the consequences of our actions are obvious and surprises limited."[72] Arguing that "civilizations with long nows look after things better," Brand goes on to collaborate on a project – a mechanical clock designed to run for as long as human civilization has currently existed, called "The Clock of the Long Now" – intended "to extend our concept of the present in both directions, making the present longer."[73] Our sense of now, he says, should encompass ten thousand years, which is, after all, "not all that long. It is only four hundred generations."[74] The physicist Freeman Dyson more specifically elaborates six different layers of now:

> The destiny of our species is shaped by the imperatives of survival on six distinct time scales. To survive means to compete successfully on all six time scales. But the unit of survival is different at each of the six time scales. On a time scale of years, the unit is the individual.

On a time scale of decades, the unit is the family. On a time scale of centuries, the unit is the tribe or nation. On a time scale of millennia, the unit is the culture. On a time scale of tens of millennia, the unit is the species. On a time scale of eons, the unit is the whole web of life on our planet. Every human being is the product of adaptation to the demands of all six time scales. That is why conflicting loyalties are deep in our nature.[75]

In this view, Carr's conversation with the Indigenous woman is an encounter between two different privileged layers of now. Carr's upbringing has taught her to privilege the now of the individual, while the other woman values the now of "the tribe or nation," revealing a more expansive sense of self and responsibility. One of the critical differences between this conversation and Carr's earlier encounters (with Sam and his boat, for instance) is that Carr has now become cognizant of her own cross-cultural incompetence. Instead of disparaging the woman for failing to understand the difference between old and new, Carr repeatedly asks questions to ensure her own understanding. Rather than imposing Western models of temporality, she opens herself to accepting, even admiring, the other woman's more expansive sense of time. After all, even Carr's notion that grave markers ought to be classified by year is quite arbitrary; why not classify the time of death by the minute? The sense of defamiliarization to which Carr has opened herself allows for all assumptions to be questioned, and the result of this questioning is visible in her remarkable transition over the course of the narrative, from anger over Sam's four-hour delay, to her revolutionary comment, "Years – little years – what are they?"

The final brief anecdote in *Klee Wyck*, a story called "Canoe," also highlights this sense of temporal defamiliarization, but carries a distinct note of sadness. Having hitched a canoe ride from an Indigenous family, Carr becomes mesmerized by the sedate, tranquil pace of the voyage:

Our going was imperceptible, the woman's steering paddle the only thing that moved, its silent cuts stirring phosphorus like white fire.

Time and texture faded ... ceased to exist ... day was gone, yet it was not night. Water was not wet nor deep, just smoothness spread with light.[76]

This passage contains a clear echo of Carr's statement in "Greenville,"
where "Sam and his son sauntered up and down getting things as if time
did not exist."[77] But while the "Greenville" comment accuses Sam of
failing to adhere to normative temporality, the difference here is the
absence of the "as if"; in the canoe, time *has* ceased to exist. The statement is not literal; it indicates that Carr has learned to operate outside
of her cultural-temporal assumptions about inflexibly calculated hours
and absolute distinctions between temporal markers like years, days, and
nights. At least for the moment, Carr has entered her hosts' conceptual
vehicle for moving through time, just as she has entered their physical
canoe. Continuing to frame the canoe as a profound metaphor for
Indigenous society as a whole, the final sentence of the book serves as
Carr's lament for what she sees as the inevitable demise of her hosts'
beliefs and ways of life: "Slowly the canoe drifted away from the moonlit
landing, till, at the end of her rope, she lay an empty thing, floating
among the shadows of an inverted forest."[78]

The image of Indigenous peoples drifting, emptied, at the end of their
figurative ropes appears inescapable. Throughout *Klee Wyck* Carr describes
even the natural aging process of Indigenous individuals as accelerated;
grandparents and young children alike are depicted in similar terms as
elderly, worn out, and dying. A woman named Sophie walks from door
to door selling her homemade baskets – a symbol for the womb, and for
reproduction and futurity itself – while her own babies die one after
another.[79] The image finds a notable counterpart in A.M. Klein's mid-
1940s poem "Indian Reservation: Caughnawaga," which laments the final
dying days of Indigenous people who have been reduced to caricaturing
their own cultural history "for the tourist's / brown pennies."[80] Klein
writes: "Their past is sold in a shop: the beaded shoes, / the sweetgrass
basket, the curio Indian, / burnt wood and gaudy cloth and inch-
canoes."[81] While Carr is exceptional in testing certain cultural assumptions and learning to acknowledge the validity of Indigenous conceptions
of time, she remains one of many authors who replicate what Laura
Groening calls "the most dangerous trope in Canadian literature: the
Indian as the member of a dead and dying people."[82] Of course, the fact
that this portrayal is such a long-standing trope means that the extinction
it predicts never actually comes about. Carr is not alone as an outsider
who bears witness to horrible destruction and helplessly laments the

collapse of Indigenous civilization, even as the final blow never quite seems to take place.

REINVIGORATING INDIGENOUS TEMPORALITIES

Over the last several decades authors and artists of Indigenous descent have frequently used temporal orientation as a way to articulate Indigenous modes of thought, or to challenge dominant cultural norms. Perhaps the most important function that recent Indigenous literature has filled is the assertion that Indigenous societies, while continuously faced with adversity, are *not* dying civilizations relegated to the past, but remain very much alive in the present, often with a keen awareness of the future. As we have seen in other contexts, the literary temporal resistance that has become prevalent in recent Indigenous writing can operate in two key directions: by witnessing the inequities associated with dominant concepts of time, or by witnessing the impacts that racist social structures more generally can have on the temporal experiences of individuals and communities.

Buffy Sainte-Marie, the Cree singer-songwriter and social activist, became famous in the 1960s and 1970s for her songs that protested war and helped to invigorate broad social conversations about issues of Indigenous survival and policies of forced assimilation.[83] Her song "My Country 'Tis of Thy People You're Dying," released in 1966, questions the dominant narrative of North American colonization by ridiculing and redrawing the normative temporal frame that surrounds these events. "Now that our longhouses breed superstition," she sings, "You force us to send our toddlers away." The children must spend their days in schools that insist "that American history really began when Columbus set sail out of Europe!"[84] Sainte-Marie's use of the word "now" ironizes the way the colonialist narrative presumes to modify, at an arbitrary historical moment, the cultural significance of long-standing Indigenous social institutions. Likewise, the very act of questioning when American history "really began" challenges the widely accepted foundational moment of the "New" world supposedly discovered by Columbus. The narrative that recounts the nation's history, Sainte-Marie argues, must take into account the people *before* Columbus, as well as the long history of genocidal acts *following* the arrival of Europeans.[85]

Also tied up here in the colonialist framing of settler-Indigene relations is the process by which settler culture portrays itself as native, as originary, and as the primary seat of value and power. Coleman writes that "by representing himself as already indigenous, the settler claims priority over newer immigrants and, by representing himself as already civilized, he claims superiority to Aboriginals and other non-Whites."[86] For Sainte-Marie, who writes, "Now that my life's to be known as your heritage, / now that even the graves have been robbed,"[87] this appropriation of indigeneity figures metaphorically as the theft of the past. At its most pessimistic, the song indicates that the temporal reverberations of colonialism move destructively both backwards and forwards: into the past, which "just crumbled," and into the future, which, because it is built on the past, now "threatens."[88] In another song, "Now That the Buffalo's Gone," Sainte-Marie describes the appropriation of Indigenous land as an ongoing ordeal, singing, "Oh it's all in the past you can say / But it's still going on till today."[89] By framing the threats to Indigenous lives and cultures as ongoing, as carrying consequences "still," and on into the future, Sainte-Marie's lyrics resist the notion that Indigenous people, and colonialism itself, belong to some other time in the past. The settler culture's claim to firstness is not a mere historical detail, but a deeply political act that continues to be performed and continues to cause material consequences.

In chapter 1 I briefly discussed Maria Campbell's autobiography *Halfbreed*, which highlights how federal government policy around the time of Canada's Confederation imposed arbitrary temporal restrictions on Métis land use in Saskatchewan. The majority of Campbell's narrative, though, describes her own impoverished and unstable living conditions in the middle of the twentieth century, indicating how the consequences of racist social structures reverberate through time and influence her own temporal experience. Even the first sentence of the book – "The house where I grew up is tumbled down and overgrown with bush"[90] – suggests that the comforts of the past, broadly speaking, have been lost and destroyed. Identifying the temporal fractures that emerge from racial divisions, Campbell imagines herself speaking to white Canadians as a whole: "I know that poverty is not ours alone. Your people have it too, but in those earlier days you at least had dreams, you had a tomorrow. My parents and I never shared any aspirations for a future."[91] The sense of a decayed past and hopeless future echoes Sainte-Marie's pessimistic moments as well as D.C. Scott's outlook, and during the rare moments when Campbell actually articulates hopes for the future, her dreams are tellingly modest. Desperate to maintain her standing in school despite having to raise her own younger siblings, she "even day-dreamed that I would make it through high school, and that we would all make good friends and become part of the community. But it didn't work out like that."[92] The constant experience of racism not only directs the Métis into a mentality of absent or humble futures, but even physically segregates them in time from white citizens. Reflecting on how the people from her community would often travel into the nearby town of St Michele on Saturdays to shop, drink, and watch movies, Campbell writes, "There was an unwritten law: our people never came in until after four and the whites would then turn the town over to us. They never mixed with us although their revenue depended on Native people's money."[93] The daylight hours associated with business and productivity belong to the white townspeople, leaving the late-night weekend hours associated with debauchery to the Métis who support this productivity.

When Campbell moves to Vancouver and takes up work in the sex trade, she develops a drug addiction that serves mainly as a form of temporal escapism. The drugs "helped me to sleep, they kept me happy, and most of all, I could forget about yesterday and tomorrow."[94] In a form of self-fulfilling prophecy, the expense of the pills prevents her from putting any savings aside to improve her future, "and my dreams of saving a lot of money just seemed to get farther and farther away."[95] Like some of the impoverished people and characters I discussed in chapter 3, Campbell finds that "my life became an endless circle of work, drink, and depression."[96] Gradually she works to repair her own psyche, joining an addiction support group as well as the Native movement in Alberta. By the end of the autobiography, she looks forward to a more positive time with the belief that "one day, very soon, people will set aside their differences and come together as one."[97] The hopefulness of this thought is encouraging, even if the future it envisions is more idealistic than probable.

Through much of the 1980s Campbell was also involved in an extended collaborative writing project with Linda Griffiths. In the resulting theatre production, *Jessica*, Griffiths plays a version of Campbell herself, enacting Campbell's life experiences through encounters with the figures of coyote, bear, and wolverine. In a collaborative volume called *The Book of*

Jessica, Griffiths and Campbell record the protracted debates, frustrations, and breakthroughs that surrounded the writing and production of the play. One of the transcribed conversations in this volume is particularly telling in the way it reveals differences in temporal orientation between Griffiths – a white woman who adheres to normative models of scheduling and punctuality – and Campbell herself. Maria comments that her relationship with Linda has "helped me to see the white part of myself," and that she would like Linda "to see it too." Linda responds:

> LINDA   But the white part of you knows exactly how I feel when you don't show up.
>
> MARIA   Don't pressure me with these things. You know I'm not very good with time. In fact, I'm totally unreliable. The way I feel about time or appointments is not the same way you feel about them. I respect and appreciate that those things are important to you, but they're just not very important to me. You know, like, if you were to come along and take the stuff that I picked up at the second-hand store and crap all over it or something, I could understand that, because that's important to me, but not time. I'm always here when you really need me ... I don't understand about time, stealing, yes, but not the importance you put on it ... Time – what is that anyway?
>
> LINDA   It has nothing to do with appointments. It has to do with respect – basic respect. I thought what was happening was that finally, after all this time, we were finally respecting each other, and then you didn't show up again.[98]

While the two friends are putting genuine effort into locating the source of their dispute, they stop short of uncovering the shaky racialized assumptions that frame punctuality as an intrinsically "white" quality. In Levine's terminology, Linda operates within the dominant clock time mode, while Maria operates on event time: Linda expects Maria to arrive for a particular scheduled appointment, while Maria claims to be "always here when you really need me." For Linda, Maria's failure to arrive on schedule means that she "didn't show up again" (her exasperation is reminiscent of Emily Carr's frustration over Sam's late departure in his boat) while Maria may feel that the moment at which her presence is truly necessary has not yet arrived, regardless of the hour on the clock. What is especially significant here, though, is that instead of articulating the different ways in which time *is* important to her, Maria accepts Linda's mode of time as the legitimate one, and describes herself as "not very good with time" and "totally unreliable." While Maria's application of event time itself may be flawed by her failure to realize just how important her presence was to Linda, she sees herself more as a failed clock-timer than a well-intentioned event-timer, because she perceives clock time to be the one mode with a rightful claim to social legitimacy. We can see a hint here of how entrenched models of time can serve, even unintentionally, to legitimize the subjugation of non-white races. At the same time, Maria's inability in this conversation to reclaim or advocate for her own approach to time recalls the way in which the events in *Halfbreed* work to trap Maria within damaging temporalities not of her own making. In this sense her autobiography is a narrative of how racial and economic divisions can not only fracture the experience of temporality for impoverished people, but also prevent alternative frames of temporal experience from gaining purchase.

The inherent legitimacy of Indigenous conceptual modes, and the politics of temporal assimilation, are primary concerns as well in Jeannette Armstrong's 1985 novel *Slash*, the first novel by an Indigenous woman in Canada. The novel tells the story of Thomas "Slash" Kelasket, an Okanagan Indian youth who travels through Canada and the United States in the 1960s and 1970s learning about the struggle for Indigenous rights. As a child, Slash is confused over the conflicting attitudes toward newness and oldness in his community. His friend Jimmy declares, "You guys up-the-hill is just stupid and old-fashioned. Nobody needs to talk Indian anymore. My Dad and them are smart. They are up-to-date. We are gonna get a T.V., too."[99] "Why," Slash wonders, "were my Dad and them so stubborn about new stuff anyway?"[100] The answer to this question comes to light when Slash's father expresses his anger over the imposition of English schooling, Band housing, and welfare dependency, all of which have led members of the community to "do nothing but get money and spend it drinking … Seems like the more Indians try new things, the worse things get for them."[101] Slash's grandfather Pra-cwa agrees: "Our people are two now. There is us and there is them that want to try all kinds of new stuff and be more like white people."[102] Meanwhile, Slash attends a talk by an Indigenous man who has dressed himself to appear "almost like a white man," who explains that Indigenous people are "living in the twentieth century" and "have a lot of catching up to do … We no longer need to sit back and be forgotten, second-class people stuck on reservations, living in the dark ages."[103] All of this leaves Slash unsure what to make of the conflicting advice. Newness, we come to understand, is framed broadly as an intrinsically white quality associated with the positive values of modernity, relevance, and inevitable progress, while oldness becomes a pejorative for obsolete Indian foolishness. Those who wish to question these associations, who find value in traditional approaches and remain suspicious of assimilation, find themselves in the impossible position of resisting the apparent reality of ongoing life itself.

When Slash is sentenced to eighteen months in prison for his involvement in a brawl, the incident that earns him his nickname, Armstrong casts the experience of enforced assimilation in prison as a metaphor for Indigenous life itself within a dominant white culture. "In there," Slash says, "you had to learn fast. It's like everybody had to kind of fit in somewhere. It's not a matter of wanting to. It's that you had to. You were playing their game. You had to form a new attitude. You had to, or you got swept away."[104] Once he leaves prison, though, and becomes increasingly involved in Indian rights movements, Slash questions the necessity of "playing their game" and subscribing to "a new attitude" in a broader sense. "I wondered what was so complicated," he says, "that large conferences and long resolutions had to be passed to do something for Indians. Something as simple as making a man feel good to be Indian didn't ever seem to be considered as an answer."[105] As he joins forces with a rebellious protest group that stages an occupation at the Bureau of Indian Affairs in Washington, DC, and illegally takes over land at Wounded Knee, Slash is exposed to the apparently radical thought that the protest activities cannot accurately be called a takeover at all: "This is our land," one of the protesters says, invoking an expanded sense of temporal recognition, "we have rights here. How can we take over? We're already here."[106]

As the protesters experience violence and hatred, as well as occasional successes, Slash vacillates between doubt that there can be any hope for Indigenous communities, and excitement over the thought that the real answer is to increase Indigenous peoples' pride in their own identities. Like Maria Campbell, during his periods of hopelessness Slash takes refuge in inebriation, blocking out the experience of time altogether:

I scraped pennies together with the other winos to buy bay rum and shaving lotion. I ended up in the drunk tanks and detox centres and ate whenever I thought of it at the Salvation Army. I don't remember too much, but sometimes, when I woke up in jail or in the D, I got flashes of things that I had done. Sometimes I didn't remember a thing for weeks. That was frightening but somehow comforting, too. Frightening because of what I might have done and didn't know about, and comforting that I didn't have to bear those days. They were just gone forever.[107]

After spending six months in a camp sanctuary where he gradually recovers and learns more about Indigenous culture, Slash decides that there is "something worthwhile to live for,"[108] that, "being an Indian, I could never be a person only to myself. I was part of all the rest of the people. I was responsible to that. Everything I did affected that. What I was would affect everyone around me, both then and far into the future, through me and my descendants."[109] His extended immersion in Indigenous culture has helped him to reject the notion of time as a painful, hopeless ordeal to be blocked out, and has expanded his perspective to the point where he is able to envision a deep future.

As a result of this shift Slash articulates a new goal: "I had to find out what things were left of the old ways in my own Tribe and make it usable in our modern Indian lives."[110] Visible here is an indication that the apparent division between tradition and assimilation, between old and new, is a false choice, that successful adjustment to present conditions must involve working with traditional knowledge and continuously reshaping "old" ways to ensure their continued usefulness. Newness itself, after all, is never created out of nothing, but is an ongoing emergent process. Gabriele Helms, too, finds that *Slash*, as well as Thomas King's novel *Green Grass, Running Water* "respond to the choice Aboriginal peoples have long faced in both their literary representations and their social contexts in Canada: assimilation or extermination. The novels reject this simplistic binary antagonism, which ultimately leaves Aboriginal peoples no choice because both options are forms of (self-) annihilation."[111] While Helms sees the novels' rejection of this false choice as a function of dialogism, the examination of contested temporalities in the books is also key. Slash learns that the impossible choice between old and new can be reframed by envisioning the temporality of a human life as well as a community in terms of blending, process, and renewal. A way of life must adapt over time as conditions evolve, and, importantly, this process is distinct from the idea that entirely new practices must supersede the old. In the words of an "old man" who advises Slash on how to prevent a traditional medicine place from being rezoned into a tourist attraction, "it's important that the place be protected. But the fact that it was a medicine place which once meant something to our people isn't enough. It's like an old basket on a museum shelf. You can't preserve our culture that way. It's using them things that are important. In using it, you understand it. That's what our culture is. You protect it by using it."[112] As the novel draws to a close, Slash tells his son Marlon, "You are an Indian of a special generation. Your world will be hard, but you will grow up proud to be Indian … You are the part of me that extends in a line up towards the future."[113] The notion that Indigenous modes of temporality and thought are legitimate in their own right, and are living rather than fossilized, is of critical importance here even if the broad goal of an acceptable quality of life for Indigenous peoples remains largely unrealized.

The re-legitimizing and ongoing evolution of Indigenous thought is also visible in the very form of Armstrong's novel. The narrative of Slash's experiences follows an extensive string of events tied to the history of Indigenous activism in the 1960s and 1970s – he attends meeting after meeting, travelling from city to city – and while Armstrong describes many changes in her protagonist over the years of the story, the narrative does not adhere to the typical Western framework in which events are shaped into rising actions that lead toward a definitive climax, making the form of the novel disconcertingly "flat" for many Western readers. As Helen Hoy points out, the fact that *Slash* is "not readily assimilable into a western literary tradition" has often caused readers to question the value of the book altogether.[114] Caught up in these issues is the broader historical link between print literacy and linearity. In his seminal comparative study of orality and print literacy, Walter Ong argues that while print culture places a strong emphasis on the "climactic linear plot" shape, oral cultures operate independently from the assumption that such a linear narrative shape is necessary or even possible.[115] Oral stories, he suggests, tend to rely more on strategic redundancies, and also place emphasis on empathetic relations rather than the production of objective distance, and on particular situations rather than abstractions.[116] While various aspects of Ong's work have been contested, his study does highlight some of the more significant idiosyncratic characteristics of oral and written storytelling.[117] Reading *Slash* through Ong's theory illuminates the fact that by using the exemplary written form of the novel, but shaping the narrative in terms more closely associated with orality, Armstrong walks a fine line. She is able to critique and reshape Western notions of linearity and narrative resolution using the very written language that has gone hand in hand with Western temporal domination, yet runs the risk of having her novel dismissed as a "failed" story because it does not fulfill the expected narrative shape of the written form. When understood as a text that intentionally challenges the assumption of linearity through the adaptation of oral methods, *Slash* can be seen as a work whose form complements its content in the project of resisting literary and temporal colonization. In this sense, the protagonist of the story and the book itself both carry out similarly precarious, and significant, articulations of alternative temporal structures.

In her essay "Land Speaking," Armstrong reflects on the way that speaking in her native N'silxchn (Okanagan) language allows her to think differently than when she speaks in English. She explains that Okanagan storytelling "relies heavily on the fluidity of time sense that the language offers,"[118] and that, when she writes in English, she attempts to echo the Okanagan emphasis on orality "to construct a similar sense of movement and rhythm through sound patterns."[119] *Slash* serves a similar function, deploying techniques of orality not necessarily primarily through sound patterns, but through the shape of the narrative itself. Armstrong's comments about the importance of understanding her storytelling from an Indigenous perspective first (rather than seeing her work simply as an adaptation of primarily Western forms) highlight the problematic tendency of Western critics to read Indigenous texts using Western criteria. Thomas King seeks to address this problem by suggesting that the diversity of Indigenous literature can usefully be described using several terms that avoid privileging European ideas of progress and colonialism. *Slash* can be said to adhere to King's concepts of polemical literature, which "chronicles the imposition of non-Native expectations and insistences (political, social, scientific) on Native communities and the methods of resistance employed by Native people in order to maintain both their communities and cultures"; interfusional literature, or "that part of Native literature which is a blending of oral literature and written literature"; and, of the most relevance here, associational literature, which tends to describe a Native community, concentrating

> on the daily activities and intricacies of Native life and organizing the elements of plot along a rather flat narrative line that ignores the ubiquitous climaxes and resolutions that are so valued in non-Native literature. In addition to this flat narrative line, associational literature leans towards the group rather than the single, isolated character, creating a fiction that de-values heroes and villains in favour of the members of a community, a fiction which eschews judgements and conclusions.[120]

By confounding the expectation, built largely into the novel form itself, of a European narrative arc, Armstrong advances Indigenous storytelling modes as legitimate in their own right, and as living systems able to reshape themselves to fit within different delivery mechanisms. Far from abandoning the Okanagan storytelling tradition in which she is trained, Armstrong engages in a productive dialogue with the form of the printed novel, an undertaking that, like Slash's life experiences, is best understood as an ongoing process rather than a neatly shaped narrative arc leading toward a definitive conclusion. If Beth Cuthand's "post-Oka" woman responds to the innovative critical questioning processes of postmodernism by saying, "What took you so long?," Armstrong likewise shows that the subversion of typical European narrative form in an Indigenous novel can be strikingly similar, in some ways, to the challenges that postmodern fiction poses to narrative traditions. The continuous remaking of "old" Indigenous storytelling modes can speak with great adeptness to present cultural circumstances.

Armstrong again takes up contested cultural temporalities in a poem memorably titled "Trickster Time." Based on a series of hassles that Armstrong and five of her writer friends experienced at the Vancouver airport, the poem describes how the group's flight to New Zealand via Los Angeles was repeatedly cancelled, rebooked, victimized by computer glitches, and transferred between different airlines at the last minute.[121]

The sequence of events creates the impression that the friends, who are "Cree Okanagan Nanaimo Salish Inuit and Mohawk,"[122] are always late and rushing to catch up, or early and having to wait, and that being unsure of whether there is anything they can do to control the situation they may as well submit to the ludicrous circumstances and endure them with grace and humour. In the first lines of the poem Armstrong personifies the chaos as the traditional trickster figure:

> We saw trickster
> there at the airport
> only he wasn't raven form
> coyote nanabush napi or wasakeja[123]

The trickster figure has taken on a new form, specially chosen for the occasion: "he looked just like one of them / behind the computers."[124] As he tap dances across luggage carousels and slides down escalator rails, trickster appears to take great pleasure in preventing the friends from reaching the moment when they will actually board a plane. At the agent's computer terminal, "trickster bounces across the screen / laughing hysterically and keeping time / from moving."[125] The brilliant line break, where trickster's clocklike act of "keeping time" transforms into the *breakdown* of time's regular forward motion, speaks to the figure's ambiguous and contradictory status as both enabler and disabler, an icon of Indigenous culture and a conspirator with colonialist power structures. Settler culture itself, which creates strict regulating mechanisms and then prevents the Indigenous friends from actually accomplishing their goal, both keeps time and keeps time from moving.

When they are finally booked onto a new flight with time to spare, the friends compose themselves and slacken their pace:

> we're not worried we can wait
> we know there must be a reason
> we can have the time to have a bite
> the time to relax that's what we needed
> boarding cards in hand we all sip coffee
> no sign of trickster[126]

Still, they agree to pass through the US customs screening "early this time just in case,"[127] and sure enough, trickster returns – "tap tap tap tap" – at the moment the immigration agent pulls aside one member of the group. "Sorry you can't go through sir," the agent says. "The U.S. classifies you as an / undesirable alien."[128] A member of Armstrong's group replies,

> "What the hell, none in this party that are aliens. YOU all are
> aliens don't you remember THAT."
> but nobody's face betrays the weak moment
> tick tick tick tick more time passes
> its hard to stay positive[129]

The contested label of "alien," which the immigration agent tries to attach to the member of Armstrong's group, is pointedly reversed; Indigenous cultures can hardly be alien compared with more recently arrived settlers. And yet, the moment betrays a weakness, as the Indigenous challenge to the dominant temporal frame and its entrenched structure of power appears futile. While the immigration agent finally concedes – "we will allow you a / temporary stop in L.A. on the way to New Zealand"[130] – this victory also reinforces the idea that the Indigenous people are mere guests, temporary visitors whose passage must be subject to bureaucratic approval and strict timing.

As the poem draws to a close, Armstrong writes:

> we six laugh running down the corridor
> "So that's what we needed the time for!"
> time to clear the path
> in good time
> Indian time
> the right time
> trickster comes just in the nick of it[131]

Keeping time once again, trickster reveals himself to have orchestrated the eventual success of the group. The frustration of coping with the absurd delays and obstructions of the dominant temporal structure is reframed as a necessary process that, in retrospect, was always leading toward a positive outcome.

Finally, an italicized note at the end of the poem casts normative temporality itself in an ironic light:

> *Jeannette Armstrong recorded this on paper*
> *somewhere in the air*
> *between Vancouver and Aoteroa / New Zealand*
> *over the international time line*
>
> *sometime between yesterday and tomorrow*
> *whichever suits you best as we seem to have lost*
> *December 1, 1990, unexplainably*
> *somewhere in the time zone she chooses that day*
> *to set this in memory in thin air*[132]

Highlighting the precariousness of assumed structures of time, the note declares that the apparently entrenched concepts of calendar dates, meridian lines, and standard time zones are in fact partial and arbitrary, framing them as inherently contradictory constructs that would be absurd to take too seriously. Even the current day's date, in the end, is something chosen and rechosen to suit particular needs. Taking this choice upon herself, Armstrong deconstructs the authority of normative time by showing, effortlessly, that it has already deconstructed itself.

Thomas King, a writer who is variously described as Canadian, Cherokee, Greek, and American, frequently uses trickster figures to satirize settler-Indigene relations in Canada, and, like Armstrong, he locates normative temporality as a particularly potent site for parody and resistance. In his short story "Coyote and the Enemy Aliens," as in many of his other stories, King writes in the first-person voice of a narrator who speaks in a colloquial style as though the words are transcribed from oral storytelling:

Sometimes that Napioa comes by my good place and says, tell us a good story. So I do. Sometimes I tell those good stories from the Indian time. And sometimes I tell those good stories from the European time. Grown-up stories. Baby stories.

Sometimes I take a nap.

Sometimes I tell Coyote stories. Boy, you got to be careful with those Coyote stories.[133]

Are we to understand that Indian stories are "grown-up," and European stories are childish? This would suggest a pointed reversal of the linear Imperial Time that frames Indigenous culture as underdeveloped and infantile. As soon as he has articulated an apparent distinction, though, between stories from "the Indian time" and stories from "the European time," King's narrator complicates the matter by introducing the notion of "Coyote stories," implying that Coyote, the trickster, plays a role that lies somewhere in between or causes a blending of Indian and European modes. The confusion of different cultural frames of time is inherently tricksterlike; it is something "you got to be careful with." King tends to use humour to both conceal and reveal matters of serious social concern, and the apparently lighthearted warning to "be careful" with Coyote stories turns out later on to signal the dangers of Canadian state racism, not only toward Indigenous peoples, but toward Japanese Canadians during the Second World War.

While the narrator warns his listeners of Coyote's tricks, and often speaks directly to Coyote to caution him against crafty or foolish behaviour, the trickster figure is at the same time inherent within the narrator himself, who intentionally conjures up the trickster by choosing to "tell you a Coyote story."[134] This particular story, the narrator explains, follows Coyote's journey west toward the narrator's house:

> That was in European time ... 1940. Maybe it was 1944. No, it was 1942. Coyote comes to my house in 1941.[135]

Like Armstrong's "unexplainable" calendar dates, King's intentional fooling with regards to the Gregorian year serves to make light of the very notion of a strictly delineated linear European timekeeping system. At the same time, the listing of dates over a five-year span of war is a reminder that the dispossession and internment of Japanese Canadians was a protracted affair. The arbitrary timing of any one particular act of dispossession during this long span makes the circumstances all the more terrifying. Working on behalf of the government, Coyote rounds up the Japanese Canadians, claiming, "This story is not a good Coyote story. This story is a good Canadian story";[136] trickery is not an accidental part of Canada's history, but is intrinsic to the nation's character. To his surprise, though, the RCMP then begin rounding up Indigenous people and Coyote himself. Insofar as Coyote is aligned with Canadian duplicity, the quick shift of power suggests that the very notion of nationhood and its associated social structures is transitory, arbitrary, and subject to continuous flux. If Canadians of particular ethnic descent can be declared aliens at any given moment, then the concept of Canada in turn is vulnerable to temperamental changes that can occur at any time. Citizenship and nationhood function as key tools of temporal power, and their strategic deployment impacts individuals across various subaltern groups. Renate Eigenbrod reads "Coyote and the Enemy Aliens," published in 2005, specifically as a caution against "the branding of all non-white people as potential 'terrorists' in 'the war against terror.'"[137] Across different eras of Canadian history, the membership of individuals within the social collective can effectively be revoked for arbitrary reasons at arbitrary times. As the poet Annharte writes, perhaps only half-jokingly, "I have provable identity in case / clan membership expires annually."[138]

King's 1993 novel *Green Grass, Running Water* also satirizes and resists European temporality, focusing especially on the role of narrative in articulating competing notions of time. Like *Slash*, the novel blends Indigenous oral and Western written storytelling forms; King's first-person narrator carries out an extended conversation with Coyote that resists the closed shape typical of linear narratives, yet the story as a whole takes the form of a novel, the exemplary Western written mode. This self-conscious negotiation with Western narrative becomes a central point of inquiry, as the characters endlessly debate whether the story has begun correctly, is proceeding correctly, or will have to begin again. When a character known as the Lone Ranger tries to begin the narrative with Western clichés such as "Once upon a time,"[139] his companions ask him to start again until, finally, he successfully launches the story with the words "Gha! ... Higayv:ligé:i,"[140] a phrasing that Jane Flick and Helen Hoy identify as "the ceremonial opening of storytelling in a Cherokee divining ceremony, divining for water and so in a sense for the future."[141] Flick goes on to note that "Higayv:ligé:i" specifically refers to First Woman or Star Woman, who falls from the sky before the creation of Turtle Island in a number of North American Indigenous cosmologies.[142] The importance of Indigenous cultural forms for shaping the narrative becomes a central motif in the novel, and the means by which King seeks to undermine the dominance of Western notions of narrative and time.

The ability of the novel to question assumed Western knowledge manifests in various ways, many of which have been the subject of abundant critical commentary. As Gabriele Helms notes, "King subverts the expectations of a white invader-settler culture by reinscribing or parodying many of its central icons: Christianity (especially the Bible), notions of progress, literary canons, history, and stereotypes of Aboriginals."[143] For Arnold Davidson, Priscilla Walton, and Jennifer Andrews, the novel thrives on the techniques of inversion, counter-discourse, and intertextuality.[144] Sharon Bailey notes that "much of the humour of the novel derives from 'orally' pointing out errors in the written stories," thus commenting on "the inflexibility of written texts and the superiority of the more plastic oral storytelling technique."[145] A special issue of *Canadian Literature* on Thomas King in 1999 covers additional critical ground. While a detailed reading of the novel would inevitably repeat much of this commentary, certain elements of the story are worth highlighting specifically in the context of critical time studies, since the politics of the representation of temporal power go beyond the most commonly cited concerns with the revision of dominant history.

Temporal politics are at work within a central conflict in the novel, the construction of the Grand Baleen Dam that promises to flood the home of Eli Stands Alone. In addition to imposing a very real physical danger, the dam serves as a lens to focus the dominant sense of temporality on the present (on the immediate expected benefit of electricity generation, lakeshore property creation, and financial profits), drawing attention away from the past and future issues necessary to Indigenous and environmental justice. Even Charlie Looking Bear, who is paid to defend the dam construction company against Eli's legal challenges, acknowledges that "once Duplessis started construction on the dam, nothing stopped it. Environmental concerns were cast aside. Questions about possible fault lines that ran under the dam were dismissed. Native land claims that had been in the courts for over fifty years were shelved."[146] Clifford Sifton, meanwhile, whose job is to return to Eli's house every day to ask Eli to relinquish possession of his property, sees the persistent legal challenge of Indigenous treaty rights as an ongoing irritation. He complains to Eli that because the government felt generous back in the last ice age, and made promises it never intended to keep, I have to come by every morning and ask the same stupid question ... Hell, Eli, those treaties aren't worth a damn. Government only made them for convenience. Who'd of guessed that there would still be Indians kicking around in the twentieth century ... You can't live in the past. My dam is part of the twentieth century. Your house is part of the nineteenth.[147]

The notion that Indigenous land ownership and treaty rights belong to a previous century, which telescopes into "the last ice age," reflects the colonialist strategy of framing Indigenous existence as hopelessly out of date, the relic of a bygone age. Sifton is one of several characters named after historical figures; Clifford Sifton was minister of the interior under Wilfrid Laurier, and advocated irrigation projects that led to the damming of rivers in southern Alberta. King's choice of names here, then, suggests that Western colonizing strategies themselves have failed to evolve with the times. It is Clifford, with his antiquated colonial attitude, not Eli, who is a relic of the past.

King also juxtaposes the politics of Western progress and Indigenous outdatedness against the tensions of Canada-US relations. When George snaps pictures of the traditional Sun Dance event despite being told that photography is not allowed, Eli exposes the camera's film, erasing the photographs. George shouts, "You can't believe in this shit! ... This is ice age crap! ... Come on! It's the twentieth century."[148] The statement echoes George's earlier claim that the United States is superior to Canada because "Americans were modern, poised to take advantage of the future, to move ahead. Canadians were traditionalists, stuck in the past and unwilling to take chances."[149] While George does not give any thought to the relationship between the two comments, King is crafting a subtle reminder that the same methods of temporal discrimination Canada has used to disempower Indigenous peoples can also belittle Canada itself.

With these insidious temporal politics at stake, the importance of King's self-conscious critique of dominant narrative structures becomes increasingly clear. Presenting alternative plotlines to the linear Imperial story is not enough; the very form of the storytelling, the way that beginnings are chosen, and the matter of who is allowed to frame the course of events, must be continuously examined and revised. As the narrator and other characters repeatedly reject the way the story has unfolded, they return again and again to new attempts at beginning. When Coyote asks, "How many more times do we have to do this?" the narrator replies, "Until we get it right."[150] This could be called an embodiment of a provisional, rather than singular or permanent, approach to temporality – a concept that I will discuss in the Conclusion.

Near the end of the story, three cars (whose names, "the Nissan, the Pinto, and the Karmann-Ghia," echo the names of Columbus's ships, the *Niña*, the *Pinta*, and the *Santa María*) float mysteriously on the water and collide with the dam, destroying it and draining the human-made lake, while "below, in the valley, the water rolled on as it had for eternity."[151] Recalling that water has been present since the "beginning" of the story, the blockage of water behind the dam (a supposed icon of progress) suggests that the construction project has served in a graceless and dangerous way to interrupt the flow of time itself; only through the dam's destruction can the normal flow be renewed. This renewal is still incomplete, though, since a tour guide had earlier described the lake as "the eleventh largest manmade lake in Alberta";[152] the drama that has played out at the Grand Baleen Dam is but one instance out of many. In another sense, just as the automobiles destroy the dam that stood as a symbol of Indigenous disempowerment, King uses the Western "vehicle" of the written novel form to dismantle and reshape the larger Western narrative structures that have reinforced racialized temporalities, a project that must continuously be reworked, begun again, and applied to different situations.

In the final lines of the novel Coyote complains that "there is water everywhere," to which the narrator replies, "'That's true,' I says. 'And here's how it happened.'"[153] Even the ending, then, is another beginning, reshaping the narrative into a circle of continuous renewal where the work of storymaking continues. Is it a coincidence that the Houghton Mifflin hardcover edition runs precisely 360 pages, echoing the shape of a complete circle in which any given point can serve as a beginning of the whole? King's insistence on continuous process as a necessary corrective to linear goal-based progress is visible as well in a memorable line when the old Indians are late arriving at the Sun Dance: "'We would have gotten here sooner,' said the Lone Ranger, 'but Coyote knew a short cut.'"[154] Just as racialized temporality must be corrected through an emphasis on circularity, multiplicity, renewal, and process, the idea of a shortcut whose goal is to find the shortest possible straight line between two points serves ultimately as an impediment.

Early in the twenty-first century, one of the prominent voices in Indigenous writing in Canada is that of Joseph Boyden. His first novel, *Three Day Road* (2005), traces the lives of Xavier Bird and Elijah Whiskeyjack, two young Cree men who enlist in the Canadian army during the First World War. The politics of assimilation into Western culture, symbolized monstrously through the soldiers' indoctrination into the violence of trench warfare, form a backdrop to the relationship between Elijah, a former residential school student who speaks English fluently and becomes popular among the white soldiers, and Xavier, who is much more hesitant to engage with Western military culture. As the stakes of assimilation grow into a choice between life and death, Boyden repeatedly frames the Cree characters' uneasy relationship with Western culture in terms of clashing notions of time.

For Neta Gordon, the temporal conflict in the novel lies in the relationship between Western historical time and Indigenous sacred time. Canadian society, with its emphasis on historical progress and assimilationism, frames indigeneity as backwards and outdated; however, by emphasizing the original Cree names of the characters over their anglicized names, Boyden highlights the significance of a "sacred time structure, a structure that opposes the problematic paradigms associated with historical time."[155] Gordon's analysis shows that the novel works to promote the possibility of healing through the use of "a genealogical sense of time" that identifies temporal strength in the continuity of Cree generations,[156] even while this project of escaping normative historical time exists in tension with Boyden's desire "to recover marginalized histories" by commemorating Indigenous contributions to Canada's First World War effort.[157] This analysis is significant in identifying some of the broad sociotemporal conflicts associated with linear Imperial Time and dominant historical narratives. However, Boyden also emphasizes the significance of the characters' explicit encounters with the everyday temporal structures of clocks and calendars. An examination of these direct encounters allows us to identify how the processes of temporal colonization function in a practical sense to draw the Cree characters into the Western social sphere, as well as the ways in which temporal resistance, for Xavier and his aunt Niska, in particular, operates not just through an emphasis on genealogical time, but through the everyday work of critical temporal awareness and an affirmation of the legitimacy of Cree timekeeping.

For Xavier, who is anxious over the dangers of battle, one of the significant early everyday encounters with Western temporality occurs when he asks Elijah for a distraction:

> To keep my head clear, I ask Elijah to teach me more English.
> "Good day, sir," Elijah says. "Do you know the time?"[158]

Fluency in clock time and punctuality occurs to Elijah as the first, most appropriate use for the English language, so that centring one's perspective on the hour of the clock becomes a metaphor for Western culture as a whole. Elijah's easy command of both the English language and clock time reflects the great distance he has travelled on the path of assimilation. Xavier does not yet comment explicitly on this association, but this brief conversation is a clue that Western timekeeping will become a specific site of potential resistance for Xavier later on.

Elijah's association of clock time with English lessons has a historical basis tied not only to the missionary presence in Indigenous communities that I have already mentioned, but also to the residential school system. While Boyden does not make any such specific reference, his writing recalls educational texts such as the Reverend E.B. Glass's volume *Primer and Language Lessons in English and Cree*, circa 1890. Intended as an instructional volume for speakers of the Cree language, the book offers basic English phrases with Cree syllabic translations on the facing pages. Lesson xxx, called "Time of Day," begins with the question, "What time is it?" and proceeds into a discussion of clock hours and the times of day associated with typical (i.e., ideologically based) components of everyday life such as schooling and working hours.[159] Regardless of whether Boyden had such a specific example in mind, he carefully frames Western models of timekeeping as central to the ideological goals of assimilationism. Elijah, who has been through the residential school system, has internalized clock time alongside broader Western cultural beliefs.

Later in the story, Xavier increasingly focuses on Western notions of time as encapsulations of the war-driven culture that threatens to absorb him. "I try to figure out what day today is in the English way of keeping time," he says. "It is high summer, but what day, what month? I slip into a light sleep, remembering that in the way that they keep time, it has been a year now that Elijah and I have been here."[160] Reflecting on the soldiers' marking of Christmas and New Year's Eve, he muses,

> This new year that begins they call 1918. I know that this is how many years have passed since they say their god was born as a man.
>
> This sadness and reflection rubs off on me. I do not like their way of keeping time. Their way is based loosely on the moons but is as orderly as the officers try to keep the trenches, full of meaningless numbers and different names for days that are all the same anyways. I worked it out and I have been with the *wemistikoshiw* twenty-seven full moons. I've been in the battlefields for nineteen full moons. It is a long time, and there is no end in sight for this war they have created.[161]

These passages serve a defamiliarizing function, framing Western temporality as partial and arbitrary, just as the Cree label *wemistikoshiw* challenges the ex-nomination of white people, denying their ability to frame themselves as unnamed and therefore natural. The passages also suggest a deep correspondence between the linear time-counting model and the apparent Western inclination toward perpetual warfare; the strict orderliness of numerical days mirrors the systematic efficiency of the military, denying flexibility and insisting that progress is being made. Worrying that the military culture is coming to define his own existence, Xavier says, "In the dark of night I think that my life has been divided into three for me by these *wemistikoshiw*. There was my life before them and their army, there is my life in their army, and, if I live, there will be my life after I have left it and returned home."[162]

Xavier's fraught encounter with Western society reaches its apex when he determines that Elijah's internalization of the madness of warfare has made him a *windigo* – in Vikki Visvis's words, a "cannibalistic human,

78 PRIMER AND LANGUAGE LESSONS

LESSON XXX.—TIME OF DAY.

clock watch watch-chain

1. What time is it? It is 10 o'clock.

2. When does the sun rise? It rises at half-past six.

3. At what time will you start in the morning? I shall leave at 9 o'clock and 30 minutes.

4. When does your school open? At 9 o'clock.

5. When does it close? At 3.30.

half-past three	3 o'clock and 30 minutes
twelve o'clock	12 o'clock
17 minutes to eleven	10.43
10 minutes past six	6.10
20 minutes past 4	4.20
15 minutes after 5	5.15
5 minutes past 9	9.15

6. We have dinner at 12 o'clock, and supper at 6 o'clock.

7. Every morning we eat breakfast at 7 o'clock.

8. What time do you go to bed? 10 o'clock.

9. At what time do you rise? 5 o'clock.

Figures 4.2a and 4.2b. *Primer and Language Lessons in English and Cree* (E.B. Glass, approx. 1890).

monster, or spirit, informed in this context by Cree and Ojibway beliefs."[163] Taking on his ancestral role of the *windigo* killer, Xavier strangles Elijah, an act that Visvis reads as a response to the novel's assertion that "Windigo psychosis *is* the 'invisible sickness' of the *wemistikoshiw*."[164] Xavier has

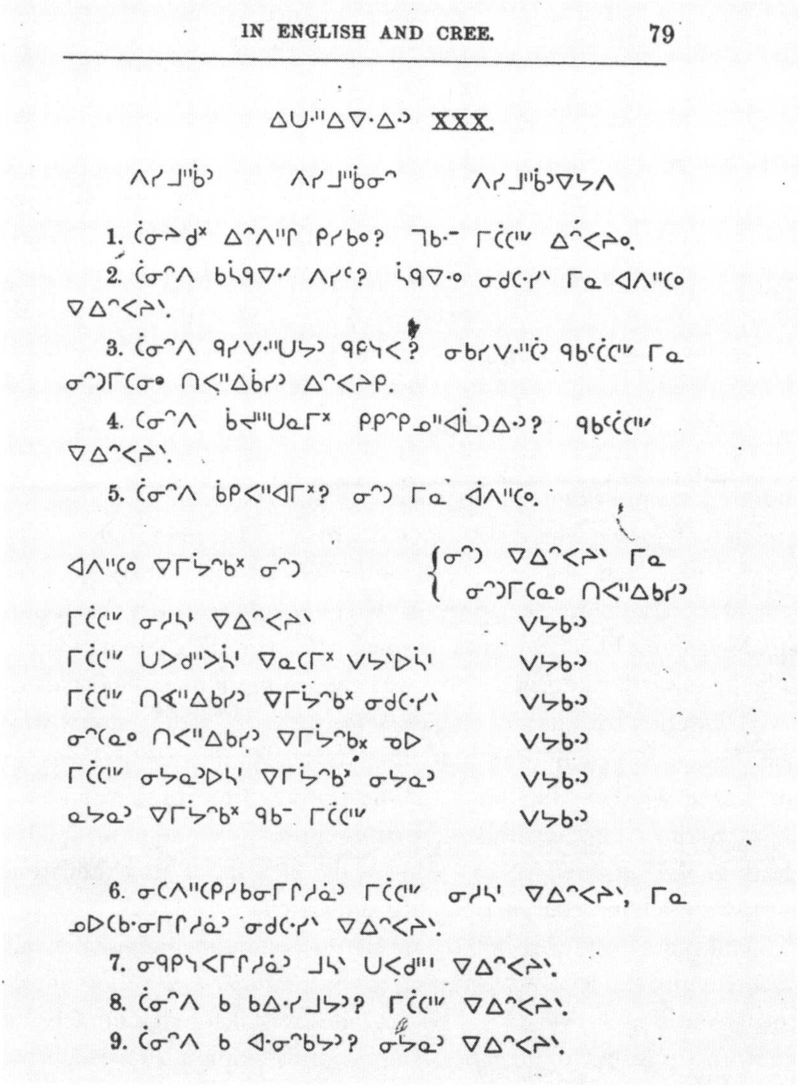
IN ENGLISH AND CREE. 79

ᐃᑌᐧᐦᐃᐁᐧᐃᐧᐤ XXX.

ᐱᓯᒧᐦᑳᐤ ᐱᓯᒧᐦᑲᓂᐢ ᐱᓯᒧᐦᑳᐤᐁᔭᐱ

1. ᑖᓂᔑᑯᕽ ᐃᐢᐱᐦᒋ ᑭᓯᑳᐤ? ᒣᑲᐧᐨ ᒥᑖᑕᐦ ᐃᐢᐸᔑᐤ.

2. ᑖᓂᐢᐱ ᑳᓴᑫᐁᐧᐟ ᐱᓯᐟ? ᓵᑫᐁᐧᐤ ᓂᑯᑕᐧᓯᐢ ᒥᓇ ᐊᐱᐦᑕᐤ ᐁᐃᐢᐸᔑᐢ.

3. ᑖᓂᐢᐱ ᑫᓯᐯᐧᐦᑌᔭᐤ ᑫᑭᓭᐸ? ᓂᑲᓯᐯᐧᐦᑖᐤ ᑫᑲᐟᑖᑕᐦ ᒥᓇ ᓂᐢᑐᒥᑕᓂᐤ ᑎᐸᐦᐃᑳᓱᐤ ᐃᐢᐸᔑᑭ.

4. ᑕᓂᐢᐱ ᑳᐘᐦᑌᓇᒥᕽ ᑭᑭᐢᑭᓄᐦᐊᒫᑐᐃᐧᐤ? ᑫᑲᐟᑖᑕᐦ ᐁᐃᐢᐸᔑᐢ.

5. ᑖᓂᐢᐱ ᑳᑭᐸᐦᐊᒥᕽ? ᓂᐢᑐ ᒥᓇ ᐋᐱᐦᑕᐤ.

ᐊᐱᐦᑕᐤ ᐁᒥᔦᐢᑲᕽ ᓂᐢᑐ { ᓂᐢᑐ ᐁᐃᐢᐸᔑᐢ ᒥᓇ ᓂᐢᑐᒥᑕᓇᐤ ᑎᐸᐦᐃᑲᓱᐤ }

ᒥᑖᑕᐦ ᓂᓱᓴᐠ ᐁᐃᐢᐸᔑᐢ ᐯᔭᑲᐧᐤ

ᒥᑖᑕᐦ ᑌᐳᑯᐦᐳᓵᐠ ᐁᓇᑕᒥᕽ ᐯᔭᐅᐳᓵᐠ ᐯᔭᑲᐧᐤ

ᒥᑖᑕᐦ ᑎᐹᐦᐃᑲᓱᐤ ᐁᒥᔦᐢᑲᕽ ᓂᑯᑕᐧᓯᐢ ᐯᔭᑲᐧᐤ

ᓂᐢᑕᓇᐤ ᑎᐸᐦᐃᑲᓱᐤ ᐁᒥᔦᐢᑲᕽ ᓅᐳ ᐯᔭᑲᐧᐤ

ᒥᑖᑕᐦ ᓂᔭᓇᐤᐳᓴᐠ ᐁᒥᔦᐢᑲᐟ ᓂᔭᓇᐤ ᐯᔭᑲᐧᐤ

ᓇᔭᓇᐤ ᐁᒥᔦᐢᑲᕽ ᑫᑲᐨ ᒥᑖᑕᐦ ᐯᔭᑲᐧᐤ

6. ᓂᑕᐱᐦᑕᑭᓯᑲᓂᒥᑭᓱᓈᐤ ᒥᑖᑕᐦ ᓂᓱᓴᐠ ᐁᐃᐢᐸᔑᐢ, ᒥᓇ ᓄᐳᑕᑲᐧᓂᒥᑭᓱᓈᐤ ᓂᑯᑕᐧᓯᐢ ᐁᐃᐢᐸᔑᐢ.

7. ᓂᑫᑭᓭᐸᒥᑭᓱᓈᐤ ᒧᓴᐢ ᑌᐸᑯᐦ ᐁᐃᐢᐸᔑᐢ.

8. ᑖᓂᐢᐱ ᑲ ᑲᐃᐧᓯᒧᔭᐤ? ᒥᑖᑕᐦ ᐁᐃᐢᐸᔑᐢ.

9. ᑖᓂᐢᐱ ᑲ ᐋᐧᓂᐢᑲᔭᐤ? ᓂᔭᓇᐤ ᐁᐃᐢᐸᔑᐢ.

killed the embodiment of Western violence and assimilation, yet while his act as a *windigo* killer may confirm his status as “a custodian of tribal values and collectivity,” in Gordon’s words,[165] it also runs the risk of descending into the same brutality that he seeks to oppose.

For Xavier and his aunt Niska, who is trained as a medicine woman, the resolution to this trauma again places temporality at the centre. The image of time and life being divided into three parts, which had threatened to absorb Xavier into Western identity, begins to carry a more hopeful sense of belonging and renewal, as Niska impresses upon him the importance of threes in *Cree* culture, and the belief that "we will all some-day walk the three-day road" that marks the transition from life into death.[166] When Niska receives word that Xavier has been killed in battle, she plans her own three-day voyage from her home in the Ontario bush to the train station to collect the wounded Elijah, a passage toward the deathly Western society embroiled in war, and one that raises temporal confusions similar to the ones Xavier has experienced. Niska says, "I had Joseph explain to me how the *wemistikoshiw* calendar worked, what month I was to be there, and I made careful preparations to journey by canoe to that town where Elijah would arrive."[167] The train station itself, which Niska reaches by learning about the Western calendar system, is an icon of strict, absolute clock time. At the station, she discovers that it is in fact Xavier, not Elijah, who has returned to Canada alive. Seeing that he is badly injured, traumatized, and addicted to morphine, she begins to travel with him back home along the same three-day path, a reverse voy-age through which Boyden hints that Xavier is undergoing a passage away from Western temporality and the deathly spectre of war, and back into traditional Cree territory – a transition that Elijah never makes, his death as a *windigo* serving in a sense as the final act of his assimilation into Western knowledge, temporality, and violence.

Significantly, as she leaves the train station behind them, Niska reveals an alternative model of timekeeping to the *wemistikoshiw* notion of cal-endars and clocks: "We do not get far," she says, "before the sun lets me know that it is time to prepare a camp."[168] This simple acknowledgment of solar time reckoning indicates that non-Western temporal emphases exist, with their own centres of accuracy and legitimacy. The importance of this idea is expanded as Niska's primary role in Xavier's life becomes clear: she is a storyteller, who enfolds her ailing nephew in recollections of his youth and her own upbringing, reminding him of the culture into which he was born – including an emphasis on the use of seasons, moons, winters, and animal behaviour to reckon time – and embodying a mode of existence that remains fully functional outside of Western culture and its assumption of inevitable assimilation.

During the critical moment of Xavier's feverish near-death struggle to recover from the physical and psychological violence of the war, Niska tells the story of Xavier's experience when, as a child of just "six winters" tracking a bull moose through a snow-covered forest, he encountered a circle of dozens of grouse "moving in unison around a tree" in a dance so mesmerizing that he "lost track of time."[169] The pattern of the dance, Niska explains, reminded Xavier of the traditional celebratory summer gathering that he had attended in the past:

> a tradition they carried on despite the stern words of the *wemistiko-shiw* church. You stared at these birds dancing in the snow, the sunlight reflecting in it in thousands of tiny ice crystals. You saw in their movement the movement of your own people as they travelled from winter to summer to winter again, dancing through the years.
>
> You saw for the first time the circle. Even though you could not yet express it in words, you understood the seasons, the teepee, the shaking tent, the wigwam, the fire circle, the *matatosowin*. You saw all of life is in the circle, and realized that you always come back, in one way or another, to where you have been before.[170]

While Xavier had learned to associate Western time reckoning with violence and assimilation, it is only through Niska's storytelling that a full appreciation of the possibilities of Cree time reckoning returns to him. Cree temporality is primarily understood here not insofar as it opposes Western time, but rather as its own legitimate and self-sufficient mode. The only way in which Cree time is connected to Western society in this scene is in the fact that the Cree mode continues to operate, and to function as a celebratory embodiment of a way of life, *despite* the "stern words" of Western colonialism, which, referred to only briefly, fade immediately into obscurity. Likewise, the division of time into three parts, which threatened to define Xavier's life in *wemistikoshiw* terms, is now reappropriated into Cree culture through Xavier's three-day journey into his traditional territory, a journey that becomes his rebirth into a continuing familial cycle, as the novel ends with a hazy vision of his own children to be born in the years to come.

Daughters are Forever (2002), a novel by Stó:lō author Lee Maracle, also articulates the temporal disruptions that have accompanied the colonization of Indigenous populations. Like Boyden's investigation of clashing notions of time, *Daughters are Forever* acknowledges both the traumas and the forms of agency and cultural affirmation that can emerge from such conflicts. Maracle, though, focuses more intensively on how a concentrated process of grappling with past and passing time can allow for time itself to become a productive force once more. The protagonist, Marilyn, is a Salish social worker in late twentieth-century Vancouver, but the narrative opens with a description of the beginning of creation and the first emergence of human life and culture through the productive energies of Westwind and Sky Woman. This idealized society of Turtle Islanders is then shattered by the arrival of hungry, diseased "newcomers" who slaughter and scalp countless members of the Indigenous population for hundreds of years, leaving the survivors shocked and immobilized. "Women," Maracle writes, "the keepers of cultural survival, passed on stillness as the ultimate way to protect their daughters."[171] These women begin to be abused by their own men, who in turn are filled with shame:

> It needs to be expressed, pushed up and out so they may sing again, but five centuries of "Hush, don't cry" holds the expression of their shame still. Under it lies a dangerous grief ... Their world has lost its future. Cut off from considering their past, they list in the momentary context of the present ...
> They mark time. Time is the enemy of the dispirited. Those who dare not make use of it mark time for death, for murder. These men wander aimlessly, killing time in small pieces.[172]

Only after this introductory section does the narrative pick up the story of Marilyn's present-day life as a social worker who is haunted by her fractured relationships with her grown-up daughters even as she helps other Indigenous mothers whose children have been apprehended by child services. This narrative feat of establishing many centuries of context for the present situation affords a radically long historical perspective, and frames the crises of abuse in Native communities – child abuse, spousal abuse, and alcohol abuse – not as the result of innate characteristics or simple personal failures, but as the ongoing consequences of five hundred years of colonization. If there is a dominant ideological belief that abusive behaviour must be understood at the level of the individual and within the time frame of a particular person's life, Maracle's expansive narrative emphasizes a broader context of time, shifting the understanding of abuse toward a temporal frame that sees experiences and decisions at the level of the individual always in negotiation with long-standing social histories.[173]

The experience of time for Marilyn – and, the narrative suggests, for colonized Indigenous populations at large – is one of paralysis, confrontation, confusion, and perhaps madness. As she travels the country giving speeches on the need for Indigenous communities to engage in the long process of healing themselves, Marilyn questions her own work: "Her presentations seemed stupid just now. Time was killing families while she trod the lecture circuit attempting to stop the clock and turn around an impossible situation conjured from attitude, condition and history."[174] Just as the shame-filled men in the introductory section "wander aimlessly, killing time," time in turn becomes a violent opponent responsible for the ongoing destruction. Meanwhile, Marilyn's daughters Cat and Lindy are constantly anxious about their mother's well-being, causing Marilyn to lament the reversal of the generational temporality that is key to parental caregiving: "*Oh gawd, my children are taking care of me; it should be the other way around. How the hell did I ever get things so upside-down?*"[175] She begins to experience episodes of "gapping," where intense memories of the past threaten "her capacity to differentiate between past and current time. Today, yesterday, tomorrow all melded into one another."[176] Driven by an awareness that the "separation of moments in time defines sanity," Marilyn becomes obsessed with her inability to stabilize her own grasp on time.[177]

In the late stages of the novel, influenced by the energies of Westwind and her own reflections, Marilyn invites Cat and Lindy to her home, picks up the wooden spoon with which she had hit them as children after their father's abandonment, and breaks it in half, saying, "I should have done that years ago."[178] She hugs Cat and Lindy, who cry and break the spoon into smaller pieces. This moment serves as the initiation of a form of familial truth and reconciliation, and allows Marilyn to appreciate the enduring quality of family relations: "The timelessness made her feel forever alive – floating in space above time. Forever being has no beginning and is without end; it is about being. It comforted and encouraged her. She felt safe."[179] Time shifts from a site of confrontation, limitation, and pain to a source of renewal, eternity, and comfort. In the final scenes Cat announces that she is pregnant – a sign of futurity and regeneration – and the three women decide to begin family therapy sessions to continue the healing process. They walk through Vancouver's

Marpole neighbourhood toward the point where the river meets the sea, seeking what Marilyn's grandmother had described as "the ocean of love we all swam through before we arrived here."[180] As they approach this intersection of waters, Lindy and Cat reveal that a seer and healer named Dolly lives nearby. Dolly, Cat explains, "helped us to find ourselves when we were teenagers. Oddly enough, she helped us to carry on loving you, despite all the memories."[181] Overcome with tears, Marilyn embraces her own shame: "It was a good feeling, this shame. She let it sink in. It was the shame of knowing there was no excuse for what she'd done."[182] As Dolly's house comes into view, Marilyn recalls one of her grandmother's stories, where a lake says to a distressed woman, "Sometimes to go forward you have to go back to the beginning."[183] The novel ends with the remark that "Dolly's house would be a kind of beginning for Marilyn and her girls."[184] This place where the rush and turmoil of what appears to be a unidirectional linear flow of water rejoins its deep and eternal source symbolizes the family's return to a regenerative relationship with time. In the sense that Maracle's narrative attempts to articulate the broader experiences of Indigenous populations, this sequence also suggests that only by attending to the origins of the current situation – only by acknowledging the shamefulness of both imposed and self-inflicted histories – can new beginnings and renewed origins be embraced. A long view of time that acknowledges present cultural and personal traumas while simultaneously contextualizing these within broader histories allows time to reveal its productive capacities once more. The literal daughters who are born to a mother exist within individual lifespans, yet they shape the ongoing character of familial existence in perpetuity, effectively forever. And metaphoric "daughters" – the consequences or progeny of crucial events from ages ago – continue to cause repercussions through the depths of time. The assertion of *Daughters are Forever* is that present experience for an individual or a society, especially traumatic experience, can be understood and thus reshaped only through a temporal frame that expands far enough to accommodate the broad context of cultural time alongside the temporal existence of individuals.

THE ONGOING PROCESS OF RESHAPING

The Truth and Reconciliation Commission of Canada, which "hopes to guide and inspire First Nations, Inuit, and Métis peoples and Canadians in a process of truth and healing leading toward reconciliation and renewed relationships based on mutual understanding and respect," appears somewhat divided between the above description of reconciliation as a process "leading toward" a definitive outcome, and the idea of reconciliation as "an *ongoing* individual and collective process."[185] Commenting on Prime Minister Stephen Harper's public apology to those affected by the residential schools, an apology that describes the abuses as belonging to a past "chapter" in Canadian history, Matthew Dorrell argues that "the construction of the statement of apology as a narrative of progress confines the abuses of the residential schools system to the past while removing the contextual information needed to understand the schools system as a critical component of a larger and continuing colonial project";[186] what is needed, then, is "a conceptual move from reconciliation to reconciling, from a finalizing process seeking closure to one which privileges an openended, ongoing dialogue between and amongst individuals and communities."[187] The partial and gradual infiltration of non-linear temporal modes into the cultural discourse, visible in comments such as these, offers the possibility of a corrective to temporal discrimination, and encourages examination of actual ongoing consequences rather than an all too easy reliance on the metanarrative of linear progressive history.

Sioui's comment that "at this moment, Canadian multiculturalism cannot have its full meaning, because Canadian thinking is still profoundly linear and the concept of multiculturalism does not agree with linear thinking,"[188] recognizes the barriers to alternative visions of temporality, while holding out hope that temporal modes centred on Indigenous cultures have at least the potential to reshape dominant discourse over time. Taiaiake Alfred, too, anticipates a broad social movement that eventually "will transcend Euroamerican notions of time and place that constrain the recognition of Onkwehonwe identities and rights to those who act in ways and live in places sanctioned by the state."[189] To the extent that they envision a theoretically more just future, such predictions reveal that the notion of linear goal setting, in the specific rather than the metanarrative sense, has real purchase even within a conception of time that seeks to operate outside of the normative mode.

Regardless of whether their authorship is traceable through Indigenous lineage, thoughtful works of literature not only bear witness to the limitations of a singular view of time, but they also contribute toward the gradual and ongoing reshaping of social temporal discourse that Sioui, Alfred, and Dorrell advocate. Eden Robinson alludes to such a process in her novel *Monkey Beach* when the character Jimmy, who believes that giving crows "things to steal" will bring good luck, leaves "an old run-down pocket watch on our porch." A crow named Spotty picks up the watch and places it carefully on a road where it is run over by a car. Spotty then "picked at the exposed innards of the pocket watch. She gathered up some of the pieces and flew away."[190] Like Thomas King, Robinson uses an automobile, that exemplary image of progress, to smash an icon of Western temporality whose pieces can then be salvaged and reshaped into something new. Alongside the importance of respecting Indigenous modes of temporality in their own right – a project to which many of the authors discussed here contribute – the intentional reshaping of Western normative modes of time emblematized by the destruction and repurposing of Jimmy's pocket watch is a vital form of intervention into the linked processes of colonization and temporal discrimination. Everyday temporal discourse that is willing to disassemble and repurpose itself can help not only to resist temporal discrimination, but also to contextualize Canada's present-day existence within long-standing issues of contested indigeneity, ownership, and priority. Incorporating silenced temporalities into normal discourse allows the everyday language that has been complicit in temporal hegemony to transform itself, embracing a consciousness of its own embattled histories. In the final chapter of this book I will look more broadly at the possibilities of temporal reshaping in Canadian literature.

Disrupting and Remaking
Constructions of Time

It becomes clear that I must destroy my watch, that false professor of time, and free its tiny slave.[1]

Don McKay

What is time, she thought, but two hands shaking us from sleep.[2]

Sheila Watson

By now it has become apparent that literary texts have often sought not only to witness and represent temporal power relations, but also to question, test, and reshape the relationships between time, power, and everyday life. From the leap of faith that Panych's unnamed man takes in order to escape his confinement in the days of the week, to Margaret Sweatman's critique of the concentration of temporal power in the hands of the elite, to Jeannette Armstrong's and Thomas King's reshaping of Western narrative temporal sequence – literature and art have demonstrated a profound ability to articulate the often invisible impact of dominant temporal constructs and to rethink and repurpose the cultural mechanisms of time. In this final chapter I offer several case studies of works that deserve to be recognized as iconic in their self-conscious negotiations with the role of time in social interactions and their productive dismantling and reconstruction of dominant temporal codes. These texts reveal the ways in which normative time is a stronghold that protects, and is protected by, existing structures of social power, but is simultaneously a makeshift apparatus always potentially on the verge of collapse. These works also indicate that while the construction of new, more just models of time is always possible, no temporal structure is free from the politics of social power relations.

One of the themes across many works that question structures of time is the idea that moments of acute crisis – whether personal, social, or ecological – are especially amenable to temporal disruption; crises serve as potent sites for examining the limitations of dominant temporality with fresh eyes and for developing renewed forms of temporal experience. When Yann Martel's protagonist in *Life of Pi* finds himself hopelessly adrift at sea in a small lifeboat with only a deadly Bengal tiger for company – a crisis par excellence – the situation causes him, inevitably, to recognize the arbitrariness and fallibility of normative timekeeping:

> I survived because I made a point of forgetting. My story started on a calendar day – July 2nd, 1977 – and ended on a calendar day – February 14th, 1978 – but in between there was no calendar. I did not count the days or the weeks or the months. Time is an illusion that only makes us pant. I survived because I forgot even the very notion of time.
>
> What I remember are events and encounters and routines, markers that emerged here and there from the ocean of time and imprinted themselves on my memory.[3]

Only his catastrophic removal from the normal measurement of time causes Pi to realize the extent to which the everyday counting of days and weeks is "an illusion that only makes us pant." Still, though, he believes that this counting process is synonymous with time itself, that ceasing to keep track of the calendar is equivalent to forgetting "the very notion of time," an assumption that proves erroneous in the next paragraph where the passage of time clearly remains in place in his consciousness: Pi now begins to measure time through *events* that serve, like a form of calendar, to differentiate one moment from the next. While he has proclaimed himself free from the Crusoelike act of counting the days, he now counts another form of temporal sequence. A terrible crisis has revealed the limitations of normative time and has created the opportunity for a new form of time reckoning to come about, even if Pi is not fully conscious of his own temporal innovation. What is more, Pi's form of event time, while spontaneously constructed, echoes the everyday experience through which remembered events *always* shape our own personal timelines. Even while Pi's temporal adventure dismantles normative time, it also reminds us that the strictly numerical counting mechanisms that appear to rule our lives were never omnipotent but exist always in an ongoing negotiation with the subjective experiences of time that remain central to our survival. While the particular circumstances of this crisis are unique – as the maritime investigator who interviews Pi about his ordeal writes, "*Very few castaways can claim to have survived so long at sea as Mr Patel, and none in the company of an adult Bengal tiger*"[4] – its consequences have a universalizing tendency. The texts to which I now turn also investigate the dismantling and reconstruction of widely recognizable human encounters with time, but enact these temporal reconstructions through crises that more directly mirror the prevalent social anxieties of war, colonialism, and civilizational collapse.

TIME IS SHATTERED, BUT THE WATCH TICKS ON: TIMOTHY FINDLEY'S *THE WARS*

Timothy Findley's novel *The Wars*, which won the Governor General's Award, is among Canada's best-known war novels. As many critics have shown, *The Wars* offers striking commentary on masculinity, sexuality, the possibilities and limitations of the ways in which people come to know or shape the past, and of course the personal and social implications of war – or, as the title implies, the multifarious wars of loss, regret, injustice, and hierarchical social structures that exist both on and off the battlefield. Time, in its experiential, historiographical, and representational dimensions, is also a central concern in the novel, and bears commentary from various perspectives. The formal construction of the narrative, in which an archival researcher in the 1970s sorts through documents, interviews, and photographs in an attempt to piece together the life of Robert Ross, a Canadian soldier in the First World War, introduces several layers of time, so that the "reality" and the presentation of Robert's life are separated temporally from one another, and the temporal experience of reading the novel reflects this precarious, subjective reconstruction of the past. The novel seems to have several different beginnings or "false starts," each of which is interrupted or not presented chronologically in relation to the others so that, in Josef Pesch's words, "from the very start Findley forces his readers to partake in the dislocation of space and time that Robert experiences."[5] (The temporal experience of the researcher, too, is clearly a factor here.) For Diana Brydon, "the order of the telling is emotional rather than chronological,"[6] although as various critics have pointed out, the disjointed form of the narration not only reflects the emotional reality of traumatic events, but also comments on the always provisional and incomplete construction of the past and of knowledge itself.

Evelyn Cobley notes that the form of *The Wars* self-consciously departs from the writings of actual veterans of the First World War, whose tendency to construct narrative order out of "the chaos of the front" amounted to an attempt to "domesticate" the war, "thereby integrating it into the continuist image of civilization's progress."[7] The denial of such progressive order in *The Wars* suggests that linearity is simply inadequate to represent the shattering impact that the war had on its participants as well as on the broader social imagination. For Pesch, the novel quashes any tendency that members of the late twentieth century might have had to imagine that nuclear war risks unleashing a secular (and thus irredeemably ruinous) apocalypse; by reminding readers that the experience of such an apocalypse has *already occurred*, Pesch argues, *The Wars* teaches us that we are "living in post-apocalyptic times."[8] Donna Palmateer Pennee sees the fragmented narrative form of the novel as a method of questioning what Homi Bhabha calls the "evolutionary narrative of historical continuity" which buttresses the dominant sense of national identity, with the result that the novel "can help us remember the making of this nation differently" through acknowledging the complexities obscured by the dominant account of Canada's maturation into proper nationhood during the First World War.[9]

David Williams offers an account of the novel's temporality that centres on Findley's use of photography. Not only does the story draw attention to specific photographs uncovered by the researcher, but the narrative itself repeatedly presents images in photographic fashion, "isolating the moment from its context" and producing "a book of interruptions," a process that effectively disrupts received notions of temporal experience and memory.[10] "In the photograph," Williams writes, "as in its verbal equivalent, a new phenomenology of time begins to emerge, a phenomenology in which the cyclical experience of daily or yearly time, or the linear sense of time as historical continuity, gives way to an atomized sense of time where distance, difference, death, delay, danger, and discontinuity become the rule."[11] A central assertion of Williams's *Media, Memory, and the First World War* is that "the Great War fundamentally reshaped our experience of time" in large part because representations of the war in cinema and in writing cemented the social importance of a new kind of "cinematic memory" in which images of the past appear to play forward in front of the viewer as though enacted in the present.[12] However, his reading of *The Wars* shows that the atomization of time in *still* photography unsettles the expected sense of continuity, creating a situation in which the reader-viewer is positioned outside of time and sees time "as a conglomerate of particles."[13]

As the above commentaries have shown, the matter of time in *The Wars* is closely tied to the ways in which the fragmented, non-chronological, and even photographic structure of the novel works to dismantle assumed forms of temporal knowledge. The unprecedented horrors of the Great War disrupt the more traditional and comforting registers of temporality, both on the large social level of progressive linear history and on the more intimate level of the workings of memory and subjective temporal experience. What these readings have been less inclined to address, though, is the sense in which the book also insists on the inevitable perpetuation of normative, linear, objectivist time – an assertion that Findley carries out primarily through the strategic use of that exemplary image of dominant measured time, the clock. The novel indeed presents a world in which time has become fragmented or atomized, but not one where this fragmentation has entirely superseded more conventional notions of hegemonic or sequential time. Rather, the book positions these alternative modes of time in a difficult ongoing dialogue with one another. The fact that the opposing forms of time are largely incompatible does not mean that the one replaces the other, but that the fragmentation of time enters into a complex, even frustrating, but necessary negotiation with a dominant clock-based time that refuses to be silenced.

Clocks figure in *The Wars* through the actual timepieces with which the characters attempt to orient themselves in time, as well as through the formal use of specific moments of clock time as section headings during the most chaotic battle scenes. For Robert, a young civilian at home in Toronto before enlisting in the military, the death of his hydrocephalic sister Rowena sparks an encounter with a clock that anticipates the larger role that clock time will play in the narrative. After Rowena's funeral,

Robert moves her wheelchair up to his bedroom "and sat there in it with his knees drawn up till the guests had left the parlour and the clock struck two."[14] As with several other encounters with clocks in the story, this moment creates as much temporal confusion as clarity: the fact that Robert remains in his sister's chair until the clock "struck two" suggests that he remains immobile for quite some time, yet without a second point of reference we have no way to know exactly how much time has passed. The ostensible precision of the temporal marker "two o'clock" is reduced to a source of temporal confusion in the absence of the necessary context. Related to this is the sense that Robert's psychological state, his subjective reality, exists outside of clock time and cannot be measured, articulated, or made sense of through the striking of the timepiece. Finally, because the striking of the clock seems to beckon Robert back downstairs where "his family sat at the dining room table waiting for him to appear," the clock is positioned here as an arbiter of social interaction, instructing Robert to re-emerge from his private thoughts into a social sphere that is frequently characterized by brutality; Robert's mother, at this moment, is insisting that Rowena's pet rabbits "had to die – and Robert had to do it."[15] Ignoring his waiting family, Robert continues to sit in the chair until three o'clock, by which time a family acquaintance has been called in to kill the rabbits himself, a development that shocks Robert into a desperate and futile attempt to intervene. The clock's prompting to rejoin the social world is a dark invitation for Robert to be initiated, in a sense, into a form of violence that foreshadows the much larger savagery of the war itself, and one that will continue inexorably despite his attempts to resist it.

Once Robert arrives at the front lines of the war – which now serves both as a literal battlefield and as a metaphor for the "wars" that penetrate all aspects of life – the narration of the chaos of the war moves in two temporal directions: Findley shows that Robert's experience of time is shattered and disrupted by the violence, but he also continues to emphasize the presence of clock time as a faulty but relentless temporal ordering principle. The heightened intensity of each moment on the front lines is made clear when we learn that shells at Verdun are fired "at the rate of 100,000 rounds per hour" in a bombardment that lasts "for twelve hours."[16] The combination of instantaneous death lurking behind each new fraction of a second, and the exhausting prolonged duration of the intensity, make the measurement of twelve hours both highly important and utterly irrelevant. When Robert somehow survives a particularly destructive explosion, Findley writes, "He had no idea how long it had been since the mines went off, but it must have been hours. (In fact, it was twelve minutes.)"[17] This temporal telescoping echoes Robert's experience in Rowena's wheelchair, as well as Mrs Ross's experience when she learns of Robert's decision to go to war: "Mrs Ross stared at her empty glass," Findley writes. "How long had it been empty? Hours? Minutes? Years?"[18] A situation of crisis pushes subjective experience beyond the register of clock time, and yet, whether through the thoughts of a character, the striking of a clock, or the sudden voice of an omniscient narrator, the inevitable presence of clock time and its role as the normative structure of temporal articulation is quickly reinforced.

These moments of troubled temporal experience in the novel are matched in a larger formal sense by the coexistence of non-chronological narrative fragments with sections titled after specific moments of clock time. During the most chaotic events of battle in the novel, the usual numbered chapter divisions are replaced by the headings "4.25 a.m.," "5.30 a.m.," "6.10 a.m.," and so on. For Lorraine York, "The rhythm of these sections powerfully suggests the way that time alters in times of crisis," even while "the almost obsessive attention to these ticking minutes (see the headings: '4 a.m.,' '4.25 a.m.,' '5.30 a.m.' …) reproduces the very rhythm of World War I: the slow rhythms of trench warfare, where years of battle could result in a gain or loss of only a few feet."[19] Time has indeed altered during this prolonged moment of crisis, as Robert and his fellow soldiers enter a state of utter temporal confusion; and yet, far from abandoning the register of clock time in order to suggest that the influence of dominant progressive time has vanished, Findley chooses this moment to emphasize and heighten the presence of clock time. That moment when temporal chaos reigns supreme is simultaneously the moment when the enduring power of clock time is felt most acutely. Williams notes that the titling of these sections reflects a historiographical technique inspired by the frozen, disassociated instants captured in photographs, through which "the narrator's facsimile of a photographic style is what enables him to write 'history' at all."[20] In a sense, photographs, like clocks, create the precise instants that they presume to observe. The narrator's borrowing from these mediated constructions of temporality is as much a desperate attempt to render chaotic time comprehensible as it is a formal decision to demonstrate that dominant registers of time refuse to disappear – and indeed can become heightened in significance – during moments of crisis. Pesch's interpretation of these sections – "All synchrony between 'real' time and 'experienced' time has vanished"[21] – is accurate insofar as the time displayed on the clock has little connection with the experience of the soldiers, but can be complicated by the realization that a degree of synchrony between the two – albeit a troublingly inadequate synchrony – is actually enforced by the repetitious structural use of clock time to designate new moments of subjective experience. Meanwhile, the significant degree to which the two forms of time are disjointed is not a new feature introduced in this battle scene, but rather echoes the everyday experience of imperfect but inevitable clock time felt by the characters who are far removed from the actual battlefield. The synchrony between clock time and experienced time was *already* broken, and already inescapable. The clock's sheer blindness to the psychological anguish and temporal telescoping that the soldiers are experiencing is a heightened reminder that clock time always diverges radically from subjective experience, even as the clock never stops ticking in the background of Western social existence.

Pesch's comment about synchrony remains useful in characterizing war as a supreme desynchronizing force, a point that Findley makes quite explicit when he writes, "There was a lot of noise but none of it seemed to be connected with what one saw. The driven, ceaseless pounding of the guns (from both sides now) had nothing to do with the bursting of the shells and the bursting of the shells had nothing to do with the thudding of the earth beneath one's feet. Everything was out of sync."[22] If a sense of synchronization with the wider world is vital for fulfilling the human ache for belonging, as I argued in chapter 2, then the unattainability of such reassurance is made much more desperate in war, where even the physical world itself seems to abandon the laws of cause, effect, and sequence. In this sense, the sections of the narrative structured around progressive, comprehensible clock time (within which Findley's comment above takes place) provide reassurance that *not* everything is out of sync. The clocks are still ticking, counting out their familiar time from one horrible second to the next.

The close ties between inexorably continuing clock time and the violently disfigured temporality of the battlefield mean that clock time is associated with trauma even while it remains insistently present as a dominant structuring principle. This figuring of clock time as a gruelling spectre explains the peculiar choice of similes when Findley writes, "Robert's footsteps and the water oozing from the wrung-out earth fell into puddles loud as clocks."[23] It also explains an event that perplexes the young Juliet d'Orsey, who, after spending time with Robert during one of his leaves, recalls that he "*would throw things down and break them on the ground. He broke his watch that way. I don't know why.*"[24] Robert's symbolic destruction of the watch is almost immediately neutralized, though, when his lover Barbara buys him a new one.[25] Clock time cannot be removed from the register of personal experience any more than it can be excised from the form of the narrative itself. When Robert wakes up in the dark, his new wristwatch is both reassuring and disconcerting, a source of knowledge as well as confusion: "He looked at his watch. 1:30. When? He crossed to the window, strapping the watch to his wrist ... Robert felt as if he had been drunk and a long way off. He even wondered if he'd lost a day."[26] The precise temporal information that the watch provides is incomplete, leaving him lost in time. Nevertheless, he fixes the watch to his body, where it is intended to be and where it resumes its place as an authoritative if limited temporal yardstick.

This scene echoes a scene earlier in the story when Robert's mother, upon reading that the Parliament Buildings in Ottawa have burned down, is "impressed by the fact that when the bells in the centre tower fell they were in the process of striking twelve o'clock – but had only tolled eleven times when they crashed to the ground. She wrote in the margin alongside this information – '*No more midnight.*' It was like a prayer."[27] With the recent death of her daughter and the expected death of her son in the war, Mrs Ross's psychological clock has metaphorically been tolling midnight for a long time – she is in the darkest period of despair. Her wish here is that the stopping of Canada's most iconic physical timepiece could somehow correspond to the end of her mental anguish, that its destruction might end the inexorable counting of her own agonizing days. However, the image also inevitably suggests a freezing of time at the moment of greatest distress, a melancholic fixation on the darkness that will never become light; as long as her son's fate is in question, *every* moment will be the moment just before the clock strikes midnight. When Mrs Ross receives the news several months later that Robert has indeed gone missing in action, she sits, nearly lifeless, at the bottom of the staircase, and discovers that she has actually gone blind. At this moment Findley writes, "In the distance, the traffic on Yonge Street and Bloor Street rumbled and clattered. Everyone was going home. All the clocks were striking."[28] Her symbolic paralysis within time has not stopped the inexorable progress of wartime devastation any more than it has stopped the city's everyday mechanical timepieces or the rush hour traffic taking "everyone" (except Robert and his fellow soldiers) home. Like the Hydra whose heads regrow as they are cut off, clock time and the agonies that it measures cannot be stopped through the destruction of a wristwatch or even of the largest, most iconic timepiece in the nation.

There is one more significant clock in *The Wars*: the wristwatch worn by the researcher – "you" – who is poring through the archival records of Robert's life. "Spread over table tops," Findley writes, "a whole age lies in fragments underneath the lamps. *The war to end all wars*. All you can hear is the wristwatch on your arm."[29] The news clippings and photographs appear to splinter the historical era of the war into messily curated pieces, reflecting what Williams calls the atomization of time as well as the postmodern awareness of the inevitable partialness and partiality of knowledge. And yet, the insistent sound of the timepiece that is physically attached to the researcher's body – *your* body – measures out the ongoing construction of perfectly regular sequential seconds. The ticking of the watch drowns out the notion that the Great War was the "war to end all wars"; time keeps moving, and along with it the human propensity for violence and domination. It also shows that the much-discussed fragmentation of time in this and other works of postmodern fiction does not supersede clock time, but enters into a complex negotiation with the objectivist model of time that refuses to be silenced.

Just as Robert's destruction of his wristwatch results only in his strapping a new watch to his wrist, just as Mrs Ross's prayer about the destruction of the Parliament timepiece leads only to her sitting, numb, while all the clocks in Toronto strike the hour, and just as Findley's use of a fragmented, non-chronological narrative partially retains objectivist sequential time as a structuring principle, so too are the researcher's intense efforts to engage with atomized, subjective time themselves measured against the constant ticking of his own watch. Cobley's comment that "*The Wars* seems characterized by the contradictory desire both to assert and to contest the power of conventional literary devices"[30] is also true of the novel's approach to the power of conventional temporal devices. The novel and its characters are torn between the need to escape the limitations of clock time and the inevitable presence of the clock in Western experience. Even the final scene of the novel sees the researcher and her atomized notes being shooed out of the archive as the archivist "moves among the tables – turning out lights and smiling – telling us gently 'Late. It's late.'"[31] The recognition of the inadequacy of clock time – an objectivist temporality that has always both succeeded and failed in measuring out human time – does not render clock time obsolete. Even intentional efforts to destroy, escape, freeze, or otherwise deconstruct clock time, while vital for articulating alternative forms of temporality and fostering a recognition of multitemporality, are themselves partially measured out against the insistent ticking of the clock.

In her book *Civil War Time*, Cheryl Wells argues that the sense of "battle time" brought about by chaotic conflict in the American Civil War "superseded watches' and clocks' ability to order society,"[32] but that this disruption was only momentary: "At the war's conclusion, antebellum American temporalities reemerged to organize life in the post-bellum era."[33] This argument makes for an illuminating comparison with Williams's view that the First World War and its contemporaneous forms of media *enduringly* changed Western society's relation to time and memory, collapsing to a certain extent the conceptual timeline from past to present. Reading Findley's use of clock time in *The Wars* suggests, in a sense, that both of these perspectives can shed light on the conflicted structure of postmodern time, where fragmented or collapsed temporalities and desynchronization enduringly question the authority of a progressive clock time that nevertheless refuses to go away. At the same time that it is shown to be inadequate, clock time in *The Wars* becomes heightened in significance through the very fact that it persists in the face of such devastating temporal disruption. The shattering violence of war makes clearer what had been true all along: clock time, in its distortions and erasures of subjective experience, consistently fails us as the ultimate arbiter of temporality, yet for all of postmodernity's recognition of this fact and of the significance of different temporal modes, we continue both literally and figuratively to strap the watch to our wrists.

THE END OF TIME: MARLENE NOURBESE PHILIP'S *LOOKING FOR LIVINGSTONE*

In chapter 3 I mentioned Marlene NourbeSe Philip's comment that, for people of African descent in the New World, "tomorrow is a constant problem," that because Western culture's promises of progress are founded on exclusionary principles of white authority, "time and its representations present a constant challenge."[34] In her 1991 volume *Looking for Livingstone: An Odyssey of Silence*, Philip imagines a radical reconstruction of the normative Western temporality that has served to cement and legitimize the status of white English colonialism as the sole driver of progress and authoritative universal timekeeper. While Findley examines the desperate but ultimately conflicted and unsuccessful attempt to destroy the clock whose perfectly uniform seconds are inadequate to articulate human and social experience, *Looking for Livingstone* is an attack directed at the Gregorian calendar system whose cultural hegemony operates in concert with the violence of global colonization. More than that, if the very notions of commonsensical linear counting and everyday language are tied inextricably to normative understandings of time, then Philip's book explodes the very nature of time itself.

I refer to *Looking for Livingstone* as a "volume" and a "book" partly because the genre and form of the writing (as with Marlatt's *Ana Historic* and Gunnars's *The Prowler*) are difficult to define. Just as the work troubles the linear distinctions between past, present, and future, it also reveals that the boundaries between prose and poetry were never clear to begin with. The story follows the journey of a narrator, known only as The Traveller, in her efforts to find Dr Livingstone, the famed explorer of Africa. From the very beginning, starting with the heading of the first section of the book, the narrative deconstructs and refigures the normative model of time:

THE FIRST AND LAST DAY OF THE MONTH OF NEW MOONS
(OTHERWISE KNOWN AS THE LAST AND FIRST MONTH)
IN THE FIRST YEAR OF OUR WORD
0300 HOURS[35]

It seems that the month in question has a duration of only one day, and that the year itself contains only the one month; the entire annual cycle is compressed into a single day, in which there is a new moon. Either the physical motions of the earth's rotation and revolution have been radically altered, or the meanings of familiar terms like "day," "month," "year," "first," and "last" have been refashioned into a new temporal vocabulary that twists and disfigures normative timekeeping. The *Anno Domini* signifier that is typically attached to historical dates of the last two millennia and means "year of Our Lord," is here modified to "year of our word," and while the notion of "the Word" carries a deep association with Christ in the New Testament, "*our* word" appears to be something different; the label throws the authority of the Gregorian calendar into question along with its Christian foundations, ringing in the axial moment of a novel calendrical system. Only the "0300 hours" appears, for the moment, to follow a familiar pattern.

Below this heading, the narrative immediately takes issue with the cultural politics involved in Dr Livingstone's "discovery" of African geographical features, pointing out that the process through which explorers like Livingstone find, identify, name, describe, and become famous for their discovery of rivers and resources requires the assistance of Indigenous people who have known about these features for ages:

David Livingstone, *Dr* David Livingstone, 1813–73 – Scottish, not English, and one of the first Europeans to cross the Kalahari – *with* the help of Bushmen; was shown the Zambezi by the indigenous African and "discovered" it; was shown the falls of Mosioatunya – the smoke that thunders – by the indigenous African, "discovered" it and renamed it. Victoria Falls. Then he set out to "discover" the source of the Nile and was himself "discovered" by Stanley – "Dr Livingstone, I presume?" And History. Stanley and Livingstone – white fathers of the continent. Of silence.[36]

The colonialist vision of temporality, in which prior human knowledge of a river or waterfall is suppressed beneath the defining moment of the first European sighting – a "watershed" moment, indeed – serves to silence alternative histories, to cast one particular frame around the order and timing of selected events. According to the mythology that Philip identifies surrounding these explorations, the world's largest waterfall was obscured from human history and knowledge for all time until Livingstone himself arrived to dis-cover it. Meanwhile, UNESCO reports that "stone artefacts of *Homo habilis* from 3 million years ago ... have been found near the falls," along with other tools providing extensive evidence of "prolonged occupation" by hunter-gatherers, farmers, and villagers up to the modern era.[37] The intention of Philip's reconfigured calendrical system now becomes clear, since the European reckoning of dates is inseparable from the biases and erasures of the colonialist vision of time.

In the second dated section of the narrative – "THE FOUR HUN-DREDTH DAY IN THE SIXTEENTH MONTH / OF THE TEN THOU-SANDTH YEAR OF OUR WORD" – we learn that the narrator has been "travelling in circles these past hundred years – circle upon circle – ever widening."[38] The description not only further distorts the usual concepts of months, years, and age, but also confounds linear thought. While the act of travelling in circles at first sounds like a failure, the accidental retracing of steps, we learn that the circles are actually building upon one another, widening the path of their motion; circularity becomes not the shape of failed linear motion, but its own constructive form. The line also responds to Yeats's ominous "widening gyre" in his poem "The Second Coming"; while for Yeats "the centre cannot hold,"[39] Philip's line suggests that the centre retains its hold despite the widening circle, and leaves open the possibility that an unbounded trajectory may actually be desir-able. Sure enough, at this point The Traveller begins a series of productive encounters with various groups of people – the ECNELIS, the SINCEEL, the LENSECI – whose names are rearranged letters from the word "silence." The ECNELIS believe that God "first created silence: whole, indivisible, complete," but has since cursed the world with words.[40] Others believe that "the first act of God was to create the word – primary and indispensable"; the ancestors of these people, "so their stories tell, mounted armies of words to colonise the many and various silences of the peoples round about, spreading and infecting with word where before there was silence."[41] Just as non-linear, non-Gregorian models of time are figured within some of these contested narratives as legitimate constructs in their own right, silence is represented not as a lack of language but as a primary and powerful aspect of existence. And just as non-Gregorian temporality faces obstruction and damage at the hands of colonizing

temporality, silence is a contested ground always at risk of linguistic inva-
sion; the narrative repeatedly casts words as violent masculine entities
penetrating and appropriating silence. Philip describes a Museum of
Silence whose curators insist that "the silences were best kept there where
they could be labelled, annotated, dated, catalogued" – to which The
Traveller says, "You must return these silences to their owners. Without
their silence, these people are less than whole."[42] While recognizing that
colonization has rendered silent pre-existing histories and temporalities,
the narrative also reclaims the notion of silence, casting it not as a weakness and an absence but as a strength and a presence. The Traveller's
dawning recognition of the power of silence lies in tension with her
refusal to be silenced; her telling of her own narrative, her construction of
her own story and reckoning of time, enacts a powerful form of resistance. Findley's *The Wars* is also characterized by what Diana Brydon calls
"its obsession with what 'could not be told' – the limitations, even treach-
eries of language" through which Robert Ross "remains forever trapped
in his silence."[43] Like *Looking for Livingstone*, *The Wars* works through an
attempt to break these cultural silences. In Philip's book, though, the
speaking out of silenced temporalities and silenced experiences coincides
with a recognition of the significance of these silences themselves. Those
times and experiences that remain unsaid, or unheard, are just as worthy
of attention, respect, and myth as the visions of time that become spoken,
let alone those that are enshrined in dominant Western history.

Just as the narrative relegitimizes silenced modes of language and time,
it also ironizes Livingstone's language of civilizing discovery through
which he incorporates Africa into European frameworks of knowledge.
Livingstone, The Traveller notes, has "a sextant, a chronometer watch –
with a stop second hand no less! an artificial horizon, *and* a compass. And
finally his arrogance."[44] His technological tools, which include his instruments for measuring seconds and degrees – time and space – are paired
with his belief that these forms of reckoning, of naming, are primary and
absolute. As The Traveller notices that time appears to move at different
rates for her than for other people, she begins to speak in terms of relative
time and multiple calendars, further destabilizing the singular authority
of Gregorian time: "I had been with the LENSECI three years and three
days – by my calendar."[45] The very phrase "my calendar" opens up a discourse of multitemporality. When Mary Livingstone, David's wife who

has been left behind in London, writes a letter to him dated *"Friday the eighteenth day of January, 1859,"*[46] we understand that she, too, has been colonized by the masculine power of Gregorian time. Of course, throughout *Looking for Livingstone* the usual problem of resistance applies: by putting so much effort into subverting and discrediting normative time, the narrative partially reinforces the existing structure of power. This power is already so entrenched, though, that the acts of resistance are more notable for their gradual chipping away at normative temporal authority.

As her journey to find Dr Livingstone continues, The Traveller moves through vast, unthinkable quantities of time. "Five thousand years – that's how long I had been travelling when I arrived in the land of the SCENILE," she says, under a heading that signifies an even more expansive, completely incongruous, amount of time: "THE TWENTY-FIFTH DAY IN THE TWO THOUSANDTH MONTH / OF THE TWO BILLIONTH YEAR OF OUR WORD."[47] Dorothy Jones comments that time in The Traveller's narrative "is portrayed as malleable since the standard ways of reckoning its passing become irrelevant when measuring the psychological and spiritual journey Philip chronicles here."[48] Certainly, some subjective experiences of time operate on a different register from the rigidly computed calendar, but the standard ways of reckoning time are entirely relevant: they are invoked again and again precisely so that they can be resisted, twisted, and overcome. The dominant temporal ideology is so powerful that it cannot be countered and dismantled in one blow; The Traveller grapples with it continually, in a process that eventually encompasses *all* time: "I had been searching for him for an eternity, it seemed – eighteen billion years – the age of the universe."[49]

In the final section of the book The Traveller and Livingstone finally encounter one another, and their two calendrical systems collide: "THE FIRST AND LAST DAY OF THE MONTH OF NEW MOONS (OTHERWISE KNOWN AS THE FIRST AND LAST MONTH) IN THE EIGHTEEN BILLIONTH YEAR OF OUR WORD, WHICH IS THE SAME AS THE END OF TIME, WHICH IS THE SAME AS THE FIFTEENTH DAY OF JUNE, NINETEEN HUNDRED AND EIGHTY SEVEN IN THE YEAR OF OUR LORD."[50] The Gregorian date – 15 June 1987 – is more than a century after Livingstone's death, which is appropriate in the sense that Philip herself is able to encounter only the ghost (the reputation, the writings, the memory) of the explorer; *Looking for Livingstone* was first published in 1991, so the writing likely occurred mainly in the late 1980s. By having this Gregorian date coincide with an entirely different calendrical date in the eighteen billionth year, Philip again casts each time-reckoning system as partial. The collision of the two calendars brings about "the end of time" not only because the age of the universe has been reached, but also in the sense that the long-standing notion of singular temporal dominance, of absolute colonialist timekeeping authority, has been dealt a crippling blow.

The clock time at this moment – "0000 HOURS" – also enacts a resetting of counted time. Catching sight of Dr Livingstone, The Traveller notes, "We looked at each other... across a distance of some three feet – the infinite in time – my silence. I looked at my cheap, digital watch – I had picked it up somewhere along the way – it was 2800 hours exactly."[51] Like The Traveller's calendar that serves mainly to warp Gregorian time, her wristwatch, after the symbolic zero-hour reset, now displays a time that violates the usual strictures of the twenty-four-hour clock. This violation of normal clock time recalls the opening line of Orwell's *Nineteen Eighty-Four*: "It was a bright cold day in April, and the clocks were striking thirteen."[52] For Philip's Traveller the transgression of normative time is triumphant, while in Orwell's text the line reveals that something appallingly unfamiliar has happened to the measurement of time and, we surmise, to society as a whole. The contrast illustrates how the disruption of normative time can be at turns liberating or distressing depending on social context and personal perspective. For the Traveller, the desirability of destabilizing colonialist time is visible in her tendency to emphasize the fact that the "explorer" is a recent arrival in a land that has been inhabited for millennia. Her first words to Livingstone are "You're new here, aren't you?"[53]

Up to this point the narrative has been fairly relentless in its criticism of Livingstone and the colonizing impulse he represents. When they actually begin speaking with one another, though, Livingstone and The Traveller find that they get along reasonably well, laughing and having their picture taken together, although The Traveller maintains a sardonic tone toward his accomplishments. When Livingstone is skeptical about The Traveller's claim that she has discovered silence, she angrily responds, "You ask for proof that I discovered my Silence – my very own Silence – when you're sitting right there in front of me? You want facts, dates and years – the time down to the last millisecond – don't you?"[54] A "fact," The Traveller declares, "is whatever anyone, having the power to enforce it, says is a fact. Power – that is the distinguishing mark of a fact."[55] Livingstone's discovery of Victoria Falls "is a lie, *and* a fact, because you and your supporters, your nation of liars, had the power to change a lie into a fact. Those falls had a name long before you got to them."[56] Like the "facts" of European discoveries of African landmarks, the authority of normative timekeeping itself is a matter of power, and The Traveller's questioning of the legitimacy of this power reaches a climax in her confrontation with Livingstone. The meeting between The Traveller and Livingstone involves both critique and conciliation, both a meeting and a separation of different temporal systems. By articulating alternative visions of time with potentially competing claims to legitimacy, these scenes hint at the necessity of multitemporality (a concept that will become especially significant in the closing sections of this book).

Finishing her conversation with Livingstone, The Traveller embraces silence once more and the narrative draws to a close:

> I touched something warm familiar   like my own   hand   human
> something I could not   see in the SILENCE   reaching out   through
> the SILENCE of space   the SILENCE of time   through the silence of
> SILENCE   I touched it   his hand   held it   his hand   *and* the
> SILENCE
> I surrendered   to the SILENCE   within[57]

These final words speak, paradoxically, to the power of non-representation, gesturing toward a time and space before language and culture, so that the tension that exists throughout the story between normative time, alternative times, and silence, is not resolved but reinforced. The word "of" in "the SILENCE of time" turns the phrase in two directions: time both possesses silence and *is* silence. There is an aspect of time and space that cannot be encompassed by language and representation, so that the colonizing appropriation of other times, like the appropriation of silence, can never be complete. Just as resistance always risks reinforcing the power it seeks to subvert, the colonization of time and silence, being incomplete, makes visible its own inadequacy and its dependence on the colonized.

At the end of the book an ostensible "author's note" describes the original leather-bound volumes, held at the Bodleian Library in Oxford University, that contain The Traveller's diary, notes, and maps. "The diary," the note explains, "is arranged in chronological order, according to present calendar time; this conflicts with the time through which The Traveller journeyed."[58] This mysterious "author," then, is sympathetic to the multiplicitous subjective temporalities embodied in The Traveller's narrative, and goes on to quote The Traveller's statement that the diaries are in fact *"a facsimile of my odyssey into Silence. The original diaries, including maps of these travels, were given to the CESLIENS for safe keeping, since they were the only ones who kept their Silence."*[59] However, in one final twist, the author's note ends by quoting another note attached to the display case that contains the diaries: *"Contrary to the statement on the last page of Volume II, these volumes comprise the only and original copy of the* Diary of a Traveller. *– William D. Boyd, Chief Archivist and Librarian."*[60] This bizarre series of claims and contradictions has the appearance of a real-world example of contested notions of priority, ownership, and authority of narrative. While the form of the book, in which the idiosyncratic experiences of The Traveller are collected in a jumble of narrative fragments that are challenging to piece together, had always been a key method through which Philip works to operate outside of the dominant temporal and narrative modes, this note on the display case draws particularly self-conscious attention to the matter of form, suggesting that even the experiences of The Traveller remain at risk of appropriation into dominant forms of archival record keeping. While The Traveller may very well feel that the "original" narrative is the record of experiences stored within her own memories, of which the written, dated description is an inadequate reproduction, the archivist sees the officially registered publication as the one factual version. His statement echoes Livingstone's tendency to associate facts with dated records, and also recalls the Museum of Silence where colonized silences are stored and labelled. Homi Bhabha's assertion that the disjunctive temporalities associated with the margins of society form a "distracting presence" that works to break down the authority of normative, singular time[61] – the idea that, in Wai Chee Dimock's words, alternative temporalities challenge the ability of the nation "to standardize, to impose an official ordering of events"[62] – is haunted by the spectre of appropriation by which the normative archive can claim alternative experiences as mere contributions to its authoritative collection. Jones notes that "the voice of what is supposedly authoritative, male, white scholarship has the last word, appropriating the Traveller's silence."[63] And yet, even William D. Boyd's note appears *within* the "author's note" and ultimately within Philip's creation itself, adding another layer of ambiguity to this appropriation. The questions of authority, ownership, and voice associated with the articulation of alternative temporalities remain at stake as the book draws to a close.[64]

Jones self-consciously sees the ironic quotation on the museum display case as "a warning which places literary conferences, and particularly anyone giving a paper on Marlene Nourbese Philip in a most invidious position, for which the only solution is silence."[65] My initial reaction to such a conundrum would be to say (and already I have broken the silence) that the text does not so much require silence on the part of the reader as it asks readers to become self-conscious of the colonizing power of their own narratives and constructions of time. Such a response is indeed likely to prove productive, and yet, like the museum, it risks incorporating alternative forms of knowing into a discursive system not fully equipped to understand them. Like Emily Carr in *Klee Wyck*, who not only gains awareness of the time-reckoning forces that she carries with her into Indigenous communities but also goes so far as to let her clock wind down and stop, readers of *Looking for Livingstone* may find that addressing the power imbalances implicit in their own models of time requires not only articulating the limitations of these structures, but also embracing the silences that they have interrupted. Yes, we should be conscious of the impositions of our clocks and calendars, but it is another thing entirely to shut them down, even for a moment, and listen.

IMAGINING MULTITEMPORALITY:
MARGARET ATWOOD'S MADDADDAM TRILOGY

In the opening scene of Margaret Atwood's 2003 novel *Oryx and Crake*, we meet a man who calls himself Snowman, who has survived a global pandemic apocalypse, and is now looking at his wristwatch. "Out of habit he looks at his watch – stainless-steel case, burnished aluminum band, still shiny although it no longer works. He wears it now as his only talisman. A blank face is what it shows him: zero hour. It causes a jolt of terror to run through him, this absence of official time. Nobody nowhere knows what time it is."[66] Somebody, Snowman's panic implies, *ought* to know what time it is; the absence of a strict, authoritative, "true" clock time is not a liberation but a deprivation. Here, on the first page of *Oryx and Crake*, Atwood identifies a concern with the social role of temporality that remains prominent throughout the series of novels that would later become known as the MaddAddam trilogy. While the novels relate to one another with a high degree of complexity, we might say that the central question about temporality in *Oryx and Crake* is, "What does it mean for a dominant social model of time to break down?" In the second novel, *The Year of the Flood* (2009), the question becomes, "How might social constructions of time be reconfigured?" And finally, the third novel, *MaddAddam* (2013), asks us to envision how new forms of blended and provisional temporalities might adapt themselves to the realities of a radically reconfigured society. Taken together, the novels form a powerful speculation on both the inevitability and the difficulties of multitemporality within a complex society – especially a society undergoing fragmentation and collapse. Indeed, the massive civilizational upheaval to which Atwood subjects her characters allows her to craft a thought experiment in radical multitemporality, demonstrating how the flexible recognition of multiple temporalities is fundamentally important to the forging of social arrangements, but also showing that the coexistence of multiple temporalities can be deeply unsettling, opening the door to dangerous conflicts, misunderstandings, and power struggles as well as to more positive forms of multicultural sociality.

The books' responses to the above questions hinge partly on the assertion that the human experience of temporality involves a contradiction. While the human desire to escape the constraints of timekeeping and of mortality – to "break the shackles of time"[67] – is apparently universal, so too is the deep psychological need to remain bound by discrete, comprehensible, and above all predictable socially shared units of time. The specific nature of these units, though, remains open to question; like Philip and other writers, Atwood promotes the notion that despite appearing to be logical and inevitable, social categories of time are in fact fragile and arbitrary. While Findley bears witness to the resiliency of normative clock time even amid massive upheaval, Atwood suggests that there is no fundamental reason why old models of time like the one symbolized by Snowman's broken watch cannot go extinct, and no reason why new models of time cannot be created – even if a global civilizational collapse seems to be the necessary catalyst. And because culturally shared ideas about time are closely tied to the politics of social relations, the destruction and reconfiguration of "official" time in Atwood's dystopian world becomes a thought experiment not only in reconstructed temporality but also in political revolution, containing the threat, or the promise, of recasting deeply held convictions along with the structure of social power hierarchies.

The personal consequences of the breaking down of predictable time units are a central source of motivation for Snowman, and a source of reader sympathy. Before the plague virus destroys civilization partway through the twenty-first century, Snowman is called Jimmy. Jimmy has desires and anxieties familiar to us, and he measures time according to normative social tools including the Gregorian calendar and standard clock time. When Jimmy's friend Crake unleashes a genetically engineered virus that appears to kill everyone on earth, Jimmy conceptualizes a break in time, a disruption that he emphasizes by renaming himself Snowman. As we join him at the beginning of *Oryx and Crake*, Snowman has grudgingly taken on the role of caretaker for the Crakers, the genetically engineered posthumans that Crake created in an attempt to supplant humanity with a superior humanoid species. When a group of young Crakers shows Snowman a collection of objects that they have found on the beach and which they consider to be incomprehensible – "a hubcap, a piano key, a chunk of pale-green pop bottle smoothed by the ocean"[68] – Snowman accepts that he will be unable to explain the provenance of such items to people who do not share his cultural memory. "These are things from before," he says simply,[69] implying the existence of a watershed moment against which all subsequent times are measured – times that cannot adequately be articulated through the now obsolete language of calendars and clocks. The dominant cultural models of time and history have ceased to exist along with their users, and, like the hubcaps and piano keys, they now carry no meaning outside of Snowman's solitary mind. He realizes to his disgust that he will now be the only person to mark the passing (in both senses of the word) of official time: "On the second Friday of March – he'd been marking off the days on a calendar, god knows why – Jimmy showed himself to the Crakers for the first time."[70] With the death of cultural time, his prospects for communicating the flow of history and even subjectivity begin to disintegrate before his eyes. While the bulk of the novel consists of Snowman's narrativized recollections of the events leading up to the pandemic, the futility of this exercise strikes him when he discovers Jimmy's scrawled explanation of the virus's origin inside Crake's destroyed bioengineering compound. Snowman "crumples the sheets up, drops them onto the floor. It's the fate of these words to be eaten by beetles."[71] He is forced to accept that the symbols through which he has always comprehended the flow of events through time will never be used again.

Oryx and Crake's ambiguous ending keeps the matter of time at the forefront. Having learned from the Crakers of the existence of three more human survivors, Snowman follows the human footprints and finally locates the unnamed trio in a forest clearing. The novel ends as Snowman peers at these people – possibly the final remnants of the human species – and tries to decide whether to kill them; if he does nothing, he reasons, they might kill him first. Again, his wristwatch is Atwood's icon of choice:

From habit he lifts his watch; it shows him its blank face.
Zero hour, Snowman thinks. Time to go.[72]

The phrase "Zero hour" may suggest that because no system of official time reckoning is in place, Snowman is empowered to determine for himself the "right" time to act. Or, he may see the lack of shared social time as a death knell: it was zero hour at the beginning of the novel, and it is still zero hour at the end; cultural time has stopped, so it is only appropriate for Snowman himself to disappear or die as well. And he does disappear: the novel ends. "Zero hour" also conjures the sense of having reached the end of a countdown; but once the countdown is over, what happens? What happens after the end of time? This depends on how we read the ambiguous final sentence, "Time to go." As J. Brooks Bouson asks, "Does 'time to go' mean that it is time to act as a peacemaker or that it is time to die?"[73] Just as The Traveller's encounter with Livingstone in *Looking for Livingstone* takes place at the end of time but simultaneously opens up new articulations of temporality, Snowman's "Zero hour" may be the end of a countdown, or the starting point for a reborn narrative of time. It is the beginning of something new, or the end of everything.

Atwood continues to address these issues in *The Year of the Flood*, which takes place in the same time frame as *Oryx and Crake* but traces the lives of characters who are minor in or absent from the first novel. The protagonists Toby and Ren belong to the God's Gardeners, an enviro-religious sect led by Adam One, who believes that a "Waterless Flood" will soon destroy all non-Gardener members of humanity. When Crake's virus strikes, the surviving Gardeners see the plague as the fulfillment of Adam One's prediction. The novel's preoccupation with the relationship between uncontrollable external events and the socially constructed nature of time is visible in its title, which names a temporal event bestowed with cultural importance. Indeed, the title of the first chapter – "Year Twenty-Five, the Year of the Flood" – introduces a watershed moment and time-reckoning system unfamiliar to readers; the Gardeners, we gradually learn, have invented an entirely new calendar. Reciting the Gardeners' rhyming oral history, Ren reveals that the axial moment in this calendar is the creation of the God's Gardeners organization itself: "*Year One, Garden just begun.*"[74,75] And while the Gardeners still use a variation on the concept of the week, participating in "Retreats and Isolation Weeks,"[76] the familiar units of months, weekdays, and numbered dates have no place in their calendar, resulting in conversations like this one between Toby and Ren:

> When I wake up, Toby's already sitting in her hammock doing some arm stretches … "What day is today?" she says.
>   I think for a moment. "Saint Terry, Saint Sojourner," I say. "All Wayfarers."[77]

As Ren explains, each day of the year carries a different name, honouring important people or concepts: "We also had to memorize every saint's day, and every single day had at least one saint and sometimes more, or maybe a feast, which meant over four hundred of those."[78]

This calendrical system borrows from the traditional Christian calendar of saints, of which there are various historical versions dedicating particular days to one or more saints. For their saints, though, the God's Gardeners have selected historical figures who are celebrated for promoting environmental sustainability, biocentrism, energy efficiency, and social justice. The Saint Terry that Ren refers to is Terry Fox, the cancer research activist who died in 1981, and he joins company, in what turns out to be a Canadian-centric list, with such figures as David Suzuki, Farley Mowat, Allan Sparrow (the Toronto city councillor who fought overdevelopment in the 1970s), Bridget Stutchbury (a York University biologist who promotes bird-friendly agriculture), and so on. An eclectic group of international names is also included: Saint Yossi Leshem of Barn Owls (Leshem is an Israeli ornithologist and owl advocate), Saint Dian Fossey, Martyr (whose research into gorilla societies ended with her murder in 1985), Saint Maria Sibylla Merian (the seventeenth-century entomologist who described insect metamorphosis), Saint Al Gore, Saint Rachel Carson, Saint Linnaeus of Botanical Nomenclature, and Gautama Buddha, the founder of Buddhism. Finally, some days are named after events such as the creation of the God's Gardeners, or after living things, as with Podocarp Day and Mole Day. This list is not exhaustive, and Atwood claims in an afterword to *The Year of the Flood* that the Gardeners "have many more saints, as well, but they are not in this book."[79] The novel's companion website, meanwhile, provided a form during the book's publicity campaign for visitors to nominate their own saints along with respective areas of jurisdiction; saint-worthy acts could "range from saving a species to planting a tree or setting up a backyard bird feeder."[80] Visitors could purchase a God's Gardeners' Scroll to certify the nomination, with a percentage of the fee going toward Atwood's chosen charities.

The Gardeners' calendar performs several functions. It establishes the types of values to which the Gardeners aspire; it allows Atwood to publicize and endorse selected real-world environmentalists and social figures, some of whom are known only within specialized disciplines; it potentially encourages readers to learn more about the saints and their work and to become active in social concerns outside of the text itself; it serves as a type of authorial wink by portraying present-day figures as the deceased and anointed heroes of a religious sect that is both insightfully forward-looking and somewhat ridiculous;[81] and finally it serves as an example of a radically reconstructed model of social time reckoning, demonstrating how such a refashioning could conceivably function.[82]

Further details of Gardener temporality are gradually revealed through sermons delivered by the leader Adam One, who, in his warnings about the coming Waterless Flood, frequently speaks about the significance of time:

> While the Flood rages, you must count the days, said Adam One. You must observe the risings of the Sun and the changings of the Moon, because to everything there is a season. On your Meditations, do not travel so far on your inner journeys that you enter the Timeless before it is time. In your Fallow states, do not descend to a level that is too deep for any resurgence, or the Night will come in which all hours are the same to you, and then there will be no Hope.[83]

Throughout these speeches the importance of time reckoning, of counting the days of lived experience, is paramount. The danger of a Fallow state (the Gardener euphemism for depression and other psychological disorders) is the onset of undifferentiated time, since hope in the face of devastation requires the careful marking of sequential moments. While the Gardeners' calendar, then, in some ways departs radically from normative Gregorian time, the two systems share a deep investment in the psychological and practical necessity of the categorization of human-scale temporal units.

In contrast to the Gardeners' quasi-Christian interpretation of the sacred implications of time reckoning, Crake's atheist-materialist view holds that the idea of immortality is "a consequence of grammar. And so was God, because as soon as there's a past tense, there has to be a past before the past, and you keep going back in time until you get to *I don't know*, and that's what God is."[84] For Crake, God is at heart a cultural model for understanding time; God explains the past before the past as well as the potentially transcendental future. And the anxiety that the idea of mortality produces in human beings, in addition to fuelling religious devotion, is a potent site for profit making. When Jimmy is awed by the state-of-the-art luxuries in Crake's genetic engineering compound he asks, "What pays for all this?" Crake responds, "Grief in the face of inevitable death ... The wish to stop time. The human condition."[85] The AnooYoo corporation similarly profits from its customers' dread of "the whole signs-of-mortality thing," offering intensive spa treatments and conducting research into age reversal.[86] Even Jimmy halfheartedly preys upon these anxieties and desires; when he is hired to write advertising slogans for sex-enhancement products, he produces such lines as, "*Live in the moment*," and "Why chain your body to the clock, you can break the shackles of time."[87] The observation that serves as the foundation for all of these corporations' business models is one that is shared by Adam One, even though his conclusions are non-commercialist. The natural human response to death, he says, is "the universal protest against Time," the cry, "Why now?"[88]

This "universal protest" is one reason why, despite the different calendars and widely varying approaches to sacred and secular time that Atwood's characters take, they perceive the destruction of social time reckoning in strikingly similar ways. When we meet Snowman in the opening scene of *Oryx and Crake* we see that despite his advertising slogans he has clearly failed to remove the shackles of time from his own feet, or rather, his wrist. And several months into his post-apocalyptic life he continues to brood anxiously over the passing of time: "He doesn't know which is worse, a past he can't regain or a present that will destroy him if he looks at it too clearly. Then there's the future. Sheer vertigo."[89] The Gardeners, meanwhile, have ostensibly received some degree of psychological inoculation against the effects of complete social breakdown. Speaking on humanity's "brutal history" of violence toward living things, Adam One urges his followers to "take comfort in the thought that this history will soon be swept away by the Waterless Flood."[90] His words turn out to be cold comfort for Toby, though, whose meticulous recording of the saints' days in a notepad after the Flood does not spare her the thought that her continued existence is futile. "This thing I'm doing can hardly be called living," she thinks. "Instead I'm lying dormant, like a bacterium in a glacier. Getting time over with. That's all."[91] Her despair echoes Jimmy's quandary nearly thought for thought: "She can't live only in the present, like a shrub. But the past is a closed door, and she can't see any future."[92] Like Jimmy, Toby faces a form of temporal vertigo brought on by the isolation of social collapse. Both characters have had their respective societies destroyed, and both now experience time as a constrictive and painful presence that the act of counting days cannot alleviate, whether these days are Gregorian days of the month or Gardener saints' days.

There are moments when these characters experience the absence of social time as a relief because it allows for intense personal freedom.

Snowman initially relishes the power of historical invention that he holds over the Crakers; realizing that there is no one to contradict him, he fabricates mythical events to explain the time before the Crakers' existence: "In the beginning, there was chaos ... And then Oryx said to Crake, *Let us get rid of the chaos* ... And this is how Crake did the Great Rearrangement and made the Great Emptiness."[93] For Ren – who wakes up one post-Flood morning crying, "Oh shit, oh shit ... I'm late! What time is it?" – relief comes in the realization that shift work is a thing of the past. "'You're not late for anything,' says Toby, and for some reason both of them laugh."[94] These temporary moments of solace, though, serve ultimately as melancholic reminders of a deeper distress. Not being late for anything indicates freedom, but also a profound loneliness. While they can be oppressive, social time conventions are necessary for coordinating everyday life with other people, so that escaping social time reckoning leads to alienation as much as liberty.

Meanwhile, there is a third cultural model of time reckoning in the novels, and this belongs to the Crakers. Like the not-quite-human Crakers themselves, their relationship with time is eerie and defamiliarizing. "They're programmed to drop dead at age thirty," Crake explains, "suddenly, without getting sick. No old age, none of those anxieties. They'll just keel over. Not that they know it; none of them has died yet."[95] What is more, Crake sees this lack of temporal anxiety as a way to avoid mortality altogether, in a manner of speaking. "Immortality," he explains, "is a concept. If you take 'mortality' as being, not death, but the foreknowledge of it and the fear of it, then 'immortality' is the absence of such fear. Babies are immortal."[96] If the AnooYoo spa remained operational in a world populated by Crakers it would surely go out of business. Snowman encounters a frustrating consequence of this lack of temporal anxiety when he discovers to his astonishment that the Crakers have recently seen a group of humans, and asks them to describe the encounter:

> "When did they come here?"
> "Oh, the day before, maybe."
> Useless to try to pin them down about any past event: they don't count the days.[97]

Even the counting of lineage lines is absent from Craker culture. The Craker women enter sexual "heat" at regular intervals and engage in what

Crake calls "guilt-free promiscuity."[98] As a result, "It no longer matters who the father of the inevitable child may be, since there's no more property to inherit, no father-son loyalty required for war."[99] The degree to which the Crakers deviate from normal human thought and practice makes them uncanny and somewhat repulsive to Snowman, and perhaps to Atwood's readers as well. It is difficult to relate to people who have no desire to count time.

When we reach the final scene of *The Year of the Flood* – the same scene that ends *Oryx and Crake*, but told from Ren's point of view – three fragile cultural models of time coexist: Snowman's Gregorian time, Ren and Toby's Gardener time, and the Crakers' unmeasured "immortal" time. Once again, though, the outcome is ambivalent. The narration in *The Year of the Flood* takes us a little further, perhaps a few hours beyond the ending of *Oryx and Crake*. The three people in the forest clearing who remain unidentified in *Oryx and Crake* are now revealed to be Ren's friend Amanda and her violent male captors, the "Painballers." Ren and Toby arrive, manage to take the two men captive, and prevent Snowman – now delirious from an infected foot and psychological trauma – from killing anyone. In the final paragraph, Ren hears distant music: "It's faint and far away, but moving closer. It's the sound of many people singing. Now we can see the flickering of their torches, winding towards us through the darkness of the trees."[100] While readers may surmise from Atwood's clues that the shadowy figures are the Crakers, approaching with the intention of helping Snowman and the other humans – and indeed this interpretation is confirmed early on in *MaddAddam*[101] – a group of faceless individuals holding torches carries inevitable associations of violent mob justice. The hopeful swelling of music and spilling of light at the end of *The Year of the Flood* remains troubled and uneasy.

We may be able to read this uneasy coexistence through the theories of multiple temporalities that I have discussed earlier, such as Coleman's call "to develop an awareness of contending, rather than single, civilities" – a position that "will involve cognizance of multiple, contemporaneous chronotopes."[102] Since multiple conceptualizations of time are inevitable, Coleman says, "a diverse civil society cannot establish any one of these chronotopes as its sole narrative."[103] The language of multiculturalism is not far from the surface here, nor is it far removed from Levine's appeal for what he calls multitemporality. Examining the conflicts that can arise between clock time and event time, he concludes, "The person, or the culture, who combines both modes in a temporal repertoire – or even better, who can draw upon a multiplicity of modes – is more likely to be up to all occasions."[104] His final chapter describes strategies for adapting to unfamiliar temporal systems, offering suggestions for recognizing cultural distinctions between work time and social time, considering the different weights that may be assigned to time in which "nothing" happens, and anticipating accepted sequences of social events. Like Coleman, Levine locates an important measure of cultural resilience in the capacity to conceptualize the flow of time in multiple ways. Both authors recognize, though, that highly ingrained power relationships are at stake in the cultural negotiation of temporalities, and that multitemporality, like multiculturalism, is not a discrete, stable condition, but involves an ongoing process of complex interactions.

The Year of the Flood is in some ways a fictional companion piece to cultural studies such as those carried out by Coleman and Levine. By the end of the novel, Atwood's readers are cognizant of three contemporaneous chronotopes, even if each temporal mode contains its own biases and each character remains invested in only a single one. The hopefulness inherent in the multitemporal ideal is present in the novel mainly through the capacity of the Gardeners to reconstruct and refashion cultural models of time in the face of anticipated catastrophic upheaval. But just as the novel's ending is made uneasy by the approach of potentially ominous strangers, the hopefulness of multitemporality is troubled by the fact that the characters tend to naturalize their own cultural norms and see other temporal systems as inferior or nonsensical. The Craker time system in particular is so alien to Snowman that he finds it difficult to carry out a simple conversation with his posthuman companions, and he continually disparages them in his mind. Crake's own materialist vision of time, meanwhile, and its profit-driven offshoots that capitalize on the human fear of mortality, arguably led to the collapse of civilization in the first place.

In her own descriptions of *The Year of the Flood*, Atwood takes up the language of multitemporality, even producing a temporal neologism to describe the novel's relationship to *Oryx and Crake*: "It's not a sequel and it's not a prequel – it's a 'simultaneouel' in that it takes place during the same time span and with a number of people in it who are peripheral in *Oryx and Crake* but are central in *The Year of the Flood*."[105] By narrating a single time span twice, in two books, Atwood indicates that different experiences of time coexist in her fictional world, just as they do in reality, and that these multiple visions of time have the potential to be hopeful or ominous, cooperative or destructive. Not only are different grand social systems of time reckoning possible, but every fully realized character – every person – inhabits her own personal calendar, her own timeline. Just as Atwood's characters experience a break in the dominant model of time only to create and encounter alternative temporalities, her simultaneouel narratives tell us that there is no singular story of time, but always multiple intertwined ones.

In *MaddAddam*, which takes place after the events of the first two books, a new hybrid society begins to take shape as the cluster of surviving humans starts to integrate – both socially and procreatively – with the Crakers. The gradual blending of these two societies is precarious, confusing for everyone involved, and very much incomplete, yet also apparently inevitable given the fact that the humans and Crakers share the same new landscape and generally wish to help one another. In terms of time reckoning, there are several ways in which the humans begin to move more toward a Craker form of temporality, both socially and biologically. Noticing that she and her human companions have developed a habit of "slacking off" as they gradually work to tend their garden and enlarge their shared cobb house, Toby muses that "it's tempting to drift, as the Crakers seem to. They have no festivals, no calendars, no deadlines. No long-term goals."[106] The "drifting" of the Crakers is effectively a highly pronounced form of event time, and one that becomes increasingly alluring given the absence of the intensive time pressures of modernity. The encroaching of the Crakers' accelerated biological time into human bodies, however, is more worrying. When Amanda becomes pregnant with a child that may be half Craker, the humans worry about the physical danger: "The Craker children are on a different developmental clock, they grow much faster. What if the baby gets too big, too fast, and can't make its way out?"[107] This particular fear is alleviated when three of the human women successfully give birth to four human-Craker hybrid babies near the end of the novel, although the future implications of this genetic mingling remain unknown.

While Craker temporality works its way into the human world in the above ways, the much more significant change in *MaddAddam* is the transition of the Crakers themselves toward a much more recognizable human time. When Toby starts to teach the young Craker called Blackbeard how to read and write, Blackbeard begins to gain consciousness of a historical past and an envisioned deep future. He gradually takes over from Toby the duties of keeping a journal of daily events as well as telling the evening story to the rest of the Crakers. By the final chapters of the book, Toby has fallen into silence altogether; the final scenes are scraps from Blackbeard's oral stories and journal entries, which lead us to understand both formally and through the content of the journal that his voice has taken over (Toby eventually commits suicide with poppy extract after the apparent death of her lover Zeb). Adopting Toby's methods of time reckoning, Blackbeard's journal entries name each Gardener festival or feast day, as well as the current phases of the moon. While such timekeeping systems had previously been meaningless to the Crakers, Blackbeard's new skills of literacy lead him to realize that his written voice can form an ordered ongoing story of significant events, and will persist into the future to be heard even after he has passed away. Toby worries, at least momentarily, that by teaching Blackbeard to read and write she may have contaminated the Craker society with particularly human failings; "What comes next?" she wonders. "Rules, dogmas, laws?"[108] But whether the transition is seen as a rise to enlightenment or a fall from grace, literacy gives the Crakers an ordered consciousness of the past, a systematized sense of both sequence and recurrence, an awareness of the implications of present actions for future generations, and an understanding of mortality. Drawing from Toby's directive that each Craker who learns to write should transcribe a new copy of the Book containing Toby's and Blackbeard's account of history and Craker cosmology, Blackbeard explains to the other Crakers that this method of textual reproduction will ensure that the writings "would always be there for us to read."[109]

When a final battle against the two escaped Painballers near the end of the novel results in the death of Jimmy, his earlier prediction of the demise of the Gregorian calendar and clock time finally comes to pass. But the universal human need to count the days is renewed through the development of the nascent human-Craker society, symbolized especially by the four hybrid infants. This new society is one in which the counting of Gardener feast days and moon phases, and thus the systematizing of time and history, is combined with the Crakers' "drifting" which, while compromised by an awareness of the future and of mortality, remains prominent due to the absence of clocks and the time pressures of modernity. In this way, *MaddAddam* can be said to imagine how new provisional forms of blended temporalities can adapt themselves to radically transformed social circumstances.[110] While the ending of *MaddAddam* through the forward-looking voice of Blackbeard is more hopeful than the troubled endings of the first two novels, the trilogy still ends with a significant degree of uncertainty and anxiety; violent strangers and vicious animals still roam the landscape, and the ability of the Crakers and humans to maintain a stable hybrid society remains unproven. Still, this new society appears to be flourishing in its own fragile way, and the tentative willingness of its members to modify their own modes of time – to understand social time reckoning as multiple and provisional rather than singular and absolute – is key to the fostering of respectful, productive social arrangements. Multitemporality, by its very nature, must be a provisional form of time.

Provisional Time

Like so many articulations of temporality, this book remains inevitably provisional. There will always be more to learn from the particular ways in which experiences of time are tied, for instance, to spatial regions of human activity or to the ecological and geological matrices of the natural world. Rather than accounting for every possible model of time within Canada, though, my goals here have been to offer a framework for understanding the major cultural structures of time that have taken hold in the nation; to articulate the ways in which social patterns that may appear unconnected to temporality can in fact profoundly influence the experience of time for individuals; to recognize that literary authors have been highly adept at witnessing, questioning, and shaping these connections; and finally to demonstrate how the above frameworks can be used to develop politically aware forms of critical temporal literacy, and to construct informed readings of temporal power relations in literature and culture.

I will close with a comment on the opportunities afforded by ongoing conversations on temporal discrimination and multitemporality. The concept of temporal discrimination, which I have advanced here as a means of identifying and responding to inequitable valuations of different times, offers one possible framework for working toward a heightened consciousness of temporal injustice. I offer it in the hopes of attaching a coherent name to the multifarious ways in which certain times are considered natural, correct, and righteous while other times are considered backward, self-destructive, fanciful, and wrong; to the ways in which the rights of the future – of our own future selves – are silenced and sacrificed for the enrichment of the short term; to the ways in which forms of social hierarchization built on categories of age, class, race, and gender serve as foundations for the unquestioned reduction of temporal agency in those groups and individuals excluded from elite status. I offer the term temporal discrimination in order to articulate the necessity of working toward equitable temporal agency for those who have been, are being, and will be excluded from dominant narratives of progress, and to prompt an opening within our social configurations to make room for the intrinsic value of alternative visions of time.

The notion of multitemporality remains a promising one for identifying and advocating flexible structures of time reckoning that remain sensitive to the repressive forms of power tied to dominant temporalities. Multitemporality reminds us that the apparently monolithic time of accelerative productivity, seven-day weeks, and economic progress was never uniform or totalizing to begin with, but consists of many interrelated temporalities that themselves form shifting and difficult relationships with personal experiences of time and alternative cultural valuations of slowness, recursion, justice, work, and leisure. In advocating flexible conceptualizations of the multiplicity of social and personal temporalities, though, I am conscious of the unequal distribution of power alongside which normative models of time have become entrenched. Any call for increasing awareness of multiple temporalities must recognize that a slanted playing field of temporal difference coexists with the imbalances that have afflicted the notion of multiculturalism.

Eva Mackey has cogently identified the key problems with Canada's implementation of multiculturalism, and these concerns are worth enumerating here to acknowledge the similar pitfalls to which a concept of multitemporality may be vulnerable. Noting that Prime Minister Trudeau's announcement of an initial multiculturalism policy in 1971 sought to help cultural groups "overcome cultural barriers to full participation in Canadian society," Mackey writes that the "Canadian society" in question is one in which the English and French cultural-linguistic groups maintain central and primary status: "Therefore, acceptable cultural diversity must buttress the project of nation-building and national unity in Canada."[1] Within this framework, minority cultures risk being framed "as fragments of cultures, constructed from folkloric and culinary remnants," which in turn "become conceptually divorced from politics and economics, and become commodified cultural possessions."[2] Compared with the initial 1971 policy, the Canadian Multiculturalism Act of 1988 shifts the focus more toward combatting racism and democratizing the responsibility for shaping society, yet Mackey finds that the Act "is still primarily concerned with mobilising diversity for the project of nation-building, as well as limiting that diversity to symbolic rather than political forms,"[3] and that the economic discourse surrounding the Act "proposes that multiculturalism is a national resource in the context of global capitalism."[4] At the same time, the policy is not equipped to counter the particular marginalization of Indigenous groups, and "has been criticised as a means to undercut Québec's demands for special recognition by bestowing recognition on other cultural groups."[5] The "key issue," Mackey writes, "is that despite the proliferation of cultural difference, the power to define, limit and tolerate differences still lies in the hands of the dominant group. Further, the degree and forms of *tolerable* differences are defined by the ever-changing needs of the project of nation-building."[6]

Mackey's criticisms are well placed, but Canada's multiculturalism policy still retains value in its attempt to recognize a plurality of cultural experiences even if this attempt suffers from flaws and biases. We might say that the problems associated with multiculturalism can productively be addressed through a "politics of fulfillment" that remains conscious of a "politics of transfiguration." Borrowing these terms from Paul Gilroy's commentary on the African diaspora, Daniel Coleman explains that a politics of fulfillment calls "upon bourgeois civil society to live up to its own declared egalitarian, universal values," while a politics of transfiguration is "radically utopian, aspiring to transcend the limits of the existing social order."[7] In calling for a broad social recognition of contending civilities to take the place of an assumed singular measure of civility, he suggests that such a desire "leans more towards the politics of fulfillment" by aiming to live up to the admirable promise of equitable civil protections, even while it remains conscious of the utopian desire for profound changes to underlying assumptions.[8] Given the more draconian social policies that have been and are being implemented in various political spheres, the effort to create improvements within a flawed vision of cultural equity may promise more benefits, at least for the time being, than the abolishment of this vision altogether.

I would like to understand the politics of multiculturalism as a lesson in thinking through a politics of multitemporality. One possible response to the inequalities tied to dominant models of time would be the attempt to abolish standardized notions of time altogether, leaving a vacuum of temporal power. This approach, though, suffers from two serious problems. The first problem is the same one that Patrick Lewis, the protagonist of Michael Ondaatje's novel *In the Skin of a Lion*, encounters during his mission to blow up the Toronto water purification plant and its iconic tower clock. While Patrick despises the clock because it represents, for him, the dominant forms of history and timekeeping that glorify the grand notion of progress while silencing the working classes, he seems in the end to realize, through his decision not to detonate the bomb, that even if the destruction of dominant forms of time is possible, it may not be desirable. Destroying normative time will not create a neutral situation from which all people can benefit equally, but will inevitably impose differently biased forms of temporal structures. This in turn reveals the second problem: shared understandings of time are necessary for the coordination of sociality, and the abolishment of social temporal agreements would, like the abolishment of language, result in an untenable loss of cooperativeness and stability. As Coleman asks, "How can you meet to discuss differences if you don't know when the people will be gathering to discuss it?"[9]

This is why a politics of fulfillment can offer a useful paradigm in the fight against temporal discrimination. An equitable approach to cultural constructions of time can acknowledge the need for socially shared temporal coordination and also understand temporal constructs as provisional frameworks to be re-evaluated and reshaped on an ongoing basis in the service of social justice. Provisional time remains alive, always present out of necessity, and always ready to undergo new rounds of questioning and negotiation. If a politics of multitemporality is to engage legitimately with differing temporal experiences and work toward a public sphere of equitable temporal agency, it must be founded on a deep valuation of the legitimacy of multiple temporalities, must recognize the provisional and temporary nature of cultural constructs, and must be willing to recognize and question existing patterns of inequitable temporal power and pressures. A politics of multitemporality must be able to perform critical readings of the time socialization stories we tell ourselves every day, and imagine new, adaptive ways of socializing ourselves into equitable forms of time. One of the goals of this book has been to open up new spaces for multiple experiences of time to make themselves heard, and to identify the necessity of recognizing diverse and shifting temporalities while enhancing our consciousness of entrenched hierarchies of temporal power. To this end, listening to one another's stories, to one another's distinctive and collective articulations of time, enacts a powerful resistance against inequitable temporal power and allows for sensitive conversations about the shared responsibility for social temporal justice. The study of literature contributes to these conversations by identifying and testing multiple registers of temporal experience, by providing a critical vocabulary for discussing the ways in which these experiences are inevitably articulated through the structures of narrative, and by fostering a habit of slow and thoughtful contemplation informed by the tools of critical temporal literacy – a habit of reading that counteracts hasty assumptions and clarifies the provisionality of normative time.

Notes

ACKNOWLEDGMENTS

1 New, *Land Sliding*, 5; emphasis in original.

INTRODUCTION

1 Panych, *7 Stories*, 91.
2 Zerubavel, *Seven Day Circle*, 14.
3 Ibid., 55, 11, 28.
4 Friedman, *About Time*, 73.
5 Copway, *Life, History, and Travels*, 78; emphasis in original.
6 Qtd. in Semmens, "Who Owns the Forest?"
7 Zerubavel, *Seven Day Circle*, 2.
8 Fabian, *Time and the Other*, 28.
9 Ibid., ix.
10 Friedman, *About Time*, 5.
11 Ibid.
12 Allen, *Republic in Time*, 217.
13 "The OEC."
14 Frye, *Bush Garden*, 222.
15 Elias, *Essay on Time*, 75.
16 Aristotle, *Physics*, IV.12.
17 Augustine, *Confessions*, Book XI.
18 Bergson, *Time and Free Will*, 232.
19 Easthope, *Literary into Cultural Studies*, 184.

20 Qtd. in Kern, *Culture of Time and Space*, 11.

21 Ibid., 19.

22 Benjamin, "Theses on the Philosophy of History," XIII.

23 Easthope, *Literary into Cultural Studies*, 182.

24 Benjamin, "Theses on the Philosophy of History," XIV.

25 Anderson, *Imagined Communities*, 24–5.

26 Thompson, "Time, Work-Discipline, and Industrial Capitalism," 90–1; emphasis in original.

27 Urry, "Speeding Up and Slowing Down," 186.

28 Innis, *Empire and Communications*, 22.

29 Ibid., 5.

30 Ibid.

31 Ibid., 169.

32 Innis, "A Plea for Time," 47.

33 Despite the fact that radio broadcasts are presumably even more light and ephemeral than newspaper editions, Innis argues somewhat strangely at the end of *Empire and Communications* that the new medium of the radio *checks*, rather than exacerbates, the emphasis of the newspaper on problems of space. His comment quoted above in "A Plea for Time," to the effect that radio and cinema dangerously neglect the concerns of durability and future orientation, seems much more in line with his larger thesis.

34 Innis, *Empire and Communications*, 169.

35 Rosa, *Social Acceleration*, 21; emphasis in original.

36 Adam, "Perceptions of Time," 519.

37 Ibid., 509; emphasis in original.

38 Urry, "Speeding Up and Slowing Down," 189.

39 Ibid.

40 During, *Cultural Studies*, 65.

41 Qtd. in Blaise, *Time Lord*, 35.

42 Bakhtin, "Forms of Time," 84.

43 Ibid., 85.

44 Ibid., 250–1.

45 Allen, *Republic in Time*, 4.

46 Kern, *Culture of Time and Space*, 1.

47 Ibid., 3–4.

48 As I explain in chapter 2, the desire for simultaneity, for social synchronization, remains powerful and important even if it is difficult to achieve.

49 L. Pratt, *Archives of American Time*, 16.

50 Ibid., 15.

51 Goodin, "Temporal Justice."

52 Adam, *Timescapes*, 124, 125.

53 Researchers in health and psychology have used the idea of temporal framing in their efforts to convince individuals to make choices with long-term benefits. For instance, people who are deemed to have a low tendency to consider future consequences may be more likely to make positive long-term health decisions (such as going for colorectal cancer screening or applying sunscreen before sun exposure) if health providers manipulate these patients into believing that the positive consequences of the decision will operate in the short term, and the negative consequences will operate in the long term (see Orbell and Kyriakaki, "Temporal Framing," for an example). My use of the phrase "temporal framing" is quite different. On a side note, it is important to realize that while the classification of individuals as likely or not likely to consider future consequences can be important, such categorizations easily neglect the social and cultural factors that help to shape people's temporal orientations, a problem I discuss in chapter 3.

54 This particular statement was made by Ontario Premier Kathleen Wynne in November 2013, in relation to the troubling and illegal behaviour of Toronto Mayor Rob Ford ("Rob Ford Scandal"). While this statement is relatively innocuous, it uses the same method of temporal framing that has been central to some of the major acts of temporal injustice discussed in chapter 1.

55 Keightley, "Introduction," 10.

56 Zimbardo and Boyd, *Time Paradox*, 44.

57 Ibid.

58 Finance Minister Jim Flaherty made this statement in March 2012, upon reducing the maximum length of time for the environmental assessment of major resource development projects from six years to two years (qtd. in Paris, "Budget Shortens").

59 Levine, *Geography of Time*, 82.

60 Ibid., 217, 219.

CHAPTER ONE

1 Wright, *Stolen Continents*, 5.

2 Aristotle, *Physics*, IV.12.

3 New, *Land Sliding*, 5.

4 Ibid.; emphasis in original.

5 King, *Inconvenient Indian*, 217.

6 Fabian, *Time and the Other*, 144.

7 Ibid.; emphasis in original.

8 Frye, *Bush Garden*, 137.

9 Szeman, "Belated or Isochronic?" 188; emphasis in original.

10 Ibid., 191–2.

11 Crocker, "Hauled Kicking and Screaming," 425.

12 Ibid., 426, 427.

13 Ibid., 431.

14 Vassanji, *No New Land*, 35–6.

15 Söderlind, "Ghost-National Arguments," 675.

16 Ibid., 689.

17 Frye, *Bush Garden*, 138.

18 Coleman, "From Contented Civility," 231.

19 Ibid., 232.

20 Ibid., 233.

21 Ibid., 235.

22 Sioui, *Histoires de Kanatha*, 124.

23 Ibid., 83.

24 Ibid., 278–9.

25 E.J. Pratt, *Towards the Last Spike*, 44.

26 Ngũgĩ, *Decolonising the Mind*, 17.

27 Copway, *Life, History, and Travels*, 96.

28 Ibid., 144.

29 Meckler and Weisman, "Obama Warns of 'Lost Decade.'"

30 Kirby, "A Lost Decade of Growth."

31 Roger Sauvé, qtd. in Kirby, "A Lost Decade of Growth."

32 A list of local TimeBanking affiliates including branches in Vancouver, Winnipeg, Toronto, and several other Canadian cities is offered at community. timebanks.org.

33 Coleman, "From Contented Civility," 237.

34 Zerubavel, *Seven Day Circle*, 83; emphasis in original.

35 Ibid., 83–4.

36 Coleman, "From Contented Civility," 231.

37 Levine, *Geography of Time*, 219.

38 Ibid., 217.

39 Bhabha, "DissemiNation," 143.

40 Levine, *Geography of Time*, xv.

41 Cartier, *Voyages of Jacques Cartier*, 26. Bracketed clarifications by editor H.P. Biggar.

42 Champlain, "Carte Geographiqve."

43 Ricoeur, *Time and Narrative*, 3: 106.

44 Landes, *Revolution in Time*, 33.

45 The use of sequential dates in Canada's early history is complicated by the fact that France adopted the Gregorian calendar upon the calendar's creation in 1582, while England and its colonies did not follow suit until 1752. This switch from the Julian to the Gregorian calendar required making up the difference in dates that had accumulated over the previous centuries, with the result that within the British Empire 2 September 1752 was followed immediately by 14 September 1752, an example of the arbitrariness of seemingly inevitable forms of temporal accounting. In England, the Calendar (New Style) Act 1750 was drawn up to orchestrate the switch. Amid fears that landlords would attempt to collect an entire month's rent for September 1752, the Act dictated that "Times of payment of rents, annuities, andc. or of delivery of goods, commencement or expiration of leases, andc. or of attaining the age of 21 years" would accrue according to "the true number of natural days" (provision 6).

46 King, "Godzilla vs. Post-Colonial," 242.

47 Ibid., 243.

48 The increasing visibility in Canada of events such as Chinese New Year may suggest that the Gregorian calendar's dominance is not absolute, though even Chinese Canadian associations publicize Chinese New Year as beginning on, say, 26 January rather than on the first day of the traditional Chinese calendar. Also notable is the reversal, in 2008, of York University's policy of cancelling classes on days marked as holidays in the Hebrew calendar, after a human rights complaint (see Louise Brown, "York U").

49 King, "Godzilla vs. Post-Colonial," 248.

50 Dohrn-van Rossum, *History of the Hour*, 18.

51 Lombardi, "Why Is a Minute."

52 Landes, *Revolution in Time*, 6.

53 Ibid., 12.

54 Ibid., 116.

55 Levine, *Geography of Time*, 57.

56 Sobel, *Longitude*, 106.

57 Franklin, *Narrative of a Journey*, 62.

58 Landes, *Revolution in Time*, 7; emphasis in original.

59 Dohrn-van Rossum, *History of the Hour*, 2.

60 Ibid., 283.

61 Rosa, *Social Acceleration*, 279.

62 Levine, *Geography of Time*, 52.

63 Mumford, *Technics and Civilization*, 14.

64 Allen, *Republic in Time*, 60.

65 Ibid., 8.

66 Ibid., 2.

67 Adam, "Perceptions of Time," 510, 513; emphasis in original.

68 Woodcock, "The Tyranny of the Clock," 46–7.

69 Haliburton, *Clockmaker*, 8.

70 Ibid., 103.

71 Ibid., 115.

72 Qtd. in S. Brand, *Clock of the Long Now*, 66.

73 Levine, *Geography of Time*, 56.

74 Haliburton, *Clockmaker*, 8.

75 Ibid., 11.

76 Ibid., 13.

77 Ibid., 8.

78 Ibid., 24.

79 Ibid., 27; emphasis in original.

80 Godeanu-Kenworthy, "The Political Other," 206.

81 Ibid., 208.

82 Ibid., 219.

83 Qtd. in Levine, *Geography of Time*, 67.

84 Galison, *Einstein's Clocks*, 104.

85 Dewdney, *Soul of the World*, 64.

86 Galison, *Einstein's Clocks*, 107.

87 Kern, *Culture of Time and Space*, 1.

88 Ibid., 69.

89 Ibid., 316.

90 Blaise, *Time Lord*, 86, 103.

91 Through an archival study of the documents associated with the 1884 conference, Adam Barrows upsets more than a century's worth of historical

knowledge in his finding that the conference "did not in fact achieve the goal for which it is credited. It did not advocate the use of the Greenwich meridian as a universal time-reckoning tool." While the conference is typically cited as having implemented global time zones alongside the choice of the prime meridian, Barrows shows that the proposal for global standard time was rejected at the conference, and caught on only gradually over the following years through sustained efforts by the primary supporters of the idea, including Sandford Fleming. Barrows, *Cosmic Time of Empire*, 36.

92 Kern, *Culture of Time and Space*, 15.

93 Ibid., 34.

94 Barrows, *Cosmic Time of Empire*, 7.

95 Galison, *Einstein's Clocks*, 110–11.

96 Stein, "Dislocations," 119.

97 Ibid., 120.

98 Qtd. in Blaise, *Time Lord*, 35.

99 Ibid., 34–5.

100 Ibid., 188.

101 Barrows, *Cosmic Time of Empire*, 4, 46.

102 In a sense, Canada's lack of control over clock time forms a parallel to the linguistic conundrum identified by Dennis Lee, that as inhabitants of a culturally subordinate colonial space, Canadians "have no terms in which to speak that do not issue from the space we are trying to speak against" (Lee, "Cadence, Country, Silence," 52). "No terms" is an exaggeration, but just as our language's historical and cultural centre lies closer to England and the United States than it does to Canada, so too does our temporal vocabulary.

103 We can see similar tension at work in the fact that the Gregorian calendar, which was created by the Catholic Church mainly to regulate the scheduling of Easter, forms a strict template within which Canada has been able to make minor localized adjustments such as Canadian Thanksgiving and the gradual secularization of Sundays.

104 Rudy, "Do You Have the Time?" 534.

105 Ibid., 537.

106 Ibid., 532, 537–8.

107 Ibid., 534.

108 Ibid., 535, 550.

109 Ibid., 547.

110 Ibid. 541–2.

111 Ibid., 553.

112 Ibid., 554.

113 Ibid., 553.

114 Ibid., 548.

115 "Time Stands Still on Parliament Hill."

116 Rosa, *Social Acceleration*, 64.

117 Ibid., 156.

118 Ibid., 159.

119 Ibid., 115.

120 Ibid., 148.

121 Levine, *Geography of Time*, 8–9.

122 Ibid., 9.

123 Ibid., 131–2. Various nuances are involved in these rankings. Ireland, for instance, placed first in walking speed, which Levine attributes to the cold climate, but 11th in clock accuracy. Ibid., 131, 133.

124 Ibid. 154, 159.

125 Ibid., 155, 158.

126 Rosa is especially critical of Levine's study, arguing that the variables Levine measures cannot be expected to reflect the overall pace of life of the society in question, and that "the action tempo of an entire series of very diverse processes from different fields of action must be considered and aggregated" (Rosa, *Social Acceleration*, 121). Presumably Levine would be the first to agree that his research should be funded well enough to allow for such measurements. Rosa's point that Levine fails to account for the more complex implications of time pressure is another significant criticism.

127 Sitney, *Visionary Film*, 352.

128 "WVLNT."

129 The Time Use Surveys do break down the results on "employed" and "unemployed" Canadians, predictably demonstrating that employed people have less free time. But the data do not reveal more detailed socio-economic differences.

130 See Table 1 in each study, Table 2 in the 1998 and 2005 studies, and Table 3.1 in the 2010 study. A comment on time stress as it relates to the aging population appears on p. 9 of the 2010 study.

131 Statistics Canada, *General Social Survey – 2010*, 7.

132 Statistics Canada, *General Social Survey: Overview of the Time Use of Canadians in 1998*, Table 1.

133 Statistics Canada, *General Social Survey – 2010*, Table 1.1.

134 Tallying a population's working time and free time is not quite equivalent to counting the "episodes of action and / or experience per unit of time" that Rosa identifies as a measure of the pace of life (Rosa, *Social Acceleration*, 64), but identifying the amount of free time available to the Newfoundland and Labrador population would still help to clarify whether the abundant leisure time in the advertisements has some reflection in reality.

135 "Two Brand New Tourism TV Ads."

136 Ibid.

137 Statistics Canada, *General Social Survey on Time Use: Overview of the Time Use of Canadians: 2005*, Tables 1.1 and 1.2.

138 White, *Tropics of Discourse*, 91.

139 Ireland, *Subaltern Appeal to Experience*, 133–4.

140 Stock market news websites tend to offer different options for the time axis on stock charts, with the maximum viewable time ranging from five days to 30 years. However, the longer time frame options are typically buried beneath several layers of links.

141 Campbell, *Halfbreed*, 2.

142 Ibid., 4.

143 Ibid., 6.

144 Ibid., 7–8.

145 Ibid., 8.

146 Ibid.

147 Immigration Act [1952], 4.1, 4.2.a.

148 Ibid., 5.a, d, e, m.

149 Keung, "Immigration Waiting Times Cause Frustration."

150 I am grateful to Malissa Phung for pointing out this confusion to me.

151 D. Brand, *What We All Long For*, 214.

152 Lawson, "Postcolonial Theory and the 'Settler' Subject," 29.

153 Morton, *Short History of Canada*, 82.

154 Clements, *Burning Vision*, 56.

155 Morton, *Short History of Canada*, 290.

156 MacIvor, *Never Swim Alone*, 72–3.

157 Traill, *Backwoods of Canada*, 94.

158 Morton, *Short History of Canada*, 79.

159 Milton, *Paradise Lost*, 5.855.

160 Demos, *Circles and Lines*, 31.

161 Ibid., 38–9, 47–51.

162 Fabian, *Time and the Other*, 31.

163 D. Brand, *Map to the Door*, 82.

164 Alfred, *Wasáse*, 152–3.

165 Lai, *Salt Fish Girl*, 244.

166 In her international study of the motivations that lead societies to address
particular historical injustices over others, Katharine McGregor finds that each
case of redress involves "a struggle over historical memory and over the extent
and form in which events or people are recorded in national histories." More
than this, she determines that the decision of whether to apologize is often
made through a cost-benefit analysis, taking into account, for instance, the
trade value that might be won by mending a particular international relationship, or the tally of how many remaining domestic victims might qualify for
compensation. McGregor, "Time, Memory and Historical Justice," 17, 18.

167 "Statement of Apology."

168 Dorrell, "From Reconciliation to Reconciling," 32.

169 "GG Relaunches Truth and Reconciliation Commission."

170 Alfred, *Wasáse*, 157.

171 Sioui, *Histoires de Kanatha*, 123.

172 Ibid., 93.

173 Ibid., 207.

174 D. Brand, *Land to Light On*, 34.

175 Dimock, *Through Other Continents*, 4.

176 McKay, "Ediacaran and Anthropocene," 24.

177 Alfred, *Wasáse*, 27.

178 Ibid., 28.

179 Morton, *Short History of Canada*, 26.

180 Ibid., 158.

181 "Haida Nation."

182 Morton, *Short History of Canada*, 140.

183 "A Destructive Force."

184 Healey, Mason, and Ricou, "'hardy/and unkillable clichés,'" 294.

185 Traill, *Backwoods of Canada*, 106.

186 Ibid., 17.

187 Ibid., 115.

188 Doyle, "Against Dislocation," 71. Doyle uses the term "English speakers" to
reflect the fact that her informants identified themselves with a greater degree

of multiplicity and heterogeneous complexity than the terms "anglophone" and "allophone," with their respective connotations of "white and Protestant" and "newly-arrived immigrants," would easily allow for. Ibid., 63.

189 Ibid., 63.
190 Atwood, *Payback*, 165.
191 McKay, *Deactivated West 100*, 46.
192 "Canadian Makers."
193 "Galleries."
194 Atwood, *Payback*, 168.
195 Bartlett, "Time Stands Up for Itself," 116–17.
196 Panych, *7 Stories*, 95.
197 Ibid., 98.
198 Ibid., 100–1.

CHAPTER TWO

1   Ondaatje, *In the Skin of a Lion*, 143.
2   Kamboureli, "Politics of the Beyond," 48.
3   Atwood, *Wilderness Tips*, 257.
4   Ibid., 265.
5   Ibid., 269.
6   Ibid., 282.
7   Ibid., 283–4.
8   Dewdney, *Soul of the World*, 10.
9   Ricoeur, *Time and Narrative*, 3: 246.
10 Ricoeur's definition of narrative emphasizes the same characteristics but centres on the importance of story-creation rather than the potentially simpler accounting of connected events. For him, the necessary condition of narrative is that it "tells a story, otherwise it would not be a narrative." Ricoeur, *Time and Narrative*, 2: 82.
11 Ibid., 1: 3.
12 Ibid., 1: 72.
13 Eakin, *Living Autobiographically*, 2; emphasis in original.
14 Ibid., 4.
15 Ibid., 23–4.
16 Ibid., 32.
17 Newlands, *Canadian Art*, 247.

18 New, *Along a Snake Fence Riding*, 6.

19 Ibid. The six voices are perhaps reminiscent of the "characters" in Luigi Pirandello's 1922 play *Six Characters in Search of an Author*, which interrogates the concepts of art, life, authority, and relativistic experience. The play begins and ends with characters looking at their watches, arguing over the appropriate action for the present time of day.

20 Qtd. in New, *Along a Snake Fence Riding*, 7; emphasis in original.

21 Bergson, *Time and Free Will*, 232.

22 Flaherty, *A Watched Pot*, 2.

23 Riegel, "Toward a Dialectical Interpretation of Time and Change," 101.

24 New, *Along a Snake Fence Riding*, 35.

25 Ibid., 109.

26 White, *Tropics of Discourse*, 91.

27 New, *Along a Snake Fence Riding*, 22.

28 Ricoeur, *Time and Narrative*, 2: 62.

29 Ibid., 2: 73.

30 Munro, *Runaway*, 308.

31 Fraser, *Poor Super Man*, 159.

32 Martel, *Self*, 267.

33 Atwood, *Wilderness Tips*, 183.

34 Atwood, *Negotiating with the Dead*, 178.

35 Newman, Clayton, and Hirsch, *Time and the Literary*, 1.

36 Paul and Sanger, *Stone Canoe*, 64.

37 Dewdney, *Soul of the World*, 95.

38 Alfred, *Wasáse*, 32.

39 Ibid. Alfred Metallic, the first PhD candidate at York University to write and defend his dissertation in an Indigenous language, similarly observes that "in the Mi'gmaw language, the action comes first, then the person. It's the opposite with the English language." McLean, "PhD Student Defends Thesis."

40 Taylor, "Politics of Recognition," 102.

41 Ibid., 111.

42 Evernden, *Natural Alien*, 40.

43 Munro, *Hateship*, 212.

44 Munro, *Runaway*, 235.

45 Munro, *Hateship*, 244.

46 Ibid., 245.

47 D. Brand, *In Another Place, Not Here*, 44.

48 Ibid., 233.

49 D. Brand, *What We All Long For*, 59.

50 Ibid., 113.

51 D. Brand, *Land to Light On*, 73.

52 D. Brand, *Map to the Door*, 25.

53 Ricoeur expands this idea by quoting Saint Augustine's description of a three-fold present: "The present of past things is the memory; the present of present things is direct perception ... and the present of future things is expectation" (Ricoeur, *Time and Narrative*, 1: 11). Freud's concept of melancholia, of the persistent shadow of a lost love object over a person's ego, is another way to articulate the negative aspects of "the present of past things." Ricoeur later goes on to suggest with reference to Heidegger that the profound unity of the past, the present, and the future in human experience may "require that the very terms 'future,' 'past,' and 'present' be abandoned, terms that Augustine never felt obliged to question, out of respect for ordinary language, despite his audacity in speaking of the present *of* the future, the present *of* the past, and the present *of* the present" (ibid., 3: 68; emphasis in original). While justification may exist for abandoning the terms "past," "present," and "future," the words carry enough of a practical distinction that their continued use is in little doubt. Heidegger's difficult quest to construct new language that better represents phenomenological experience results, Ricoeur says, in the belief that "temporality is then the articulated unity of coming-towards, having-been, and making-present, which are thereby given to be thought of together" (ibid., 3: 70). This alternative vocabulary appears to maintain a threefold temporal distinction, yet privileges the present as the phenomenological vantage point for human experience. Like Augustine, Heidegger, and Ricoeur, literature often seeks to articulate the deep, inevitable connections in human experience between the past, the present, and the future, whether this is accomplished through questioning the conventions of language or through representations of the associative processes of subjective time.

54 Coleman, *White Civility*, 12.

55 Coleman, "From Contented Civility," 231.

56 Williams, *Confessional Fictions*, 178.

57 Ibid.

58 Lynch, *One and the Many*, 18.

59 Ibid., 23–4.

60 Roy, *Road Past Altamont*, 71.

284 NOTES TO PAGES 87–90

61 Franco Moretti argues that the Bildungsroman, as a story of youth, became the "symbolic form" of modernity in the nineteenth century largely because modernity "perceives the experience piled up in tradition as a useless dead-weight, and therefore can no longer feel represented by maturity, and still less by old age" (Moretti, *Way of the World*, 6). He traces the disappearance of the Bildungsroman form primarily to the onset of the First World War, whose social trauma presented an "insoluble problem" to the Bildungsroman: "The trauma introduced discontinuity within novelistic temporality, generating centrifugal tendencies toward the short story and the lyric" (ibid., 244). In this sense, the use of a short story cycle to articulate new socio-temporal realities in the twentieth century is entirely appropriate. And yet, Moretti's insight that the Bildungsroman structure itself is "*intrinsically contradictory*" because it is based on "dynamism and limits, restlessness and the 'sense of an ending'" (ibid., 6; emphasis in original) suggests that the transition from the Bildungsroman toward forms that more strongly emphasize discontinuity was more of an evolution rather than a complete break. The focus on youth in a *Künstlerroman* such as *The Road Past Altamont* also mirrors the focus on youth in the classic Bildungsroman, suggesting that in the transition from modern to modernism, and perhaps to postmodernism, youth remains among the most appropriate figures for examining rapidly changing social circumstances.

62 Williams, *Confessional Fictions*, 187.

63 Nodelman, "Gabrielle Roy's *La route d'Altamont*," 219.

64 Ibid.

65 Williams, *Confessional Fictions*, 187.

66 Adam, "Perceptions of Time," 519.

67 Roy, *Road Past Altamont*, 29–30.

68 Ibid., 30.

69 Felski, *Doing Time*, 3.

70 Roy, *Road Past Altamont*, 61.

71 Ibid., 77.

72 Ibid., 77–8.

73 Commentary on this scene has usually focused on Christine's question of whether they are looking at the end of the lake or the beginning, and the old man's response: "The end or the beginning? Such questions you ask! The end or the beginning. And if they are fundamentally the same … […] Perhaps everything finally forms a great circle, the end and the beginning coming together" (ibid., 68). As I have suggested, while cyclical aspects of generational time are

significant in the book, it is important to consider the temporal experiences of synchronization and simultaneity rather than leaning excessively on quotations such as this one to identify a strictly cyclical (or otherwise spatial) mode of time.

74 Williams, *Confessional Fictions*, 182.

75 Roy, *Road Past Altamont*, 83.

76 Ibid., 112.

77 Ibid., 125–6.

78 The gulf that exists here between Christine and Maman, between the older generation and the younger, between Quebec and the prairies, suggests a longing for continuity that is somewhat reminiscent of the desire for cultural and linguistic continuity among much of the population of Quebec itself (a desire that is famously articulated within the context of traditional, rural Quebec in Louis Hémon's *Maria Chapdelaine*). Such longing seems inevitably to embody a form of synchronous non-synchronicity, as Christine feels anchored to her contemporary Manitoba, while her mother feels a deep pull toward the Quebec of her memories.

79 Roy, *Road Past Altamont*, 122.

80 Ibid.

81 Ibid.

82 Ibid., 130.

83 Ibid., 145.

84 Ibid., 135.

85 Bush, *Minus Time*, 6.

86 Ibid.; emphasis in original.

87 MacKinnon, "Risk and Resilience," 107.

88 Bush, *Minus Time*, 41; emphasis in original.

89 Ibid., 214.

90 Ibid., 137.

91 Ibid., 178.

92 Ibid., 231.

93 Ibid., 322.

94 Ibid., 276; emphasis in original.

95 Ibid., 277.

96 Ibid., 326.

97 Ibid., 308.

98 Ibid., 282.

99 Ibid., 313.

100 Ibid., 334.

101 Ibid., 55.

102 Ibid., 334. Commenting on the iconic sound of Big Ben in Virginia Woolf's *Mrs Dalloway*, Ricoeur asks whether we can say of the characters, at the moment the clock strikes, "that the hour is the same for all? Yes, from outside; no, from inside. Only fiction, precisely, can explore and bring to language this divorce between worldviews and their irreconcilable perspectives on time, a divorce that undermines public time" (Ricoeur, *Time and Narrative*, 2: 107). As Bush's novel shows, though, the proliferation of global travel and digital communication makes apparent the fact that people inhabit different hours even from the "outside." The divorce between personal temporalities is compounded by the relativity of time itself, and while the visible impact of such relativity on human affairs is a fairly recent development, fiction's toolbox appears up to the task of articulating these complications.

103 Bush, *Minus Time*, 338; emphasis in original.

104 Ibid.

105 Ricoeur, *Time and Narrative*, 3: 132.

CHAPTER THREE

1 D. Brand, *What We All Long For*, 264; emphasis in original.

2 Wyatt, *Time's Reach*, 104.

3 Dewdney, *Soul of the World*, 15.

4 Clements, *Burning Vision*, 13.

5 Hargreaves, "A Precise Instrument for Seeing," 51.

6 Commenting on the frustration that the "double and triple exposure" of scenes and time periods in *Burning Vision* caused one of her colleagues who was responsible for costume design in a production of the play, Theresa J. May decides that the play is best understood as "*ecodramaturgy*: that is, play-making (script development and production) that puts ecological reciprocity and community at the centre of its theatrical and thematic intent." The play "makes visible a web of human agency that binds together places, people, and creatures" (May, "Kneading Marie Clements' *Burning Vision*"). By also binding together *times*, the play emphasizes the importance of temporal intersectionality to human experience as well as to political responsibility and ecological fallout.

7 Clements, *Burning Vision*, 20–1; ellipses in original, emphasis in original.

8 Ibid., 71.

9 Ibid., 44.

10 Ibid., 81.

11 Ibid., 29.

12 Ibid., 34.

13 Ibid., 84.

14 Ibid., 92.

15 Ibid., 109; emphasis in original.

16 Ibid., 110.

17 Ibid., 16. Sandy Pool's poetry in *Undark: An Oratorio* also takes up the voices of the radium painters, leaving readers to consider the deadly ties between the rush to exploit technological innovations and the lasting impacts of environmental injustice.

18 Clements, *Burning Vision*, 112.

19 Ibid., 109; emphasis in original.

20 Ibid., 119; emphasis in original.

21 Ibid., 75.

22 For an important discussion of geological ages, which are outside of my scope here, see Don McKay's "Ediacaran and Anthropocene: Poetry as a Reader of Deep Time."

23 The linear notion that certain cultures are more "developed" than others is closely related to concepts of age, leading to cases where dominant representations tend to infantilize or portray as antiquated people belonging to "backward" cultures. I will discuss contested ideas of social and biological maturity in this chapter's section on race, as well as in chapter 4.

24 DeFalco, *Uncanny Subjects*, xv, 13.

25 Ibid., 19.

26 Ibid., 30.

27 Ibid., xii–xiii.

28 Zimbardo and Boyd, *Time Paradox*, 44.

29 Ibid., 45–6.

30 Montgomery, *Anne of Green Gables*, 2.

31 Alexander, "Anne with Two 'G's," 45.

32 Ibid., 43.

33 Montgomery, *Anne of Green Gables*, 30–1.

34 Ibid., 139.

35 Ibid., 63.

36 Ibid., 89.

37 Ibid., 90–1.

38 Ibid., 214.

39 Ibid., 114.

40 Ibid., 131.

41 Hoy, "'Too Heedless and Impulsive,'" 66, 68, 70.

42 Zimbardo and Boyd, *Time Paradox*, 99, 141.

43 Hoy, "'Too Heedless and Impulsive,'" 79.

44 Montgomery, *Anne of Green Gables*, 207.

45 Ibid., 235.

46 Ibid., 237.

47 Ibid., 239–40.

48 Zimbardo and Boyd, *Time Paradox*, 141, 288.

49 Montgomery, *Anne of Green Gables*, 248.

50 Ibid., 255.

51 Zimbardo and Boyd, *Time Paradox*, 44.

52 One of the novel's more surprising features is that at the same time that Anne
    begins largely to accept normative adult temporality, openings of imaginative
    contemplation begin to appear in Marilla's psychological armour of temporal
    discipline. "Dear me," Marilla says to Matthew after witnessing one of Anne's
    typical early excited monologues, "it's only three weeks since she came, and it
    seems as if she'd been here always. I can't imagine the place without her"
    (Montgomery, *Anne of Green Gables*, 89). A few years later, we are told that
    Marilla "felt a queer regret over Anne's inches. The child she had learned to
    love had vanished somehow and here was this tall, serious-eyed girl of fifteen"
    (ibid., 252). Marilla finally admits her feelings to Anne, crying out, "I was wish-
    ing you could have stayed a little girl" (ibid., 276). By entertaining thoughts of
    imagined and emotionally driven timelines, Marilla echoes the child's inven-
    tive, often counter-logical framing of the world. To an extent Montgomery is
    taking advantage of ageist stereotyping to tug at her readers' heartstrings, yet
    through these scenes the desirability of partially escaping wholly practical time
    resonates, at least briefly, within the adult world just as it does within the world
    of the child.

53 Wyatt, *Time's Reach*, 166.

54 Coupland, *Generation X*, 86.

55 Rosa, *Social Acceleration*, 273.

56 Coupland, *Generation X*, 3.

57 Ibid., 20, 21.

58 Ibid., 5.

59 Ibid., 41.

60 Ibid., 171.

61 Ibid., 61.

62 Ibid., 175.

63 Ibid., 177.

64 Ibid., 181–2.

65 "Generation A."

66 Stone, "The Children of Cyberspace."

67 Ricoeur, *Time and Narrative*, 3: 111.

68 Ibid.

69 Gorman and Wessman, "Images, Values, and Concepts of Time," 234.

70 Gurvitch, *Spectrum of Social Time*, 87.

71 Ibid., 94–5.

72 Qtd. in Levine, *Geography of Time*, 188.

73 Gurvitch, *Spectrum of Social Time*, 59.

74 Qtd. in Levine, *Geography of Time*, 188.

75 Friedman, *About Time*, 115.

76 Ibid.

77 Zimbardo and Boyd, *Time Paradox*, 101.

78 Ibid. Zygmunt Bauman differs in his assessment of the relationship between class and time perspectives, arguing that "inhabitants of the first world live in a perpetual present, going through a succession of epochs hygienically insulated from their past as well as their future. These people are constantly busy and perpetually 'short of time,' since each moment of time is non-extensive – an experience identical with that of time 'full to the brim'" (Bauman, *Globalization*, 88). The impoverished, meanwhile, "are crushed under the burden of abundant, redundant and useless time they have nothing to fill with. In their time 'nothing ever happens'" (ibid.). Going on to label the first group "tourists" and the second group "vagabonds," Bauman manages to articulate the polarizing consequences of globalization in terms of these drastically different temporal experiences, and accurately concludes that wealthy investors are increasingly able to enjoy a "disconnection of power from obligations … towards yet unborn generations and towards the self-reproduction of the living conditions of all" (ibid., 9). By focusing so heavily on this polarization, though, he may lose sight of some of the complexities of temporal experience for the

wealthy, whose consciousness of at least a personal future is necessary to ensure that wealth is extended and retained, and for the poor, who on the one hand may indeed spend time on productive and enjoyable pursuits, and on the other hand may still be "subject to the faceless rhythm of factory time" that Bauman sees as a relic of the past (ibid., 88).

79 Ireland, *Subaltern Appeal to Experience*, 170.

80 Ibid., 158.

81 Newlands, *Canadian Art*, 181.

82 Ibid.

83 Laliberté's *The Slave to Machinery* is roughly contemporary with Charlie Chaplin's film *Modern Times* (1936), which opens with the face of a clock signalling the start of the workday, followed by a running flock of sheep juxtaposed against the rush of workers arriving at the factory. Chaplin's character soon finds himself being pulled through the enormous gears of a relentless machine.

84 Rosa, *Social Acceleration*, 64.

85 Ibid., 64–5; emphasis in original.

86 Ibid., 321, 21; emphasis in original.

87 Zimbardo and Boyd, *Time Paradox*, 101.

88 Levine, *Geography of Time*, 14.

89 Ibid., 12.

90 Dohrn-van Rossum, *History of the Hour*, 289.

91 Ibid., 9.

92 Levine, *Geography of Time*, 68, 70.

93 Ibid., 12–13.

94 Rosa, *Social Acceleration*, 157.

95 Qtd. in Levine, *Geography of Time*, 13.

96 Morton, *Short History of Canada*, 7.

97 Levine, *Geography of Time*, 141.

98 Ibid., 141–3.

99 Ibid., 103.

100 Statistics Canada, *General Social Survey on Time Use: Overview of the Time Use of Canadians: 2005*, Table 1. I am using the 2005 study for these figures because the 2010 study does not break responses down by region.

101 Ibid., Tables 1.6, 1.10.

102 Ibid., Table 2.

103 "More Canadians Pressed for Time."

104 Rosa argues that traditional forms of time management and planning in people's lives are "being replaced by flexible time arrangements that (similar to the processing of digital computers) involve microtemporal oscillation between the demands of distinct functional spheres that are all running as 'non-stop' enterprises" (Rosa, *Social Acceleration*, 192). As one result of this, "It might very well turn out that the survey instruments of time use research are a manifestation of highly temporally differentiated 'classical' modernity but are only of rather limited value for analysis of the time structures of late modernity" (ibid., 130). This conclusion certainly applies to university instructors and other people whose work is not always clearly delimited by the hours of the clock, but as with some of his other comments, Rosa may underestimate here the lingering significance of the punch clock for many other types of workers.

105 "Nice Work if You Can Get Out."

106 Ibid.

107 Martel, *Self*, 266.

108 Rosa, *Social Acceleration*, 192.

109 Wayman, "Factory Time," 101–3. Excerpts reproduced with permission from the publisher.

110 New, *Along a Snake Fence Riding*, 85.

111 Mackenzie, *Recession-Proof*, 3, 4.

112 Ibid., 3.

113 I. Brown, "Sleep Deprivation Is a National Epidemic."

114 Wayman, "Overtime," 20.

115 I. Brown, "Sleep Deprivation Is a National Epidemic."

116 Gurvitch, *Spectrum of Social Time*, 100.

117 Coupland, *Generation X*, 147.

118 Kramer, "1919 Winnipeg General Strike," 60.

119 Wyile, *Speculative Fictions*, 104.

120 Ibid., 98.

121 Helms, *Challenging Canada*, 125.

122 Ibid., 127.

123 Ibid., 128–9.

124 Sweatman, *Fox*, 73.

125 Ibid., 36.

126 Ibid., 37.

127 Ibid., 78; emphasis in original.

128 Ibid., 81; emphasis in original.

129 Ibid., 84; emphasis in original.

130 Ibid., 88–9.

131 Ibid., 132; emphasis in original.

132 Ibid., 187.

133 Ibid., 188.

134 Vassanji, *No New Land*, 85.

135 Ibid., 88.

136 Mootoo, *Cereus Blooms at Night*, 26. Eviatar Zerubavel highlights how the "lack of synchrony between the week and the month" can be a particularly problematic temporal feature for workers attempting to calculate their budgets: "Consider, for example, how inconvenient it is for employees paid by the month to budget their expenses on a regular weekly basis, when, out of the very same paycheck, they have to make four weekly trips to the supermarket on some months yet five on others. Employees paid by the week, however, do not have an easier time having to pay their monthly telephone, gas, and electric bills sometimes out of five paychecks yet sometimes out of only four." Zerubavel, *Seven Day Circle*, 61.

137 Mootoo, *Cereus Blooms at Night*, 28.

138 I discuss this scene in the "Gender and Sexuality" section of this chapter.

139 Richler, *Apprenticeship of Duddy Kravitz*, 204–5.

140 Ibid., 285.

141 Fennario, *Balconville*, 35.

142 Gurvitch, *Spectrum of Social Time*, 99.

143 Felski, *Doing Time*, 1.

144 Kristeva, "Women's Time," 861. For Kristeva, first-wave feminism, "as the struggle of suffragists and of existential feminists, aspired to gain a place in linear time as the time of project and history" (ibid., 864), while the second phase in the 1960s and 1970s is one in which "linear temporality has been almost totally refused, and as a consequence there has arisen an exacerbated distrust of the entire political dimension" (ibid., 864). While Kristeva, writing in 1979, can only speculate on the emergence of a "third attitude" that is more interested in questioning binary thinking, Felski, writing two decades later, in many ways both validates and extends Kristeva's line of inquiry.

145 Felski, *Doing Time*, 17–18.

146 Ibid., 82.

147 Ibid.

148 Ibid., 20.

149 Ibid.
150 Felski notes, "There is something very familiar about this division between linear and cyclical time. It is also the way we often distinguish between industrial and agricultural societies" (ibid., 18). Following Barbara Adam and Akhil Gupta, Felski argues that this kind of stereotypical cultural division of temporal modes, like the division of temporal modes between men and women, cannot hold up under detailed analysis: "Western culture, in spite of its strong reliance on linear time, is also saturated with time cycles, from the boom-bust rhythms of economics to the annual rites of Christmas, Hanukkah, and Thanksgiving, to the small-scale routines of everyday life. On the other hand, the non-Western world cannot simply be seen as dwelling in archaic, non-linear time" (ibid., 19). In the next chapter I will more closely examine the interdependent nature of cyclical and linear time.
151 Ibid., 21.
152 Ibid.
153 Ibid.
154 Ibid.
155 Ibid., 21–2; emphasis in original.
156 Ibid., 22.
157 Ibid., 3.
158 Ibid., 26.
159 Kristeva, "Women's Time," 873.
160 Traill, *Backwoods of Canada*, 17.
161 Ibid., 18.
162 Atwood, "Further Arrivals," lines 17–18.
163 Traill, *Backwoods of Canada*, 121.
164 Felski, *Doing Time*, 82.
165 Zimbardo and Boyd, *Time Paradox*, 101. Analyzing the results of their long-running time perspective survey, Zimbardo and Boyd also claim that "on average, men tend to be more present-hedonistic and women more future-oriented. Generations ago, this difference undoubtedly carried a survival advantage" (ibid., 248). Such a claim is difficult to analyze: is the primary responsibility for child rearing an inherent difference that causes women in general to act more with a view to future consequences? What role do changing educational, social, or family structures play in these survey results? Isolating cultural and generational variables in such a study would be very difficult.
166 Montgomery, *Anne of Green Gables*, 304.

167 Ibid.

168 Ibid., 305.

169 Ibid., 306.

170 Ibid., 307.

171 Munro, *Hateship*, 224.

172 Qtd. in Levine, *Geography of Time*, 58.

173 Landes, *Revolution in Time*, 7.

174 Rosa, *Social Acceleration*, 167; emphasis in original.

175 Marlatt, *Ana Historic*, 47.

176 Ibid., 28.

177 Ibid., 124, 125.

178 Wyile, *Speculative Fictions*, 148.

179 Ibid., 144. For Gabriele Helms, dialogism is key to understanding these concerns: "Dialogic relations institute a strategy for inscribing voices previously unheard, and this strategy deprivileges dominant discourses of patriarchy and compulsory heterosexuality as well as the hegemonies they support" (Helms, *Challenging Canada*, 77). For Rebecca Waese, on the other hand, *Ana Historic*'s transgression of traditional literary form has more to do with the use of the dramatic mode. Through the way in which "historical moments are 're-enacted' in the mind's eye of the protagonist," as well as through the novel's focus on bodies and bodily expression, "Marlatt challenges and transgresses conventional boundaries of genre by utilizing conventions from drama and the theatre" (Waese, "Dramatic Mode," 100). These interpretations, the latter of which especially differs from the usual commentary on Marlatt's unconventional use of narrative, reflect the multiple ways in which Marlatt carries out her critique of historiographical conventions.

180 L. Pratt, *Archives of American Time*, 15.

181 Kamboureli, "Politics of the Beyond," 48.

182 Marlatt, *Ana Historic*, 37.

183 Helms, *Challenging Canada*, 67.

184 Bhabha, "DissemiNation," 145.

185 Ibid., 143.

186 Dimock, *Through Other Continents*, 129; emphasis in original.

187 Gunnars, *Prowler*, section 81.

188 Cook, "Love and Other Unofficial Stories," 35. Janice Keefer expands the potential form or genre of *The Prowler* even further: "Text, memoir,

autobiography, theory, detective story, novel. *The Prowler* is all and thus none of the above." Keefer, "The Prowler," 90.

189 Cook, "Love and Other Unofficial Stories," 35.

190 Gunnars, *Prowler*, section 25.

191 Carse, *Finite and Infinite Games*, 3.

192 Ibid., 4.

193 Ibid., 8.

194 Gunnars, *Prowler*, section 25.

195 Felski, *Doing Time*, 22.

196 Gunnars, *Prowler*, section 120.

197 Atwood, *Cat's Eye*, 222–3.

198 Ibid., 292.

199 Ibid., 382.

200 Ibid., 371.

201 Ibid., 453.

202 Ibid., 463; emphasis in original.

203 Ibid., 498.

204 Ibid., 500.

205 Ibid., 501.

206 Ibid., 460–1.

207 See the discussion of working time and sex in Statistics Canada's Time Use Surveys in chapter 1.

208 Atwood, *Cat's Eye*, 143.

209 Ibid., 153.

210 Ibid., 161.

211 Ibid., 188.

212 Ibid., 231.

213 Ibid., 234.

214 Ibid., 22.

215 Ibid., 152.

216 Ibid., 353.

217 Ibid., 270.

218 Ibid., 537.

219 Sheckels, *Political in Margaret Atwood's Fiction*, 101.

220 Ibid. Sheckels notes that familial paternal power in *Cat's Eye* operates in such a way that "girls are beaten if they do what is perceived as wrong," that "they are

scolded and demeaned," and that Cordelia in particular "is made to feel that she will never meet the established standard and thereby earn the love of her father" (ibid., 101) – a clear echo of the situation into which Cordelia traps Elaine.

221 Atwood, *Cat's Eye*, 444.

222 Tolan, "*Cat's Eye*: Articulating the Body," 192.

223 Marion Wynne-Davies argues that *Cat's Eye* investigates the subjective nature of memory, and works "to explore the inner-self as a means of fragmenting and undermining any fixed interpretation of the past" (Wynne-Davies, "The Mysteries of Time and Memory," 46). While I agree that the slipperiness of memory and of the past is a central concern in the novel, it is also important to acknowledge the emphasis that the novel places on the very concrete consequences that past events have for personal agency.

224 Findley, *Stillborn Lover*, 1.

225 Cavell, "Introduction," 16.

226 Findley, *Stillborn Lover*, 150.

227 "Same-Sex Rights."

228 Ibid.

229 Freeman, *Time Binds*, xxii.

230 Ibid.

231 Ibid.

232 Davies and Funke, "Introduction: Sexual Temporalities," 3; emphasis in original.

233 Ibid.

234 Ibid., 10.

235 Ibid., 3.

236 Martel, *Self*, 9.

237 Ibid., 22.

238 Ibid., 108.

239 Ibid., 286.

240 Ibid., 287.

241 Ibid., 40.

242 Ibid., 190.

243 Ibid., 331.

244 Gerry Turcotte writes in the *Sydney Morning Herald* that *Self* suffers "from a serious identity crisis," and that "one of the problems with this work is that Martel is trying hard to be idiosyncratic and innovative" (Turcotte, "Self").

These comments are similar to those of various reviewers and critics, many of whom point out that Martel himself later expressed a wish to distance himself from the novel. Smaro Kamboureli is also highly critical – perhaps too critical – of the novel, but for her it is the ethical implications of the text that pose a problem. She argues that Martel "takes ethical action by telling a story that involves rape but relinquishes the imperative of considering the contingencies informing this act: how to tell it and what 'moral risks' it involves" (Kamboureli, "Limits of the Ethical Turn," 951). She also argues that Martel replicates, but fails to question, racist assumptions in the scenes that deal with racial conflict, so that his "troping towards a feminist ethics is mitigated by the novel's racial politics" (ibid., 953). She points specifically toward a scene where Martel's protagonist, some time after her own rape, violently assaults an Indigenous man. While Kamboureli reads this scene as a failure to critique racism, and even as an implicit condoning of racist violence, the shock of the scene and the pain of the victim could instead be understood as narrative elements that portray racist violence as a horrible crime on par with sexual assault.

245 Findley, *Wars*, 193.

246 Ibid., 193–4.

247 Ibid., 37.

248 As I will show in chapter 5, Findley goes even further in identifying the violence of the battlefield itself as a site of devastating (but not absolute) temporal dislocation.

249 Mootoo, *Cereus Blooms at Night*, 228.

250 Ibid., 127.

251 Ibid., 132.

252 Newlands, *Canadian Art*, 120.

253 Ibid.

254 Ibid.

255 Fraser, *Poor Super Man*, 122.

256 Ibid., 172.

257 Ibid., 179.

258 Ibid.

259 Coleman, *White Civility*, 10; emphasis in original.

260 Ibid., 11, 12.

261 Ibid., 12. As Fabian points out, the concept of allochrony carries its own dangers; the tendency of twentieth-century anthropologists to deny coevalness (the sharing of a common time) to other cultures is established through

"a persistent and systematic tendency to place the referent(s) of anthropology in a Time other than the present of the producer of anthropological discourse" (Fabian, *Time and the Other*, 31; emphasis in original). Referring to "the denial of coevalness as the *allochronism* of anthropology" (ibid., 32), Fabian notes that such allochronism has been complicit in "placing the Now of the primitive in the Then of the Western adult" (ibid., 63). The intention of Coleman's argument, though, is to recognize that a single linear scale cannot adequately assess the "development" of different cultures, a notion that is largely compatible with Fabian's insistence that different cultures exist in the same moment. In a sense, Fabian and Coleman are simply using different metaphors to resist the same problematic vision of primitive cultures as delayed travellers on the dominant timeline; Fabian promotes an image in which all cultures exist at the same "now" within actual time, while Coleman promotes the recognition of multiple coexisting timelines.

262 Hill, *Book of Negroes*, 111.

263 Ibid., 206.

264 Ibid., 255.

265 Ibid., 409. While Aminata enters the country after her emancipation, Canada has its own often-silenced history of slavery. Quoting an unnamed "standard history of the country," which says that Canadians can "claim the proud distinction for their flag ... that it has never floated over legalized slavery," George Elliott Clarke points out that this interpretation involves its own sly manipulation of temporal accountability: "The claim is literally true, but only because Canada did not yet exist when the enslavement of Natives and Africans flourished on what is now Canadian soil" (Clarke, "White Like Canada," 103). Clarke goes on to note that a "1995 poll conducted by the Canadian Civil Liberties Association found that 83 percent of Canadian adults did not know that slavery was practiced in pre-Confederation Canada until 1834, when Britain abolished the institution throughout its empire" (ibid.).

266 Hill, *Book of Negroes*, 134.

267 Ibid., 189.

268 Frye, *Words with Power*, 255.

269 Stephanie Yorke notes that Aminata's narrative reflects, but also circumvents, the traditional form of the slave narrative, a literary form that was shaped largely to fulfill the political goals of white abolitionists. Yorke points out that when "campaigning abolitionists" pressure Aminata "to make her story conform to both the pre-existing model and their manumission campaign,"

Aminata "(and perhaps a spectral Hill) complains of their interference and chooses to set down her narrative independent of their leadership" (Yorke, "Slave Narrative Tradition," 131). By telling her story on her own terms, Aminata in a sense resists not only the temporal disempowerment of slavery, but also the colonial control of narrative identity.

270 Coleman and Goellnicht, "Introduction," 4.

271 Qtd. in ibid.

272 Choy, *Paper Shadows*, 72–3.

273 Ibid., 74; emphasis in original. The Immigration Act of 1910, for instance, states: "Canadian domicile is acquired for the purposes of this Act by a person having his domicile for at least three years in Canada after having been landed therein within the meaning of this Act" (Immigration Act [1910], 2.d.). This statement is modified, though, near the very end of the Act, where provision 79 clarifies that "[a]ll provisions of this Act not repugnant to the provisions of *The Chinese Immigration Act* shall apply as well to persons of Chinese origin as to other persons."

274 Davis, *Begin Here*, 120.

275 Choy, *Paper Shadows*, 246.

276 Ibid., 243.

277 Ibid., 247.

278 Ibid., 74.

279 Ibid., 75.

280 Ibid., 75–6.

281 Ibid., 76.

282 Coleman, "From Contented Civility," 233.

283 Choy, *Paper Shadows*, 75.

284 Ibid., 5.

285 Ibid.

286 Ibid., 248.

287 Ibid.

288 Ibid., 338; emphasis in original.

289 Coleman, "From Contented Civility," 225.

290 Ibid.

291 Kogawa, *Obasan*, 92, 95.

292 Ibid., 218.

293 Ibid., 219.

294 Ibid.

295 Ibid., 94.

296 Ibid., 45.

297 Ibid., 29.

298 Ibid., 54. Helena Grice writes that the contrasts, in *Obasan*, "between Naomi's personal ruminations and recollections and the various reported accounts of that history reflect the juxtaposition of private and public temporalities" (Grice, "Reading the Nonverbal," 95). While Naomi and her aunt Obasan measure time subjectively with reference to the events of their own lives, "Aunt Emily's letters, reports and newspaper articles represent the public, verbalised chronology of Japanese Canadian history" (ibid., 95). Grice concludes that critical readings of *Obasan* need to acknowledge the alternative forms of knowledge and communication that Kogawa emphasizes – body language, sensory perception, and alternative models of space and time – and that these often non-verbal forms must not be mistaken for mere silence (ibid., 93). Grice eloquently highlights the importance of Naomi's resistance of normative temporality; still, though, this partial resistance serves also to emphasize and reinforce her dependence on normative time. Naomi's narrative begins, for instance, with the time stamp, "9:05 p.m. August 9, 1972." Kogawa, *Obasan*, 1.

299 Lefebvre, "In Search of Someday."

300 Coleman and Goellnicht, "Introduction," 7.

301 Vassanji, *No New Land*, 116.

302 D. Brand, *Map to the Door*, 5.

303 Ibid.

304 Ibid., 24.

305 Visvis, "Traumatic Forgetting."

306 Philip, "Taming Our Tomorrows," 271.

307 D. Brand, *In Another Place, Not Here*, 8.

308 Ibid., 41.

309 Ibid., 43.

310 Ibid., 32.

311 Ibid., 126–7.

312 Ibid., 131.

313 Ibid., 159.

314 Ibid., 185–6.

315 Ibid., 190.

316 Ibid., 215. Verlia's comment about "doing time," like Jackie's parents' comment in Brand's *What We All Long For* that life in Toronto is "hard time" (D. Brand,

What We All Long For, 179), alludes to the disproportionate representation of racial minorities in actual correctional facilities. While the overrepresentation of African Americans in the US prison system has often been discussed, Correctional Service of Canada (csc) notes that "relatively little research has been conducted on visible minority offenders under the supervision of the correctional system in Canada" (Trevethan and Rastin, *Profile of Visible Minority Offenders*). In a 2004 report, the csc finds that "in comparison to their proportion in the Canadian population, Caucasian and Asian offenders are underrepresented, while Black offenders are disproportionately represented" – this despite the fact that "visible minority offenders seem to be less 'entrenched' in a criminal lifestyle than Caucasian offenders." The report indicates that while Black Canadians represent 2% of the general population, they represent 6% of the incarcerated population, and that while Aboriginal persons comprise 3% of the general population, they represent a stunning 18% of the incarcerated population (ibid., Figure 3). Caucasian Canadians, who make up 84% of the general population, account for only 71% of the incarcerated population. In other words, despite the fact that average aggregate sentences for Black inmates are actually slightly shorter than for Caucasians (ibid., Tableau 3-A), proportionally speaking, Black and Aboriginal persons in Canada *do more time*. Of course, other factors are also involved; the majority of inmates are young, male, and unemployed at the time of arrest (ibid., Figure 6).

317 D. Brand, *In Another Place, Not Here*, 246–7.
318 Visvis, "Traumatic Forgetting."
319 D. Brand, *In Another Place, Not Here*, 213.

CHAPTER FOUR

1 Robinson, *Monkey Beach*, 2.
2 Cuthand, "Post-Oka Kinda Woman," 133.
3 Sioui, *Histoires de Kanatha*, 124.
4 Justice, "Renewing the Fire," 52.
5 Sioui, *Histoires de Kanatha*, 279.
6 Adam, "Perceptions of Time," 519.
7 Jameson, *Archaeologies of the Future*, 199.
8 Newlands, *Canadian Art*, 21.
9 Sanger, "Looking for Someone Who Sees," 17.
10 Sanger, guest lecture.

11 Paul, "From the Mouth of Susan Barss," 68, 69.

12 Ibid., 69.

13 Sanger, "Riding the Stone Canoe," 149.

14 Ibid.

15 Fausto-Sterling, "Dueling Dualisms," 15.

16 Hallowell, "Temporal Orientation," 670.

17 Ibid., 654.

18 Ibid., 656.

19 Ibid.

20 Ibid., 660.

21 Ibid., 662.

22 Ibid., 650.

23 Ibid., 651.

24 Ibid., 666–7.

25 Ibid., 665–6.

26 Ibid., 667.

27 Ibid., 668.

28 Ibid.

29 Friedman, *About Time*, 110.

30 Ibid., 111.

31 Adam, "Perceptions of Time," 519; emphasis in original.

32 Sioui, *Histoires de Kanatha*, 104.

33 Demos, *Circles and Lines*, 4–15.

34 Ibid., 47–51, 74–6.

35 Coleman, *White Civility*, 14, 30.

36 Sioui, *Histoires de Kanatha*, 278–9.

37 Ricoeur, *Time and Narrative*, 3: 68.

38 The question of which emerges "first" in Western civilization – the articulation of fundamentally discrete categories of time, or the idea that one particular cultural embodiment of time is natural and superior – likely does not have a simple answer. Commenting on the history of anthropological discourse that distances "primitive" Indigenous cultures in time, Johannes Fabian offers a preliminary approach to such a discussion by arguing that "the idea of a knowledge of Time which is a superior knowledge" was "prefigured in the Christian tradition, but crucially transformed in the Age of Enlightenment." Fabian, *Time and the Other*, 10.

39 Sioui, *Histoires de Kanatha*, 279.

40 Copway, *Life, History, and Travels*, 144.
41 Johnson, *Moccasin Maker*, 89.
42 Ibid., 92; emphasis in original.
43 Ibid., 93; emphasis in original.
44 Ibid., 83.
45 Strong-Boag and Gerson, *Paddling Her Own Canoe*, 5.
46 Salem, "'Her Blood Is Mingled.'"
47 Qtd. in ibid.
48 Scott, "Onondaga Madonna," line 2.
49 Ibid., 10.
50 Ibid., 12.
51 Salem, "'Her Blood Is Mingled.'"
52 Criticism on Emily Carr's writing has tended to focus on the construction of Carr's autobiographical self, her representations of the natural world, and the ethics and politics of her troubled empathy toward (or appropriation of) Indigenous cultures. On the latter concern, see Janice Stewart's article "Cultural Appropriations and Identificatory Practices in Emily Carr's 'Indian Stories.'" For a discussion of this issue in Carr's larger body of visual art, see Gerta Moray's book *Unsettling Encounters*.
53 Carr, *Klee Wyck*, 33.
54 Ibid., 34.
55 In his discussion of time discipline in factories during the Industrial Revolution, David Landes notes that, for the workers who had moved into factory employment "from cottages and fields" where they could work largely at their own pace, the new requirement "to appear by a set time every morning and work a day whose duration and wage were a function of the clock" was often exceptionally difficult. "Their unfamiliarity with or resistance to the new discipline," he writes, "found its most frequent and powerful expression in their inability or reluctance to show up on time" (Landes, *Revolution in Time*, 229). Considering the experiences of these factory workers alongside the experiences of the Indigenous schoolchildren in *Klee Wyck* provides further support for the idea that Carr is witnessing the compulsory imposition of time discipline onto a group of people who had previously developed their own rich (but not clock-based) approach to time. She is not, as she at first assumes, meeting people who simply have no understanding of time.
56 Carr, *Klee Wyck*, 40.
57 Ibid., 79.

58 Ibid., 81.

59 Ibid., 82.

60 Ibid., 83.

61 Levine, *Geography of Time*, 82.

62 Ibid., 91.

63 Carr, *Klee Wyck*, 83.

64 Adam, "Perceptions of Time," 509; emphasis in original.

65 Carr, *Klee Wyck*, 85.

66 Ibid., 86. Carr does not often specify which Indigenous culture or language she is referring to. Aside from occasional references to Chinook and Haida, she more often uses the general term "Indian."

67 Ibid.

68 Ibid., 87.

69 Ibid., 135.

70 Ibid., 136.

71 Ibid., 136–7.

72 S. Brand, *Clock of the Long Now*, 29; emphasis in original.

73 Ibid.

74 Ibid., 30.

75 Qtd. in S. Brand, *Clock of the Long Now*, 35.

76 Carr, *Klee Wyck*, 151–2 (ellipses in original).

77 Ibid., 79.

78 Ibid., 152.

79 I am grateful to Roger Hyman for pointing out the significance of this image to me.

80 Klein, "Indian Reservation: Caughnawaga," 304.

81 Ibid.

82 Groening, *Listening to Old Woman Speak*, 21.

83 Born on the Piapot Cree First Nation in Saskatchewan, but having spent most of her life in the United States, Sainte-Marie has ties to the Cree, American, and Canadian nations. "My Country 'Tis of Thy People You're Dying," for instance, focuses explicitly on the United States, though Sainte-Marie herself was inducted into the Canadian Music Hall of Fame in 1995 and received a Lifetime Achievement Award in Arts at the National [i.e., Canadian] Aboriginal Achievement Awards in 1998.

84 Sainte-Marie, "My Country," lines 10–11 and 14.

85 Jeannette Armstrong makes a similar point in her poem "History Lesson," which portrays the European colonization of the Americas as a violent journey toward death, characterized by protracted assaults on the land and its people.

86 Coleman, *White Civility*, 16.

87 Sainte-Marie, "My Country," lines 45–6.

88 Ibid., line 37.

89 Sainte-Marie, "Now that the Buffalo's Gone," lines 25–6.

90 Campbell, *Halfbreed*, 1.

91 Ibid., 9.

92 Ibid., 86.

93 Ibid., 110.

94 Ibid., 136.

95 Ibid.

96 Ibid., 158.

97 Ibid., 184.

98 Griffiths and Campbell, *Book of Jessica*, 77–8.

99 Armstrong, *Slash*, 11.

100 Ibid.

101 Ibid., 25.

102 Ibid.

103 Ibid., 25, 26.

104 Ibid., 44.

105 Ibid., 62.

106 Ibid., 87.

107 Ibid., 159–60.

108 Ibid., 163.

109 Ibid., 164–5.

110 Ibid., 171.

111 Helms, *Challenging Canada*, 99.

112 Armstrong, *Slash*, 171.

113 Ibid., 206–7.

114 Hodne and Hoy, "Reading from the Inside Out," 68.

115 Ong, *Orality and Literacy*, 140.

116 Ibid., 38, 45, 49.

117 Gabriele Helms dismisses Ong's work as one of the "universalist" theories of orality "which posit a linear progression from a primitive oral to a superior

literate consciousness. These deterministic models have often informed the paternalistic attitudes of Western critics towards the literary accomplishments of Aboriginal peoples" (Helms, *Challenging Canada*, 106). Certain of Ong's statements do make his work vulnerable to such criticism; he does refer to "the earlier oral world" (Ong, *Orality and Literacy*, 15) and claims that "without writing, human consciousness cannot achieve its fuller potentials, cannot produce other beautiful and powerful creations. In this sense, orality needs to produce and is destined to produce writing" (ibid., 14). At the same time, though, Ong's study identifies unique forms of value in orality, and highlights some of the significant characteristics of oral storytelling that cannot translate into written language. He argues passionately that oral traditions must not be analytically reduced "to variants of writing" (ibid., 12), and that scholars of orality should avoid writing-centric terms such as "preliterate" (ibid., 13). A Jesuit scholar, Ong also had an interest in re-establishing the oral basis of Catholicism. While it is important to recognize the deficiencies of Ong's work, aspects of his study still hold value.

118 Armstrong, "Land Speaking," 194.

119 Ibid., 192.

120 King, "Godzilla vs. Post-Colonial," 244–6.

121 See Karin Beeler's interview with Armstrong, titled "Image, Music, Text," for details on the events that inspired the poem.

122 Armstrong, "Trickster Time," 1. Excerpts from "Trickster Time" published with permission from the author, sourced from *Voices: Being Native in Canada*, edited by Linda Jaine and Drew Hayden Taylor, pages 1–5. University of Saskatchewan, Extension Division, 1992. ISBN 0888802692.

123 Ibid.

124 Ibid., 5.

125 Ibid., 2.

126 Ibid., 3.

127 Ibid.

128 Ibid., 4.

129 Ibid. Odd use of "its" in original.

130 Ibid.

131 Ibid., 5.

132 Ibid.

133 King, "Coyote and the Enemy Aliens," 50.

134 Ibid.

135 Ibid., 51 (ellipses in original).

136 Ibid., 58.

137 Eigenbrod, "The 'Look of Recognition.'"

138 Annharte, "In the Picture I Don't See," 15.

139 King, *Green Grass, Running Water*, 7.

140 Ibid., 11.

141 Flick, "Reading Notes," 144.

142 Ibid., 147.

143 Helms, *Challenging Canada*, 118.

144 See Davidson, Walton, and Andrews, *Border Crossings*.

145 Bailey, "The Arbitrary Nature of the Story," 43.

146 King, *Green Grass, Running Water*, 100.

147 Ibid., 117, 119.

148 Ibid., 321.

149 Ibid., 134.

150 Ibid., 194.

151 Ibid., 346–7.

152 Ibid., 337.

153 Ibid., 360.

154 Ibid., 318.

155 Gordon, "Time Structures," 127.

156 Ibid., 130.

157 Ibid., 120.

158 Boyden, *Three Day Road*, 58.

159 Glass, *Primer and Language Lessons*, 78–9.

160 Boyden, *Three Day Road*, 223.

161 Ibid., 307–8.

162 Ibid., 245–6.

163 Visvis, "Culturally Conceptualizing Trauma," 225.

164 Ibid., 239; emphasis in original.

165 Gordon, "Time Structures," 131.

166 Boyden, *Three Day Road*, 246.

167 Ibid., 5.

168 Ibid., 8.

169 Ibid., 328, 331.

170 Ibid., 331.

171 Maracle, *Daughters are Forever*, 22.

172 Ibid., 24–5.

173 Paula Farca argues that time and memory in *Daughters are Forever* are best
understood in terms of place, displacement, and the imaginative desire to
reclaim lost places (see Farca, "Traveling through Memory"). This interpretation leads to valuable insights on the relationship between identity and place,
but obscures some of Maracle's more direct concerns with temporality itself
through temporal framing and the fraught experience of time for members of
historically colonized populations.

174 Maracle, *Daughters are Forever*, 57.

175 Ibid., 63; emphasis in original.

176 Ibid., 64.

177 Ibid.

178 Ibid., 233.

179 Ibid., 239.

180 Ibid., 246.

181 Ibid., 248.

182 Ibid.

183 Ibid., 250.

184 Ibid.

185 "About Us" (emphasis added).

186 Dorrell, "From Reconciliation to Reconciling," 29–30.

187 Ibid., 30.

188 Sioui, *Histoires de Kanatha*, 107.

189 Alfred, *Wasáse*, 206.

190 Robinson, *Monkey Beach*, 125.

CHAPTER FIVE

1 McKay, "Quartz Crystal," 15. Excerpted from *Strike/Slip* by Don McKay.
Copyright © 2006 Don McKay. Reprinted by permission of McClelland and
Stewart, a division of Penguin Random House Canada Limited, a Penguin
Random House Company.

2 Watson, *Double Hook*, 101.

3 Martel, *Life of Pi*, 212.

4 Ibid., 354; emphasis in original.

5 Pesch, "When Time Shall Be No More?" 87.

6 Brydon, "'It Could Not Be Told,'" 65.

7 Cobley, "Postmodernist War Fiction," 120.

8 Pesch, "When Time Shall Be No More?" 86.

9 Pennee, "Imagined Innocence, Endlessly Mourned."

10 Williams, *Media, Memory, and the First World War*, 167, 162.

11 Ibid., 162.

12 Ibid., 271.

13 Ibid., 167.

14 Findley, *Wars*, 18.

15 Ibid., 18.

16 Ibid., 91.

17 Ibid., 125.

18 Ibid., 23.

19 York, *Introducing Timothy Findley's* The Wars, 42.

20 Williams, *Media, Memory, and the First World War*, 179.

21 Pesch, "When Time Shall Be No More?" 88.

22 Findley, *Wars*, 126. Findley's writing here echoes the description in Charles Yale Harrison's 1928 novel *Generals Die in Bed* of shells that move faster than sound, disrupting normal causality. When Harrison's unnamed narrator first arrives in the trenches, he recalls the brief and disconcerting advice with which his military superiors have equipped him: "The shriek of the shell, the instructor in trench warfare said, was no warning because the shell traveled faster than its sound. First, he had said, came the explosion of the shell – then came the shriek and then you hear the firing of the gun." Harrison, *Generals Die in Bed*, 22–3.

23 Findley, *Wars*, 132.

24 Ibid., 174; emphasis in original.

25 Ibid., 184.

26 Ibid., 184–5.

27 Ibid., 152; emphasis in original.

28 Ibid., 205.

29 Ibid., 3; emphasis in original.

30 Cobley, "Postmodernist War Fiction," 113.

31 Findley, *Wars*, 218.

32 Wells, *Civil War Time*, 5.

33 Ibid., 1.

34 Philip, "Taming Our Tomorrows," 271.

35 Philip, *Looking for Livingstone*, 7.

36 Ibid.; emphasis in original.

37 "Mosi-oa-Tunya / Victoria Falls."

38 Philip, *Looking for Livingstone*, 10.

39 Yeats, "The Second Coming," lines 1, 3.

40 Philip, *Looking for Livingstone*, 11.

41 Ibid., 11, 12.

42 Ibid., 57.

43 Brydon, "'It Could Not Be Told,'" 64, 69.

44 Philip, *Looking for Livingstone*, 16; emphasis in original.

45 Ibid., 14.

46 Ibid., 29; emphasis in original.

47 Ibid., 19.

48 Jones, "Writing the Silence," 200.

49 Philip, *Looking for Livingstone*, 61.

50 Ibid., 60.

51 Ibid., 61.

52 Orwell, *Nineteen Eighty-Four*, 7.

53 Philip, *Looking for Livingstone*, 61.

54 Ibid., 67.

55 Ibid.

56 Ibid., 68; emphasis in original.

57 Ibid., 75.

58 Ibid., 77.

59 Ibid., 78; emphasis in original.

60 Ibid.; emphasis in original.

61 Bhabha, "DissemiNation," 143.

62 Dimock, *Through Other Continents*, 129.

63 Jones, "Writing the Silence," 206.

64 In some ways, Philip's project in *Looking for Livingstone* echoes Hubert Aquin's attempt in his 1965 novel *Prochain Épisode* (*Next Episode*) to articulate through narrative form the necessity of revolution against a dominant colonizing force. In *Next Episode*, a revolutionary Québécois separatist awaiting trial in a psychiatric institution invents a narrative about a similar Québécois revolutionary caught up in a complex web of espionage in Switzerland, resulting in a narrative whose vision of a desired revolutionary future is so twisted that it verges on the incomprehensible. By the narrator's own account the story is a disorganized and nonsensical distraction from the collapse of the revolutionary goal; it is a "broken book" that "resembles me" and "embraces the very shape of the time

to come" (Aquin, *Next Episode*, 64). If the Traveller in *Looking for Livingstone* takes up residence in a defamiliarized time for the purpose of twisting, ironizing, and partially escaping the dominant time of colonization, Aquin's protagonist becomes lost in a twisted, incomprehensible time as a representation of the *failure* of the revolutionary to subvert dominant power. Arguing that the inertia that grips Aquin's narrator is a reflection of Quebec's confinement to the Constitution of Canada, which defines it as merely one province among many, David Williams writes, "No wonder that the fate of an imprisoned narrator should resemble the fate of a nation confined to this prison of print" (Williams, *Imagined Nations*, 154). While both books are highly conscious of both the promise and the limitations of temporal resistance, Philip may be more willing to see within the reconfiguration of dominant temporalities the potential for productive new conversations to occur.

65 Jones, "Writing the Silence," 206.

66 Atwood, *Oryx and Crake*, 5.

67 Ibid., 320.

68 Ibid., 9.

69 Ibid.

70 Ibid., 414.

71 Ibid., 413.

72 Ibid., 443.

73 Bouson, "'It's Game Over Forever,'" 153.

74 Atwood, *Year of the Flood*, 60. Atwood never explicitly aligns the events of the trilogy with actual Gregorian calendar dates. Bouson, drawing clues from Atwood's media interviews after the publication of *Oryx and Crake*, pegs the pandemic around 2027 (Bouson, "'It's Game Over Forever,'" 140), which would place the creation of the God's Gardeners near 2002. In *MaddAddam*, however, we learn that much of urban California as well as New York City are already underwater before Adam becomes Adam One and founds the Gardeners, meaning that the fictional timelines are inconsistent either with themselves or with reality. Atwood may have revised her envisioned timelines during the decade in which she wrote the three novels. In the end, the novels are intended to connect what she sees as the trajectories of our present reality with a speculative future scenario, but the fictional events understandably resist being mapped onto the timeline of historical reality.

75 The Gardeners' decision to create a new Year One echoes the short-lived attempt by the leaders of the French Revolution to implement a "revolutionary

calendar." According to this system, "The year 1792 of the Christian era would be the year one of the new Republican calendar," and new measurements would be used to count weeks, months, and hours (Levine, *Geography of Time*, 78). This new calendar proved unpopular largely because it reduced the number of holidays and violated the counting of the Sabbath; like Stalin's revolutionary calendar in Russia, it was abandoned after a few years (ibid., 78–9).

76 Atwood, *Year of the Flood*, 100.

77 Ibid., 407.

78 Ibid., 61.

79 Ibid., 433.

80 "Enroll a Saint." The portion of Atwood's website allowing visitors to nominate a "saint" was deactivated sometime after the publicity campaign for *The Year of the Flood*.

81 Ultimately, Adam seems to create the God's Gardeners as a very practical attempt to survive what he understands as the likely disastrous outcome of the corporate creation of horrifying bioengineered diseases for profit. Whether he "really" believes the content of his sermons, or whether his teachings are designed purely for their survivalist benefit, is an open question even for his brother Zeb, who reflects, "I never knew myself how much of it he really believed himself" (Atwood, *MaddAddam*, 228). The closest the novels come to resolving this question is Toby's recollection that Adam One "said that if you acted according to a belief, that was the same thing. As having the belief" (ibid., 228).

82 Writing prior to the publication of the MaddAddam series, Alice Ridout notices that many of Atwood's earlier stories experiment with temporal reconstructions, at least on the level of individual characters whose life stories "move away from depicting female victims of the linear narrative of marriage and family towards more complex relationships with 'multiple futures'" (Ridout, "Temporality and Margaret Atwood"). While Ridout focuses on Atwood's short stories, Atwood's early novel *Surfacing* is also notable in its protagonist's explicit rejection of the normative, colonizing temporality associated with patriarchy and Americanization. At the end of the novel the narrator decides to "re-enter my own time" (Atwood, *Surfacing*, 191). The ambition of the Gardeners' calendar, then, can be seen as an extension of Atwood's long-standing interest in the reconfiguration of social temporality.

83 Atwood, *Year of the Flood*, 163.

84 Atwood, *Oryx and Crake*, 316; emphasis in original.

85 Ibid., 352.

86 Atwood, *Year of the Flood*, 264.

87 Atwood, *Oryx and Crake*, 319–20; emphasis in original.

88 Atwood, *Year of the Flood*, 326.

89 Atwood, *Oryx and Crake*, 179.

90 Atwood, *Year of the Flood*, 312.

91 Ibid., 95.

92 Ibid., 96.

93 Atwood, *Oryx and Crake*, 124–5.

94 Atwood, *Year of the Flood*, 383.

95 Atwood, *Oryx and Crake*, 364.

96 Ibid.

97 Ibid., 434.

98 Ibid., 203.

99 Ibid., 202.

100 Atwood, *Year of the Flood*, 431.

101 Atwood, *MaddAddam*, 5.

102 Coleman, "From Contented Civility," 231.

103 Ibid., 237.

104 Levine, *Geography of Time*, 219.

105 Qtd. in Coyne, "Atwood's Songs of Praise."

106 Atwood, *MaddAddam*, 136.

107 Ibid., 215.

108 Ibid., 204.

109 Ibid., 386.

110 Even the genetically engineered pigoons – dangerous pigs with human prefrontal cortex tissue – enter the protocols of temporal negotiation when they enlist the help of the human-Craker alliance to kill the Painballers who have been slaughtering their young. Serving as a translator for the "Pig Ones," Blackbeard explains that they "will never again try to eat your garden. Or any of you ... And they ask that you must no longer make holes in them, with blood, and cook them" (Atwood, *MaddAddam*, 270). Like treaties between colonizers and Indigenous peoples, this pact envisions a shared future scenario of perpetual cooperation, but remains fragile and presumably necessitates periodical reassessment. Exactly which humans and Pig Ones are included in this envisioned cooperative future, and how long is "never"?

CONCLUSION

1 Mackey, *House of Difference*, 66.
2 Ibid.
3 Ibid., 67.
4 Ibid., 70.
5 Ibid., 64.
6 Ibid., 70; emphasis in original.
7 Coleman, "From Contended Civility," 229.
8 Ibid.
9 Coleman, "Timing Question."

Bibliography

"About Us." Truth and Reconciliation Commission of Canada. Accessed 20 May 2011. http://www.trc.ca/websites/trcinstitution/index.php?p=4.

Adam, Barbara. "Perceptions of Time." In the *Companion Encyclopedia of Anthropology: Humanity, Culture and Social Life*, ed. Tim Ingold, 503–26. London: Routledge, 1994.

– *Timescapes of Modernity: The Environment and Invisible Hazards*. London: Routledge, 1998.

Alexander, Joy. "Anne with Two 'G's: Green Gables and Geographical Identity." In *100 Years of Anne with an 'e': The Centennial Study of Anne of Green Gables*, ed. Holly Blackford, 41–60. Calgary: University of Calgary Press, 2009.

Alfred, Taiaiake. *Wasáse: Indigenous Pathways of Action and Freedom*. Peterborough: Broadview, 2005.

Allen, Thomas M. *A Republic in Time: Temporality and Social Imagination in Nineteenth-Century America*. Chapel Hill: University of North Carolina Press, 2008.

Anderson, Benedict. *Imagined Communities: Reflections on the Origins and Spread of Nationalism*. 2nd ed. New York: Verso, 1991.

Annharte. "In the Picture I Don't See." In *Exercises in Lip Pointing*, 12–15. Vancouver: New Star Books, 2003.

Aquin, Hubert. *Next Episode*. 1965. Translated by Sheila Fischman. Toronto: McClelland and Stewart, 2001.

Aristotle. *Physics*. Translated by R.P. Hardie and R.K. Gaye. The University of Adelaide Library, 30 June 2012. Accessed 20 Sept. 2012.

Armstrong, Jeannette. "History Lesson." In *Native Poetry in Canada: A Contemporary Anthology*, ed. Jeannette C. Armstrong and Lally Grauer, 110–11. Peterborough: Broadview, 2001.

– "Land Speaking." In *Speaking for the Generations: Native Writers on Writing*, ed. Simon J. Ortiz, 174–94. Tucson: University of Arizona Press, 1998.
– *Slash*. 1985. Penticton: Theytus, 2007.
– "Trickster Time." In *Voices: Being Native in Canada*, ed. Linda Jaine and Drew Hayden Taylor, 1–5. Saskatoon: University of Saskatchewan, Extension Division, 1992.
Atwood, Margaret. *Cat's Eye*. Toronto: Seal Books, 1988.
– "Further Arrivals." In *A New Anthology of Canadian Literature in English*, ed. Donna Bennett and Russell Brown, 784–5. Don Mills: Oxford University Press, 2002.
– *MaddAddam*. Toronto: McClelland and Stewart, 2013.
– *Negotiating with the Dead: A Writer on Writing*. New York: Anchor, 2002.
– *Oryx and Crake*. Toronto: Seal Books, 2003.
– *Payback: Debt and the Shadow Side of Wealth*. Toronto: Anansi, 2008.
– *Surfacing*. Toronto: McClelland and Stewart, 1972.
– *Wilderness Tips*. Toronto: Seal, 1991.
– *The Year of the Flood*. Toronto: McClelland and Stewart, 2009.
Augustine, Saint, Bishop of Hippo. *The Confessions of Saint Augustine*. Translated by Edward B. Pusey. New York: Modern Library, 1999.
Bailey, Sharon M. "The Arbitrary Nature of the Story: Poking Fun at Oral and Written Authority in Thomas King's *Green Grass, Running Water*." *World Literature Today* 73, no. 1 (1999): 43–52.
Bakhtin, Mikhail. "Forms of Time and of the Chronotope in the Novel: Notes Toward a Historical Poetics." In *The Dialogic Imagination: Four Essays by M.M. Bakhtin*, edited by Michael Holquist, 84–258. Translated by Caryl Emerson and Michael Holquist. Austin: University of Texas Press, 1981.
Barrows, Adam. *The Cosmic Time of Empire: Modern Britain and World Literature*. Berkeley: University of California Press, 2011.
Bartlett, Brian. "Time Stands Up for Itself." In *The Watchmaker's Table*, 116–17. Fredericton: Goose Lane, 2008.
Bauman, Zygmunt. *Globalization: The Human Consequences*. New York: Columbia University Press, 1998.
Beeler, Karin. "Image, Music, Text: An Interview with Jeannette Armstrong." *Studies in Canadian Literature* 21, no. 2 (1996): 143–54.
Benjamin, Walter. "Theses on the Philosophy of History." In *Illuminations: Essays and Reflections*, edited by Hannah Arendt, 245–55. Translated by Harry Zorn. London: Pimlico, 1999.

Bergson, Henri. *Time and Free Will.* 1913. Translated by F.L. Pogson. Mineola: Dover, 2001.

Bhabha, Homi K. "DissemiNation: Time, Narrative and the Margins of the Modern Nation." In *The Location of Culture*, 139–70. London: Routledge, 1994.

Blaise, Clark. *Time Lord.* Toronto: Vintage, 2001.

Bouson, J. Brooks. "'It's Game Over Forever': Atwood's Satiric Vision of a Bioengineered Posthuman Future in *Oryx and Crake.*" *Journal of Commonwealth Literature* 39, no. 3 (2004): 139–56. Accessed 16 Aug. 2011.

Boyden, Joseph. *Three Day Road.* Toronto: Penguin, 2005.

Brand, Dionne. *In Another Place, Not Here.* New York: Grove, 1996.

– *Land to Light On.* Toronto: McClelland and Stewart, 1997.

– *A Map to the Door of No Return: Notes to Belonging.* Toronto: Vintage, 2001.

– *What We All Long For.* Toronto: Alfred A. Knopf, 2005.

Brand, Stewart. *The Clock of the Long Now.* New York: Basic Books, 1999.

Brown, Ian. "Sleep Deprivation Is a National Epidemic. And It's Killing Us." *Globe and Mail*, 13 May 2011. Accessed 13 May 2011.

Brown, Louise. "York U to Stop Cancelling Classes on Jewish Holidays." *Toronto Star*, 28 Oct. 2008. Accessed 30 Oct. 2008.

Brydon, Diana. "'It Could Not Be Told': Making Meaning in Timothy Findley's *The Wars.*" *Journal of Commonwealth Literature* 21, no. 1 (1986): 62–79.

Bush, Catherine. *Minus Time.* Toronto: HarperCollins, 1993.

Calendar (New Style) Act 1750 (c.23). *Legislation.gov.uk.* The National Archives, UK. Accessed 1 May 2010. http://www.legislation.gov.uk/apgb/Geo2/24/23.

Campbell, Maria. *Halfbreed.* Halifax: Goodread Biographies, 1973.

"Canadian Makers: The Arthur Pequegnat Clock Company." The Canadian Clock Museum. Accessed 24 Oct. 2011. http://www.canclockmuseum.ca/ Canadian_Makers/The_Arthur_Pequegnat_Clock_Company.html.

Carr, Emily. *Klee Wyck.* 1941. Vancouver: Douglas and McIntyre, 2003.

Carse, James P. *Finite and Infinite Games.* New York: Ballantine, 1986.

Cartier, Jacques. *The Voyages of Jacques Cartier.* Edited by Ramsay Cook and Henry Percival Biggar. Toronto: University of Toronto Press, 1993.

Cavell, Richard. "Introduction: The Cultural Production of Canada's Cold War." In *Love, Hate, and Fear in Canada's Cold War*, ed. Richard Cavell, 3–32. Toronto: University of Toronto Press, 2004.

Champlain, Samuel de. "Carte Geographiqve de la Novvelle Franse Faictte par le Sievr de Champlain Saint Tongois Cappitaine Ordinaire Povr le Roy en la

Marine." Public domain image. *Wikipedia*. 15 May 2005. Accessed 30 Oct. 2008. http://commons.wikimedia.org/wiki/File:Samuel_de_Champlain_Carte_geographique_de_la_Nouvelle_France.jpg.

Chaplin, Charles, director. *Modern Times*. Performed by Charles Chaplin and Paulette Goddard. United Artists, 1936. Film.

Choy, Wayson. *Paper Shadows: A Chinatown Childhood*. Toronto: Penguin, 1999.

Clarke, George Elliott. "White Like Canada." *Transition* 73 (1997): 98–109. Accessed 15 July 2011.

Clements, Marie. *Burning Vision*. Vancouver: Talonbooks, 2003.

Cobley, Evelyn. "Postmodernist War Fiction: Findley's *The Wars*." *Canadian Literature* 147 (1995): 98–124.

Coleman, Daniel. "From Contented Civility to Contending Civilities: Alternatives to Canadian White Civility." *International Journal of Canadian Studies* 38 (2008): 221–42.

– "Re: Paul's Fifth Chapter, and Timing Question." Email message to the author. 28 Dec. 2011.

– *White Civility: The Literary Project of English Canada*. Toronto: University of Toronto Press, 2006.

Coleman, Daniel, and Donald Goellnicht. "Introduction: 'Race' into the Twenty-First Century." *Essays on Canadian Writing* 75 (Winter 2002): 1–29.

Cook, Méira. "Love and Other Unofficial Stories: Narrative Prowling in Kristjana Gunnars' *The Prowler*." In *Writing Lovers: Reading Canadian Love Poetry by Women*, 34–58. Montreal: McGill-Queen's University Press, 2005.

Copway, George. *The Life, History, and Travels of Kah-Ge-Ga-Gah-Bowh, George Copway: A Young Indian Chief of the Ojebwa Nation, A Convert to the Christian Faith*. 1847. Whitefish: Kessinger, 2006.

Coupland, Douglas. "Generation A: 10 Questions for Douglas Coupland." Video interview. *YouTube*. Crush Inc., 30 Sept. 2009. Accessed 8 July 2010. https://www.youtube.com/watch?v=SKCVxd2SOsQ.

– *Generation X*. New York: St Martin's, 1991.

Coyne, Katie. "Atwood's Songs of Praise." *Bookseller*, 8 June 2009. Accessed 16 Aug. 2011. http://www.thebookseller.com/profile/atwoods-songs-praise.

Crocker, Stephen. "Hauled Kicking and Screaming into Modernity: Non-Synchronicity and Globalization in Post-War Newfoundland." In *Canadian Cultural Studies: A Reader*, ed. Sourayan Mookerjea, Imre Szeman, and Gail Faurschou, 425–40. Durham: Duke University Press, 2009.

Currie, Mark. *About Time: Narrative, Fiction and the Philosophy of Time*. Edinburgh: Edinburgh University Press, 2007.

Cuthand, Beth. "Post-Oka Kinda Woman." In *Native Poetry in Canada: A Contemporary Anthology*, ed. Jeannette C. Armstrong and Lally Grauer, 132–3. Peterborough: Broadview, 2001.

Davidson, Arnold, Priscilla Walton, and Jennifer Andrews. *Border Crossings: Thomas King's Cultural Inversions*. Toronto: University of Toronto Press, 2003.

Davies, Ben, and Jana Funke. "Introduction: Sexual Temporalities." In *Sex, Gender and Time in Fiction and Culture*, ed. Ben Davies and Jana Funke, 1–16. New York: Palgrave Macmillan, 2011.

Davis, Rocío. *Begin Here: Reading Asian North American Autobiographies of Childhood*. Honolulu: University of Hawai'i Press, 2007.

DeFalco, Amelia. *Uncanny Subjects: Aging in Contemporary Narrative*. Columbus: Ohio State University Press, 2010.

Demos, John. *Circles and Lines: The Shape of Life in Early America*. Cambridge: Harvard University Press, 2004.

"A Destructive Force Has Met Limited Resistance." Office of the Auditor General of Canada. 22 Oct. 2002. Accessed 30 Oct. 2008. http://www.oag-bvg.gc.ca/internet/English/mr_20021022_e_15433.html.

Dewdney, Christopher. *Soul of the World: Unlocking the Secrets of Time*. Toronto: HarperCollins, 2008.

Dimock, Wai Chee. *Through Other Continents: American Literature across Deep Time*. Princeton: Princeton University Press, 2006.

Dohrn-van Rossum, Gerhard. *History of the Hour: Clocks and Modern Temporal Orders*. Translated by Thomas Dunlap. Chicago: University of Chicago Press, 1996.

Dorrell, Matthew. "From Reconciliation to Reconciling: Reading What 'We Now Recognize' in the Government of Canada's 2008 Residential Schools Apology." *English Studies in Canada* 35, no. 1 (2009): 27–45.

Doyle, Judith. "Against Dislocation: Narratives of the Future, Identity and Politics among English Speakers of Montreal." *British Journal of Canadian Studies* 14, no. 1 (1999): 63–72.

During, Simon. *Cultural Studies: A Critical Introduction*. London: Routledge, 2005.

Eakin, Paul John. *Living Autobiographically: How We Create Identity in Narrative*. Ithaca: Cornell University Press, 2008.

Easthope, Antony. *Literary into Cultural Studies*. London: Routledge, 1991.

Eigenbrod, Renate. "The 'Look of Recognition': Transcultural Circulation of Trauma in Indigenous Texts." *Canadian Literature* 215 (Winter 2012): 16–32.

Elias, Norbert. *An Essay on Time: The Collected Works of Norbert Elias*, vol. 9. Edited by Steven Loyal and Stephen Mennell. Dublin: University College Dublin Press, 1992.

"Enroll a Saint." Margaret Atwood: The Year of the Flood. Accessed 12 May 2010. http://yearoftheflood.com.

Evernden, Neil. *The Natural Alien: Humankind and Environment*. 2nd ed. Toronto: University of Toronto Press, 1993.

Fabian, Johannes. *Time and the Other: How Anthropology Makes Its Object*. New York: Columbia University Press, 1983.

Farca, Paula Anca. "Traveling through Memory and Imagination in *Daughters are Forever* by Lee Maracle." In *Identity in Place: Contemporary Indigenous Fiction by Women Writers in the United States, Canada, Australia, and New Zealand*, 57–75. New York: Peter Lang, 2011.

Fausto-Sterling, Anne. "Dueling Dualisms." In *Sex, Gender, and Sexuality*, ed. Abby L. Ferber, Kimberly Holcomb, and Tre Wentling, 6–21. Oxford: Oxford University Press, 2009.

Felski, Rita. *Doing Time: Feminist Theory and Postmodern Culture*. New York: New York University Press, 2000.

Fennario, David. *Balconville*. Vancouver: Talonbooks, 1980.

Findley, Timothy. *The Stillborn Lover*. Toronto: HarperPerennial, 1993.

– *The Wars*. 1977. Toronto: Penguin, 1996.

Flaherty, Michael G. *A Watched Pot: How We Experience Time*. New York: New York University Press, 1999.

Flick, Jane. "Reading Notes for Thomas King's *Green Grass, Running Water*." *Canadian Literature* 161/162 (Summer/Autumn 1999): 140–72.

Franklin, John. *Narrative of a Journey to the Shores of the Polar Sea, in the Years 1819–20–21–22*, vol. 1. 3rd ed. London: William Clowes, 1824. *Project Gutenberg*. 3 Aug. 2006. Accessed 16 Aug. 2011. http://www.gutenberg.org/files/18979/18979-h/18979-h.htm.

Fraser, Brad. *Poor Super Man*. Edmonton: NeWest, 1995.

Freeman, Elizabeth. *Time Binds: Queer Temporalities, Queer Histories*. Durham: Duke University Press, 2010.

Friedman, William. *About Time: Inventing the Fourth Dimension*. Cambridge: MIT Press, 1990.

Frye, Northrop. *The Bush Garden: Essays on the Canadian Imagination*. 1971. Toronto: Anansi, 1995.

– *Words with Power*. San Diego: Harcourt Brace, 1990.

Galison, Peter. *Einstein's Clocks, Poincaré's Maps: Empires of Time*. New York: W.W. Norton, 2003.

"Galleries: The Arthur Pequegnat Clock Company." The Canadian Clock Museum. Accessed 24 Oct. 2011. http://www.canclockmuseum.ca/gallery/ THE_ARTHUR_PEQUEGNAT_CLOCK_COMPANY/1725.html# largeimage.

"GG Relaunches Truth and Reconciliation Commission." CBC News, 15 Oct. 2009. Accessed 15 Oct. 2009.

Glass, E.B. *Primer and Language Lessons in English and Cree*. Translated by John McDougall. Toronto: William Briggs, n.d. (approximately 1890). *Early Canadiana Online*. Accessed 16 Jan. 2011. http://eco.canadiana.ca/view/ oocihm.30552/3?r=oands=1.

Godeanu-Kenworthy, Oana. "The Political Other in Nineteenth-Century British North America: The Satire of Thomas Chandler Haliburton." *Early American Studies* 7, no. 1 (2009): 205–34. Accessed 16 Aug. 2011.

Goodin, Robert E. "Temporal Justice." *Journal of Social Policy* 39 (Jan. 2010): 1–16. Accessed 28 Nov. 2013.

Gordon, Neta. "Time Structures and the Healing Aesthetic of Joseph Boyden's *Three Day Road*." *Studies in Canadian Literature* 33, no. 1 (2008): 118–35.

Gorman, Bernard S., and Alden E. Wessman. "Images, Values, and Concepts of Time in Psychological Research." In Gorman and Wessman, eds., 217–63.

Gorman, Bernard S., and Alden E. Wessman, eds. *The Personal Experience of Time*. New York: Plenum, 1977.

Grice, Helena. "Reading the Nonverbal: The Indices of Space, Time, Tactility and Taciturnity in Joy Kogawa's *Obasan*." *MELUS* 24, no. 4 (1999): 93–105. Accessed 15 July 2011.

Griffiths, Linda, and Maria Campbell. *The Book of Jessica: A Theatrical Transformation*. 1989. Toronto: Playwrights Canada, 1997.

Groening, Laura Smyth. *Listening to Old Woman Speak: Natives and AlterNatives in Canadian Literature*. Montreal: McGill-Queen's University Press, 2005.

Gunnars, Kristjana. *The Prowler*. Red Deer: Red Deer College Press, 1989.

Gurvitch, Georges. *The Spectrum of Social Time*. Translated by Myrtle Korenbaum. Dordrecht: D. Reidel, 1964.

"Haida Nation: Backgrounder." Union of BC Indian Chiefs. Mar. 2004. Accessed 29 July 2011. http://www.ubcic.bc.ca/files/PDF/2004Mar_ HaidaNationBackgrounder.pdf.

Haliburton, Thomas C. *The Clockmaker*. 1836. Toronto: McClelland and Stewart, 1958.

Hallowell, A. Irving. "Temporal Orientation in Western Civilization and in a Pre-literate Society." *American Anthropologist* 39, no. 4 (1937): 647–70. Accessed 10 Feb. 2011.

Hargreaves, Allison. "A Precise Instrument for Seeing: Remembrance in *Burning Vision* and the Activist Classroom." *Canadian Theatre Review* 147 (Summer 2011): 49–54.

Harrison, Charles Yale. *Generals Die in Bed*. 1928. Toronto: Annick, 2002.

Healey, Michael, Travis V. Mason, and Laurie Ricou. "'hardy / and unkillable clichés': Exploring Meanings of the Domestic Alien, *Passer domesticus*." *ISLE* 16, no. 2 (2009): 281–98.

Helms, Gabriele. *Challenging Canada: Dialogism and Narrative Techniques in Canadian Novels*. Montreal: McGill-Queen's University Press, 2003.

Hémon, Louis. *Maria Chapdelaine*. 1916. Translated by W.H. Blake. Toronto: Dundurn, 2007.

Hill, Lawrence. *The Book of Negroes*. Toronto: HarperCollins, 2007.

Hodne, Barbara, and Helen Hoy. "Reading from the Inside Out: Jeannette Armstrong's *Slash*." *World Literature Written in English* 32, no. 1 (1992): 66–87.

Hoy, Helen. "'Too Heedless and Impulsive': Re-reading *Anne of Green Gables* through a Clinical Approach." In *Anne's World: A New Century of Anne of Green Gables*, ed. Irene Gammel and Benjamin Lefebvre, 65–81. Toronto: University of Toronto Press, 2010.

Hughes, Aaron W. *The Invention of Jewish Identity: Bible, Philosophy, and the Art of Translation*. Bloomington: Indiana University Press, 2011.

The Immigration Act [1910]: An Act Respecting Immigration. Ottawa: C.H. Parmelee, 1910. *Early Canadiana Online*. Accessed 15 July 2011. http://eco.canadiana.ca/view/oocihm.9_07184/2?r=0ands=1.

The Immigration Act [1952]: An Act Respecting Immigration. Government of Canada. Ottawa: E. Cloutier, 1952. *Early Canadiana Online*. Accessed 15 July 2011. http://eco.canadiana.ca/view/oocihm.9_08041/2?r=0ands=1.

Innis, Harold. *Empire and Communications*. 1950. Edited by David Godfrey. Victoria: Press Porcépic, 1986.

– "A Plea for Time." In *Canadian Cultural Studies: A Reader*, ed. Sourayan Mookerjea, Imre Szeman, and Gail Faurschou, 37–53. Durham: Duke University Press, 2009.

Ireland, Craig. *The Subaltern Appeal to Experience: Self-Identity, Late Modernity, and the Politics of Immediacy*. Montreal: McGill-Queen's University Press, 2004.

Jameson, Fredric. *Archaeologies of the Future: The Desire Called Utopia and Other Science Fictions*. New York: Verso, 2005.

Johnson, E. Pauline. *The Moccasin Maker*. 1913. Charleston: BiblioBazaar, 2006.

Jones, Dorothy. "Writing the Silence: Fiction and Poetry of Marlene Nourbese Philip." *Kunapipi* 26, no. 1 (2004): 196–206.

Justice, Daniel Heath. "Renewing the Fire: Notes toward the Liberation of English Studies." *English Studies in Canada* 29, nos. 1–2 (2003): 45–54.

Kamboureli, Smaro. "The Limits of the Ethical Turn: Troping towards the Other, Yann Martel, and *Self*." *University of Toronto Quarterly* 76, no. 3 (2007): 937–61.

– "The Politics of the Beyond: 43 Theses on Autoethnography and Complicity." In *Asian Canadian Writing beyond Autoethnography*, ed. Eleanor Ty and Christl Verduyn, 31–53. Waterloo: Wilfrid Laurier University Press, 2008.

Keefer, Janice Kulyk. "The Prowler." In *Kristjana Gunnars: Essays on Her Works*, ed. Monique Tschofen, 90–107. Toronto: Guernica, 2004.

Keightley, Emily. "Introduction: Time, Media, Modernity." In *Time, Media, and Modernity*, ed. Emily Keightley, 1–24. Hampshire: Palgrave Macmillan, 2012.

Kern, Stephen. *The Culture of Time and Space 1880–1918*. 1983. Cambridge: Harvard University Press, 2003.

Keung, Nicholas. "Immigration Waiting Times Cause Frustration." *Toronto Star*, 22 Oct. 2010. Accessed 10 July 2012.

King, Thomas. "Coyote and the Enemy Aliens." In *A Short History of Indians in Canada*, 50–70. Toronto: Harper Perennial, 2005.

– "Godzilla vs. Post-Colonial." In *New Contexts of Canadian Criticism*, ed. Ajay Heble, Donna Palmateer Pennee, and J.R. Struthers, 241–48. Peterborough: Broadview, 1997.

– *Green Grass, Running Water*. Boston: Houghton Mifflin, 1993.

– *The Inconvenient Indian: A Curious Account of Native People in North America*. Toronto: Anchor, 2012.

Kirby, Jason. "A Lost Decade of Growth: Many Real Indicators Put Us Back to Where We Were 10 Years Ago." *Maclean's*, 12 Aug. 2009. Accessed 15 Oct. 2009.

Klein, A.M. "Indian Reservation: Caughnawaga." In *The Collected Poems of A.M. Klein*. Edited by Miriam Waddington, 304–5. Toronto: McGraw-Hill Ryerson, 1974.

Kogawa, Joy. *Obasan*. Toronto: Penguin, 1981.

Kramer, Reinhold. "The 1919 Winnipeg General Strike and Margaret Sweatman's *Fox*." *Canadian Literature* 160 (Spring 1999): 50–70.

Kristeva, Julia. "Women's Time." In *Feminisms: An Anthology of Literary Theory and Criticism*. Rev. ed. Edited by Robyn R. Warhol and Diane Price Herndl, 860–79. New Brunswick, NJ: Rutgers University Press, 1997.

Lai, Larissa. *Salt Fish Girl*. Toronto: Thomas Allen, 2002.

Landes, David S. *Revolution in Time: Clocks and the Making of the Modern World*. Cambridge: Belknap, 1983.

Lawson, Alan. "Postcolonial Theory and the 'Settler' Subject." *Essays on Canadian Writing* 56 (1995): 20–36.

Lee, Dennis. "Cadence, Country, Silence: Writing in Colonial Space." In *Unhomely States: Theorizing English-Canadian Postcolonialism*, ed. Cynthia Sugars, 43–60. Peterborough: Broadview, 2004.

Lefebvre, Ben. "In Search of Someday: Trauma and Repetition in Joy Kogawa's Fiction." *Journal of Canadian Studies* 44, no. 3 (2010): 154–73.

Levine, Robert. *A Geography of Time: The Temporal Misadventures of a Social Psychologist, or How Every Culture Keeps Time Just a Little Bit Differently*. New York: Basic Books, 1997.

Lombardi, Michael A. "Why Is a Minute Divided into 60 Seconds, an Hour into 60 Minutes, Yet There Are Only 24 Hours in a Day?" *Scientific American*. 5 Mar. 2007. Accessed 3 June 2014.

Lynch, Gerald. *The One and the Many: English-Canadian Short Story Cycles*. Toronto: University of Toronto Press, 2001.

MacIvor, Daniel. *Never Swim Alone*. In *2 plays: Never Swim Alone and This Is a Play*. Toronto: Playwrights Canada, 1991.

Mackenzie, Hugh. *Recession-Proof: Canada's 100 Best Paid CEOs*. Ottawa: Canadian Centre for Policy Alternatives, 2011. Accessed 15 July 2011. http://www.policyalternatives.ca/sites/default/files/uploads/publications/National%20Office/2011/01/Recession%20Proof.pdf.

Mackey, Eva. *The House of Difference: Cultural Politics and National Identity in Canada*. Toronto: University of Toronto Press, 2002.

MacKinnon, John E. "Risk and Resilience in Catherine Bush's *Minus Time*." *Journal of Commonwealth Literature* 41, no. 2 (2006): 101–20.

Maracle, Lee. *Daughters are Forever*. Vancouver: Polestar, 2002.

Marlatt, Daphne. *Ana Historic*. Toronto: Coach House, 1988.

Martel, Yann. *Life of Pi*. Toronto: Vintage, 2001.

– *Self*. Toronto: Vintage, 1996.

May, Theresa J. "Kneading Marie Clements' *Burning Vision*." *Canadian Theatre Review* 144, no. 1 (2010): 5–12.

McGregor, Katharine E. "Time, Memory and Historical Justice: An Introduction." *Time and Society* 21, no. 1 (2012): 5–20.

McKay, Don. *Deactivated West 100*. Kentville: Gaspereau, 2005.

– "Ediacaran and Anthropocene: Poetry as a Reader of Deep Time." *Prairie Fire* 29, no. 4 (2008–9): 4–15.

– "Quartz Crystal." In *Strike/Slip*, 15–16. Toronto: McClelland and Stewart, 2006.

McLean, Sandra. "PhD Student Defends Thesis in Mi'gmaw Language, a York First." *YFile*. York University. 24 Nov. 2010. Accessed 25 Nov. 2010. http://yfile.news.yorku.ca/2010/11/24/phd-student-defends-thesis-in-migmaw-language-a-york-first/.

Meckler, Laura, and Jonathan Weisman. "Obama Warns of 'Lost Decade.'" *Wall Street Journal*. 10 Feb. 2009. Accessed 15 Oct. 2009.

Milton, John. *Paradise Lost*. In *John Milton: The Complete Poems*. Edited by John Leonard. London: Penguin, 1998.

Montgomery, L.M. *Anne of Green Gables*. 1908. New York: Seal Books, 1996.

– *Rilla of Ingleside*. 1920. Toronto: McClelland and Stewart, 1947.

Mootoo, Shani. *Cereus Blooms at Night*. London: Granta Books, 1996.

Moray, Gerta. *Unsettling Encounters: First Nations Imagery in the Art of Emily Carr*. Vancouver: UBC Press, 2006.

"More Canadians Pressed for Time." CBC News, 15 June 2010. Accessed 15 June 2010.

Moretti, Franco. *The Way of the World: The Bildungsroman in European Culture*. 1987. London: Verso, 2000.

Morton, Desmond. *A Short History of Canada*. 6th ed. Toronto: McClelland and Stewart, 2006.

"Mosi-oa-Tunya / Victoria Falls." UNESCO World Heritage Centre. United
　　Nations. Accessed 15 Jan. 2015. http://whc.unesco.org/en/list/509.

Moss, Laura, ed. *Is Canada Postcolonial? Unsettling Canadian Literature.*
　　Waterloo: Wilfrid Laurier University Press, 2003.

Mumford, Lewis. *Technics and Civilization.* 1934. Chicago: University of
　　Chicago Press, 2010.

Munro, Alice. *Hateship, Friendship, Courtship, Loveship, Marriage.* Toronto:
　　Penguin, 2001.

– *Runaway.* Toronto: McClelland and Stewart, 2004.

Munsch, Robert. *Love You Forever.* Illustrated by Sheila McGraw. Richmond
　　Hill: Firefly, 1986.

"Narrative." *The Canadian Oxford Paperback Dictionary.* Don Mills: Oxford
　　University Press, 2000.

New, W.H. *Along a Snake Fence Riding.* Lantzville: Oolichan, 2007.

– *Land Sliding: Imagining Space, Presence, and Power in Canadian Writing.*
　　Toronto: University of Toronto Press, 1997.

Newlands, Anne. *Canadian Art from Its Beginnings to 2000.* Toronto: Firefly,
　　2000.

Newman, Karen, Jay Clayton, and Marianne Hirsch. "Re-Reading the
　　Present." In *Time and the Literary*, ed. Karen Newman, Jay Clayton, and
　　Marianne Hirsch, 1–7. New York: Routledge, 2002.

Ngũgĩ wa Thiong'o. *Decolonising the Mind: The Politics of Language in African
　　Literature.* London: East African Educational Publishers, 1986.

"Nice Work if You Can Get Out: Why the Rich Now Have Less Leisure than
　　the Poor." *Economist*, 19 Apr. 2014. Accessed 22 Apr. 2014.

Nodelman, J.N. "Gabrielle Roy's *La route d'Altamont* and Canadian Highway
　　Narrative." *Studies in Canadian Literature* 33, no. 1 (2008): 211–28.

"The OEC: Facts about the Language." Oxford Dictionaries. Oxford University
　　Press. Accessed 9 Jan. 2010. http://www.oxforddictionaries.com/words/
　　the-oec-facts-about-the-language.

Ondaatje, Michael. *In the Skin of a Lion.* Toronto: Vintage, 1987.

Ong, Walter. *Orality and Literacy: The Technologizing of the Word.* 1982. 3rd ed.
　　Florence: Routledge, 2012.

Orbell, Sheina, and Maria Kyriakaki. "Temporal Framing and Persuasion to
　　Adopt Preventive Health Behavior: Moderating Effects of Individual
　　Differences in Consideration of Future Consequences on Sunscreen Use."
　　Health Psychology 27, no. 6 (2008): 770–9.

Orwell, George. *Nineteen Eighty-Four*. Harmondsworth: Penguin, 1949.

Panych, Morris. *7 Stories*. Vancouver: Talonbooks, 1990.

Paris, Max. "Budget Shortens Environmental Review Process." CBC News, 29 Mar. 2012. Accessed 29 Mar. 2012.

Paul, Elizabeth. "From the Mouth of Susan Barss." In Paul and Sanger, 67–81.

Paul, Elizabeth, and Peter Sanger. *The Stone Canoe: Two Lost Mi'kmaq Texts*. Illustrated by Alan Syliboy. Kentville: Gaspereau, 2007.

Pennee, Donna Palmateer. "Imagined Innocence, Endlessly Mourned: Postcolonial Nationalism and Cultural Expression in Timothy Findley's *The Wars*." *English Studies in Canada* 32, nos. 2–3 (2006): 89–113.

Pesch, Josef. "When Time Shall Be No More? The Narration of Apocalypse in Timothy Findley's *The Wars* and Joy Kogawa's *Obasan*." *British Journal of Canadian Studies* 14, no. 1 (1999): 85–98.

Philip, Marlene NourbeSe. *Looking for Livingstone: An Odyssey of Silence*. 1991. Toronto: Mercury, 1997.

– "Taming Our Tomorrows." In *Literary Pluralities*, ed. Christl Verduyn, 270–7. Peterborough: Broadview Press and the *Journal of Canadian Studies*, 1998.

Pirandello, Luigi. *Six Characters in Search of an Author*. 1922. In *Stages of Drama: Classical to Contemporary Masterpieces of the Theater*, 2nd ed., ed. Carl H. Klaus, Miriam Gilbert, and Bradford S. Field, Jr, 678–708. New York: St Martin's, 1991.

Pool, Sandy. *Undark: An Oratorio*. Gibsons: Nightwood, 2012.

Pratt, E.J. *Towards the Last Spike*. In *E.J. Pratt: Selected Poems*. Edited by Sandra Djwa, W.J. Keith, and Zailig Pollock, 155–204. Toronto: University of Toronto Press, 2000.

Pratt, Lloyd. *Archives of American Time: Literature and Modernity in the Nineteenth Century*. Philadelphia: University of Pennsylvania Press, 2009.

Richler, Mordecai. *The Apprenticeship of Duddy Kravitz*. New York: Paperback Library, 1959.

Ricoeur, Paul. *Time and Narrative*. 3 vols. Vols 1 and 2 translated by Kathleen McLaughlin and David Pellauer; vol. 3 translated by Kathleen Blamey and David Pellauer. Chicago: University of Chicago Press, 1984–88.

Ridout, Alice. "Temporality and Margaret Atwood." *University of Toronto Quarterly* 69, no. 4 (2000): 849–70.

Riegel, Klaus F. "Toward a Dialectical Interpretation of Time and Change." In Gorman and Wessman, eds., 59–108.

"Rob Ford Scandal 'Truly Disturbing,' Wynne Says." CBC News, 14 Nov. 2013. Accessed 27 Nov. 2013.

Robinson, Eden. *Monkey Beach*. Toronto: Vintage, 2000.

Rosa, Hartmut. *Social Acceleration: A New Theory of Modernity*. Translated by Jonathan Trejo-Mathys. New York: Columbia University Press, 2013.

Roy, Gabrielle. *The Road Past Altamont*. 1966. Translated by Joyce Marshall. Toronto: McClelland and Stewart, 1989.

Rudy, Jarrett. "Do You Have the Time? Modernity, Democracy, and the Beginnings of Daylight Saving Time in Montreal, 1907–1928." *Canadian Historical Review* 93, no. 4 (2012): 531–54.

Sainte-Marie, Buffy. "My Country 'Tis of Thy People You're Dying." In *An Anthology of Canadian Native Literature in English*, 4th ed., ed. Daniel David Moses, Terry Goldie, and Armand Garnet Ruffo, 172–3. Don Mills: Oxford University Press, 2013.

– "Now that the Buffalo's Gone." In *An Anthology of Canadian Native Literature in English*, 4th ed., ed. Daniel David Moses, Terry Goldie, and Armand Garnet Ruffo, 173–4. Don Mills: Oxford University Press, 2013.

Salem, Lisa. "'Her Blood Is Mingled with Her Ancient Foes': The Concepts of Blood, Race and 'Miscegenation' in the Poetry and Short Fiction of Duncan Campbell Scott." *Studies in Canadian Literature* 18, no. 1 (1993): 99–117.

"Same-Sex Rights: Canada Timeline." CBC News. 1 Mar. 2007. Accessed 15 July 2011.

Sanger, Peter. Guest lecture. McMaster University, 23 Oct. 2008.

– "Looking for Someone Who Sees." In Paul and Sanger, 15–57.

– "Riding the Stone Canoe." In Paul and Sanger, 133–80.

Scott, Duncan Campbell. "The Onondaga Madonna." In *Duncan Campbell Scott: Selected Poetry*. Edited by Glenn Clever, 14. Ottawa: Tecumseh, 1974.

Semmens, Grady. "Who Owns the Forest?" *OnCampus Weekly*. University of Calgary. 16 Sept. 2005. Accessed 22 Jan. 2012.

Shakespeare, William. *Macbeth*. Edited by Nick de Somogyi. London: Nick Hern, 2003.

Sheckels, Theodore F. *The Political in Margaret Atwood's Fiction: The Writing on the Wall of the Tent*. Abingdon: Ashgate, 2012.

Sioui, Georges. *Histoires de Kanatha: Vues et contées / Histories of Kanatha: Seen and Told*. Ottawa: University of Ottawa Press, 2008.

Sitney, P. Adams. *Visionary Film: The American Avant-Garde, 1943–2000*. 3rd ed. Oxford: Oxford University Press, 2002.

Sobel, Dava. *Longitude*. New York: Walker, 1995.

Söderlind, Sylvia. "Ghost-National Arguments." *University of Toronto Quarterly* 75, no. 2 (2006): 673–92.

"Statement of Apology." Aboriginal Affairs and Northern Development Canada. 15 Sept. 2010. Accessed 22 Jan. 2012. https://www.aadnc-aandc.gc.ca/eng/1100100015644/1100100015649.

Statistics Canada. *General Social Survey: Overview of the Time Use of Canadians in 1998*. Ottawa: Minister of Industry, 1999. Accessed 22 Jan. 2012. http://www.statcan.gc.ca/pub/12f0080x/4194543-eng.pdf.

– *General Social Survey on Time Use: Overview of the Time Use of Canadians: 2005*. Ottawa: Minister of Industry, 2006. Accessed 22 Jan. 2012. http://publications.gc.ca/Collection/Statcan/12F0080X/12F0080XIE2006001.pdf.

– *General Social Survey – 2010 Overview of the Time Use of Canadians*. Ottawa: Minister of Industry, 2011. Accessed 10 July 2012. http://www.statcan.gc.ca/pub/89-647-x/89-647-x2011001-eng.pdf.

Stein, Jeremy L. "Dislocations: Changing Experiences of Time and Space in an Industrialising Nineteenth-Century Ontario Town." *British Journal of Canadian Studies* 14, no. 1 (1999): 115–30.

Stewart, Janice. "Cultural Appropriations and Identificatory Practices in Emily Carr's 'Indian Stories.'" *Frontiers: A Journal of Women Studies* 26, no. 2 (2005): 59–72.

Stone, Brad. "The Children of Cyberspace: Old Fogies by Their 20s." *New York Times*, 9 Jan. 2010. Accessed 22 Jan. 2012.

Strong-Boag, Veronica Jane, and Carole Gerson. *Paddling Her Own Canoe: The Times and Texts of E. Pauline Johnson (Tekahionwake)*. Toronto: University of Toronto Press, 2000.

Sweatman, Margaret. *Fox*. Winnipeg: Turnstone, 1991.

Szeman, Imre. "Belated or Isochronic? Canadian Writing, Time, and Globalization." *Essays on Canadian Writing* 71 (Fall 2000): 186–94.

Taylor, Charles. "The Politics of Recognition." In *New Contexts of Canadian Criticism*, ed. Ajay Heble, Donna Palmateer Pennee, and J.R. Struthers, 98–130. Peterborough: Broadview, 1997.

Thompson, E.P. "Time, Work-Discipline, and Industrial Capitalism." *Past and Present* 38 (1967): 56–97. Accessed 18 Sept. 2012.

"Time." *The Canadian Oxford Paperback Dictionary*. Don Mills: Oxford University Press, 2000.

"Time Stands Still on Parliament Hill." CBC News, 25 May 2006. Accessed 22 Jan. 2012.

Tolan, Fiona. "*Cat's Eye*: Articulating the Body." In *Margaret Atwood: Feminism and Fiction*, 174–98. Amsterdam: Rodopi, 2007.

Traill, Catharine Parr. *The Backwoods of Canada*. 1836. Toronto: McClelland and Stewart, 1966.

Trevethan, Shelley, and Christopher J. Rastin. *A Profile of Visible Minority Offenders in the Federal Canadian Correctional System*. Ottawa: Research Branch, Correctional Service of Canada, 2004. Accessed 6 July 2011. http://publications.gc.ca/collections/collection_2010/scc-csc/PS83-3-144-eng.pdf.

Turcotte, Gerry. "Self." *Sydney Morning Herald*, 2 Aug. 2003. Accessed 30 Apr. 2014.

"Two Brand New Tourism TV Ads." Newfoundland and Labrador, Canada – Official Tourism Website. 17 Jan. 2011. Accessed 10 July 2012. http://www.newfoundlandlabrador.com/TheLatest/NewsArticle/47.

Urry, John. "Speeding Up and Slowing Down." In *High-Speed Society: Social Acceleration, Power, and Modernity*, ed. Hartmut Rosa and William E. Scheuerman, 179–98. University Park: Pennsylvania State University Press, 2009.

Vassanji, M.G. *No New Land*. Toronto: McClelland and Stewart, 1991.

Visvis, Vikki. "Culturally Conceptualizing Trauma: The Windigo in Joseph Boyden's *Three Day Road*." *Studies in Canadian Literature* 35, no. 1 (2010): 224–43.

– "Traumatic Forgetting and Spatial Consciousness in Dionne Brand's *In Another Place, Not Here*." *Mosaic* 45, no. 3 (2012): 115–31.

Waese, Rebecca. "Dramatic Mode and the Feminist Poetics of Enactment in Daphne Marlatt's *Ana Historic*." *Studies in Canadian Literature* 37, no. 1 (2012): 100–22.

Watson, Sheila. *The Double Hook*. 1959. Toronto: McClelland and Stewart, 1989.

Wayman, Tom. "Factory Time." In *Did I Miss Anything? Selected Poems 1973–1993*, 101–3. Madeira Park: Harbour, 1993.

– "Overtime." In *Free Time: Industrial Poems*, 18–20. Toronto: Macmillan, 1977.

Wells, Cheryl. *Civil War Time: Temporality and Identity in America, 1861–1865*. Athens: University of Georgia Press, 2005.

White, Hayden. *Tropics of Discourse: Essays in Cultural Criticism*. Baltimore: Johns Hopkins University Press, 1978.

Williams, David. *Confessional Fictions: A Portrait of the Artist in the Canadian Novel*. Toronto: University of Toronto Press, 1991.

– *Imagined Nations: Reflections on Media in Canadian Fiction.* Montreal: McGill-Queen's University Press, 2003.

– *Media, Memory, and the First World War.* Montreal: McGill-Queen's University Press, 2009.

Woodcock, George. "The Tyranny of the Clock." In *The Rejection of Politics*, 46–50. Toronto: New Press, 1972.

Wright, Ronald. *Stolen Continents: 500 Years of Conquest and Resistance in the Americas.* New York: Houghton Mifflin, 1992.

"WVLNT (Wavelength For Those Who Don't Have The Time)." Art Metropole. Accessed 22 Jan. 2012. http://www.artmetropole.com/index.cfm?fuseaction= shop.FA_dsp_browse_detailsandInventoryUnitsID=633e194f-f331-4979-8294- e2c5439cb06aandCategoryID=andUnitsType=0_0.

Wyatt, Rachel. *Time's Reach.* Lantzville: Oolichan, 2003.

Wyile, Herb. *Speculative Fictions: Contemporary Canadian Novelists and the Writing of History.* Montreal: McGill-Queen's University Press, 2002.

Wynne-Davies, Marion. "The Mysteries of Time and Memory: 1988–1999." In *Margaret Atwood*, 42–66. Tavistock: Northcote House, 2010.

Yeats, W.B. "The Second Coming." In *The Collected Poems of W.B. Yeats.* Edited by Richard J. Finneran, 187. New York: Scribner, 1996.

York, Lorraine M. *Introducing Timothy Findley's* The Wars. Toronto: ECW, 1990.

Yorke, Stephanie. "The Slave Narrative Tradition in Lawrence Hill's *The Book of Negroes.*" *Studies in Canadian Literature* 35, no. 2 (2010): 129–44.

Zerubavel, Eviatar. *The Seven Day Circle: The History and Meaning of the Week.* New York: Free Press, 1985.

Zimbardo, Philip, and John Boyd. *The Time Paradox: The New Psychology of Time that Will Change Your Life.* New York: Free Press, 2008.

Index